THE HEREAFTER BYTES

A FUNNY SCI FI NOVEL

VINCENT SCOTT

Thinking Ink Press
P.O. Box 1411
Campbell, California 95009
www.ThinkingInkPress.com

THE HEREAFTER BYTES. Copyright © 2020 by Vincent Scott. All rights reserved.

For more information, contact editorial@thinkinginkpress.com.

Published by Thinking Ink Press
P.O. Box 1411
Campbell, California 95009
www.ThinkingInkPress.com

ISBN 978-1-942480-30-3 (hardback)

ISBN 978-1-942480-28-0 (paperback)

ISBN 978-1-942480-29-7 (ebook)

Printed in the United States of America.

Project Credits

Cover illustration: Ivreese Tong

Cover design and ebook formatting: Streetlight Graphics

Author's head shot: Aaron Wheetman

Editor: Betsy Miller

Copy Editor: Ellen Bond

Early Readers: John Lahey and Tessa Miller

Sensitivity Reader: Chris Lahey

Kickstarter Advisor: Madeleine Holly-Rosing

All jokes aside, this book is dedicated to the hope that humanity might still get its shit together.

1

PING PONG

June 18th, 2063 4:37 p.m. PST

A passenger drone whirred past the bus window two stories above the river of autonomous cars below. I glanced out the window following the drone's path as far as I could from my vantage point. Crammed as I was, in between a sweating bicyclist and a man who smelled like beef stock in the middle aisle, there wasn't a lot of room to maneuver. The drone vanished beyond the windowsill. Someone was going somewhere important, leaving me behind. That felt on point for the day. My phone chirped. I brought up the notification in my smart contact.

Can you talk?

The social faux pas of using the phone on mass transportation was not something I would normally do, but I wanted to talk. It had been a bad day.

Sure, I sent.

My phone rang and I nearly dropped it, recovered, checked the caller, remembered that I knew who was calling, nearly dropped it again, recovered again, and answered the call. A nearby passenger looked at me like my last several moments had destroyed her flagging faith in humanity. I shrugged apologetically.

"Hey, Abigail."

"Hey, Romeo. Just wanted to see if you were okay. Izy said you were making it official today."

"Yeah, just did. I'm ... I'll be okay."

"I'm really sorry."

"It's not your fault."

"You sure you don't want me to help out. Izy would understand."

"No," I said. "Izy deserves to run her own business."

"I could invest in her business in a few years."

"Visual Arts isn't exactly a lucrative major, Abigail. I was going to be just as employable with the degree as I am now."

She snorted.

"I mean look," I said. "Is this the end of my life? Yes. Am I going to end up going to prison for stealing a loaf of bread? Undoubtedly. Will I escape and go on a long adventure fleeing from an over-dedicated police officer who doesn't believe in a person's ability to reform? Only time will tell."

"Isn't that the plot of *Les Misérables*?"

"How would I know? I didn't graduate from college."

"Okay," Abigail said. "You're really okay?"

"I'll survive."

"Hey," she said. "Lots of successful people dropped out of college."

"I think most of them had marketable skills."

"Yeah, I think they probably did," she said. "You could come and work for me."

I laughed.

"You know I would," I said. "But I just don't look good in leather."

"Latex?"

"I think I might be allergic."

"Excuses, excuses. You're never going to get hired with an attitude like that."

Another passenger shot me a dirty look for talking on my phone. I tried to work up the courage to roll my eyes at them. My work was in vain. The courage would not rise.

"I should go," I said.

"Okay," Abigail said. "How about a 'fuck the system' drink this evening?"

"I can't really—"

"I'm buying obviously. I know your broke ass can't afford it."

"Oh, in that case, great."

"Talk to you later, dropout."

"Bye."

I fumbled trying to put the phone back in my pocket. I looked up to see if any passengers were still giving me dirty looks. Several of them were.

I don't remember what happened next, but I've seen the security footage. Brace yourself. Things get grizzly.

There was a bang, the bus lurched to the left, a crash, and my body covered the distance from the middle of the bus to the front windshield as if I'd been fired out of a cannon. My elbow hit the front window first. At this conference of physics, my joint and the glass decided to compromise. The window shattered, my elbow exploded.

I flew—or perhaps hurtled, there was very little in the way of aerodynamic grace involved—over the car we collided with. (Its occupants were ... indisposed. Self-driving vehicles have allowed people to fill their time on the freeway with all sorts of activities they didn't used to. Hey, at least they died happy.) I hit the cargo truck behind that car and, thanks to the curvature of its hood, bounced. High. Fifty-one feet according to the security footage (which went viral in darker corners of the Internet.) My pelvis was turned into a collection of bone toothpicks, my still-intact arm broke, and my right knee decided bending 90 degrees in only one direction was for squares.

Don't worry, at this point, I was profoundly unconscious.

If you're a compassionate person you might be thinking, 'surely this is over, how much pain can one roguishly handsome, shockingly intelligent man take?' Nice description, totally inaccurate, but nice. The problem is, compassion is something humans made up. Gravity doesn't give a shit about compassion. If gravity was capable of caring about anything, I think it would be a very simple life principle. What goes up, must come down—unless it reaches escape velocity but, unfortunately, this is not a story about my daring adventures in space.

I fell 51 feet back down to Earth into the lane adjacent to the stopped traffic. I sprawled like a handful of wet noodles just in time for a soccer mom's self-driving minivan to run over both my legs and, check the geometry on this one ... break my nose. Pretty wild, right? Apparently, I missed out on a career as a contortionist.

If you're a reasonable person, you might be thinking at this point, 'My goodness, I didn't know I could commune with the dead, but I must be able to because this human lawn dart is decisively deceased.' First of all, shut up. I let the first thought pass, but I'll do the thinking in this story. Second, yeah, you're right. I'm dead.

Is that freaking you out? Don't panic. I'm not here for your soul—like I'd tell you if I was.

I died. Not actually on the freeway. After I left the soccer mom with the uncomfortable responsibility of explaining to her kids what that bump, bump sound was, I was whisked away to the local hospital. I clung to life like a pro athlete clings to the fiction that they've never taken performance enhancing drugs, not once, never, okay fine, many times over a period of years. With that concession, my heartbeat stopped.

It was 2063 and modern medicine can do some pretty impressive things, but when providence throws you through an improvised meat grinder, that's for keeps. So anyway, that's my story, thanks for stopping by. That's all there is. The rest of the pages are blank. See ya later.

What? You're still here? Fine, I'll tell you what happened next.

I warn you now, this story only gets weirder. I want you to know, I didn't ask for any of this. I'm not weird. There was a time when I was just your run of the mill asexual college dropout, working at a server farm full of dead people, whose best friend is a dominatrix. Totally normal ... okay, I mean, normality is subjective.

2

ROSA GALAN'S ROSA GALAN

Month Day, Year --:-- press 1 for a.m. press 2 for p.m. select region

In 2051, a woman named Rosa Galan made a historically significant announcement. Her start-up ReMind, Inc. had invented a scanner that could capture enough detail of the functioning mind to recreate it on a computer. Further, they had managed to simplify many of the lower functions of the brain, which radically reduced the amount of processing power necessary to simulate it. Using this technology, they had created a copy of Rosa Galan.

The world was astounded. While people working on AI had been arguing for decades about whether conscious AI had already been invented, was soon to be invented, or was impossible to invent, Rosa Galan and her company had recreated consciousness inside digital space. They had leapfrogged the entire process of actually understanding what consciousness was and just copied nature's homework.

Things took a strange turn shortly after. Rosa Galan's copy sued the real-world Rosa in court. The copy argued that they were essentially the same person, therefore the copy had as much right to control the company and their personal assets as the biological Rosa. The biological Rosa's lawyers said this was ridiculous, but when asked by the judge why, they found themselves struggling to find a cogent reason.

The case immediately became a national sensation. Human rights organizations and religious groups got involved on both sides. Every news outlet in the world had daily coverage of the case. (I was in high school at the time, so I was obviously taking an avid interest in ... literally anything else.)

In the midst of the legal proceedings, congress decided that having two of the same person was too disruptive, regardless of what the courts decided. A law passed that outlawed copying a living person. Scientists objected that this could fatally stifle the search for the mechanism of consciousness.

A few months later, the Rosa copy suggested a solution. (By that point, The Supreme Court had decided that the copying would be handled like a divorce, with assets split between the two Rosas.) Now, with a significant stake in the company, the copy suggested a bold new direction. If you can't copy living people, why not copy dead ones.

The company rebranded itself as EternityNet and offered to copy the minds of anyone who wanted some version of themselves to live on after death. Philosophers assured the public that this was about as much like an afterlife as a sailboat is like a spaceship. The public didn't listen. In a country where people had spent millions on cryogenics, the idea of having some consciousness outlast death was too exciting to ignore.

People did it by the thousands, then tens of thousands. Over the next decade more than 18 million people worldwide had copied their minds, to be stored inertly, until the time of their deaths. They had all kinds of elaborate explanations for why it wasn't just a copy. I saw a news report where a man insisted he thought his soul was pretty clever, and it would figure out how to jump from his biological mind to the digital one.

Questions started to emerge like, should they vote? Should they pay taxes? What social programs should they receive? As the primary things the digital copies needed were power, hard drive space, software, and processing capacity, it opened up an entirely new can of resurrected worms.

It has long been understood by learned people that the Congress of the United States only takes action when a lot of people are yelling at it, and people were yelling. Some wanted the technology banned outright as the work of the devil. Others wanted the technology made universally available to every American. What did the congress do? What has the US Congress always done when there was a difficult choice to be made? They made it a states' rights issue.

Washington State, where I'm from, took a hands-off approach at first. Then the family members of someone who had intended to get copied, but was bucked by a horse before they could get around to it, sued the hospital who refused to copy their loved one's comatose mind. Shortly after, by which I mean two years later—hey, that's fast in government time—a law was passed that required that all accident victims be copied. Now, if you don't want to be copied, you have to fill out paperwork. It's like 'do not resuscitate,' 'do not copy.'

So now there are a lot of us. Nobody has an exact number, but tens of millions worldwide. As these copies became an increasingly important force in the digital world, people started asking what to call them. The answer was obvious. The first usage is debated, but the name seemed to emerge everywhere all at once; the copies were called, 'ghosts.'

3

BIOS ARE GROSS

March 3rd, 2064 8:37 a.m. PST

I woke up. With a mental command I rendered my avatar around my consciousness. It looked like me before the accident. It was thin shouldered and black haired, with brown eyes spaced a little too close together. My face was pale and freckled, and there was a birthmark on the side of my forehead that looked like a pineapple. I looked around. Hovering in an eternal abyss, I decided to load some surroundings.

A second later, a virtual reality apartment appeared around me. Upside of digital space, nice digs are cheap. Maybe that's because they're basically useless. Still, when I was alive, I lived in a roach-infested apartment with a beautiful view of the back of a hedge. In my digital apartment, the windows showed downtown Seattle. I don't know why I've always stuck with my hometown. I could change the preferences to include a view of any city or anything in the world, but there's no place like home. The gang of wild baboons using vines to swing from building to building, that's a third-party program I added for my own amusement.

I glanced out the window contemplating the beauty of the sun reflecting off a skyscraper, and I did my best to ignore the alpha male baboon banging on the outside of my window and puffing up his chest. I flicked open my social media. A page appeared in my vision blocking the apes and their journey toward the Space Needle. A new ex-GIF was the top link. I clicked it.

I found myself low to the ground, surrounded by savannah grass and gnarled trees. I looked around. There didn't seem to be anything interesting in the GIF. I felt the wind against my skin. The smell of hot earth filled my nostrils. I looked down. I appeared to be ... a hunk of meat. There was the faintest rustle to my left. I turned toward it. Something was moving through the grass, getting closer to me.

Two eyes blinked. A fat, pink tongue lashed out to lick lips.

"Oh no," I said.

The lioness started creeping forward. I spotted another set of eyes, then another.

"Oh no."

The lions pounced out of the grass, springing on me, their teeth bared.

"Waaaah."

The first lioness sunk her teeth into me. I jerked back, I was back in my apartment.

"What kind of monster makes you a hunk of meat without warning?"

Ex-GIFs, or experience GIFs, really put you in the middle of the moment they capture.

I flicked down the line of links that made up my social media feed with a little more caution. There was some

real-world news. Climate change had created unprecedented refugee crises on almost every continent, one of
Russia's nuclear missiles had gone missing, and a movie
star had decided to name their new baby Gorf. I closed the
page.

The simulated alpha baboon was getting pretty aggressive on the other side of the window. I reached out and with
a thought conjured a cornucopia of fruit into being. The
mollified alpha started digging through the multicolored
heap.

I checked the clock on my wall. It was almost time for
work.

You might think digital space sounds like a restric-
tion-free utopia, a binary bacchanal, a worldwide
Woodstock, a virtual Valhalla, sorry, I'll stop (a shareable
Shangri La, sorry, last one.) You'd be right to a point. The
point would be the real-world infrastructure needed to
enjoy all that no-holds-barred freedom. Every ghost needs
a certain amount of processing power to keep their brain
simulation running. On top of that, if you want to render
in flawless detail things like apartments, cityscapes, and
hordes of aggressive baboons, you've got to have the real-
world computers that run that software. Those computers
cost money.

I booted up the interface on my robot.

And I was back in the real world in a modified errand
robot. It was a spindly thing. Vaguely humanoid in the basic
construction. I had two arms, and two legs. The bottoms of
my legs had wheels that I could lock in place and use as
feet when doing things like climbing stairs. My hands were
missing a finger, but they were pretty dexterous as I flexed
them. My head is a screen that shows a dynamic image of
my avatar's face.

Before you go thinking I'm an unstoppable super-robot, you should know the max carrying capacity of my arms is 20 pounds. There are housecats that can overpower me.

I glanced around the office space. It was cluttered with whirring servers. In the corner sat the empty desk of my employer.

"Good morning, Romeo," Izy said, in her Kazakh accent.

"Hey Izy. Why do you look like you're planning to murder me?"

"My coffee is late."

Izy was standing by the window. Hanging off the side of the building was a one-meter-square platform. It had a series of markings on it that archeologists of the future would no doubt ascribe to some religious rite. In fact, they just guide automated drones to landing.

"Bastards."

"Yes," Izy said. "I have been standing here thinking about how I could undetectably murder the CEO of Flooffee for the last four minutes."

Flooffee is a company that delivers coffee by drone. They make more coffee in a day than their next competitor does in a month. Flooffee has zero coffee shops.

"What have you come up with?"

"Is possible. I could send a micro-drone into his office carrying a tablet of arsenic. I could drop it into his coffee. This would be suitably ironic."

"Don't most big office buildings scramble unapproved radio signals?"

"Good point," Izy said. "I would have to use a laser guidance system. That would require that I be within visible range. I might have to infiltrate Flooffee."

A buzzing sound drew her attention to the window. A brightly colored drone with the company name stenciled on the side landed. Izy opened the window, and a carrying contraption opened on top of the drone.

"Flooffee apologizes for your order's late arrival. Your next cup is half-off on us."

"Hmm," Izy said. "Very well. You may tell your employer he can live another day."

"I'll pass along that feedback."

She took her coffee and shut the window.

"You ever worry about people taking your jokes seriously?"

She looked confused.

"What joke?"

I met Izy when I was first figuring out that I was asexual. There's a point in every queer person's life where they just need to hear an actual live person tell them to their face that they're not alone, and who they are is okay. For me that was Izy. We were both at a meeting of people sharing their thoughts on asexuality. She leaned over and whispered in my ear.

"I think I got everything I need from this. I'm going to go get drunk. Want to come?"

I did.

Izy immigrated to the United States when she was a teenager in the 2050's. The massive droughts that struck Central Asia in that decade led to tens of millions of people being displaced. Most of them went to Europe. Add them to the population crossing the Mediterranean, and Europe risked turning into a crisis zone. Turns out millions of desperate people arriving in your continent all at once is bad for stability. Maybe they shouldn't have spent all those centuries arbitrarily drawing borders, extracting resource wealth, and withholding education from their slaves ... did

I say slaves? I meant second-class subjects ... did I say second-class subjects? I meant brown people.

It wasn't humanitarian concerns that finally made the United States assist in absorbing some of the refugees. It was the threat to the global economy. Waiting for visas, Izy's family went through some shit she's never talked about. Let's just say there is a star-shaped scar on her cheek that looks an awful lot like a bullet wound.

Around that scar is a set of big cheeks that swell into pontoons when she smiles, a very sharp chin—seriously, she could use it as a scalpel, short-cut black hair that she never seemed to feel like styling, light brown skin, a body that showed that her favorite weekend hobby was a semi-professional rugby team, and a sense of humor so acerbic you could use it to dissolve metal. She was joking about killing the CEO of Flooffee, I think ... pretty sure.

"What's on the docket for today?" I asked.

"I need you to be in the office this afternoon. I have dentist appointment."

"Ew. You bios are gross."

A faint smile tickled the edges of Izy's mouth.

"Oh, shut up, you poltergeist."

I gave her my most theatrical gasp.

"How dare you? That is our word."

"Yeah, yeah, why don't you go shake some furniture?"

"Why don't you put some deodorant on, you smelly bio?"

"You know you're lucky I don't use stun gun baseball bat. I scrap you for parts."

"Yeah well, you're lucky I don't ... fuck. I don't ... give me a second."

She scoffed.

"That's right. You can't hurt me. What you going to do? Annoy me to death."

I pondered for another moment. My eyebrow raised.

"I could change your default Flooffee order to decaf."

Izy's face went stern. She swallowed.

"I apologize for poltergeist comment. Let's not let this get nasty."

"Agreed."

Izy owns the server farm. It caters almost exclusively to ghosts. I work for her maintaining the hardware and doing customer support. She's the brains, I'm the ... what am I? I'm not the brawn. Damn, I think I just realized, Izy employs me out of pity.

A ding drew Izy's attention to her phone.

"There is package downstairs," Izy said. "Can you go get it?"

"Sure."

The server farm is on the seventh floor of a cheap office building in way, way south Seattle. If you're wondering what that means socio-economically, put it this way, it's where the city settled the refugees.

Over the last couple of decades climate-change fueled droughts have rocked the greater southwest like a crib attached to a paint mixer. Many of the displaced Americans and Mexicans headed north. Those that were at the mercy of the system accepted subsidized housing far to the south of Seattle's millionaires and billionaires.

Our building doesn't have much in the way of frills. We've got an elevator, but it rattles in an ominous 'you're about to plunge to your death' kind of way. I still take it. My wheel feet allow me to climb up and down stairs, but they're a little too unstable to walk upright. I have to bend over and clamber like a dog. It's not the most dignified way to travel. There is nothing quite as awkward as running into someone on the stairs when your head is at crotch level.

I arrived in the lobby and spotted a delivery robot outside the building's front entrance. It was the same model as mine. Most of the delivery companies used them. I opened the door. Rain was falling, the sky was hidden by light-grey clouds, and a car rolled through a puddle and sent a wash of water across the sidewalk. Another beautiful day in Seattle. I waved for the robot to approach. It didn't move.

"Give me the package."

It didn't respond. I sighed. Having a physical body is rare to the point of unheard of for ghosts. Most of the digital dead left themselves money when they died, and digital space is pretty much the real world, but with superpowers. Why would they leave? I have to for work. That means, I've got to deal with the physical world.

A fair amount of the real-world infrastructure just wasn't built to deal with someone in my position. The package delivery robot didn't register me as a human, so none of its numerous customer-service subroutines activated.

I rolled out the door trying to hold it open with one arm while I reached for the package with the other. I grabbed the box. The messenger robot pulled it away.

"Give me the package, you little shit."

My hand kept searching for purchase on the box. The messenger robot rolled back a few feet. I slipped, lost my grip on the door, and it clanged shut.

"You fucking bastard," I said.

Now unrestrained, I lunged at the messenger robot.

"Give it to me, damn it. Let go."

The messenger robot stared at me blankly. No part of its programming had prepared it to be attacked by a disgruntled dead man. I yanked on the box, but the carrier still wouldn't relent. We pulled up close to each other.

"Let go you fucking asshole. It's my package."

The screen that made up its face flashed a recognition. It released the box causing me to fly backward and clatter onto my bony metal ass.

"Package delivered," it said. "Have a great day."

It rolled away leaving me sprawled on the concrete of the sidewalk. I clambered to my feet, swiveled my external camera 180 degrees, and checked my posterior. It didn't look like I'd suffered any substantial damage. I glanced around to see if anyone had seen my altercation with the messenger robot.

Across the street a woman was waving her hands next to a wall like she was casting a magical spell. A notification popped up in the corner of my perception. She was creating public Graffinity street art. Graffinity is an augmented-reality app that allows people to create street art without actually painting a wall. Any good patch of wall usually has a few hundred options you can select to be your preferred street art.

Biological people have to wear some kind of Augmented Reality system to see it. Most do. They tend to go for contacts, some use glasses or even goggles. My robot's visual interface has AR built in. I selected the art she was creating.

It was the Emerald City from *The Wizard of Oz*. However, the landscape around the distant green city had changed. It was bulldozed and leveled. In every direction scaffolding was going up for boxy office buildings. Massive cranes towered over the rising structures. I examined the picture for a minute.

"Depressing," I muttered.

I flipped through the other Graffinity options. There was a picture of the president making out with the green image of Benjamin Franklin from the hundred-dollar bill. I scoffed. Nobody uses cash anymore. I flipped to the next one. A famous pop star had clearly had someone come and add a poster for their upcoming album to this wall's collection. I flipped again. The wall went blank, then an ad flashed up. A little box near the bottom of my perception said, 'you can skip this add in ...' a counter was running down from five.

"Whatever."

I turned to the building's keypad, typed in the code, and headed back up to the office.

"Took you long enough," Izy said.

I handed her the package.

"The messenger robot didn't recognize me as a person again."

"Despicable. In this day and age."

"I'd be more appreciative of your concern, except that I'm pretty sure you sent me to get the package because you knew I'd have to fight for it."

Izy looked at a nearby server bank. She seemed to find it amusing, as the edges of her mouth twitched.

"I may have, completely by accident, recorded the front door security camera."

"You don't say."

"Very unfortunately, I do say."

She blinked and I could see she had activated her AR contacts. She made a gesture with her hand and a video file appeared in my messenger app. I selected it. Sure enough, I was playing tug-of-war with the messenger robot and falling on my ass in a loop.

"If you post that anywhere—"

"Relax, it is for my personal amusement."

The package I had delivered was sitting on her desk. She picked it up and blinked again.

"Is new ghost," she said. "Hook them up to server tower 18, okay. I'll set up their interface."

I took the package from her and pried it open. A black box, very similar to the one I use, was inside. I swiveled toward the designated server, while Izy started making flicking gestures with her hands, navigating an AR world.

Ghosts are simply computer code. Zeros and ones on a hard drive that when, processed in the correct way, create a sentience. In theory, a ghost could jump from one computer to another and, as long as each computer had the requisite hard-drive space and processing power, they would continue to function, but most ghosts don't do this. Why? A little thing called the transporter problem.

You see, when a computer uploads a file, it doesn't upload the file. It uploads a copy of the file. The original file exists on the computer's hard drive. If, as very few ghosts do, you upload a copy of the ghost to another computer, then delete the original, you haven't really jumped from one server to another. You've created an entirely new entity on the distant server and killed the original, a.k.a. yourself. While the new entity's experience may be contiguous with no memory of death by file overwrite, the original is no less gone.

This freaks most ghosts out.

As a result, they want to have a permanent hard drive that is the one and only storage for the information necessary to run their simulation. Does this make any sense? Kind of. How? Let me explain. When you go to sleep, your consciousness ends. Sure, you dream and some biological processes happen, but for a sizeable portion of the night, if your definition of death is the end of consciousness, you die ... yeah, freaky right, sit with that a second.

Why don't you face every night by screaming 'the end is nigh' at the top of your lungs? Because your experience has continuity. In the morning, you will wake up. Also, because your sense of self, which is at least partially tied to your body, is reassured by the continuity of your physical form. Sure, your consciousness temporarily ended, but your heart rate kept beating along.

This sense of reassurance is probably irrational, but it's powerful, and ghosts want it too. Sure, in theory, every time the power goes out, every ghost that loses power dies. When the power returns, an entirely new entity begins that just happens to be identical to the entity that died. Just like in theory, every time you go to sleep your consciousness ends, then a new one begins when you wake up in the morning.

In practice, it's nice to know that something of yourself lingered permanently, if inertly, while the lights were out. That's why most ghosts, including myself, keep a fixed box that contains a hard drive and the processors necessary to run our simulation. A permanent real-world body, in other words. Irrational it may be, but when has that ever been enough to stop humans from doing something. They're called 'black boxes.' Mine is nestled in the frame of my robot. I carry it with me everywhere I go.

I connected the new ghost's black box. It started to whir as power brought its processors to life.

"Hello, Mr. Phillips," Izy said, back at her desk. "Yes, you are installed. My associate is going to jump into digital space to help you get acclimated. Please contact me if you have additional processing or memory needs."

She paused.

"Very good, you as well." She hung up the phone. "You heard that, Romeo?"

"Yep."

"I just sent you the connection link."

A message icon popped in the corner of my vision. I rolled over to my robot's charging station. I could connect over the WiFi, but direct cable connection is faster. I clicked the blue hypertext in Izy's message.

My robot's interface vanished and the digital world materialized around me. An old man was standing in the void of unrendered surroundings.

"Hello Mr. Phillips," I said.

He spun on his foot and a smile spread across his face.

"Oh, hello," he said. "You're here to show me how all this works?"

"I am."

"It's a little emptier than I imagined."

"Well you can load any surroundings you want."

I pulled up some basic VR surroundings that come standard with most operating systems. The Grand Canyon spread around us.

"Oh my," he said. "Very impressive."

"Yeah," I said. "It's pretty cool. You can open up settings and alter almost anything you want. Just consciously select an icon and it will open. The software that runs your neural-simulation will read your brain activity and activate whatever you select. It takes a few minutes to get the hang of, but then you'll be flying through cyber space. You can dial the temperature on your skin up or down. You can change your avatar. Have you ever wanted to have four arms, or maybe a tail? The entire digital world, both 2D and 3D is open to you. The digital world's your oyster."

"Yes, yes." He nodded. "That's all very nice. It's not exactly what I was looking for though."

"What were you looking for?"

"I was hoping to view the porn."

I coughed on nothing.

"The porn?"

"Yes. Will you show me the porn?"

"Um ... uh ... no ..."

"You're not going to show me the porn?"

"I think ... you can ... just search ... it's not hard to find."

"If you don't show me the porn, I might have to give you a bad rating for customer service."

So, it was going to be like that.

"You know, you do what you got to do."

I logged off and reactivated my robot's interface. Izy looked toward me as I moved off my charging platform.

"That was quick. Is Mr. Phillips settled in?"

"He wanted me to show him 'the porn.'"

"Another one?"

"Yeah."

"What is it about the recently deceased that makes them so frisky?"

"Working in the service sector sucks."

And that's my job. There's a little more to it. Upgrading the servers and updating the software takes a fair amount of our time. It's steady work, but if I'm honest, when it's not low-grade traumatizing, it bores the living shit out of me.

I rolled back toward Izy's desk. An app notification appeared in the corner of my eye. I paused when I recognized it. Someone was calling me, like actually calling me. It wasn't a voice message. They wanted to talk to me in real time, and they hadn't sent me a text first. Who does that? What is this, the 20th century? Something horrible must have happened. I pondered my still-living relatives. The last time I'd talked to my grandma, she hadn't been doing too well. I pulled up the app and saw the incoming caller. Not grandma. It was Abigail.

"Hello? Abigail? Did you die?"

"What?" she said.

"You're calling me."

"I know. It's weird, sorry. I need your help."

"With an organ transplant?"

"What?"

"You didn't text first."

"I know. I'm sorry. Stop being annoying," she said. "Can I come and see you?"

"Well," I said. "You sure you didn't die?"

"I'm not the one around here who has a history of dying."

"Ooh, damn, dark."

"Can I come and see you?"

"I guess. I just ... I'm still reeling. I feel like a messenger just rode up on a horse to hand-deliver a scroll."

"You are the reason I get migraines. Can I come see you, now?"

"When now?"

"Right now. I'm outside your building."

"Right now?"

There was an audible sigh on the other side of the line.

"Romeo, you know I'd generally be game for this back and forth, but seriously, I need your help. I kind of, might have, fucked up. I'm not sure."

There was earnest worry in her voice.

"Okay," I said. "Yeah, come on up. Just, leave the horse tied up outside."

"Fuck you."

She hung up.

"Abigail's here," I told Izy. "I assume that's not a problem."

She looked up from some AR distraction and nodded.

"No, no problem. Honestly, if I could hire her and fire you, I probably would."

"You know," I said. "I made one little comment about bios being gross."

4

ABIGAIL'S DUPLICITY

March 3rd, 2064 9:14 a.m. PST

Abigail looks like exactly what you'd expect a dominatrix to look like. It's pretty much a necessity, if not to survive, then to thrive in the sex-work industry. You've got to appeal to somebody's sexual fantasy. That's the thing about beauty standards. Everybody objects to the arbitrary standards imposed on them, but ignores the standards they impose on others. So, the standards keep everybody running in a circle like a group of drunk wedding guests trying to do the conga. Sex workers are like the wedding DJ. They take advantage of the fact that people can't help but dance. That's probably why they've always been so stigmatized.

She's got long, black hair, pale skin, austere cheekbones and chin, and shoulders that have the same kind of toned musculature as a pitcher in baseball (from all the flogging.) Contrary to what you might think, she doesn't spend every waking moment walking around in black leather and latex.

She was wearing a pair of fashionable slacks, a dark blue sweater, and a pair of running shoes with silver streaks along the sides.

"Hello, Izy," Abigail said. "Sorry for dropping in unannounced."

"Not a problem."

She turned toward me.

"Can we talk in private?"

My digital eyebrows raised.

"Okay," I said.

I was beginning to feel a bit of genuine worry. Swiveling on the spot, I led her toward one of the server rooms. I shut the door behind us.

"What's up?" I asked.

Whatever had brought her here was clearly weighing on her. She burst into speech.

"I did something bad. Well, not bad, really. That's totally subjective. I don't think it was bad. Just because something's illegal doesn't make it wrong. The law doesn't have a monopoly on morality. Just look at history. What I did was risky. But it was so much money, and the law is so ridiculous. Trust America to overreact. But now I've taken the risk, and it might have blown up in my face, but maybe not. I don't know."

This is a side to Abigail that most people never see. She is smart. Very smart. 'Built a propensity for bondage into a small empire,' smart. When her brain gets going it can be hard to keep up with the variables she's throwing out.

Most people don't see this because when she's stressed, and she doesn't know someone, she clams up. This coupled with her austere cheekbones makes her an intimidating presence. Very useful in her line of work. When she trusts you, however, you get to find out that Abigail has quite the capacity for incoherence.

"I just can't be sure. It's just that what I did is a little illegal. Okay, very illegal. It doesn't seem like it should have gotten dangerous, but—"

"Dangerous?"

"Yeah dangerous. Aren't you listening?"

"Okay, Abigail. Slow it down for me. What's going on?"

She sighed, winding her brain down to Romeo speed.

"Alright. About three months ago, I got a new client. He was a referral. A software engineer for a big medical technology company called Maddoc Technologies. He had a very specific proclivity."

"You know I don't like to hear about this kind of thing."

"Toughen up, my dainty flower, it's important. There was a very specific kind of kink he was into. It's called interrogation play, and it's exactly what it sounds like. We establish a secret. We enter the scene. He withholds the secret. I use various forms of pain to entice him to reveal it. He reveals the secret, the scene ends. No big deal."

"So, he paid you to torture him?"

"No." Abigail sounded irritated. "It's a lot more complicated than that. You have a lot of conversations about boundaries and pain levels. There are safe words. I don't inflict pain randomly. I have to be acutely aware of where they are at every moment, their pain level, and their emotional state. As the dominant, it's my responsibility to give the other person a gratifying session. It takes a lot of creativity and empathy. Don't boil my business down to simplistic—"

Abigail saw me smiling. She scowled.

"You were goading me."

"Sorry," I said. "Sometimes it's fun to see scary Abigail."

"Careful what you wish for," she said. "Scary Abigail does things like disconnect your battery, then replace your arms and legs with little doll arms and legs, then reconnect your power and let you struggle."

"Okay, well, thanks for the nightmares."

"Yeah."

"So, how does this get dangerous?"

"Right, so, I'm doing a couple of sessions a week with this guy. All is going well. Then about a month ago, he doesn't reveal the secret we established. It's usually some little tidbit of childhood, or a random piece of information. The secret doesn't normally matter. Except this time he revealed a real secret. A work secret he wasn't supposed to tell me. It didn't turn out to be important, but he freaked and left. I was pretty sure I'd never see him again. Not a big problem, my client list is pretty full. I wrote it off. Too bad, no harm no foul. Except a few days later, he calls."

"What did he want?"

"To do it again. Revealing the real secret was more gratifying for him than any of our sessions where he revealed something pointless."

I pondered that.

"Sex is ... weird."

"You think it's weird? Imagine what it's like to people having it."

"Touché."

"Besides, what I do isn't legally sex."

"Right, sure, whip away, but you touch someone's genitals and you're a criminal."

"Yeah."

"The law is weird."

"No argument on that one."

"So, besides the threat to my delicate sensibilities at some point this story gets dangerous, yes?"

"I'm getting there," she said. "He wanted to keep revealing secrets, but be sure I wouldn't tell anyone. I assured him I wouldn't. That wasn't good enough. So, he made a suggestion."

She paused.

"What?" I asked.

"He had access to an EternityNet scanner. He wanted to make a copy of me. With a little bit of software you can modify a ghost so they can selectively delete things from their memory. He wanted to do that."

I stared at her.

"You didn't."

"Well ..."

"Abigail!"

"What?"

"That's a felony. A federal felony, which seems like it's extra bad."

"Oh, come on, it's legal in the Netherlands."

"Everything is legal in the Netherlands. We're not in the Netherlands."

"Stop freaking out."

"Why should I? It's ... it's unethical."

"Oh bullshit. Who could possibly know better than me if I would be okay with being created? Consent is literally built into the creation process. There's more consent in an adult creating a copy of themselves, than there is in a parent deciding to have a child. The kid didn't ask to be born, but I knew that my digital-me would be cool with this arrangement, because my digital-me is me."

"You ... well, that's actually kind of a good point, but illegal!"

"It's a pointless law."

"So, you disagree with a law, and it doesn't apply to you."

"Pretty much."

"I think the government would disagree."

"They'll have to catch me."

"They might."

"They'll have to convict me."

"They might."

"Nah, they won't."

"How ... wha ... why?"

She smiled and shrugged like that answered everything. I covered my face with my hands. My robot phalanges clacked against my face screen. It wasn't as comforting a gesture without the tactile response. I lowered my hands.

"Why are you telling me this? Wait, this happened a month ago? There's been a copy of you for a month? Why didn't you tell me this? Another copy of my best friend is running around? Didn't ghost Abigail want to see me? What the fuck, Abigail? I thought we were friends. Wait, knowing this makes me an accomplice. I could go to prison. Prison, Abigail. Why did you tell me this? I can't go on the lam. It's really hard to find places to charge your battery when you're running from the law ... I assume. Why didn't you tell me you were going to tell me this?"

Okay, so Abigail's not the only one capable of incoherence.

"I think I'm going to pass out."

"Can ghosts pass out?" Abigail asked.

"I'm not sure."

"Deep breaths."

"I'm not capable of breathing."

She shrugged.

"So, what happened?" I asked. "I assume something happened?"

"Yeah. The copy was doing this guy's sessions. He used AR goggles to see the digital-me, and we rigged up a robot that could administer the pain. It was going great. Actually, better than great. There's a huge untapped market for this internationally. Abi and I—"

"Abi?"

"That's what we decided she would go by."

"I see."

"She and I decided to become partners and start expanding the business internationally. Imagine a service where you could send a BDSM-bot right to a client's house, then they could have a real, digital dominatrix run the sessions in augmented reality. I can't believe nobody is doing this yet."

Abigail started out as a simple dominatrix, but she's ambitious. She currently runs three private BDSM clubs in the greater Seattle area and has 22 employees who discreetly provide every legal BDSM service you can imagine to the rich and kink closeted.

"I'm glad business is going well," I said. "But please leave your venture capitalist streak out of this for the moment."

"Right, sorry," she said. "Two days ago, she sent me this."

Abigail pulled her phone out of her pocket and showed it to me. It was displaying an anonymous messenger app.

Abigail, things have gotten weird. Maybe, dangerous weird. Steer clear of George Washington. I've got to disappear for a while. Don't look for me. I'll get in touch when I figure things out. Seriously, just stay out of this. I know right now you're thinking about how you're going to try to find me. Don't. Damn it. Fuck off. You know I'm at least as smart as you. You're still thinking you can outsmart me you arrogant ass. I'm going to be hiding. Searching for me will probably make things worse. Abi.

"George Washington?"

I looked at Abigail.

"The software engineer's name was George. I change the surname of clients in my records so they've got the same name as someone famous. It's funny and adds a little extra security."

"Spanking George Washington. Yeah, I can see how that could be funny."

"Right."

"She seems to think you should stay out of this."

Abigail rolled her eyes.

"Are you rolling your eyes at yourself?"

She squinted.

"I guess."

"So, this is why you freaked out and drove here?"

"No." Abigail took a bracing breath. "George Washington is dead."

I tried to resist. It was a serious situation. Someone was dead. I tried.

"Well I guess I assumed so after three hundred years."

"Romeo."

"Sorry, sorry. When did you find out?"

"I went to talk to him this morning. Last night he fell to his death out of his office window."

"Suicide."

"Maybe. The office window didn't open. He'd have to smash the glass to jump through it."

"Is that something he might do?"

"I don't think so. Besides there's a public balcony four floors up. If he wanted to kill himself, why not just head up there?"

"You think someone helped him through the window?"

"I think I really need to talk to Abi."

"Okay," I took a moment. "Okay, so why are you telling me this? Don't get me wrong, I'm mad you didn't tell me sooner, and terrified that you told me at all. But why did you rush straight here?"

"Abi and I have talked about the digital world and ghosts," Abigail said. "She said ghosts are a little suspicious of people in the real world."

"Yeah, well, you won't let us vote."

The Supreme Court is pointedly ignoring three separate cases on Digital American voting rights.

"Hey, that's not me," Abigail said.

"Oh, isn't that always what the stooges of 'The Man' say? I'm not to blame. It's just the system."

Abigail cocked her head.

"Romeo, I appreciate you're freaking out, and humor is where you go when you freak out, but can you try to take this seriously for a minute?"

I sighed. I didn't want to. It was all very scary. Most people faced with fear scream. Not me, not usually. The first time a bully told me he was going to beat me up, I gave a shrill laugh and chucked a chocolate milk at him. My heart beats to the tune of a one-man band falling down a flight of stairs. When I'm scared, he just falls faster.

"You want me to help you look for Abi?"

"Yes."

"Because I'm your ghost buddy who'll vouch that you're down with the cause."

"Basically, yes."

"You bios are all alike."

"Romeo."

"Fine, I'll help."

"Thank you."

I wheeled backward and forward in the room. I reached out a hand and leaned against a server. A lot had happened, very quickly.

"Did you have any ideas where to start looking?" I asked.

"Yes, Abi and I bought her a fake identity together. I was thinking she might go back to the same person. His name is Sanav. He lives in the DOA Republic."

"The DOA Republic?"

"You know it?"

"I've spent a little time there."

Abigail smiled.

"You applied to live there?"

I grimaced.

"I'm on the wait list."

"So, can we go?"

"You want to go now?"

"No Romeo, I want to sit around here for a few hours and panic."

"Oh good, that's what I was planning."

"I know it was. Let's go."

"Okay," I relented. "How are you getting online?"

"I'll use my phone."

Abigail pulled the flexible plastic out of her pocket. She pressed a button and it straightened into a flat plane.

"Ugh, 2D interface," I said. "All the other ghosts are going to think I'm a jackass hanging out with you."

"Well then, you'll know how I felt hanging out with you in high school."

"Okay, ouch, and fair enough."

I zipped outside. I took a moment to calm down before getting Izy's attention.

"Hey Izy, Abigail needs my help. Mind if I hop on the net for a few minutes?"

"Why would I mind?" she said. "I'm just paying you for this time."

"Please. I'll help you plan how to kill the CEO of Flooffee. You know, in case tomorrow's coffee is late."

"Hmm. Very well."

I rolled to my charging station and plugged my robot into the server connection.

I rubbed my hands together nervously. They clicked and clacked. I was a part of a conspiracy. We were conspirators, who had conspired. I thought through all the successful criminal conspiracies I had ever heard about. It seemed to me like we didn't have nearly enough elected officials involved for a high chance of success.

I closed out my robot's interface and connected.

5

DRINKS ON ARRIVAL

March 3rd, 2064 9:36 a.m. PST

I was floating in an abyss again. It was a lot more tense after my conversation with Abigail. Usually the unfettered emptiness of unrendered digital space feels like it's a mental command away from a good time. Now it felt like there was something ready to strike, like a jungle cat, a clown, or the workers of the world, finally united.

A link request appeared from Abigail. I accepted it. A city started rendering before me. A blank canvas of terrain spread out in all directions. A flat, rocky outcropping appeared in front of us. Buildings popped into existence like frat bros at lady's night. Not for the first time, Abigail and I were surrounded.

She was floating in the air, a 2D video being captured from her phone. Her 2D presence vanished as she turned away. She spun and looked back at me.

"You're still freaking out, aren't you?"

"What?" I said. "No. No. No? No."

She sighed.

"We're going to find Abi and figure this out. George Washington was probably embezzling from the company or something."

"Do companies usually throw embezzlers out of office windows?"

Abigail looked away for a moment.

"Okay, so maybe it's something else."

The structures around us had white plaster walls and clay tile roofs. A large, many-pillared temple perched on the flat rock formation overlooking the city below. It was ancient Athens. Well, I'm not sure the ancient Athenians had cracked space elevator technology. A long semi-transparent cable stretched into the sky. Every once in a while, people were shooting up and down inside it like it was a massive pneumatic tube. A frozen tundra extended to the north, a thick jungle to the east, the swirling dunes of a desert to the west and, to the south, a port filled with a menagerie of sea vessels. Like I said, rules are pretty thin on the ground in cyber space.

I set off toward the port with Abigail in tow, the DOA Republic sprawling out around us.

The republic had appeared a decade ago when people playing games against AI was a big deal. Chess and Go were popular mechanisms for humans to prove how much smarter they were then computers. Then people started losing. They started losing chess first. As soon as this happened, humans decided chess was a lame game for losers. Go, an ancient strategy game from China, allowed humans to hold onto their flagging sense of self-importance. Many people decided that Go was the only true test of human strategic ability. Then humans started losing to computers. People decided Go was a simple game, that only losers liked. Apparently the most important quality of being human was whatever AI hadn't beaten us at yet.

This process continued for decades. Humans finding things they could still do better than AI and bragging about it, until AI beat them, then suddenly that thing became, like, totally pointless, and humans never cared about it anyway. These days AI is nipping at humanity's heels in almost every area of life.

The DOA Republic was founded and paid for by an anonymous administrator. The purpose was to test humans against AI in one of the greatest games ever invented, governance. Every two years the reins of power were handed back and forth from a democratically-elected group of humans to an AI, called DOA. Citizen satisfaction was the metric for victory. At first, humans won, and they were very pleased with themselves. Then the AI tied the humans. The humans became less enthusiastic. These days, well, a lot of the DOA Republic's citizens thought governance was, like, totally pointless, and they never really cared about it anyway.

It's gradually dawning on humanity that the robot uprising won't be an uprising. It'll just be the day AI sits us down and says, 'Yeah so, we're going to have to let you go.'

I took a deep breath. The air smelled like a fantasy of bracing sea air. The salty tang had undertones of cinnamon and juniper. Upside of being a ghost, you can get taste, smell, and touch in digital space without specialty equipment. Activate the right set of simulated neurons and any sensation can be experienced.

Abigail and I arrived at the beach. Some locals were surfing massive wave breaks on the backs of sharks, Jet Ski. I sent a request to the DOA Republic's servers to render the new vehicle. A notice popped up.

You are NOT currently a guest of a DOA Republic citizen. Your vehicle will be rendered at the lowest resolution settings.

A pixilated blob appeared in the water a few feet away. Something to understand about the digital world, you can render anything, so the only thing that matters is the resolution. Driving around on a pixilated Jet Ski is like driving around in a car painted with house paint.

"Where are we headed?" I asked.

"The little boat on the right."

Near the edge of the crowd of hulls, decks, and cannonry was a tiny wooden sailboat.

It took me a moment to identify the handlebars on the Jet Ski. I climbed aboard and Abigail climbed on the back. I gunned the vehicle's engine and took off toward the tiny sailboat. A massive wave struck the side of the Jet Ski. We flipped and were washed up on the beach.

"Want me to drive?" Abigail asked.

"If you feel strongly about it."

We set off again, this time with Abigail driving. She waited for a wave to crash, then gunned the vehicle over the forming crest of the next. It was strange watching her pilot with no visible hands or legs. After a few seconds of maneuvering, we set off across the bay. Crystal-blue water showed off the kind of established coral that wasn't found in the real world anymore. A sea turtle the size of a small whale breached ahead of us. Abigail narrowly dodged it.

"Whoa, close one," the turtle shouted.

"Sorry," I shouted, as we zipped away.

We pulled alongside the tiny sailboat. It was made entirely of varnished wood. A little hatch covered the entrance to the cabin.

"Sanav?" Abigail said.

There was a clang from inside the boat that echoed like the inside of a cavern. The tap tapping of feet on a stone floor approached. The door flew open. A brown-skinned man wielding a cutlass sprang into the bright sun.

"Avast, ye land lubbers, give over yer doubloons."

We starred in silence. He smiled a little awkwardly.

"Just fucking with ya. Come on in."

"Hey, Sanav," Abigail said. "You remember me, I take it?"

Sanav gave a toothy grin full of crooked teeth. His avatar's black hair was cut short but bounced as if it were in zero-g. He pitched the cutlass over his shoulder. It clattered on the sailboat's deck, then vanished from sight.

"I remember you, and I know why you're here. You're looking for Abi."

"How did you know?" Abigail asked.

Sanav's eyes flashed with excitement.

"She swung by and warned me not to help you find her."

"Fuck."

"Yeah. You should still come in though, I'll make margaritas."

"Ooh, margaritas," I said.

Abigail caught my eye. I leaned toward her.

"This is how we do things in digital space," I said. "Things take a little more time. He wouldn't invite us in without a good reason. Trust me."

"Really?"

"Well, do you have somewhere else we should look?"

On the other side of her 2D screen, she looked away from the phone.

"No."

"Well then, the fact that I'm not sure shouldn't be a problem."

I clambered off the Jet Ski. Abigail looked like she was going to object, then she shrugged. We climbed through the hatch in the sailboat into an entryway the size of a tennis court. I didn't even blink at the defiance of physics. On the other hand, the massive moving sculpture of a photorealistic steampunk submarine and a giant squid battling to the death, that slowed me down for a second.

"The Nautilus, *Twenty Thousand Leagues Under the Sea*, pretty cool, right," Sanav asked, shutting the hatch with a quiet click.

"Yeah," I said. "Kind of a lot for the front entrance, but cool."

"I've always loved the sea." He rested an arm on my shoulder and looked wistfully at the battling leviathans. "I used to sail competitively. It's just so beautiful. I feel like understanding the ocean is as close to understanding infinity as humans can get. Of course, I did die in a boating accident, so maybe the sea was trying to tell me something. 'It needs space. Back off, I hardly know it.' What does it say about me that I have a codependent relationship with a geographical feature?"

"Uh, I guess it makes you sound like an old-timey sailor," I said.

Sanav contemplated that for a long moment.

"I can live with that. This way."

He led us around the digital battle and down a flight of stairs. We entered what appeared to be a luxury submarine. A set of floor-to-ceiling windows showed the nearby coral reef. The plush furniture was all curves and soft angles. It was a bright cornucopia of colors like the reef outside. Sanav waved a hand and a full bar appeared along the back wall. He sprang over the counter and lifted two pitchers.

"Lime or pomegranate?"

"Pomegranate," I said.

He poured a stream of pink slushy onto the counter. Just before it struck the marble and splattered, a glass appeared. Once full, Sanav snapped his fingers and a ring of salt materialized around the rim. I took a sip. It was delicious. Three or four years after ghosts were created someone came up with a third-party software that allowed for the creation of simulated ethanol molecules. It's supposed to be bad for your simulation. It risks data corruption or something. That stopped very few ghosts from downloading the software. I, for one, am not spending the rest of existence without the occasional wine cooler. (Yeah, that's right, wine coolers. What? They're a delicious beverage at a reasonable price.)

Sanav poured himself a lime margarita. He glanced at Abigail.

"Sorry," he said. "I can't give you anything in the physical world."

"It's fine," Abigail said. "It's not what I'm here for."

On the screen, she crossed her arms and gave Sanav a look designed to level a repressed politician.

"Your friend is pretty intimidating," our host said.

"This is actually her at like a 2. She hasn't even narrowed her eyes yet."

Abigail narrowed her eyes at me.

"Oh, yeah," Sanav said. "That's good stare."

Our host smiled.

"I can't tell you where Abi went."

"Why not?" I asked.

"She asked me not to."

"Damn, she's always one step ahead."

Sanav snorted.

"Look," I said. "Abi might really be in trouble. Abigail really does want to help. Why can't you help us find her? They're the same person."

His face went dark.

"Being the same person doesn't mean anything," he said. "In the criminal world, people make copies of themselves then use them as free labor. You know there is a software that can inflict pain on a ghost. People use it to force their ghosts to work for them."

My eyes went wide.

"They enslave themselves," I said. "That's messed up. And profound? I don't know. Maybe it's just messed up."

"Just messed up. How do I know that's not what's happening here?"

"Abigail would never do that," I said. "All the pain she inflicts is consensual."

He looked at Abigail.

"What about you, tall, dark, and silent lady? Abi is a copy of you. You can be pretty sure that if the roles were reversed, you'd do the same thing she's doing. Don't you trust yourself?"

Abigail's jaw twitched.

"Abi is an asshole who's cutting me out of whatever's happening because she thinks she knows better."

"Ouch. Don't be so hard on yourself," Sanav said.

"She's being protective, that's my fucking job."

"I'm not sure that's a good enough reason to breach a trust."

"Fine. If you're not going to tell us anything, we're wasting our time here."

Abigail's screen turned toward the exit. It would have been a decisive move if she'd been there in person. As a 2D image, turning away just made her disappear. Despite the less than dramatic visual, it had the intended effect on Sanav.

"I might ..." he took a sip from his margarita. "Be persuaded to share something if I knew what was so urgent.

Tell me what the big deal is, maybe I'll decide to point you in the right direction."

Abigail turned back, her eyes narrowed.

"You don't know anything," she said, dawning realization in her voice. "You don't know where she is. She just stopped by and warned you I might be coming. You're needling for information because you're curious. Damn it. We're wasting our time here, Romeo. Let's go."

I took a last sip of the margarita and shrugged.

"Thanks for the drink."

I followed Abigail toward the flight of stairs.

"Wait, wait," Sanav said. "I know something."

Abigail turned back.

"What?"

"Okay, full disclosure, I have no idea where Abi went. She wouldn't tell me."

"Fucking lying—"

"But I do know something."

"What?"

"My business, selling fake ID's, it requires that I have my ear to the ground. I have friends in low places, and a few high ones. After Abi stopped by, I got word that someone is looking for her. Someone who is willing to pay tens of thousands of dollars to find her."

"So, you thought you'd pump us for information so you could sell Abi out?"

Abigail's eyes went wide and wrathful.

"Whoa, no, no, no," Sanav said. "Not selling Abi out. I would never do that to a fellow ghost."

"What then?"

"The rumors that I heard didn't say why Abi was being hunted."

"So?"

Our host shrugged.

"I'm curious. I thought you guys might know."

"You've been wasting our time because you're a busybody?"

My head ping-ponged back and forth.

"I wouldn't say wasting. I make a mean margarita."

"It was goo—"

I saw Abigail's face and fell silent.

"What do you know about the people looking for Abi?"

"Not a lot," Sanav said.

The confident swagger he'd had before was crumbling. Abigail has this effect on people.

"There's a man named Yam. He's one of the brokers for whoever is offering the reward. I know him a little bit. I can't help you find Abi, but I might be able to help you find out who's chasing her."

"Yam?"

"Root vegetable. 'Cause he's underground."

"Really?"

"I suspect it's not his given name."

"You think?"

"I could point you in his direction."

Abigail raised an eyebrow.

"Or I could introduce you," Sanav said. "If you tell me why Abi is running."

Abigail opened her mouth to snap.

"That seems fair," I interrupted. Abigail looked at me. I leaned toward her. "What harm can it do? He already knows you made an illegal copy of yourself. That's the only law you broke. Right? Right ... right?"

"Yes."

Abigail sighed.

"Fine. I'll tell you what I know. You take us to meet this, ugh, Yam."

"Great." Sanav smiled. "Let me just finish my margarita."

I shook my head vigorously.

"Or we could just go now."

I nodded vigorously.

"Let's," Abigail said. "Where are we headed?"

"How would you guys like to go shopping?"

Sanav chucked his margarita glass over his shoulder. It smashed and vanished.

6

HOUNDED

One person's trash is another's gold. By this logic, all flea markets are full of alchemists. For the 3D internet, this particular form of magic was performed on a site called Consumerama.

A crowded market popped into existence around us all at once. Each shop was outlined by a tent made out of brightly-colored cloth. Their awnings extended over the aisles and blocked out the sky. The low ceiling made the whole place feel claustrophobic. The confined space filled the air with an urgency, a need to buy, buy now, now, before it's too late.

Despite the cramped quarters, each row of shops seemed to extend to infinity. Customers filled those rows. They jostled and bustled, buying and selling. Every avatar imaginable was flitting through and around each other. Two tumbleweeds were rolling along, stopping at window after window. They bumped into a man wearing a purple pajama set. Two tango dancers did a spinning flourish and a gathered crowd clapped. A cat was sitting in front of a tent. It winked at me, then hissed.

"What did I do?" I said.

The noise was cacophonous. Rules on noise pollution either didn't exist or weren't enforced. I heard shouts, barks, bugles, and baritones. People everywhere were browsing, arguing, needling, wheedling.

"Volume, volume. Pump up the volume."

A nearby peddler was selling audio software. Beside it, a shop was selling digital interior decorating. Every genre of music was blasted from all directions. Art of all kinds filled the displays around me. Art done by famous artists, and nobody artists. There was a portrait done by Manet, next to a portrait of Monet, next to a portrait of a pile of money. Some products were purely digital, others had physical equivalents that could be shipped for a low, low cost to any real-world address.

Another shop window advertised personalized film re-editing. It showed several famous film sequences altered by the purveyor. A comedy played out like a horror film, a drama as bawdy farce.

'Get the ending you want,' a sign read.

The tango dancers were selling software that would make any avatar a great dancer. Next to their shop, an old woman was offering to read ghosts' fortunes to see if their soul had, in fact, connected with their digital copy. She had a crowd waiting to be served.

Every once in a while, a grey mannequin avatar wandered past. It was the default avatar for people that didn't have one. It was haunting. One looked at me as it passed. I didn't scream. It was more of a muffled squeak. Most of the patrons were floating along in low-res versions of their personal avatars. I looked around and found that was true for me and Sanav. Abigail's video had lost a little of its crispness.

"Where to?" Abigail asked.

It was clear from her voice she hadn't quite forgiven Sanav for lying to us.

"We'll have to browse for a while?"

"Why?"

"Yam's business isn't exactly legal. To stay anonymous, he changes store fronts regularly. Don't worry. He's always selling a book called *Surprisingly Legal*. That's how we find him."

"*Surprisingly Legal*?" I said.

"Yeah, it's a book about banking in the 21st century."

He made a few gestures with his hands as he entered the book title into the Consumerama interface. The world around us flickered for a moment, then reappeared. It was still a crowded mess of various shops and services, however they were all pulled together by a similar quality. They all looked pretty shady to me. My guess, *Surprisingly Legal*, was used as a locator for a lot of illegal merchants. The percentage of grey mannequin avatars had jumped to almost half.

"Are you sure we can trust these people?" Abigail asked.

"Oh no, not at all," Sanav said. "You might want to turn your phone camera off. Yam has a picture of Abi. He might recognize you."

Abigail nodded and her screen went blank. It was now an ominous floating black square. Sanav set off down one of the rows of shops. I fell into step beside him. He leaned in close.

"Your friend is still mad I lied, isn't she?"

"Yeah."

"Is she ever going to let me off the hook?"

"I don't know," I said.

"I hate it when people are mad at me."

"You could try apologizing."

He nodded and turned back.

"I'm sorry I lied before, Abigail."

"It's fine."

Sanav turned back to me.

"It doesn't feel like it's fine."

I winked.

"Hey, Abigail?"

"Yeah."

"Sanav really seems like he's sorry."

Abigail sighed.

"It's really fine. Blank slate. Let's just find this Yam person."

I turned back.

"I think that's the best you can hope for, at least for now. Abigail has a tendency to hold grudges, but eventually she gives up on them."

"You realize I can hear everything you're saying," Abigail said.

"I ... did ... not," I said.

There's a software that modulates your volume based on distance. I had forgotten that 2D interfaces weren't compatible with that software. We might as well have been whispering directly into Abigail's ear.

"So, can you tell me why Abi is running?" Sanav asked, diving in to change the subject.

I glanced back at the ominous black square.

"I guess we did promise." Abigail's voice had softened a bit. "Yeah, go ahead."

I conveyed the tale of George Washington the kinky software engineer. Sanav made a great audience. His eyes widened. He gasped. There was even a moment where he stopped mid-step and turned to me mouth open.

"So, you think the person who killed George Washington is looking for Abi?"

"Maybe, or maybe it's a coincidence. That's why we need to talk to her."

"This is like a mystery."

"Right?"

Sanav turned back to Abigail.

"You have no idea what George Washington might have told Abi?"

"No idea," she said. "The whole point of the setup was that not even she would know."

"So, why is somebody looking for her?"

"We don't know," I said.

"Oh wow, this is super real."

"Yeah."

"How are you not freaking out?" Sanav asked.

"Oh, I am."

"How is she not freaking out?"

"Abigail goes quiet and intimidating when she's worried."

Sanav took a moment. He nodded.

"Wow."

We walked in silence for a few seconds. I kept an eye on our guide, trying to gauge how well he was coping. Aside from a slightly wide-eyed look, Sanav seemed to be alright. He paused outside a bright purple tent.

"I think this is it," he said.

"Why?" Abigail asked.

Sanav pointed to a yam sitting in the front display.

"Of course."

"Hey Abigail, you probably want to let me and Romeo do the talking," Sanav said. "I don't know if Yam knows what Abi sounds like."

"Okay," Abigail said. "Romeo, you think you're up to this?"

"No, fuck no. Absolutely not."

"Romeo."

"I mean, sure, absolutely."

"Great. Exactly what I wanted to hear."

I rubbed my hands together. I was feeling an anxious, fractious kind of unease. I looked at Sanav.

"Let's go," I said.

We ducked into the tent. We entered an office. The moment the tent flap closed the cacophony of the market went silent. The interior was decked out in black leather upholstery. The walls were covered in red velvet with black trim. A massive black mahogany desk was dead ahead of us.

"Are you serious?" I asked.

"It's a bit much, I know," Sanav said.

"It's like a cartoon gangster's office."

"I put a lot of myself into this office, stranger."

The voice came from behind the desk. The large black leather chair facing away from us swiveled.

"No," I said. "He did not just do the swivel reveal."

Sanav coughed meaningfully.

"Right, serious. Sorry."

Sitting in the chair was a man wearing a pinstriped suit. He had, no joke, a fat cigar in his mouth. As far as I know, nicotine for ghosts hasn't been programmed yet, but there it was, smoking away. His eyes were beady and persistently narrowed. Beneath them was a wide cleft nose and an even wider cleft chin. He looked suspicious. There's no other word for it. He looked like a criminal.

"Hey, Yam," Sanav said. "How's business?"

"Good, Sanav," he said, in a sing-song, sinister voice. "Things must not be so hot for you, tooling around with a bio. Who's your obelisk?"

He gestured at Abigail's floating black square.

"Just a client who would prefer to remain anonymous."

"What? They don't trust me?"

Yam said the words like he was offended, but also like it totally made sense to him. He stood up from the desk, his arms spread. The gesture on anyone else would have implied they meant no harm. Yam made his open hands look like switchblades waiting to lash out. I was impressed. He had created this avatar, and this was what he'd gone for. Yam was so disreputable in appearance, so shady and duplicitous in his every look and gesture, that I found myself respecting his honesty. It takes a special kind of integrity to be such an obvious crook.

"Who's this?" Yam asked, looking at me.

"This is Romeo."

"Hello, Yam," I said.

"That's Mr. Yam to you, stranger."

I choked.

"Mr. Yam, then. Hello."

The digital gangster didn't seem to mind my amusement. Sanav on the other hand looked worried. He took my arm and turned me away from Yam.

"I know he's ridiculous, but that's kind of his deal," he said. "You can't really threaten dead people all that much, so he goes ridiculous to put ghosts off their guard. He can still do quite a lot of digital damage though."

"What can he do?" I asked.

"Want to spend the rest of your life having your identity perpetually stolen? Over and over and over again?"

"Shit. No."

"Be respectful."

We turned back to Yam.

"I apologize for my comment about your office, Mr. Yam," I said. "Everybody goes post-futurism in the digital world, I appreciate you have classic taste in interior design."

"Thank you," he said. "So, why are you here?"

"We're actually here about that ghost, Abi," Sanav said. "I think you're offering a reward for information about her."

"You have information? You're here to collect?"

"No," Sanav said.

Yam's face fell.

"Then what?"

"We were wondering who your client is?" I said.

Sanav looked at me like I'd just blown my nose on Yam's tie. Yam didn't look pleased either.

"Why?" he asked.

Sanav sighed.

"I know Abi a little bit. She's a decent kind of person. I'm just curious why somebody is looking for her."

Yam raised an eyebrow. He ran a finger along the cleft of his chin.

"You thought I would tell you who my client is?"

"Maybe, or at least why they were looking for her."

His face was migrating from cartoon villainy to actually sinister.

"Would you burn a client for me, Sanav?"

Sanav looked uncomfortable.

"No, you wouldn't," Yam answered for him. He looked up at the ceiling. "Look, you helped me get out from under my bio. Got me this shiny new identity. I feel a sense of gratitude."

He leaned forward.

"So, here's what I will tell you. If you do know this Abi, tell her to run. Far and fast. The people who are looking for her aren't fucking around."

He leaned back. It was amazing to me how oppressive the furnishing had become. The black and red had all seemed a bit ridiculous. Now all I could see was blood and abyssal darkness.

"You shouldn't have come here, Sanav," Yam said. "My clients put a keyword search on the conversations in my office. They think I don't know. Arrogant pricks. I turned it off a few moments ago, but your friend already said the name Abi. If you know what's good for you, you'll run. Right now."

Sanav's eyes went wide and he nodded.

"Time for us to go," he said.

"Wait, what?" I said.

He didn't answer, but instead, turned toward the exit. Yam had already turned back to his desk. Abigail's hovering square and I burst out of the tent after Sanav. The world outside had changed. The endless row of flea market tents had vanished. It was now just the one tent, and an endless grey plane. Standing in a semicircle around the tent entrance, to my horror, were six of the featureless grey default avatars. They stood out a little darker against the infinite, bland expanse.

"Oh, shit ... I think," I said.

"Pretty sure: oh, shit.," Sanav said.

The central grey avatar stepped forward. Its featureless face looked us over in a way that made my spine tingle.

"Well hello there, where are you all off to?" The lead avatar had a thick Australian man's accent.

"Fuck off," Sanav said.

"I thought that might be your perspective." He looked behind Sanav. "Who's the chokkie Tim Tam?"

"What?" I asked.

"The black square who's floating about with you. A bio, I presume. Let's see."

The lead avatar made a gesture. Abigail's blacked-out screen turned back on. I was too shocked to react at first. Whoever this anonymous avatar was, he was using some very high-level software and a lot of processing power to hijack a phone and turn on its camera with only a few seconds notice.

"Well, hello," the lead avatar said. "Don't you look familiar? You know I'm looking for a ghost that looks an awful lot like you."

We all sat in silence for another several seconds.

"Fuck," I said.

"Well summarized," the avatar said. "But don't yet despair. I'm not getting paid to track a bio. In fact, I didn't know this Abi was a copy of a living person. So why would I care? My paycheck comes from one thing, and one thing only, finding Abi the ghost. Help me with that, and we'll all be happy to pretend none of this ever happened."

"We're not helping you find Abi," Abigail said.

"Really?" The grey avatar advanced. "You might want to recon—"

"I'm sorry," I interrupted, as the grey figure drew closer. "I'm just, these avatars. While we have this conversation, do you guys have alternative avatars you could use? The matte-grey, faceless mannequin thing is really freaking me out."

Sanav looked at me.

"Really?"

"It's just weird. I feel like I should focus, and I'm just not going to be able to. I'm sorry, I appreciate it's my problem."

Sanav looked at the lead avatar questioningly.

"Fucking sure, whatever," he said.

"Ugh, go to preferences for Consumerama," Sanav said.

"Are you kidding me?" Abigail grumbled.

In the top corner of my perception was a box containing three horizontal lines. With a thought I selected it.

"Got it."

"Change default avatar."

The option wasn't there.

"That's not an option."

Sanav sighed.

"Yes, it is. It's near the bottom."

"It's not here."

"Look again."

"I really can't see it."

"It's there."

"Oh, I found it," I said. "I found it."

"There should be options."

"Let me see."

An array of generic avatars appeared.

"Yup, let me see. Ooh, clowns."

I looked up. A series of circus clowns were grinning maniacally at me.

"Not clowns," I said. "Definitely not clowns. How about, raptors?"

A half-dozen ancient predators surrounded me.

"Okay nope, nope. I am so sorry about this."

"Is he for real?" the lead avatar asked.

"I am sorry," Sanav said. "I don't know him very well."

"Business men in suits," I said.

I looked up.

"Okay, somehow that's more creepy. Give me a second here. Okay, okay, got it."

I looked up to see six Golden Retrievers wagging their tails happily.

"Hey, why are you looking at my crotch?" the lead avatar asked.

"Oh, sorry," I said. "You're a Golden Retriever to me, so that's where your head is."

"Well, change the avatar then, 'cause now you're freaking me out."

I looked in preferences.

"Ah, there's a standing option."

The Golden Retriever was now hopping on its back legs.

"Is that better?" I asked.

"Well, now you're starring at my chest, but yeah that's fine."

I snorted.

"What?" he said.

"I'm sorry, I just noticed the dog's mouth moves when you talk," I said.

"Can we please focus?" Abigail asked.

"I'm sorry, I'm sorry," I said. "I realize what we're doing is very serious, and I've disrupted that. I'm good now."

"Fucking hell," the lead Golden Retriever said. "Where the fuck was I?"

"You were about to try and get us to sell out Abi," I said. "Which is never going to happen. This is digital space. What are you going to do, send us spam? Identity theft? An inconvenience, but I'm not selling out a friend for that. Even if she's a friend I haven't met yet."

I looked pointedly at Abigail. She ignored the look.

"He is right," she said. "You don't have any leverage. So, unless you want to tell us who's looking for Abi or why, there's no reason for us not to just leave."

"I wouldn't be so sure about that. Leverage is what you make of it. For example, I may not know a lot about you all, but I do know that you are from America, that you've made a copy of yourself which is illegal in that country, and

I know the IP address from which you are connected to the Internet. With those pieces of information, I could say, drop an anonymous tip to the FBI, perhaps."

"You're bluffing," Abigail said. "You don't know where we are."

"Well, this gentleman here is running on a server farm in international waters." He indicated Sanav. "You two, however, are in Seattle, Washington. Makes sense. His name I don't know. The account on your cell phone however." He stepped toward Abigail. "Says it's registered to one, Abigail Page. Abigail to Abi, how cute."

"Why does that make sense?" I asked.

"What?"

"That we're in Seattle?"

The Golden Retriever shot me a look, then pulled back his lips in frustration.

"Whoever hired you is in Seattle," Sanav said.

"Fuck off," the golden-haired dog said. "Very clever. Like it will make any difference. Give up Abi and the FBI need never know you were involved. She'll just disappear. Problem solved for you."

"Get fucked," Abigail said.

"Yeah," I added.

"I would have preferred to do things kindly," he said.

A jolt of pain shot up and down my body. It was like my entire digital skeleton had been turned into one giant funny bone and every square inch of it had been banged into a sharp corner. I collapsed in agony and screamed. It wasn't a scream for help. It was the kind of sound your body makes when some primordial part of you knows you're doomed and thinks, 'well might as well warn the other apes not to come this way because agony and death are what awaits them.' I looked over to see Sanav was in the same condition.

"Now," the retriever said. "I don't want to have to do that again, but I definitely will. So, tell me where Abi is."

The other Golden Retrievers moved in a little closer to loom over us. I saw Abigail was unaffected but also unable to do anything.

"Let's get out of here," I said.

"Yes," Abigail said.

"Trying," Sanav said.

My mind reached for the command that would allow me to disconnect from Consumerama. I selected it. An error message popped up in my screen.

"Sorry about that," the lead retriever said. "I wouldn't want you lot to fuck off too soon. I may have blocked the disconnect command on your interfaces."

There are a lot of upsides to being a ghost in digital space. There are also a few downsides. As an electronic entity, my entire interface with the world is run through software. Software can be hacked. A human can always disconnect themselves from the Internet because if worst comes to worst, they can just walk to their modem and unplug the thing. For me, if the electronic command doesn't work, I'm trapped. I looked up at the looming pack of standing Golden Retrievers.

"What can I do?" Abigail asked.

"You can tell me where Abi is," the pack leader said.

"Not you, asshole. I'm done talking to you."

"I've got software that will get me out of here," Sanav said.

"I don't," I said.

"Get out of here," Abigail ordered. "I'll help him."

Sanav vanished, as did Abigail's phone screen. I felt very alone surrounded by a bunch of thoroughbred show dogs. Another jolt of pain ran up my body.

"Where is Abi?"

I looked up at my torturer.

"Why don't you go lick your—."

The world vanished. My Internet interface crashed. I booted my robot interface. Abigail was crouched in front of me. She had yanked the cable connecting me to the Internet out of the server. Izy was standing behind her, confusion and concern on her face. I looked at Abigail.

"I feel like we should have listened to Abi when she said, 'searching for me will probably make things worse,'" I said.

Abigail looked at the floor.

"I hate it when she's right."

7

VANDERWALL BERRYS

March 3rd, 2064 11:05 a.m. PST

"What is happening?" Izy asked.

I looked at her. Not having a throat, I was incapable of gulping. I have knees, but they don't have enough lateral flexibility to really rattle.

"So, Izy—"

"It's my fault," Abigail said. "I dragged Romeo into this."

"Well, dragged? I think I pretty much rose to the occasion."

Abigail looked at me.

"I'm trying to help you out here."

"Oh sure, sorry."

She looked back to Izy.

"But no," I said.

They looked at me again.

"For a good reason this time. I can't let you go down alone, Abigail. It's in moments like this where we need courage." I looked at my boss and friend, ready to level headedly convey recent events. "Help! Izy, we fucked up. The FBI are on the way. It was Abigail's fault ... okay I admit it, I'm to blame too. Why is everybody pointing fingers? Who's to blame isn't what's important, right now. Help, help, I don't know what to do, please help."

"You're the only one pointing fingers, Romeo," Abigail said.

"Well, now you're pointing the finger at me for pointing the finger. So, who's really pointing the finger here."

"I feel a migraine coming on."

"The FBI?" Izy asked, cutting off my retort.

"Possibly." Abigail said. "We should assume so."

Izy's poker face is so immovable it could be used as the anchor point for a space elevator. It flickered.

Abigail's phone buzzed.

"It's Sanav," she said. "I'm going to send him a message saying we're fine, and that he should lay low."

"Tell me what happened," Izy said. "Fast."

We did. Izy's face somehow became progressively less expressive as the story continued.

"You should have told me what was going on," Izy said.

She squared her substantial, rugby-ready shoulders. Her eyes were a little wider, the muscles in her jaw flexed.

"I'm really sorry, Izy," Abigail said. "I just didn't want to get you involved."

"Objective failed, it would seem."

"I know. I didn't think it would spin into this. I'm so sorry."

"I am too," I said. "Really, really, sorry."

Izy surveyed us. I clasped my mechanical hands.

"You know about cyber security, Izy," I said. "Can we do anything to make sure the FBI don't actually connect Abigail to Abi?"

"No," Abigail said.

"What?" I asked.

"Abi and I communicated a lot. It might take them a few days, but if the FBI really look, they'll find evidence of that contact. I need to get out of here. The best I can do is not get you dragged into this, Izy."

"Do you have somewhere to go?" Izy asked. "They will check your home."

"I could go to one of my clubs," Abigail said. "My name's not legally attached to them."

"I would take your battery out of your phone," Izy said.

"Thanks."

"What can I do?" I asked.

"I don't think there's anything," Abigail said. "I shouldn't have gotten either of you involved. I really thought we'd just find Abi and sort this out. I'm sorry."

"You should go, Abigail," Izy said.

"Right."

Abigail started for the door. She took her phone battery out as she went.

"Did you drive here?" Izy stopped her.

"Yes," Abigail said.

"Drive some distance away from here," Izy said. "Then park your car. Take mass transit the rest of the way to your club."

"Okay," Abigail said.

She started for the door. Stopping halfway through, she looked back at both of us. She seemed to be looking for something to say. Instead she just nodded. Izy didn't respond. I waved. I wasn't exactly sure what else to do. Abigail shut the door as she left.

"Can I do anything?" I asked.

"I don't know, Romeo. Can you?"

"Okay, still angry, I see. I'm very sorry."

"It doesn't feel like you're sorry enough."

"You want to get the stun gun baseball bat, don't you?"

"Don't tempt me, metal man."

"Am I still employed?"

"We'll see."

"I'll just shut up."

"At last, wisdom manifests."

Izy started making flicking gestures with her hands. She was doing something with her AR interface.

"How bad is this?" I asked.

"I have no idea."

"But you seem worried."

"Yes. I am here on Green Card. The FBI could make many problems for me."

My non-existent stomach lurched.

"Shit, that didn't even occur to me."

"It would seem not."

It's difficult to tell with stoics, but it was beginning to dawn on me how pissed Izy was. Even more uncomfortable, her anger was completely justified. There are few fates in life worse to suffer than having a good person angry at you for good reason. Well, actually, there are plenty of fates worse to suffer. (Shark attacks, flesh-eating bacteria, sitting through school plays.) Still, I felt like shit.

"Izy I'm going to fix this."

"What?"

"I've decided, whatever it takes, I will make sure this doesn't mess with your life. Even if I have to turn myself in and confess."

"What would you confess to, exactly?"

I paused. It hadn't occurred to me, but I was only barely a criminal.

"I don't know. I'll think of something. Worse comes to worse, I'll commit a crime and confess to it."

"Don't be foolish."

"I can't help it. I mean, I'm not ... sorry I thought you were going to say brave or something."

"Does that sound like something I would say?"

"Well, in retrospect, obviously not."

Izy looked at me like she imagined a jingly jester's hat on my head.

"Things might be fine," she said. "The FBI probably doesn't respond to every anonymous tip. Is possible, they won't even show up."

An hour later the FBI showed up.

They manifested in the form of two young agents in cheap suits. One was a black woman, the other a white man. In every other way they seemed to be identical. Equally tall, their shoulders were the same width. They had the same kind of aggressive fitness. The kind of body that makes you think they've spent a significant amount of time in the gym with someone shouting in their face, 'push it!' Their suits were black and had the same blue shirt. They were each wearing trench coats that hung to the same point on their calves. As they entered the office, their footsteps were in sync. They glanced around, their heads turning together, first to their right, then to their left.

"Agents Vanderwall and Berrys," Izy said, examining their badges. "What brings you to this little server farm?"

Nothing in the way Izy said the names indicated which agent was which.

"We're here looking for someone."

"A someone named Abigail Page."

"We got a tip that she might be here."

"She was online using an IP address associated with your server farm."

"Is she here?"

"Ever heard of her?"

Izy blinked in the face of the barrage.

"Which question would you like me to answer first?"

"Go in order."

"No. Yes," Izy said.

"Darn."

"Great."

"What was she doing here?"

"Where did she go?"

"Visiting. I don't know," Izy said.

"Visiting?"

"Darn."

"Yes." Izy paused. "Is, darn, something I should respond to?"

"No."

The two agents stepped further into the office. They had a rhythm about their speech that made them seem like a single entity. They did a second scan of the room like a Hydra with two heads.

"Why did she visit?" the female agent asked.

"We are friends," Izy said.

"She came to visit you?" the male agent asked.

"And my employee, Romeo."

"I'm not flirting with you," the male agent said.

"I think the employee's name is Romeo," the female agent said.

"It is," Izy said.

The male agent seemed embarrassed.

"Good. As long as we're clear."

"Very clear," Izy said.

"Where is Romeo?"

"He is a ghost."

"You employ a ghost?"

"Yes."

"How progressive."

"Sure," Izy said.

"Can we speak to Romeo?"

"He's standing right in front of you."

I waved. Both agents jumped.

"I thought that was an errand robot."

"As did I."

"I've heard of ghosts with robotic bodies."

"Not common."

"Very strange."

"Hello," the male agent shouted at me.

I paused for a moment, confused. Some people don't know how to handle talking to a dead person. It seems to trigger the same response in them that being an English speaker in a non-English speaking country has triggered in generations of American tourists. They shout. In the face of that, I have found there is only one reasonable response.

"Hello," I shouted back.

"We need to ask you about Abigail Page," the female agent shouted.

"Okay," I shouted back.

I raised my eyebrows at Izy over the two agent's shoulders. She shrugged.

"Do you know where Mrs. Page went?"

"No."

"Do you know how to contact Mrs. Page?"

"Her phone number," I shouted.

"We have that."

"Her phone is off."

"We couldn't GPS locate it."

"Battery pulled out."

"Almost like she's hiding."

"Any idea why she might be hiding?"

"No," I said. "Why are we shouting?"

"I thought it might help us to understand each other."

"Okay," I shouted.

"Do you know if Mrs. Page has much interaction with ghosts?" the female agent said, still shouting.

"Me."

The male agent turned to his partner.

"I don't understand," he said, at a normal volume.

"He's saying she interacts with him," the female agent replied.

"I see."

They turned back to me.

"You don't know where Mrs. Page might be?" the female agent shouted.

"Her apartment," I shouted.

"We checked on the way over."

"No answer when we buzzed."

"Then I don't know."

The two agents turned back to Izy.

"Did Mrs. Page access the Internet while she was here?" the male agent said, at a normal volume.

"Possibly," Izy said. "I didn't track her every move."

It was clear the agents were bristling at our lack of helpfulness.

"Did Mrs. Page say where she was going?"

"No, she just left," Izy said.

"Is that right?"

"Yes."

Vanderwall and Berrys looked around the office, now suspicious. Their collective eyes fell on a set of security cameras in opposite corners of the room.

"You have security cameras."

"Yes."

"We'll need to see the footage."

"Hmm." Izy looked down at the ground. She shook her head. "Small problem."

"What?"

"You have warrant?"

"We can get a warrant," the female agent said.

"But you not have one?"

Both agent's jaws tightened.

"This is problem," Izy said. "Company policy, I cannot show security footage without warrant."

"Can we speak to your boss then?"

"I am boss."

"You're the boss."

"Yes," Izy said. "I wrote policy. I am a stickler for the rules. Very unfortunate."

"Then we'll get a warrant."

"Good. Small problem."

"What, now?"

"No security footage is stored here."

"I'm sorry?"

"Yes, very unfortunate. Is all uploaded to a server in Taipei."

"Taipei?"

"Is the capital of Taiwan."

"We know where Taipei is. Fine, international warrants are a little more trouble, but we'll get one all the same."

"Good. Small problem."

"What?" the male agent snapped.

"This server farm in Taipei is very unreliable. There is history of data being corrupted. Specifically, when they respond to international warrants. They are dubious business people. I am small business owner. What can I do? But, good luck with getting footage."

Vanderwall and Berrys had the exact same vein pulsing in the center of their foreheads. Izy looked like they were having a conversation about the weather.

"What's your name?"

"Elisabetta Aliyev."

"Aliyev?"

"Yes, is Russian by way of Kazakhstan."

"Are you a citizen of the United States, Mrs. Aliyev?"

"No."

"Are you sure you want to obstruct a federal investigation?"

"I don't believe asking for a warrant is obstruction."

"People believe a lot of things, Mrs. Aliyev."

"Is true," Izy said. "I have noticed this."

I didn't like the direction the conversation was headed. I rolled forward.

"Excuse me," I said.

"Shit," the female agent said, as both agents jumped.

"Snuck right up on us."

I was still ten feet away.

"Uh, sorry."

"Do you understand the consequences of impeding a federal investigation?" the male agent shouted at me.

"Yes," I shouted.

"Do you know if Abigail Page has ever been involved in the copying of a living human?" the female agent shouted.

"I just wanted to inform you agents that this entire conversation is being recorded," I shouted, hoping that would dodge the question.

I tapped the side of my screen. Both agents straightened up.

"I see," the male agent said.

"Good to know," the female agent said.

Their shouting had stopped.

"We're going to continue to investigate."

"If we discover you withheld pertinent information ..."

"We'll be back."

Vanderwall and Berrys headed for the door.

8

THINGS INTERNETTED

March 3rd, 2064 12:25 p.m. PST

Izy was still mad. She wasn't yelling or shouting. She wasn't even refusing to talk to me. Instead, she was utilizing the ability that every stoic person seems to pick up at some point. The ability to make the air in the room seem several degrees colder than comfortable. As I didn't have skin to feel the air, I was pretty sure it was psychosomatic. Izy wasn't just living in my head rent-free. She was messing with the thermostat.

"Do you need anything?" I asked.

"No, all good."

Not bitter, not angry. Just icy.

"I was thinking I would do research on George Washington. See if I can figure out what Abi is running from."

"Good idea."

"If you need me—"

"I will call," she said.

"Okay."

I rolled to my charging station and connected myself directly to the server. I'd have to find some way to make things up to Izy. What do you give the friend you may have inadvertently embroiled in a criminal conspiracy? A Thompson machine gun in a violin case? Maybe a black-and-white-striped sweater with a matching balaclava?

Closing out my robot interface, I booted my home apartment. The baboons had moved on to terrorizing the apartment building next door. With a thought, I converted the windows into a series of blank screens.

Researching a person online is a little like fumbling around an unfamiliar room in the dark. For the most part you run into recognizable shapes: chairs, tables, that crush from college they never got over. You just hope, as you fumble, you don't run into anything sharp or sticky. Considering the FBI were investigating, and a pack of Australian Golden Retrievers were tracking me, my life was already pretty sticky and fairly sharp. I couldn't imagine knowing more about George Washington would make things worse. In perhaps not my finest moment, I'd actually typed the name and hit search before I remembered that wasn't the software engineer's real name. With several money-green depictions of the first president looking down on me, I pondered how to find the more modern George.

I looked up local news coverage and quickly found a story about the software engineer. At 10:45 pm his body had been found on the sidewalk beneath his office. He had clearly fallen to his death. The article referred to his death as a suicide though the police hadn't made any formal statements. His real name was George Frederick. I decided to keep calling him George Washington.

A few quick searches and I was looking at a variety of social media profiles. Most were private. A professional page listed his position as 'Researcher' at Maddoc Technologies. I threw that profile page to one of the big screens and opened a new search page. I looked up the company.

It was an accidental success of the medical research world. It had developed a medication that's intended purpose was to treat muscular dystrophy. In a market teaming with competition, the medication had failed spectacularly. However, in the midst of the FDA trials, a side effect had been noted by many of the researchers, effortless weight loss. The company quintupled in value almost the moment this news became public.

"Interesting," I said.

I opened up a new tab and spent ten minutes watching clips of adult cats meeting new kittens. They were delightfully disgruntled.

"Shit, focus," I said.

I scrolled through a few more pages, but besides the weight-loss medication, the company didn't have much of a public profile. They'd developed a medication that lowered blood pressure, a high-end brain scanner, and three different kinds of tumor-suppressing gene therapy. It was all the kind of stuff that's boring until it's saving your life.

"Aha," I said to myself. I tapped my fingertips together triumphantly. "I have no idea what any of this means."

Investigating is hard.

I flipped through the pages looking for something else to connect. Lamenting my lack of thumbtacks and red yarn, I had to settle for bookmarking all the pages and putting them in a folder. I titled the folder, 'Investigation.' I paused for a moment then retitled it, 'Secret Investigation.' I paused again then retitled it, 'Tax Documents.'

I went back to the news article about George Washington's death. The Maddoc Technologies' headquarters were in downtown Seattle. Abi was in the wind, and I had no other direction to look. My only two options were to stop or move forward. A real detective would head down to the main building and ask around. I didn't even need Abigail to remind me I wasn't a real detective, still something had to be done.

Opening up a new page, I spent ten minutes watching GIFs of surprised monkeys.

"Focus," I told myself.

I closed my web browser and started my robot interface. The office reappeared around me. Izy was at her desk talking on the phone. Her back was to me. I approached, backed away, pretended to look at a server for a moment, realized she wasn't looking at me so acting casual was pretty pointless, approached again, then listened.

"I might need your legal services," she said. "I may be running into immigration troubles." She paused. "Something at my work."

She was calling a lawyer. This is what I had done to my friend. I'd brought lawyers into her life. All the courage I'd been fostering vanished like it had suddenly been adopted by an eccentric, bald billionaire. I bolted for the door. I wasn't sure what I was going to do, but I couldn't sit around. Izy had been better to me than almost anyone I knew. I couldn't drag her deeper into this mess.

I slipped through the office door, down the elevator, and out onto the street. A fleeting ray of sun cut through the clouds. I took this as a sign. As soon as I rolled outside, it started raining again and the clouds closed and seemed to darken. I ignored this. Fuck signs.

Pausing for a moment, I pondered where to go. There was really only one place I thought might help. The office where George Washington had died. Maybe that kinky, no teeth having software engineer had something at his office that could help me figure out what was happening.

(It's possible at this point I was mixing up my Georges.) I headed toward the light rail that went into downtown.

I guessed it would take Izy 20 minutes to realize I'd gone. She would be mad, but I didn't think madder than she already was. If she was going to fire me, then so be it. I cared about her more than my job. Even if my job was working for her. I paused on the sidewalk to consider. I decided it was better for her to be ignorant, irritated, and not deported, then illuminated, deported, and determined to seek revenge. Morality is a real head-scratcher at times.

The light-rail station was covered in both physical and AR graffiti. A collection of commuters were staring at phones, watches, tablets and, failing any of these, the ground. All of them were committed to ignoring the existence of other humans. I feel like cars have cluttered the roads of America for decades in large part because people can't stand dealing with strangers on mass transportation. If that's true, social anxiety was a pretty significant cause of climate change.

I rolled up the wheelchair ramp to the station. Near the end of the platform, I spotted a familiar heap of fabric. The ticker board on the wall informed me the next train was eleven minutes away. With time to spare, I rolled down to the end of the platform and greeted the human clothesline.

"Hey, Chester," I said.

"What?" A dreamy voice said.

"Hello, Chester. It's me, Romeo."

The heap of fabric shifted.

"Romeo of fair Verona?"

"Nope, he's dead."

"When did that happen?"

"Technically never."

"In that case, give him my best next time you see him." I grinned.

"How are things?"

"On course to meet the inevitable fate of entropy."

"Right. Uh, but in the meantime, more immediately."

"They're good."

A cardboard sign was propped up against his clad and reclad body. He shifted the sign and the cloth layers fluttered. The cardboard read, 'Chester184@helpthehomeless. org. All forms of payment accepted.' Nobody uses cash anymore so somebody got creative and made an app for electronic individual donations.

"So, any big thoughts today?" I asked.

"Always, man."

Well, let me hear it?"

Chester sat up and took a deep, decisive breath.

"We're going through a flux. Whole world is changing."

"Oh yeah?"

World changing rants were always Chester's best.

"Yeah," he said.

"How so?"

"Well, way back, we came up with this idea. We called it 'God.'"

"I'm familiar."

"Well, 'God' was the center of everything. Why's that dude king? 'Cause 'God' said he should be. Why do we do things this way? 'Cause 'God' said so. Then, someone asked if everybody was sure 'God' was around. And lots of people weren't sure. So, people asked should we organize everything around something we're not sure exists. And people were like, 'maybe not.'

"Then we organized everything around people, 'cause we were sure they were around. How humans felt about stuff became the center of everything. We made ideas like democracy. Let's take what everybody thinks and just do that. If what we do doesn't work, at least most people will be wrong and feel embarrassed about it and not complain so much."

"Democracy works okay though. Wisdom of the crowd and all that."

"Oh sure, it's okay sometimes. But sometimes it's not. It messes up a lot. So, something new is coming."

"What's that?"

"What's more true than what people want?"

"I don't know."

"The data. The flow."

"The data?"

"Yeah, man. Information from every corner of the world. It's coming all the time, but before we can make it the center of everything, we got to have a way to process it. It's not going to be people that do that. Leastways not bios. Maybe ghosts, but I don't think so."

"So, AI, then. You think computers are going to be in charge of the future."

"Nah, nah man. You're not seeing big enough. It's not going to be AI that controls everything. They'll be a part of it, but they won't be in control. Everything will be in control. We're going to become one big thing. Not just humans and AI, but the birds and the bees and the trees too. A network. We just got to build the ties that bind us. The groundwork's already being laid. You won't have to vote, 'cause the network will know what you want by your wanting it. You'll know what the network wants. You'll know what the birds and the bees and the trees want.

"Imagine if a tree could tell you it needs water. A bird could tell you it needs a place to build its nest. You could tell it, 'yeah little bird, it's totally chill if you build your nest here.' It would know if you were lying."

"How would it know exactly?"

"We're already developing tech that will let people send thoughts from one to the other. You think we're going to stop with people. It'll be pets first, then smarter wild animals. We'll work our way down the food chain."

I pondered that for a moment.

"Will that be better?"

"Who knows, Romeo?"

I nodded.

"That was a good one. I liked that thought."

"Thanks."

"Chester?"

"Yeah?"

"Are you currently on any mind-altering substances?"

"Oh yeah."

I opened up an app and made a donation to Chester's account. A small electronic beep sounded from deep within the swaddling fabric.

"Thanks, Romeo," Chester said.

"No problem."

"Where are you headed?"

"To do something really dangerous and probably ill-conceived."

"Oh, cool. Good luck, man."

"Thanks."

The train pulled into the station and the waiting commuters begrudgingly acknowledged each other. It was clear, were it not for the need to navigate, they would never have done something so indecent. I rolled onto the train.

"Hey, Chester?"

"Yeah?"

"When does this all happen?"

Chester laughed.

"Look around buddy. It's been happening for decades."

9

FRESH WATER

In 2048, a drought started in the Southwest and the Great Plains of the United States. Nobody was too worried that year, droughts happen. Climate scientists went, 'this could be bad.' Society ignored them. Everything was pretty normal. The drought stuck around into 2049. It lingered through 2050, 2051. At this point, a few people suggested it might be a problem. A few minor irrigation reforms were passed to ensure the aquifers wouldn't be drained dry for a few years. 2052, 2053. People started to freak out a little. Small towns started to dry up. Water was trucked in. 2054, 2055. The Ogallala, America's largest aquifer, ran dry. By the summer of 2056, the Great Plains were a desert, and ten million people had lost everything.

Cities were abandoned. Big ones.

Turns out that nature doesn't give a fuck about national boundaries and the same drought extended into Mexico. Five million people crossed the border in six months. I'm pretty sure Border Patrol just collectively pretended to have gout that year.

Where did everybody go? Everywhere.

Seattle and the greater Puget Sound area found themselves with 1.2 million people to deal with. The population of a city wanted to move into an area already pretty populated. Like a dehydrated marathoner's side, it was going to be a bit cramped. Western Washington's cities scrambled to figure out a way to shift the burden of the refugees onto the other cities. Then there was a riot and a sizeable portion of Bellevue was destroyed. (Don't worry, Bellevue's not that great a loss.) Washington State and its major cities decided cooperation might be in order.

This was a pretty chaotic time. I was still living with my parents. There was a curfew for a few weeks. (If I'd been cool enough to have some place to go, I would have been so pissed. Abigail was so pissed.)

The cities created a refugee distribution system. Each city had a quota for how many people they would take. The refugee's information was collected: family size, professional qualifications, socioeconomic status. Then cities would offer invitations. The refugees could decide where they wanted to go based on which cities invited them. Seattle pushed very hard for this system. Can you see why? It's subtle. Take a minute. Imagine you're evil. Now, think about it.

Seattle, as the richest city, was also the city most people wanted to be settled in. It had the most jobs and, at least initially, the refugees wouldn't be paying the ludicrous housing costs. So, Seattle could just look over the socioeconomic information and professional qualifications of the refugees and invite the richer and more easily employed ones. Cagey bastards. Racism being a socioeconomic force as much as it is a cultural one, this pretty rapidly manifested into a pattern. For the most part, Seattle was taking the rich—'less poor' would be more accurate—white refugees.

Even as people in real-time pointed out the racism of the policies, Seattle's majority white population repeated their children-of-the-corn mantra, "But I'm not racist. But I'm not racist, though. But I'm not racist." Some people suggested that a racial quota system be put in place to compensate for the obvious bias in refugee processing. This idea was immediately shot down with the charge of—Can you guess? Can you guess what the charge was?—reverse racism.

Seattle obviously did this thinking the richer, more employable, refugees would be easier to settle. At first, they were right.

Renton, Kent, and Tacoma (those are cities around Seattle) turned into disaster zones, but in the midst of that disaster, an aggressively innovative set of mayors and city councils, that could see their respective cities were teetering on the edge, moved fast. Turns out, threat of total societal breakdown really silences detractors. They instituted a bunch of civilian work programs, that were decried as communism, but rapidly stabilized the situation as they alleviated desperation and allowed for the rapid expansion of those three cities' infrastructures.

Meanwhile, the techno-capitalists of Seattle were trying to figure out a way to magic their predominantly white refugee population into prosperity in some way that didn't, in any way, ever, EVER, require raising taxes. Don't get me wrong, the southern Puget Sound was still on a knife edge and Seattle was still the wealthiest city for a thousand miles, but Seattle was the only one with a genuine ghetto these days.

Oh yeah, the next year, another million people showed up.

10

THE RESURRECTION OF THE ROI

March 3rd, 2064 1:10 p.m. PST

The subway doors shut in my face and the train lurched into motion. There was a squeal, a rattle, and we were off. Campaigning on improving mass transportation systems was the kind of reasonable thing politicians do in the dreams of civics professors. Because I don't live in the orderly nighttime fantasies of tweed-wearing academics, the local mass transportation system was falling apart. I glanced around the train car. People were staring at their phones, tablets, and some just stared into the distance, AR contacts or glasses making their eyes go unfocused.

Dancing cartoon advertisements were leering at me and encouraging me to play a game or press a button to see if I had won something. Every inch of flat space had ads displayed by tiny micro-projectors. I opened up my app files and found one called Adarter. I turned it on and every advertisement around me vanished in my AR display. Adarter was adblocking software that replaced ads with various works of art. The app allows the user to go into the art collection and select favorites. I've never done that. It was just a mishmash of various eras and styles. 8-bit Nomofomo (nostalgic modernist formulated moods) pieces from the 2030s sat next to Renaissance art, which hung above a collection of impressionistic paintings of trees. Now, with the inner walls of the train car covered in beautiful works of art, I looked out the window.

South Seattle was whizzing past. The area was densely cluttered with rapidly-built subsidized housing packed to overflowing with refugees from other states and countries. Graffinity notifications popped up on most walls offering to cover up the regular old graffiti that ornamented everything in sight. A 2040s-era car had been set on fire. It was in flames as its AI software drove it around and around a parking lot. A group of neighborhood teenagers watched, drinking from bottles wrapped in reusable tote bags.

I settled in for the ride to downtown.

The engineers and accountants that had arrived in the big refugee surges, and had been so covetously snapped up by Seattle, had arrived at exactly the wrong moment. The 2050s saw the rollout of several pieces of software that made it possible for one engineer or accountant to do the work of ten. Stockbrokers, architects, and pretty much all math-based professions got the same treatment. They all arrived in Seattle's supposedly thriving job market just in time for their sectors of it to shrink like wool in the wash. Actors have better job security. Take a moment to think about that ... actors. Let me tell you, there is nothing more depressing than an unemployed accountant, they know exactly how broke they are.

The train pulled into the next stop. On the platform outside a woman was holding a sign that read, 'the dividend is nigh!' Standing around her were a group of chanting people. I sighed. It was the Church of Latter-day Accountants.

In the last decade, an accountant from Utah, finding himself abandoned by the God Employment, turned to Jehovah in a big way. He founded a religion, or a cult, or a pyramid scheme, depending on who you ask. The central principle of his philosophy was that the societal dividend was too small. The payoff to the common person was too low to be worth participating in society. His belief was that a great dividend was coming. God was going to bring the faithful a return on investment that would rebalance the wrongs of the world. His followers, mainly accountants and former stockbrokers, were passionate.

The train doors opened and the crowd of CLDA members piled into my car.

"Have you heard the good word," one of them said in a bombastic, deep voice.

The members started moving awkwardly along the crowded car handing out pamphlets. I flipped into my screen controls and switched the display from the avatar of my face into a logo for a package-delivery company. It's something I do when I don't want to be bothered. People are so used to seeing delivery robots, none of the church members looked twice.

"The dividend is nigh, brothers and sisters. We have made our investment and the Lord will give us our return." The man speaking was wearing a suit and holding a Bible with a calculator attached to the cover. "Are you ready for the ROI, sister?"

The woman he was talking to kept staring fixedly out the train car window. The train doors shut and we set off again. We were trapped with the CLDA members. Undeterred by the woman's lack of interest, the preacher moved further down the car.

"Divest from sorrow, brothers and sisters? We have struggled and we have toiled and what has been our return? Nothing but red ink on our ledgers."

"Red ink, amen," his followers said in unison.

"The satanic shackles of debt have bound us to hopelessness."

"Satanic debt, amen."

The rhythmic call and response made me feel very uncomfortable. I pressed myself hard against the side of the compartment as the preacher passed.

"But the good Lord will render unto us that which we need."

"Yes, he will," one of his followers said.

"Where will he take us, brothers and sisters?"

"Into the black, into the black," the CLDA members shouted.

"That's right," the preacher said. "The good Lord will take us to the land of black ink and profit. A place where our ledgers will always overflow with more income than cost."

"I want to see that place," someone shouted.

A passenger on the train stood up from his seat. His face was scrunched as he tried to hold back tears. The preacher turned toward the man, a surprised look on his face. He clearly hadn't been expecting to actually convert anybody.

"What's that, brother?"

"I ... I'm just really having a hard time right now."

The preacher started jostling his way through the crowded car toward the man. He elbowed a woman in the face as he went, so excited to reach his new acolyte.

I rolled my digital eyes.

"Don't get converted. You'll just encourage them," I muttered.

One of the CLDA members passing by glanced at me, a confused look on their face. I scrambled.

"Error," I said, in my best impression of a robot voice. They kept looking at me. "Uh, must deliver packages."

They nodded to themselves and moved along.

The preacher had reached the swayed passenger.

"Talk to me, brother. Tell me about your troubles."

"I'm an accountant."

"Oh, so many of us are, brother. So many of us are."

"I'm on my way to my 28th job interview in two months."

"Unemployment is the tenth circle of hell, my brother."

"The tenth circle of hell," the CLDA members chorused.

"I just, I just want to ..."

"Divest from hopelessness," the preacher said.

"Yeah."

"Divest from hopelessness!" the CLDA members cheered.

"Hey, hey, what have I told you people?"

A man wearing a transit-cop uniform had just entered the compartment from the next car down.

"No proselytizing on public trains."

"Beware, brothers and sisters," the preacher said, dialing the bombast to eleven. "It is the agent of Satan."

"Agent of Satan," the church members said. They hissed at the transit cop.

"Yeah, yeah, I'm the agent of Satan," he replied. "Now, unless all of you want to go to jail, you're getting off on the next stop."

The train was slowing as the next station approached.

"That makes no never mind," the preacher said. "We have found the faithful one in this car."

He gripped the converted passenger around the shoulder. The despairing accountant's mouth spread into a hesitant smile. The train stopped and the door opened. The CLDA members filed out, shooting the transit cop dirty looks.

"Come along now, brother," the preacher said, guiding the convert out the door. "Let's talk about the membership fee."

"Membership fee?" the man yelped.

He turned to look back at the compartment just in time for the door to shut in his face. He watched the train pull away from the station. His hesitant smile faltered then vanished.

"Poor bastard," I said.

The other passengers were still staring at their devices. The CLDA pamphlets littered the floor.

11

TRIANGLES SOLVED

March 3rd, 2064 1:31 p.m. PST

Downtown Seattle's sidewalks were a roiling mass of urgency and despondency. Begging homeless were thick on the ground while frantic business people played a massive game of demolition derby as they crossed from offices to coffee shops, to bars, to restaurants designed around the concept of 'doing lunch.' Corporate America had left behind the stodgy, conformist era of everyone wearing business suits and embraced the bold, innovative era of ... everyone wearing zippered hoodies. (It was a real dark turn for western fashion.) Looking up gave me the uncomfortable feeling that I was standing at the feet of a collection of glass titans, all of whom were pondering who would get to squash me.

I considered what to do next. My plan had always been pretty nebulous: go to the office where George Washington had died and see what I could find out. I'd panicked back at the server farm. I didn't know how to face Izy or explain to her how little plan I actually had. She would have just looked at me all impassive. You know how it is with stoics, they look at you and you're like, 'are they mad at me or is it just a Tuesday?'

Flipping open my web browser I connected to the city's downtown public WiFi. (Rich people have no problem with public spending that exclusively benefits them.) The address for Maddoc Technologies wasn't difficult to find. I activated my AR GPS. A blue line appeared in the air in front of me. It led down the sidewalk and banked at the next intersection. Revving my little wheels, I headed in that direction dodging in between rich people and homeless people all of whom seemed to agree that theirs was the true plight of the modern world.

Notifications cluttered my vision as I rolled along the sidewalk. Graffinity notices popped up on every piece of unoccupied space. Shops, restaurants, and coffee shops all offered me a discount if I watched a short video describing their food or wares in sumptuous detail. People were covered in notifications as well. A man, walking down the sidewalk in a pair of black pants and a black shirt, had a notice from an AR fashion site. I selected the notification and his entire body was suddenly wreathed in blue and purple smoke. It fluttered and swirled behind him as he walked. A woman in a business suit seemed to glow the moment I clicked her notification. The effect was subtle, but it definitely made her stand out as she walked down the crowded sidewalk. I selected the notification next to a teenager waiting at a bus stop. Her eyes turned black. Threefoot horns sprouted from her forehead and smoke rose from her nostrils as she breathed. Technology has changed the world by giving humans entirely new ways to do exactly the same stuff.

I rounded the corner. A steep hill greeted me. A small Ndle service was running people up the slope. Ndle is a company that offers these little flat-topped drones that you pay to take you up steep hills. You hop on and they automatically charge your credit card a dollar. Are there people who would rather pay a dollar then walk up a block's worth of hill?

There was a line waiting for the next available drone.

Zipping past them, I followed the blue line my AR GPS was manifesting in front of me. The line was semi-transparent giving people directly in front of me blue face as I zigzagged across the sidewalk. The denizens of the tech capital of the Northwest kept bustling and pushing their way onward. Most of them ignored me, forcing me to dodge and twist around them. Adarter replaced a large bus billboard with the painting 'Scream.' I'd been downtown for less than five minutes, and I was already exhausted.

The Maddoc Technologies' building emerged from the crowd of metal and glass as I rounded another corner. A corporate logo filled the center of a small courtyard next to its entrance. A large M dwarfed a small 'Technologies,' both were gilded in a shimmering gold metal. A Graffinity notice popped up next to the logo. I selected it. There was a 'Not Safe For Work' warning. I paused. 'NSFW' is always a risky click with Graffinity. Sometimes it's a cutting piece of satire or a beautiful work of art that just happens to include nudity or some other adult material. I selected the okay button.

An artist had created a detailed 3D rendering of a giant penis draped over the Maddoc Technologies' logo. I sighed. The rest of the time 'NSFW' just means it's a giant penis. This one was pretty well rendered, which made it much worse. I turned off Graffinity and turned to the Maddoc Technologies' headquarters.

"What the fuck am I doing?" I mumbled.

The building's rotating door was a whirling dervish of flustered-looking employees. Just inside I could see a set of security gates. Employees were touching their thumbs to a small scanner next to the gate before walking through. It seemed pretty obvious now that a major corporation would have security at the entrance. This was probably the kind of thing Izy would have pointed out if I'd talked to her before leaving. Smart people are insufferable with their foresight.

A messenger robot whizzed past me on the sidewalk. It banked into the courtyard and toward the building's entrance. I contemplated exactly how it was going to navigate the large rotating door. It paused for a moment at the entrance, its head panning from left to right. After a moment or two of contemplation the little bot bypassed the main entrance. Its destination turned out to be a small portal near one corner of the glass front entrance. It was about three feet square and low to the ground, like an oversize doggy door. I watched as the robot bent low at the knees. It turned the long thin package it was carrying like it was preparing to joust. It rolled forward and into the building unhindered.

"A messenger robot entrance," I said.

I rolled toward that corner of the building. Sizing up the portal, I was sure I could slip through it without an issue. Another messenger robot rolled inside, then another left. Nobody stopped them or demanded to see credentials.

"Well suck on that foresight," I said.

I rolled forward, scrunched my body down to size, and rolled through the little entrance.

An alarm sounded and a small metal gate slammed in front of me.

"Oh fuck."

I tried to roll back, just in time to have another metal gate slam shut behind me.

"Oh fuck."

An automated voice filled the box.

"Do not attempt to escape. You are being detained for illegal trespassing."

"Um, no, no, just ... I want to leave."

"Do not attempt to escape. You are being detained for illegal trespassing," the automated voice insisted.

"Uh, that's not super convenient for me."

"Do not attempt to escape. You are being detained for illegal trespassing."

"Shit." I thought hard. "Shit." I took a deep breath. "Shit."

I gave the metal gate behind me a push. It was as quietly insistent as the automated voice was noisily insistent.

"Do not attempt to escape. You are being detained for illegal trespassing."

"Okay, I get it," I snapped.

A bored-looking security guard was crossing the lobby toward me.

"Any chance you'd reconsider?" I asked the box.

"Do not attempt to escape. You are being detained for illegal trespassing."

"You know compromise is the bedrock of civilization."

"Do not attempt to escape. You are being detained for illegal trespassing."

The security guard was getting closer. This was it. My life as an amateur detective had come to an end. My career was, let's be honest, pretty pathetic.

"What have we got today?" the security guard asked. "Animal rights? Anti-corporate? What brand of ..."

He paused when he saw me.

"What the ..."

I looked at him. Terror had turned my guts—the sensation of my guts simulated in my digital brain—upside down, or inside out. It felt like every nonexistent cell of my digestive system had decided it was the end of the world and had thrown a party to end all parties. It was not a reasonable party where everyone watches their intake. It was the kind of party where people take Ecstasy in the first hour, and someone's on the roof in their underwear by the end of it.

"Package pickup?" the security guard asked.

I stared at him. I was too scared to have any idea how to respond.

"Robot," he said. "State your current task."

My seized brain allowed the smallest of gear turns.

"Package pickup," I said. "Sixth floor, room 60 ... 4?"

He raised an eyebrow and pulled a keycard attached to his belt by a retractable string. He swiped it on something I couldn't see. There was a beep and the metal door in front of me opened. The metal door behind me was still closed. One choice. I rolled forward. The security guard turned my body and looked at a spot on my arm.

"Your RFID tag fell off."

I didn't know how to respond.

"Robot, record notice."

I took a chance.

"Recording notice."

"Your robot lost his RFID tag. It's also acting a little weird. It probably needs a software reinstall. End notice."

"Notice recorded," I said.

The security guard swiped his card on the scanner again and the outside of the small metal cage opened. He walked away. I stood dumbfounded. The partygoers in my nonexistent stomach had just found out that the ecstasy they had taken had actually been sugar pills and the apocalypse, as well as the pizza they had ordered, were not in fact coming.

"What the ..."

My eye widened. I'd never changed my screen back to the avatar of my face. I still had the delivery company logo as my exterior screen.

"I ... am ... a genius," I whispered.

Okay, not my most self-aware moment. I'd just avoided jail, cut me some slack. Before I attracted any more attention, I headed toward the building's elevators. I boarded one going up. Three other people followed me inside. They bustled and shoved me to the back without much consideration for my general, you know, existence. I looked at the panel of floor numbers and realized I had no idea which one to push. I tried to open up the webpage to see if any of the articles I had bookmarked mentioned it. I discovered that the city's WiFi was scrambled inside Maddoc Technologies' headquarters. There was a corporate WiFi, but it was password-protected.

A thought occurred to me. Izy had once told me if I was ever concerned about being tracked to turn off my robot's connectivity features. I went into my setting and flipped on airplane mode. Yes, that's right, I have an airplane mode.

My three companion passengers had pressed floors 17 and 36. I decided to get off on 36 and try to figure out where to go from there. The elevator binged on 17 and one of the three disembarked. The doors closed. The two remaining passengers took a step closer to each other. The woman was wearing a light blue designer-brand hoodie. The man's was a slate grey with a specialized pocket to hold the AR glasses resting on his nose.

"Did you hear about the guy that killed himself?" the man said.

"Yeah, George something," the woman said. "Really sad."

"Yeah," he said. "Not that surprising though, you got to wonder what project he was running that the CEO of our parent company was constantly breathing down his neck."

"She is a little ..."

"Draconian."

"I guess."

"Louis knew him apparently. Not well, but you know, to say hi to."

"How's he doing?"

"Fine, I think."

"Poor George ... whatever his name was."

"Apparently, he smashed his office window to jump. 35 floors. He must have looked like strawberry jam when he hit the pavement."

"Ugh," the woman said. "Jesus, Terry. Do you have to be so crass about it? A guy died. I'm pretty sure I met him a couple times."

"Sorry," Terry said. He paused. "Do you still want me to come over tonight?"

"Um," she said. "I don't know. I'm not feeling that well."

I looked back and forth between them. I tried to wheel a few extra steps away and bumped against the back wall.

"Come on, Ginger. I thought we were having fun."

"We were. I just ..."

I muted my external speakers.

"Oh, oh no," I said.

"What's going on," Terry said. "Let's talk about it. If there's a problem—"

"Look," Ginger said. "I've got work to do. I just can't think about this right now."

"Well, when can you think about it?"

Terry sounded hurt. I willed the elevator to move faster.

"Hey, don't act like this is just my problem," Ginger said. "When was the last time you took any real time for us? You just come over to my place, we have sex, then you run off in the morning to change at your place."

"Well, we're both busy," he said. "You can't blame me for trying to be successful here."

"I don't blame you for that," she said. "I'm just not sure—"

The elevator dinged. It was the sweetest sound I've ever heard.

"Let's talk about this later," Ginger said.

She straightened up. Terry smoothed his hoodie. The doors opened, and they whisked out, each turning in a different direction. I peeked out the elevator and shook my head. To all you people trying to navigate the dating world: my condolences. I tapped the button for the 35th floor.

The elevator dinged again. I rolled out onto the 35th floor of the building hoping Terry's offhand comment had been specific. The floors were laminate hardwood, and the walls were painted in a canary yellow. The interior design screamed, 'Hey, 50 years ago people were lucky to get better than beige paint and dark-grey carpeting, be grateful or we'll cut your pay.'

AR notices popped up next to each office indicating whose they were. I had seen George Washington's actual name during my research. Fumbling around in the recesses of my mind I couldn't quite find it. Had it been George Harrison? That seemed familiar. I decided to keep my eye out for George Harrison as I rolled along the hall. An AR panel lit up with the words 'Conference Room 35A' next to one of the doors. On the other side of the hall, 'Nolan Vance: Bio-Chemical Researcher' hovered in neon-blue letters. I rolled past, 'Supply Closet,' 'Conference Room 35A,' and 'Molly Barracuda: Public Relations.'

There was an open office door ahead of me. Voices came from within.

"Just to be clear, are we, or are we not, currently selling mayonnaise as a healthy alternative to sunscreen?"

"There's no evidence it doesn't work."

"Is there any evidence that it does work?"

The door shut as the two people inside continued their important corporate work. I kept rolling. Someone headed past me toward the elevator. He didn't even glance in my direction. His phone was pressed against his ear as he walked.

"Well, I don't know what a Synthetic Undiversified Callable Kicker Exposed Rate Stock is either, Dennis. But it's worth more today than it was yesterday, so I want five thousand of them. Make it happen."

He hung up his phone and continued his bustle toward the elevator bank. I looked back to see him straightening his hoodie in the reflective metal of the elevator doors. He gave himself one of those snap points, as if he liked what he saw. I snorted and turned away.

Rounding a bend in the hall, I pulled up short. It turned out I didn't need to know George Washington's real name. A door had a giant, flashing AR notice, 'Crime Scene: Do NOT Enter.' A few real-world strips of yellow police tape were fluttering, carried on a breeze coming through the open office door. I rolled forward trying to keep the buzzing from my electrical motor to a minimum. There were two voices inside.

"You think this is connected?" a male voice asked.

"I don't think it's not connected," a female voice answered.

"That's not an answer."

"I think we're still at the question phase."

"SPD pulled his phone records. He apparently contacted Abigail Page multiple times in the last several months."

"Were they able to trace where the messages went?"

"No. She has some kind of custom setup designed to make her hard to trace."

"We could get the NSA involved. They could probably track it."

"For a rogue digital copy? Pretty picayune."

"Right, they'd never help."

"Jackasses."

"Assholes."

"Keyboarding clicking douche-dongles."

"Nice one."

"Thanks."

"You think Abigail Page has anything to do with this guy's suicide?"

"Maybe, maybe not. I still can't figure out what she does."

"Really?"

"She's got a Massage and Bathhouse business license, but the address is tied to a rented office space. I called the landlord. He's never met the tenants of that office. As far as he knows, they've never been there."

"A front."

"But for what?"

"Good question."

"I thought so."

"So, we keep searching."

"We try to find Abigail Page's business?"

"Bingo."

I peeked around the edge of the office door. Agents Vanderwall and Berrys were staring at the window. The smashed glass had been covered by a giant sheet of thick plastic. The wind whipped the outside of the building pulling the plastic tight inside, then relented allowing the thick semi-transparent sheet to sag. I held the doorframe to steady myself as I examined the two FBI agents. They were narrowing in on Abigail. I'd have to warn her. Vanderwall turned toward George Washington's desk. I ducked back into the hall.

"So, what's next?"

"I was thinking lunch."

"Teriyaki."

"You read my mind."

"Fuck," I muttered.

I rolled back down the hall away from the door. Swiveling my head 180 degrees, I caught sight of Vanderwall and Berrys leaving the office. They were deep in conversation. I rounded the corner and started looking for a place to hide. Most of the offices and labs were occupied. 'Supply Closet' blinked up in my AR readout as I passed a door. I snatched the doorknob and yanked it open. Having the strength of an arthritic poodle, I barely managed to get it ajar. It was enough. I rolled inside and shut the door. I turned my external microphone to its max and listened as the two agents passed in the hall. I could just hear the sound of one of them tapping the elevator call button. I let out a relieved sigh. Well, I didn't obviously. I don't have lungs, but my copied brain doesn't know that. I was in the clear.

I stiffened. Footsteps were approaching. I pressed my microphone to the door. Had Vanderwall and Berrys seen me after all? I didn't know what to do. I looked around the supply closet. Shelves were stacked with spare external hard drives, cables and, on a bottom shelf, for the luddites, a stack of paper and some pens. There was nowhere to hide. I rolled away from the door, hoping the footsteps would continue past. They stopped just on the other side of the door. I rolled to the back of the room, dropped into the crouch my robot stays in while recharging, and turned off my screen. The door opened.

It wasn't Vanderwall or Berrys. It was Ginger. She glanced around the hall for a moment before stepping inside the supply closet and shutting the door. She hardly seemed to notice me crouching on the floor. She leaned against the shelf. Her face was flushed and she pulled on the string hanging down from her hoodie's collar. I had no idea what was happening. Less than a minute later, a man opened the door. It wasn't Terry. The moment the door shut behind him, he leaned forward and kissed Ginger.

I stood flummoxed and frozen. I was trapped.

The two lovers started falling backward and forward in the closet knocking wires off shelves and grunting as they went. Have you ever had one of those moments where you wish without a shadow of exaggeration that a meteorite would smash though the ceiling and kill you where you stand? As the man's ass smacked against my front screen, I had one of those moments.

"Oh Louis," Ginger said. "This feels so wrong."

"Does this feel wrong?"

I was spared the sight of whatever Louis did as his ass was blocking my camera. I was not spared the sound Ginger made. For my own sanity, I had to take a risk. I turned my external speakers on.

"Error, error, error, error," I said, in my best impression of a robot voice.

"What the fuck is that?" Ginger asked.

"Who cares?"

Louis' butt smacked against my head.

"ERROR, ERROR," I pleaded.

Ginger looked down at me.

"It's a messenger robot. Just put it out in the hall."

In that moment, I loved Ginger. I loved her like someone saved from hanging loves air. Louis heaved me, opened the closet door, and, not very gently, dropped me on the hallway floor. The door slammed. I looked around. The agents had already left.

"Fucking ... people ... and ... fucking," I said.

I turned back toward George Washington's office. I shuddered and my metal body rattled. I tabulated how much therapy it would take to get me back to okay. Too much. I rolled around the corner heading toward the now-closed door of the office. I paused before reaching to open it. I clicked and clacked my fingers together. There might be an alarm or a security camera.

I jiggled the handle.

It wasn't locked. I pressed the door inward. No alarm. I unstuck the police tape from where the FBI agents had reattached it to the frame. There's a line between reckless and audacious, and I had to be near it. Or past it. Or so far past it, I couldn't see it. With a quick glance up and down the hall, I rolled inside.

The interior decor was expensive and bland. Postmodern art adorned the walls. The kind of nebulous blob paintings that stay popular because corporate executives needed art that is at once expensive (to convey status), and so meaningless they'll never offend a potential business partner's sensibilities.

The desk had a scattering of gadgets. A projector, a few AR manipulation tools like a smart pen and, in the corner of the desk, a wireless power projector for charging any electronics placed in its vicinity. Apart from the giant sheet of plastic covering the smashed window, nothing seemed out of place.

"Okay," I whispered. "If I were a clue ..."

I knelt down and scanned the carpet beneath the window.

"I'd have already been gathered by the police."

I was beginning to doubt sneaking into a secure building and risking a trespassing charge without any plan or purpose was such a good idea.

"Come on," I muttered. "You got this. Three semesters of college have got to mean something."

I unbalanced rising up from the floor. Catching myself on the desk, I tapped a little square of plastic near the edge. It let out a pleasant pair of tones and a notification appeared in my AR display.

You have activated a personal assistant. Would you like to allow this program access to your personal calendar events, hard drive and memory, camera, browser history, professional emails, personal emails, personal medical history, criminal record, sexual preferences, family dramas, names of your bastard children, and any plans you may have to overthrow the government?

'Yes' and 'No' hovered in two boxes before my eyes. These modern apps are getting really intrusive. I selected No.

Are you sure? This software will not be able to help you optimally if you don't allow it access to all your personal information.

'Yes' and 'No' hovered before me again. I paused. Was I supposed to say No to allowing it access to my information or Yes, I'm sure I don't want it to have access? I selected Yes.

Great! We'll start downloading that information to the personal assistant.

I panicked.

"No, cancel."

A cancel button was in the bottom corner. I clicked it. The app still said, 'Preparing to download' next to its progress bar. I hoped that meant it hadn't downloaded anything yet.

"Just open the personal assistant, please."

Please remember the personal assistant software will not be able to help you optimally without access to this information.

"I understand."

The little box of plastic seemed to hear me. It made another cheerful tone and the top half of a mustachioed butler appeared before my eyes.

"Good day to you, sir," the image said. "My name is Caruthers. I am George's personal assistant."

"Hello, Caruthers. Uh ... how are things?"

"Splendid, sir. I'm afraid George is out of the office, right now."

That's one way to put it, I guess. I gulped.

"Oh, that's ... unfortunate."

"Can I take a message for you?" Caruthers said.

It dawned on me. Nobody had told the AI.

"Um, no. What's ... can I see George's schedule?"

"I'm afraid I am only authorized to reveal limited personal scheduling information. I can tell you if a specific time has a scheduling conflict, but I can't show you George's complete schedule without George's authorization. Would you like to know where George is now?"

"Yes, sure. Where's George?"

"He's scheduled to be working in his lab. Lab 39L11. Four floors up."

"Thanks."

"Can I have your name and department in case I see George before you do? I'll let him know you were looking for him."

"Caruthers, I'm afraid I've got some bad news."

"Bad news? Whatever do you mean, sir?"

"George has passed."

"A test?"

"No."

"On a promotion."

"No. George is dead."

The digital butler's face fell. His mustache wiggled back and forth.

"Oh my. That is unfortunate. I suppose this means he won't be making this month's budget meeting."

"Probably not."

"I put together such a lovely slide show for his presentation."

"That's too bad."

"No one will see it."

"No, I guess not."

"Would you like to see it?"

"I think I'm good."

"Right, of course."

I reached up to rub my chin and ended up clacking my metallic fingers against my face screen.

"Caruthers, you're always in the office, right?"

"Yes, of course."

"But you didn't see George die?"

"No."

"How is that?"

"George turned me off at 10:22 p.m."

"Do you know why he turned you off? Was he going home?"

"George usually leaves me on at night. I doubt he was going home."

"Why would he turn you off?"

"Your guess is as good as mine, good sir."

I pondered. Why would George turn off his personal assistant?

"Because he had an appointment that he didn't want recorded," I answered my own question.

"I'm sorry?" Caruthers asked.

"Nothing. Was George behaving strangely at all?"

"Strangely how?"

"Like depressed?"

"I am a personal assistant and incapable of diagnosing mental health issues."

"Sure, that makes sense."

I cast around for another line of questioning.

"What does George do, I mean, what did George do?"

"George was a software engineer."

"No, I mean, what did George do here, specifically?"

"I'm afraid I'm not allowed to talk about current projects. That is proprietary information."

"You can't tell me anything?"

"I'm afraid not."

"Can you tell me who was George's immediate superior?"

"No."

"Can you tell me what kind of technology George was writing code for?"

The butler's eyes narrowed.

"You have asked too many questions about proprietary information. My security protocols have deemed this a potential intrusion. I have alerted security."

My digital jaw dropped.

"What?"

"Please sit down and wait for them to arrive. I apologize if this alert is in error."

"Wait, really? You called security?"

"I'm afraid so, old bean."

I cast around looking for an escape hatch, failing that, a hole that would swallow me into the ground.

"Caruthers, you ..."

"Yes, sir? Can I offer you any more personal assistance?"

"More personal assistance! You're a real asshole, Caruthers. I thought you were cool."

"I'm sorry to hear you're dissatisfied with my performance."

I put my hands to my head and clutched the sides of my face screen. I was on the edge of total panic.

"Does your app have a rating in the app store?"

"Yes."

"1 star, asshole!"

"I'll pass that along."

I bolted for the door. What had I been thinking coming to a giant secured corporate office? I was going to go to jail. They were going to scrap me for parts. Whoever was after Abi and Abigail was going to find them. The FBI, the Australian Golden Retrievers, somebody was going to track them down. Izy would probably get dragged into it. We were all doomed. Doomed, I tell you. I glanced back into George's office. Caruthers was staring bemusedly at the wall. I set off back toward the elevator.

I reached the far corner and rounded it. I saw the elevator bank in the distance. Someone was exiting the elevator. I froze on the spot, terrified I might see a security guard. The guy was wearing a hoodie. My frame relaxed a bit. I started rolling forward. As I got close, I recognized the man approaching. It was Terry. He was carrying a bundle of cables underneath his arm. I slowed down as I realized where Terry was headed. The supply closet.

Gauging the distance, I knew I wouldn't pass him before he reached the door. I didn't know what to do. Had Louis and Ginger already ... moved on? Frozen on the spot, I watched things unfold as if they were in slow motion.

Terry reached the door. He opened it. I balled my hands into nervous fists.

"Ginger? Louis?"

"Terry?"

"What the fuck?"

"It's not what it looks like," Louis said.

"What the fuck else could it be, Louis?" Terry shouted. "I'm pretty sure that's not where they keep the extra power cables."

Ginger came stumbling out of the supply closet trying to fix a very disheveled hoodie.

"Lower your voice, Terry," she said.

"Lower my voice? Lower my voice? Go fuck yourself, Ginger."

People were starting to poke their heads out office doors. I looked around nervously, but nobody was paying attention to me.

"Terry you're causing a scene."

"I'm causing a scene. I'm causing a scene."

Louis stepped out of the closet pulling on his clothing. Terry eyes were tinged with madness.

"How could you do this to me?"

A small crowd of people were now watching. I stood stock still in the middle of the hallway. I had no idea what to do.

"Terry, if you'll just calm down we can go somewhere and talk."

"Don't you tell me to calm down, you bitch."

The entire hallway gasped.

"What the fuck did you just call me?" Ginger shouted.

Bam.

In that moment, the gathered audience got to discover that Ginger had quite the right hook. Terry went down hard.

"Call me a bitch, you fucking asshole. You're surprised I'm cheating on you with someone who actually gives a shit about me? It was my birthday last week. Did you even notice? You think you're the injured party here. I'll make you the fucking injured party."

Ginger dove on top of Terry and started pummeling him. Louis looked at them, looked around at the gathered crowd, then tried to pull Ginger off Terry.

"Should somebody call security?" an onlooker asked.

As if on cue, the elevator dinged. Two security guards stepped lazily onto the 35th floor. Their eyes widened when they saw the full-blown brawl filling the hallway.

"Holy cow," one of them said.

"Hey," the other said.

Ginger and Terry were past caring. Even Louis, who had caught an elbow to the jaw, had lost himself in the fray.

"Fucking asshole. Fuck you."

"Fuck me, fuck you."

"Ouch, that's my hair."

The two security guards tried to pull the three apart. Arms and legs lashed out. With the security guards outnumbered, things weren't going well. I realized that this was my chance. The scuffle was filling the hall, but I decided it was worth the risk. I revved my motor and started toward the elevator banks. I dodged a sprawled Terry leg and a flying Ginger fist. Emerging on the other side of the battle, I headed for the metal doors of the elevators. They opened as I arrived. A woman in a green hoodie stepped out and froze. I didn't hesitate, but rolled past her and into the elevator car. The doors closed, and I let out an inaudible whisper of thanks.

"What was that all about?" one of the elevator riders asked another.

"I don't know. Since Maddoc Industries was purchased, meltdowns have been happening more and more."

"The new management does like to work us."

"I get my retention bonus in eight months. Then I'm getting out of here."

"Damn, I still have fifteen months."

"Poor bastard."

I looked at the digital screen beside the door and saw that the elevator was going up. My digital throat gulped. I wasn't heading toward freedom. I was heading deeper ... or higher ... into the belly of the beast. (If that was true, it really begged the question, what hole did I enter through?)

The elevator was sailing past Floor 38. I glanced at the button for Floor 39. One of the four people in the elevator had already pressed it. George Washington's lab was somewhere on that floor. The elevator slowed to a halt and the doors parted. One of the occupants brushed past me. I hesitated. I had just narrowly avoided getting busted by the building's security. For all I knew, they were tracking me on CCTV. I needed to get out of there and warn Abigail about the FBI. I also needed to face the wrath of Izy when she found out I'd left the server farm to break into a corporate headquarters. It was that thought that made me roll off the elevator. There was no reason to rush back.

The halls on the 39th floor were more antiseptic than those below. Linoleum tiles covered the floor. Small windows in every door gave views of various laboratories. The people that passed me in the hall wore lab coats over their hoodies. It was all very, 'this is where we do the experiment we're not allowed to talk about.' I double-checked that my screen still had the delivery company's logo displayed and went forward like the mindless automaton I was pretending to be. The person I followed off the elevator stopped a half-dozen labs down the hall. She pressed her thumb into a pad beside the door. It beeped a cheery kind of 'no trespassing charge for you' kind of beep, and she slipped inside. This was pointless. Even if I could find George's lab, I wasn't going to be able to get inside. I don't even have a thumbprint to get rejected by the scanner.

I kept rolling. Maybe the police had already been there and had left the lab open. I rounded a corner in the hall and spotted the door. It was ajar. I couldn't believe my luck. Daddy rolled a straight seven again! I rolled forward almost cheering as I swerved through the open entrance. I slammed on my little robotic brakes the moment I was a foot inside. There were two people in the room. They didn't look like cops. They were wearing black hoodies, over black t-shirts. A fashion choice that was both sketchy and atrocious. Both of them were hunched over a computer terminal in the room. A loud machine was making a sinister electrical racket beside them. Thanks to the noise, neither of them seemed to notice my entrance.

I rolled back, real slow. Once I was outside, I peeked around the doorframe. The machine stopped making the angry buzzing. One of the two black-clad people pulled a hard drive out of the grey and black plastic machine and replaced it with another one from the counter. The machine started to buzz again. I was pretty proud of myself that I knew what they were doing. They were degaussing hard drives. It's how you permanently delete digital data, the 21st century equivalent of putting paper files in a furnace. They were hiding something.

I wished I had the mind for conspiracies. I was totally lost. I leaned around the doorframe and snapped a couple of screenshots from my external camera. There was a large server, a dozen screens connected to a set of computers, and some kind of full-body scanner that filled the corner of the room. None of it made any sense to me. It was time to go and brainstorm. Maybe Izy or Abigail could make something of the contents in George's lab.

A door in the hallway behind me opened and I went stiff. I looked over my shoulder. A man with big bags under his eyes and a large coffee mug in his hand stepped out into the hall. He glanced at me. I froze. He turned and started walking away like I was an extra-spindly janitorial drone. Shielded as I was from suspicion, protected by the powerful force of delivery company corporate branding, I'd gotten farther than even I would have thought. My instincts were telling me it was time to cash out. I followed the exhausted man down the hall toward the elevators. I let him climb aboard an elevator and disappear before I rolled up and summoned one for myself.

It was empty as I clambered aboard. I pressed the button for the ground floor. Ideas were bouncing around inside my head like a dozen frogs who all at once realized some bastard had turned up the heat on this pot they were all sitting in. George's suicide stank to high heaven, but what had actually happened? What did the company have to hide? And why did Caruthers have to be such an asshole?

The elevator was approaching the ground floor. When it opened on the lobby the first thing I heard was sobbing. I hesitated to leave the elevator. I ducked my head out instead. The sobbing was Terry. The cops were escorting handcuffed Ginger, Terry, and Louis toward the main entrance. They looked slightly worse for wear. Terry's hoodie had a sleeve torn off. It had bunched around his wrist where it was handcuffed. Louis had a fat lip and Ginger's hair looked like someone had set a firecracker off in it. Her bottom lip was quivering as she looked back at Terry.

"Oh Terry," Ginger said. "I'm so sorry."

"No, I'm sorry," Terry said. His right eye was bruised. "I'm the one who should be sorry. You're right. I never really appreciated you. I was so obsessed with this job. Ginger, I hate this fucking job."

"Me too."

"Me too," Louis interjected.

Tears were welling in his eyes.

"Oh Louis, I'm so sorry I got you mixed up in this," Ginger said.

"I'm sorry. I'm sorry to both of you."

The entire lobby had gone quiet. Even the cops had slowed down.

"I've always hated this job," Louis said. "I took it to pay off my student loans. My degree is in Zoology. I've always wanted to live in Costa Rica. There's so much beautiful wildlife. I went there to visit my grandparents when I was a kid. It's wonderful."

"Fuck this job. Go Louis, go to Costa Rica," Ginger said.

"I don't want to go without you. And Terry, I don't know how this happened. You're my oldest friend. I don't want to live without either of you. I ..."

He fell silent, his words choked off by fear and doubt.

"Louis," Terry said. "This is ... I've always wanted to tell you something ..."

The cops had fully stopped. Every person in the building was hanging on every word being spoken.

"Back in college," Terry said. "That night. We got drunk, then I kissed you ... we pretended like nothing happened."

Louis looked away. Terry swallowed hard.

"I've always wanted to tell you. I love you, Louis."

Louis looked up. His eyes bright as if a thousand doubts had been resolved all at once.

"You do?"

"I do."

"I love you too, Terry."

They both looked at Ginger.

"Ginger," Louis said. "Will you run away with us?"

Ginger's mouth hung open. She looked back and forth at them. Joyful tears welled in her eyes.

"Yes, yes. A thousand times yes! Let's move to Costa Rica!"

The gathered business people stared, completely flabbergasted. Mouths hung open. Someone dropped a bag they were carrying. Everyone looked at them. The man who had dropped the bag started clapping. Slow at first, then faster. The crowd, given direction, jumped onboard the bandwagon like it was heading toward happily ever after. They started clapping. Even the cops stepped back for a moment.

"We're going to Costa Rica," Terry shouted.

The crowd roared in response. The cops finally remembered their jobs and continued taking the three toward the waiting cop cars outside. The crowd cheered for the three until the cop cars had driven away.

You know as an asexual and aromantic person, there are times when I feel removed from the ups and downs people experience in their sexual and romantic relationships. They can feel very distant and not very relatable to me. But there is something about three disgruntled office employees throwing aside societal expectations and moving to Costa Rica that pulls on the heartstrings in a universal kind of way. I was rooting for those love-struck kids. I smiled as I watched them loaded into the back of the cop cars.

A heavy hand landed on my shoulder. It spun me around. A burly woman in a security guard uniform smiled down at me.

"We've been looking for you."

She lifted her hand off me. I heard the crackle of a taser behind me. Everything went dark for a second. My system rebooted. I tried to look around.

"What just—"

I heard the crackle of a stun gun again. Everything went dark for longer than a second.

12

KILLER PLAN, CHAMP

March 3rd, 2064 2:51 p.m. PST

/System rebooting ...

I woke up. I was in a concrete room handcuffed to a metal table. A security camera was mounted in the corner above the room's only door. I jiggled my wrists in the cuffs. They were clearly meant for restraining human bodies. I clamped my fingers together and wiggled my wrists right out of the cuffs. They clattered to the table. I didn't think the door was going to give that easily. I glanced up at the security camera.

"Hello?" I said.

I ran my fingertips across the table, went to cross my arms, decided against it halfway through, I went to put my wrists back in the handcuffs, realized that if someone was watching they already knew I could get out of them, and just rested my hands on the table.

"Hello?" I tried again.

Nobody answered. I rolled over to the metal door. I turned the handle. It opened. Whoever had me in their custody had left the door unlocked. A group of security guards were standing around a break room drinking coffee.

"Hello?"

They all paused in their conversation. One of them looked around.

"Hello?" she asked.

"Yes, hello," I said again.

She looked around until she found me poking out of the room.

"What the hell?"

"I'm wondering—"

"Why are you talking?"

"Uh, to communicate, I guess."

She looked at her colleagues. They all shrugged.

"Are you? You're not a delivery drone?"

"No."

"You didn't malfunction?"

"No. I'm a ghost."

Her brow furrowed.

"Crap. Um. Go back inside that room and wait."

"Well, I was wondering if I could just leave? I mean, I just got lost."

"Uh," she looked at her colleagues. They all seemed busy sipping their coffees. "No." She didn't sound certain. "I've got to text somebody."

I slumped a little.

"No need to text anyone."

"Uh, I think ... yes. I'm going to have to text my supervisor."

"You don't have to text your supervisor."

"I have to text my supervisor."

"Look, I could just get out of your hair."

"Jimmy, get the taser," she said.

"Never mind, I'll just wait in here."

I shut the door. I took my seat, and for good measure, I slid my hands back into the handcuffs. I tapped my feet against the chair leg. A few minutes passed.

"What?" the shout came from outside.

There was a muffled reply.

"You tased a ghost. You tased a ghost. Twice! Does anybody know if a ghost can die from being tased? Oh fuck, the Digital American Anti-Defamation League is going to crawl right up my ass."

There was a muffled response.

"So, he was trespassing?"

More muffled talk.

"What do you mean one of our guards let him in?"

Muffle, muffle.

"So, you're telling me we let him into the building because we assumed he wasn't a human and then we tased him because we assumed he wasn't a human. You know what ghost-rights activists really don't like to hear? That people thought they weren't human. This really isn't looking good for us, people."

Muffle.

"I don't care if you don't think it's fair, and neither will the lawyers. I gotta text somebody."

Another five minutes passed. The door to the concrete room opened and a man entered. He was short, nervous, and had a set of eyebrows that, amongst the ensemble of his facial features, seemed determined to steal the show.

"I'm Bill Beaufort, Head of Building Security," he said. "You're in a lot of trouble."

I recognized his voice as being the yeller. He slid into the chair across the table from me. He cleared his throat and flipped a tablet around to face me. It showed security camera footage of me wandering around the halls outside George Washington's office. He tapped the screen and it showed me peeking inside George Washington's lab.

"Clear evidence of trespassing. That's a very serious charge."

He gritted his teeth like he's just shown me my fingerprints on the murder weapon.

"What do you gotta say for yourself?"

"I didn't know I was trespassing."

He tried to make his face go rigid. Instead it wilted, like a puffer fish whose bluff had been called.

"I'm sorry?" he said.

"Well, when your security guard let me in, I figured it was fine for me to be here."

His mouth tensed up like he was tasting something sour.

"Uh, well, that—"

"You know you guys should really think about soundproofing this room."

He glanced at the door. His lip quivered as he realized what I might have heard. I felt the phantom sensation of my stomach giving a lurch of excitement when I saw his reaction. I'm not really someone who outmaneuvers people.

"How about this?" I hazarded. "You let me go, and I'll pretend you never tased me."

He blinked and his head cocked to the side.

"I've got to text somebody."

"Sure."

The door shut behind him as he left. A little surge of excitement shot through me. It might have just been the aftereffects of being tased, or it might have been because still sitting on the table in front of me was the tablet and the security footage. I touched the screen and an interface came up. I glanced at the security camera. Would someone intervene? I glanced over the interface and saw an option for entering a time and date. I switched to the camera that was showing the hallway outside of George Washington's office. It was showing me going the wrong way down the hall, then turning around. I set the camera to show what was happening in that hall the night before at 10:22 pm. Caruthers had told me that was when George had turned him off. I pressed play. The hallway was empty. It was late at night. The only office with a light on was George's midway down the hall.

I pressed fast forward. Still nothing happened. A flicker of motion made me slow the footage. I grunted in disappointment. It was just a janitorial robot vacuuming the hall. It looked like a big box with six spindly arms hanging off in different directions. One of the arms opened the door to one of the empty offices, and the robot disappeared inside. I glanced at the metal door. Bill would be back at any moment. I pressed fast forward again. Twenty-five minutes of empty hallway sped past my vision. Nothing happened. George's body had been found at 10:45 pm. Nobody had entered the room during that time. He really had killed himself.

I leaned back in my chair. Somehow the fact that George Washington had killed himself made me feel a little down. It had all just stunk to high heaven. Another flicker of movement drew my eye back to the screen. It was just the janitorial robot. My digital jaw dropped. The janitorial robot was coming out of another office. As in, not the one it had just entered.

"Oh my snap, crackle, and pop," I said. "I am the best detective ever."

The footage had been altered. Proof, not just suspicious people in black hoodies, or weird behavior on George's part. Real undeniable proof. There was a conspiracy. I'd cracked the case. Okay, more I'd proved that there definitely was a case. My hands trembled in excitement. The door to the little room opened and I switched the tablet back to the shot of me peeking in George's lab. Bill was back.

"You've got a deal, Mr.— I didn't catch your name?"

"Smith, Romeo Smith."

I stared him down.

"Okay, whatever. You get out of here and don't tell anyone about anything that may or may not have happened, and we won't press trespassing charges."

"Of course you won't."

"Right, because we're saying we won't."

"Of course you are."

"Just leave."

"Okay."

Here's something I've noticed since I died. Rolling around as a ghost, especially inside the jury-rigged husk of a messenger robot, I just don't fit. There's no set response for someone like me. When the system runs into a person who just doesn't fit into its predesigned patterns, it kind of freaks out. If you give the system the option for you to just go away, it will take it most of the time. People don't like to have to think up ways to respond to new stuff. It's hard and if their response doesn't work, they might get fired. Bill leaned forward to uncuff me.

"No need," I said.

I wiggled the cuffs off like bangle bracelets and nodded a farewell. Bill stared at the cuffs for a moment, then gave a resigned shrug. He escorted me out to the lobby.

"Never come back," he said.

I looked up at him.

"Never? What if ..."

He fixed me with the stare of a man deciding if spite could motivate him to do all that paperwork after all.

"Okay," I said. "Never come back, cool. See you later. I mean, no I won't. 'Cause ... uh, goodbye."

I rolled for the exit, this time going through the big revolving door. I turned back to see Bill stalking off.

I switched my screen back to the dynamic avatar of my face. Airplane mode was still activated. I switched it off and got a text notification. It was from Izy.

Where are you?

I bit my bottom lip. She was clearly enraged or irritated or just idly curious. How do you tell with these fucking stoics? I wheeled myself around and headed back toward the light-rail station. The CLDA was nowhere to be found on my return trip. I waved at Chester as I rolled off the train and headed back to the office.

"Hi, Izy," I said, as I entered.

There was no answer.

"I just stepped out for a ... soda."

That didn't make any sense.

"I mean I went for a walk, for two hours, without telling you."

Izy wasn't at her desk. She was lying in wait, to spring on me with her oft-mentioned stun gun baseball bat. I pulled my arms close to my body and peeked around a corner.

Nothing.

I rolled along the row of servers. Maybe the FBI had come and arrested her. I didn't know which was worse, the possibility that she was furious with me or the possibility that I had gotten her arrested. A whirring behind me spun me around. I looked down a row of servers. A coolant fan had just turned on, no big deal. I turned around. Izy was standing in the doorway of one of the office's extra server rooms.

"Aaah!"

"What?"

She looked at me. One of her eyebrows was raised. It was almost a complete expression. I leaned against the server bank beside me.

"You scared the crap out of me."

"Why?"

"I don't know, you weren't at your desk. I thought ... I'm not sure."

"I was replacing a component on a server tower back here."

"Sure, yeah, of course you were, it's just been a weird afternoon for me."

"Yeah? Where did you go? You should really tell me when you leave the office."

She walked back toward her desk and slumped back into her office chair. Izy placed her feet on the desk and leaned back. The frostiness from this morning had thawed. One thing I can say for Izy, she doesn't hold a grudge, or at least, she doesn't appear to. It's really hard to tell.

"I ..."

It all came tumbling out, the whole story in fits and starts. As I spoke, her other eyebrow raised. It was a complete expression.

"I guess it is true what they say," she said.

"What?"

"Is better to be lucky than to be smart."

"And both is even better."

She fixed me with a stare so immovable it could have given an unstoppable force a run for its money.

"Sure," she said, after a long pause. "So probably something stinks about this George Washington's death. But what?"

"Well, I think the techs in black hoodies indicate something is going on at Maddoc Technologies."

"Maybe, but deleting extraneous data when a research project gets handed over to a new team is probably pretty common. If project is proprietary, which the digital assistant said it was, it might just be corporate policy. It's not, not suspicious. But it's not, not, not suspicious. You understand?"

"Uh, yeah."

"Still, altered footage is very strange."

"Right, so conspiracy. Somebody from the company had to delete that footage."

"Maybe, but that doesn't necessarily mean conspiracy. Could be personal. Someone with access had grudge against George, perhaps."

"You think?"

"Could be. George might have been sleeping with someone's spouse."

"Maybe."

I glanced out the window. Raindrops were contouring the glass.

"I don't know," I said. "I got the impression from this place, when people get caught cheating on each other they just form poly triads and move to Costa Rica."

"I think that might have been a unique situation."

"Possibly. My gut still says conspiracy."

"You don't have a gut."

"I feel like I have a gut."

"Great, you're listening to your imaginary gut."

"It's not imaginary, it's just digital."

"Is psychosomatic projection of your brain simulation. Is digital and imaginary."

"Fine, but that doesn't make it wrong."

Izy sighed. She blinked and the tiny speck of light from her AR contacts appeared in both her pupils.

"I have to go to dentist appointment."

"Now?" I said. "Shouldn't we call Abigail and warn her about the conspiracy, or at least the FBI?"

"We do not know there is conspiracy, and FBI won't find her business very soon. We have a little time. She is very good at hiding it in paperwork, and I did much of her IT work to keep her online profile untraceable. At the moment, we don't really have anything worth telling her."

"Not worth telling her? I ... there were a lot a chances I took and ... really? Everything I found out was useless?"

"Not useless, just not decisively useful."

"I feel like that's a platitude."

"It is. Can you mind the office while I am at my appointment?"

I was staring at the grey carpet.

"Yeah."

Izy stood and patted me on the shoulder.

"Was very brave what you did, Romeo. You are a good friend."

"Thanks."

She left. I cast about, balling my fists. I'd felt so clever. Now it seemed obvious that what I'd learned had done nothing to answer the questions of why. Why was Abi on the run? Why had George died?

"Hello," a voice said.

I looked up. I'd spaced out for a few minutes, pondering the last few hours. Someone had entered the office while I wasn't paying attention. She was standing a few feet inside the door. She looked like a student teacher on her first day. She was wearing a pair of pleated pants, a white cotton button-down, a tan overcoat hung open loosely and a big, yellow pin of a bird was flashing on the coat's lapel. A set of thick-rimmed glasses hung halfway down her nose.

"Are you Mr. Romeo Smith?" she asked.

She had a sing-song voice that somehow managed to stay emotionless.

"Yes. Who are you?"

"I am the agent of another's will."

I pondered that for a minute.

"Uh. Is this a religious thing? 'Cause we've got a No Soliciting sign—"

"This is not a religious thing."

"Okay. You're the agent of another's will. You have a boss?"

"Yes."

"Who are they?"

"That's not important. What's important is they gave me a directive."

"What's that exactly?"

"Your being neutralized. I'm here to facilitate that."

"I'm sorry?"

She let the coat slide off her shoulders and draped it over a chair. Some kind of black metal corset was wrapped around her midriff.

"It's a beautiful day, isn't it?"

"I'm sorry, can we go back?"

"I enjoy the rain while I'm working?"

Her lips stretched into a vacant, sweet, terrifying kind of smile. She rolled her neck. Her thumbs ran up and down her fingers popping each joint.

"I'm sorry. Before, did you say you're here to kill me?"

The young woman stretched her arms straight out to either side. The corset holding her midriff started to move. It spread out into two hands each extending from the young woman's sides like bat wings. They were overlong with an extra joint per digit. They flexed and spread like they were preparing for something. My jaw dropped.

"Let's begin."

13

TIMED OUT

March 3rd, 2064 3:39 p.m. PST

My assassin rolled her shoulders and all her fingers flexed. All of them, on all four hands, in unison. She advanced.

"Aaaah," I said.

"I don't know if that's necessary."

I spun around looking for somewhere to go. The school-teacher was standing in between me and the only exit. I spotted a Flooffee cup on Izy's desk. It still had a little coffee in it when I picked it up. I spun around and hurled it in my attacker's face. Well, I tried. Remember when I said I have the physical strength of a housecat. The coffee sloshed out of the cup and fell on the floor between us. The woman flinched back.

"Why would you do that?" she asked.

I looked at the ground.

"What?"

"You could have gotten coffee on my shirt. Coffee stains are almost impossible to get out."

I stared at her.

"What? Stop acting like you're not trying to murder me."

"I'm not trying to murder you."

"Oh, have I ... shit. Have I misunderstood the situation?"

"Maybe, what do you think is happening here?"

"You're trying to murder me."

"Oh, you have misunderstood the situation."

"Oh, sorry ... then ... what is—"

"I'm here to abduct you so that you can be interrogated. You'll be destroyed later."

"Destroyed, you mean murdered."

"I hardly think it's murder."

"Why is it not murder?"

"Well," she gestured toward me.

I gasped.

"Racist, or xenophobe ... digitalist? I'm not sure we settled on vernacular for bigots like you."

"I am not a bigot. I just don't think you're human."

My avatar's jaw dropped to the bottom of my screen.

"That's literally ... that's the whole ..."

"Just stay still."

She stepped toward me.

"No. Leave me alone."

"No, Mr. Smith. I'm afraid that's not an option. You're going to have to come with me."

"Aaah."

I rolled. Revving my electric motor to the max, I achieved a brisk walking pace. I cast around the server banks looking for somewhere to hide. I opened up my phone app and tried to call 911. No connection. I tried to go online. The office WiFi was down. This woman had killed external signals. I was alone.

"Mr. Smith, please come back."

The schoolteacher was following me, also at a brisk walking pace. I dodged down a line of servers and turned, trying to double back to the door. She appeared around from another aisle ahead of me.

"Why are you doing this?" I asked.

"I was ordered to."

"By who?"

"My employer."

"How did you find me?"

"A contact gave us an IP address that led back to this building."

"You hired the Golden Retrievers."

I pointed a triumphant finger, my eyes wide.

"What?"

Her brow wrinkled.

"Mr. Smith, I understand this is very trying for you, but I have other things to do today. If you could just hold still, that would be a great help to me."

She started toward me.

"No," I shrieked.

I turned back down the aisle of server towers and banked toward the back rooms in the office. Behind me were the methodical footfalls of someone who was sure I couldn't outrun them. I made it to the back room door. A hand grabbed my arm and spun me around. She had caught up with me. She smiled a faint, oh hello, kind of smile. I swung my free arm at her. She caught it and brought it down to her side. The black metal hand extending from her side gripped my wrist tight.

"Why?" I asked. "I just want to know before I die. What does this have to do with George?"

She blinked.

"What do you know about George?"

"I know he was murdered."

"Astute."

"Wait, how do you know George was murdered?"

She raised a pitying eyebrow at me. I gasped.

"You killed George Washington."

She cocked her head.

"No."

"I mean, whatever his actual name was."

I struggled, but she held me fast. She pulled my arm not pinned in the vice grip of her black metal hand down to her other side. The second spidery appendage reached out flexing and searching for a grip. She had me pinned. Her actual hands reached down toward my chest, where my black box was housed.

"No, no," I said.

"There, there, Mr. Smith. It will be over in a moment."

I squirmed against my restraints. Casting around for some escape. The woman's head was near mine. I tried to lurch forward and crack my face screen against her face. I bumped her forehead with all the force of a swinging cabinet door.

"Ouch," she said. "Please don't do that again."

She continued fumbling with my electrical innards, leaning her head a little farther back as she did. A flash of inspiration hit me. I found the volume control on my external speakers and dialed it up to max. As fast as I could, I searched for 'scream core' on my internal music storage. A file popped up in the search results. I hit the link. A swirling buffering indicator came up.

"Come on," I said.

The sound was deafening. It was an incoherent roar of screeching instruments and shouting voices. I spared a half-second to wonder why I had this track in my music collection. The schoolteacher lurched back and her black metal hands snapped open with the movement. I was free.

I ducked underneath her arm and bolted for the front door of the office. I didn't look back. I urged my little electric motor way past the red line. The edge of the last row of server towers was just ahead. I was grabbed from behind and hurled sideways. I sprawled across the floor by the window. The song was still playing from my external speakers.

"Would you mind switching that off?" my attacker said.

"Fuck you," I boomed.

"Goodness, Mr. Smith. There's no reason to be rude."

"What is your deal?"

"I'm in the service industry. I care about good customer relations."

"I'm a customer to you."

"Technically, you're closer to the product, but that's no reason not to be polite."

I was at a total loss for words. She leaned down, heaved me up, and cracked my face screen against the inside of the office window.

"I don't know if a long fall will conceal blunt force trauma on a robot as much as it does for a human, but seeing as records of your visit to our office today have already been deleted, I don't imagine it should be a problem if suspicions are aroused. There will be no connection to my employer."

She cracked my face screen against the window again. I heard the crack of display glass. My arms and legs went limp. She'd yanked the cable out that connected my black box to my robot body. My display screen was my only connection to the outside world. In a matter of seconds she was going to yank that too, and I would be nothing but a consciousness in a box, waiting to get erased. My external speakers went silent. Another cable had been yanked.

"Stop," someone shouted.

Everything froze. The voice sounded familiar. Still pinned in the assassin's arms I was spun around. It was Izy. She'd come back. Her face was the hard granite of a cliffside that's seen a thousand millennia. She was standing beside her desk. The loud sound from my speaker had covered her entrance.

"Hello, how are you?" my assassin asked.

"My tooth hurts."

"I'm sorry to hear that. I'm right in the middle of something."

"I can see."

"It's unfortunate you returned," the schoolteacher said. "His is the only name I was given today."

"Hmm. Very unfortunate."

The schoolteacher allowed me to slump down to the ground. I fell on my side with an angular view of the room.

"I thought you had left the office."

"I had."

"You came back."

"You shut down my security system."

"Yes."

"When you did that, it sent an alert to my phone. Is a third-party software. You must have missed it."

"I must have. Very clever."

"Thank you."

I was watching the weirdest face off ever. The stoic Kazakhstani versus the sing-song schoolteacher.

"Well, I'm afraid it's very important that I don't leave witnesses."

She took a step toward Izy.

"Stop right there."

"Why?"

Izy pointed to her desk. There was a keychain dangling on the wall. A key was inserted into a keyhole in the center of an electrical panel.

"You see switch?"

"Yes."

"That's manual reset switch for security system. I turned it when I arrived, about 60 seconds ago."

"I see."

"It takes about two minutes to reset."

"I see."

The schoolteacher smiled vacantly. Izy stared impassive.

"Do you really think you can kill both of us and get clear of the security cameras in ... about 50 seconds." Izy said. "Before you answer, you should know ..."

She lifted a heavy, black implement covered with bright silver electrodes.

"I have stun gun baseball bat."

My assassin looked to the side for a moment. I have no doubt in my mind she was literally thinking through the step-by-step process of killing both of us.

"No," she said, with a slight nod. "Congratulations on your survival."

She turned and picked up her coat and looked down at me.

"I'm quite certain I'll see you again, Mr. Smith. Have a nice day."

14

GORDIAN PEARL

March 3rd, 2064 3:51 p.m. PST

"Are you alright?" Izy asked.

My would-be assassin had vanished out of the office door. Izy stepped around me so she could keep her eyes on the exit as she knelt down.

"Romeo?"

Izy noticed the yanked cables and started fumbling outside my camera's view. A cheery tone told me that my body had been reconnected. My external speakers came back online and started blaring the squealing noise.

"Fuck," Izy said.

She clamped her hands to her ears.

"Sorry," I said.

I exited the link and the noise ceased.

"What in hell was that?"

"Self-defense," I said. "Best I could do."

She nodded and wiggled one of her fingertips in her ear.

"Are you okay?"

"Not really," I said. "She said she was here to kidnap me so I could be interrogated. Then I was going to be destroyed."

"No permanent damage to your black box?"

"Well, the memories aren't going to be fading any time soon."

She nodded almost imperceptibly.

"I take back what I said before," she said.

"What?"

"Is better to be smart than to be lucky."

"Yeah."

"Your screen is broken."

I looked around. There weren't any mirrors in the office. Izy held up her phone for me to see. A web of cracks crisscrossed my avatar.

"Should we call the cops?"

"And tell them what?" I said. "My friend made an illegal copy of herself so I broke into the headquarters of a major corporation which attracted the attention of a four-handed assassin who looks like a schoolteacher."

"Is a bit tenuous. Did you take picture of her?"

My mouth dropped open.

"Uh, well, now that you say it, it feels really obvious that I should have."

Izy grunted.

"We would not have a lot for cops to go on. And with the FBI looking for Abigail, the police might see us as the criminals."

"Yeah."

"You are sure you are okay?"

"Yeah."

"Remember when I was not angry that you went to Maddoc Technologies without telling me?"

"Yeah?"

"I am angry now."

"That's fair," I said. "What should we do?"

"I don't know. I'm not sure that's even the first question we should try to answer."

"Why does Abigail copying herself lead to assassins trying to kidnap me?"

"Okay. That's the second question we should ask. The first question we should ask is, are we safe here?"

"Oh yeah, good question. How do we answer it?"

Izy's eyes went blank as her AR contacts started to flicker.

"Shit," she said.

"What?"

"Look at the front door security feed."

Everyone in the building had access to the front door's feed. I pulled it up. The sidewalk in front of the entryway was empty.

"What am I looking for?"

"Look across the street. The black car."

Three people were sitting in a black vehicle. I zoomed in a little and blinked.

"Is that a steering wheel?"

"Yes."

"That's a manual car?"

"Yes."

"Is that legal?"

"Yes, if you have special license."

"You think they're here for us?"

"No, I think three people are sitting outside our building in a manual car because is such a nice neighborhood."

"I mean property prices have been going up lately."

"They are here to watch us, Romeo."

"Right," I said. "So, what do we do?"

"If they are just watching, then my security system has them on the back foot for now. We have time."

"To do what?"

"To answer question number two."

"Why are assassin's trying to kill us?"

"Yes."

"How?"

"Let's start with why did you go to Maddoc Technologies?"

"I don't know. Abigail's copy told her to stay away from George. I thought maybe he was the cause of all this."

"Did the assassin say anything that supported that theory?"

"No," I said. "She mentioned our IP address. I think she was sent here by whoever hired the Australian Golden Retrievers."

Izy looked away.

"What has my life become?" she muttered.

"I know the feeling."

She walked over to the office exit, glanced down the hallway, then closed and locked the door.

"I can't believe someone wanted to kidnap you."

"Then interrogate and probably kill me, don't forget."

"Oh, that I can believe. I have wanted to dismantle you many times."

"That's not so funny for me right now. I almost died."

"Sorry."

She scratched her chin.

"So, all we know is someone is after Abi, and Abi thought it had to do with George."

"Yeah," I said.

"There must be more. You didn't see anything, hear anything at Maddoc that might be useful?"

"Uh ..."

I tried to remember the details of my trip to the corporate headquarters. The saga of Ginger, Terry, and Louis loomed large. A dim, dusty bulb lit up in the back of my mind.

"I did take some pictures of George's lab," I said.

Izy's facial features seemed to rise in excitement. It might have just been the lighting.

"We should take a look. I've got access to some software that might help."

She flicked her hand and her eyes went distant. An invitation to an AR space popped up in my view. I selected it, and it closed my robot interface. In the space between heartbeats, the world around me had turned into a digital sitting room. There were plush chairs, couches, and divans scattered around. Each was upholstered in exotic fabrics. A painting on the wall showed a bunch of 19th-century French people drinking tea and wine. They all looked shocked at something being said by a wig-wearing young man in the center of the room. He had a single finger pointed up in the universal symbol of 'QED motherfuckas.'

"Over here, Romeo," Izy said.

She was standing in a corner. Her digital avatar was the spitting image of her. Her body wobbled weirdly as she moved, trying to orient itself based on the location of her hands and eyes. I could see how she in the real world was moving, and how her digital avatar was trying to compensate and match her smoothly. It was close. The biggest limitation was that her face was completely impassive. On any other person it would have been unsettling. On Izy it was just par for the course.

"Send me the pictures you took," she said.

I flipped through my camera app.

"What is this place?" I asked.

I attached the photos to an email and sent them to Izy.

"Is a chat room I administrate."

"What do you chat about?"

"I don't want to talk about it."

"Why? What is it?"

"Is not important."

"Okay."

She waved her hand and several of the paintings on the wall went blank. The photos I'd sent her were appearing blown up on the screen. While she was distracted, I walked over to one of the nearby bookshelves. *Cast on for Coziness: A Beginner's Guide to Knitting* was emblazoned on the spine of a digitally-rendered leather book. The book beside it was called, *Purls, Knits, and Chablis: Knitting for the 21st Century Enthusiast*. I walked over to another bookshelf.

"What are you doing?" Izy asked.

I glanced at another book spine, 'Knitting into the Now.' I turned to Izy. My jaw hanging open.

"These books are all about knitting," I said.

"So?"

"You said you administrate this chat room."

"So?"

"Izy, do you knit?"

"Shut up."

My eyes went wide. I looked around the room instinctually looking for someone else who could appreciate the wonder of my realization.

"You knit?"

"Maybe."

"You ... uh ... with needles, the whole thing. You knit?"

"What's the big deal?"

"I mean, it's not a big deal. It's fine. It's just, you knit?"

"My grandmother taught me how when I was a kid."

"That's so adorable."

"Shut up."

"Holy crap, you saved my life a few minutes ago, and this is still the thing about you I like the most."

"Shut up."

"Wait, why are you embarrassed?"

"I don't know, you're freaking out about a small hobby I have."

"Well, yeah, it's kind of out of character."

"Ugh, 'out of character.' What is this 'character' that every time someone does something interesting, they are 'out' of?"

"Aw, now I'm sad. Did you not tell me you like knitting because you were embarrassed?"

"No. Is hobby. There is not much to talk about if you're not a knitter."

"Knitter," I squeaked.

"Oh, for fuck's sake."

"And you administrate a chat room for all your knitting pals."

I brought my knuckle to my mouth and bit it in unbridled joy.

"I am remembering why I never told you."

"Don't be embarrassed. It's not a big deal. It's great."

"Clearly, that's why you're freaking out."

Her voice was low and resentful. My face fell.

"I'm sorry. I don't want you to feel bad, Izy."

"I don't feel bad."

"You sound like you feel bad."

"No."

"A little?"

"Is just ... sometimes you want to be a thing without it being like, 'oh you're that thing, and this other thing, how weird, those two things are different.' People demand you justify having interests. Knitting is good hobby."

"I'm sure it is."

"Is meditative."

"I'm sure."

The chat room fell silent. I looked down at my feet. I sidestepped toward Izy.

"Sorry."

"Is fine."

"Will you knit me a scarf?"

"Ugh, scarves are for amateurs. I'll make you a hat."

I smiled.

"So why did you bring me here?"

"We have software that uses predictive algorithms to turn 2D images into their 3D counterparts."

"What do you use that for?"

Izy paused.

"So people can show off their recent, real-world knitting in digital space."

"Aw."

"Shut up."

"Do you guys have competitions?"

"No."

She looked away.

"There might be a Secret Santa exchange in December."

Glee forced me to double over entirely.

"Oh, it's too much. I can't take it."

"You just survived a near death experience, are you angling to go through another?"

"No," I said. "I'm sorry. It's just … all so cute."

Izy waved her hand and one of the pictures in front of us expanded until it was filling the wall.

"Let's just focus," she said.

"Sure."

I bit my bottom lip.

The expanding picture was an image of George's lab. The two black hoodie-wearing techs were in the center of the screen, their backs to the camera. Izy touched a space in the air in front of her and the 2D image before me distorted. It seemed to elongate and stretch. The flat plane had formed into a fully-dimensional hologram. I stepped closer to the edge of the image.

"That's so cool," I said.

Izy stepped past me into the picture. She was standing in the digitally-recreated room. After a moment's hesitation, I followed through the frame into George's lab. The rendering was high-resolution. My external camera is pretty good and the software had refined it further. I walked toward the back of the room. Bizarre, black shadows appeared behind every object. They hovered in the air on the opposite side from the camera's POV.

The amorphous shadows became more pronounced as I followed Izy toward the still image of the two lab techs. Their faces came into view. With both their backs to the camera, the software had nothing for its algorithms to predict. Instead the front of their faces blurred into an uneven oval of black space that extended several inches out from where the edge of where their faces should be.

"Evil blob faces," I said. "That seems appropriate."

"Hmm."

Izy was looking at the electronics arrayed across the lab counters. She picked up something that looked like an external hard drive.

"Wow, you can pick things up?"

"Yes," Izy said. "The software compensates somewhat."

She spun the carbon fiber box she was holding. The curvy blob sticking out the side of the hard drive spun as if it were a fixture on the otherwise impeccably-rendered object. I walked over to one of the lab techs. It was hard to tell with just their backs toward me, but it looked like a man. I reached up and poked the side of his head. The whole body moved sideways on the floor. He bumped into the other lab tech. Both objects wobbled, and the one I'd poked twisted sideways toward me. I was staring into an inky abyss as the entire unrendered side of the tech was facing me.

"That is disturbing."

"How about you do not touch things?" Izy said.

"I'm not a child," I said.

The other lab tech toppled under the weight of the first and they both fell to the ground.

"I'll just not touch things."

Izy waved her hand, and the two lab techs reset to their original positions.

"What should I be looking for?" I asked.

"Anything that tells us what George was doing."

I walked along the counter glancing at the various pieces of electronic equipment. Working for Izy, I knew a little about computer components. There were a lot of spare hard drives around. A computer in the corner had the kind of bulky case designed to accommodate significant upgrades. None of it indicated what skullduggery George was perpetrating.

A collection of books was sitting on a shelf above the counter. In the picture they looked like actual paperback published books. They were the kind of high-quality reprint favored by people who wanted a status symbol. The first title read, *Atlas Shrugged*. I winced. I glanced at the next book. *The Fountainhead* was emblazoned in gold on the spine. I looked down the rest of the line of books.

"Ugh," I said. "I found evidence."

"What?"

"The complete works of Ayn Rand."

"Fuck."

"Yeah. George was clearly a monster."

I continued down the counter. The big body scanner loomed ahead of me.

"What do you make of this?" I asked.

Izy walked over to the contraption.

"Looks like an MRI machine. They use it to scan a person's body."

"Why would George have one?"

"You tell me. You were in his office. Was there anything there that mentioned MRIs?"

"No."

"What could you be doing in medical research that gets you killed?"

I glanced over the degaussing machine the black-clad techs had been using.

"I don't know."

Izy's avatar glitched and wobbled as she turned. Her hands and eyes led the rest of her body away. I glanced over the counter beside me. There was a tablet, but it was facing the ceiling so its screen hadn't been captured by my camera. I walked down the length of the counter.

"So," I said. "Did you hear that new single by Bwa Bwa?"

"Try to stay focused, Romeo."

"So, no?"

"Is bumping track. Now pay attention."

I looked down at the counter in front of me and sighed. I picked up another of the hard drives Izy had handled earlier. It was just a white plastic box with a few cable ports on the back. I sighed again. Izy kept scanning the other side of the counter. At long last, she sighed.

"Nothing," she said. "At least I think nothing."

"Yeah."

I walked back toward the techs. Izy met me in the middle.

"So, what do we do now?" I said.

Izy scratched her chin and looked at the ceiling.

"I don't know."

I glanced at the image of the tech beside me. The resolution was amazing. I really wanted to just poke it again. I reached up a finger and something caught my eye. The two techs were sitting in front of computers. Because they had been between the camera and the computers most of the screens had been obscured. There was a small corner of display visible in the top right. I leaned forward. The sliver of the screen was showing a calendar app reminder. The words were small. I leaned forward farther. I didn't want to knock the lab techs over again. I paused.

"What the fuck am I doing?" I said.

I knocked the two techs aside. Because they were imbued with a low mass only digital space could achieve, it was a pretty boss move. They banged and rolled across the counters then bounced into the center of the room. Izy looked down at me.

"What are you doing?"

"I noticed something."

"Okay. Why did you knock the techs around again?"

I pointed at the computer monitor. Izy followed the digit.

"There's a calendar notification on this computer screen," I leaned forward. "It says, 'Tell RG servers in 92031A need to be expanded.'"

I felt a little deflated.

"Okay, I was hoping for something more."

"Hmm," Izy said. "Is something. RG. I wonder what that is? Person? Position?"

"Organization? Royal Guard. You think the British aristocracy is involved? I never trusted those furry-hat-wearing guards they employ. What's so important about them not moving?"

Izy tried her best to keep the edges of her mouth from twitching. Every once in a while I get the best of her stoicism. She glanced away and turned back stern.

"No, I think probably not."

"Well, it's a thought."

"Is it?"

"Hey, I found the clue. I get to be glib."

"How about, you found the clue, so that redeems you from bringing an assassin down on our heads?"

"I will take that deal."

Izy cocked her head. She shook it after a moment.

"There wasn't any mention of an RG with the personal assistant?" she asked. "Think, Romeo."

I threw myself back to my time in the Maddoc Technologies' building. My brain kept gravitating to the sight of Ginger clocking Terry. I chuckled.

"What?" Izy said.

"Sorry, I got distracted."

"Three seconds have passed. How did you get distracted in three seconds?"

"I'm sorry, give me a minute."

I mulled over my entire time in George's office and his lab. There was nothing that seemed to matter. A little snippet of conversation rose to the front of my brain. Terry, before he and Ginger had gotten all late-night soap opera, he had said something about ...

"There was one thing."

"What?"

"While I was in the elevator, Terry said something about George answering to the CEO of Maddoc Technologies' parent company."

Izy's eyes widened.

"You didn't think to mention this when you told me what happened?"

"Well, it didn't seem like the most important thing Terry did. I prioritized."

"Ugh, Romeo," Izy said. She rubbed her fingertips against her temples. "You've ... CEO's don't micromanage projects at subsidiary companies. That's weird. Like suspicious weird."

"How would I know that?"

"I don't know, by having a general sense of how the world works."

"What about me makes you think that's a realistic expectation?"

She tipped her head to the side and shrugged.

"Fair enough."

She flicked her hand and the wall beside her turned into a screen. She started typing into a search engine.

"What are you doing?"

"I'm looking up what company owns Maddoc Technologies."

She hit search. A few articles were the first links on the page. They were from a couple of years back. Izy selected the first one. The headline read, 'Maddoc Technologies acquired by EternityNet.'

"Oh crap," Izy said.

"If Maddoc Technologies is owned by EternityNet, then the CEO George was answering to was ..."

"Rosa Galan. RG."

"George was working for one of the richest people in the world."

15

AERIAL CAVALRY

March 3rd, 2064 4:21 p.m. PST

"Izy, is Rosa Galan trying to murder us?"

"I think so."

"No, no, that's not okay.

"But still true."

"Do we run? We run right? Bora Bora, Toledo, Timbuktu. It's 'go to a place that you've only vaguely heard of, change your name, and sell trinkets to tourists time,' right?"

"I'm pretty sure Rosa Galan has access to the resources and technology to find us anywhere."

"Fucking big data."

Izy waved her hand. The lab around us faded, and I booted up my robot interface. She was staring at a blank wall when her eyes focused.

"Rosa Galan," she said.

"What do we do now?"

"I do not think there is a prescribed course of action for when a multibillionaire is trying to kill you."

"FEMA never has plans for the stuff you really need."

Izy looked over at me with an eyebrow barely raised.

"Sorry," I said. "I'm kind of panicking."

She nodded.

"That is reasonable."

We stood in silence for a few seconds.

"I think we should go warn Abigail," she said.

"Yeah?"

"Rosa Galan is ... we need to make sure Abigail knows."

"Okay," I said. "So, let's go to her downtown club. That's where she said she'd be."

"Small problem."

"What?"

"The building is under surveillance. They might snatch us in the street, or follow us to Abigail."

"Shit."

"We need to slip past anyone watching."

"How?"

"I do not know."

"Is there any way to leave the building besides the front and back door?" I asked.

"I don't think so. There are windows, but the ground-floor windows do not open. I'm guessing us jumping out from the second floor might be a little conspicuous."

"Also, you might break an ankle and I might break an axle."

"Hmm." Izy chewed on the inside of her cheek.

"Could we disguise ourselves somehow? Slip out looking like someone else."

"Like who?" she asked. "Another retrofitted delivery robot and another tall woman with broad shoulders?"

"We are a little distinct."

"A little."

Izy eyebrows furrowed a millimeter. She was really stressed.

"Do you actually think the people watching the building would snatch us off the street?" I asked.

"When one of the richest people in the world wants you dead, you assume the worst."

She looked up at the ceiling, lost in thought. I glanced out the office window. It was late afternoon. The light from the sun was just starting to turn orange. I looked at the drone pad on the other side of the glass. I laughed.

"What?" Izy said.

"I just had a really ridiculous idea."

"What?"

"No, it wouldn't work."

"No offense, Romeo, but let me be the judge of that."

"Hey."

She blinked at me expectantly.

"Alright," I said. "Fair point. I weigh about 60 pounds right."

"About that."

"What's the max weight on one of those express package delivery drones?"

"I think max carrying capacity on drone is 18 pounds. Something like that."

"So, if we could break me into pieces."

Izy looked toward the window. She looked back at me, then turned back toward the window. She laughed, like fully laughed. It was pretty amazing. She scanned my skinny frame with an appraising eye.

"We would have to put your black box, battery, external camera, and speaker system in the same package so you could communicate with whoever receives packages at Abigail's club."

"Yeah."

"But the legs, your frame, your backup battery, and the arms we could divvy up."

"Uh huh."

"That is by far the most ridiculous idea I have ever heard." She nodded. "Let us do it."

"Really?"

"I don't have anything better. We could send you straight to Abigail's club."

"Okay. I'll see if I can find some boxes in the back."

Izy placed the order for drone package pickup. Same-hour pick-up was absurdly expensive. I found some old delivery boxes in one of the server rooms in back and brought them to Izy. She lifted her tool box out from behind the desk and pulled a socket wrench from among the precisely organized collection.

"Be gentle with me," I said.

"Don't make this weird."

She found the bolts that secured my left leg to my frame.

"What about you?" I asked, as she started ratcheting the wrench. "You'll be here alone."

"We can't leave the ghosts on our servers unguarded. If that woman comes back and trashes the place looking for evidence of Abi or Abigail's whereabouts, she could kill someone. I will set up extra security protocols on the office video cameras. That should keep them at bay."

"Are you going to be okay?"

"I do not know. At the moment, I am more worried about you."

"Rest assured. If they find me, they'll never take me alive."

I giggled maniacally.

"Panicking."

"Oh yeah."

We started by removing my legs. It wasn't that diffi-cult. The delivery robot my body was retrofitted from was designed to have components easily replaced. The first leg came loose and the control line and power cable popped out of their sockets. I was seated on the office chair while Izy lifted the now limp extremity and placed it into one of the boxes.

"This is a little disturbing," I said.

"Seems cathartic to me," Izy said.

She started working on my other leg.

"While you're gone, I will see if I can't come up with something we can add to your robot to give you some self-defense."

"That would be nice, thanks," I said. "Like giant machine-gun hands, or maybe a missile launcher attached to my shoulder. Just spitballing. Think overkill."

Izy let out the first single breath of a chuckle.

"I'll see what I can do."

She removed my black box and battery from the frame of the robot. All that was left of me was the top bar of my frame that my arms attached to and my screen. She removed the arm, then my screen.

"You still okay?" Izy asked.

"Feeling a little all over the place."

There was a long silence. Izy was a little bent at the waist as if she was suffering from some sudden abdominal pain.

"You really want to goad me with that kind of joke while you are helpless before me?"

"Sorry," I said.

"Is fine."

"In moments like these, I really fall to pieces."

"You are a monster."

Izy checked a time readout on her desk.

"The delivery drones will be arriving soon," she said. "I'll send your other body parts first. When you arrive they'll already be there. I'm sending you straight to Abigail's downtown club."

"Great."

"Nervous."

"What? You act like I've never disassembled myself and sent myself by automated drone across the city. Remind me, just curious, no real reason for asking, what's the delivery failure rate on these drones?"

"I do not think it would be a good idea to check now."

A loud whirring sound came from outside. Izy picked up one of the boxes and opened the window. She placed the box in the carbon-fiber cage beneath the drone.

"Thank you for using Swiftdrop Delivery," the drone chirped.

"That name is a little unsettling," I said.

"Why? Because it evokes the image of you dropping to the ground and smashing on the pavement?"

"That's not what I need to hear right now."

"What? I cannot make joke?"

I stifled a snort.

"How's the CEO of Flooffee doing?"

"His days are numbered."

The drone took off and within a minute another had landed. Izy handed off another package. She walked back to the desk and lifted me into a waiting box.

"Good luck," she said. "Tell Abigail that she has to get out of the club and go ... I do not know where. She cannot stay there."

"Okay."

"Here is the socket wrench. You can get someone to put you back together once you arrive."

"Okay."

She paused.

"Good luck."

"You too," I said.

Izy nodded at me and closed the box. Everything went dark. I heard tape getting pulled off its roll and the box lid rustled as it was fastened shut. Izy stuck the delivery sticker she had printed onto the outside of my box and I was up and jostling. I heard the whirr of an arriving drone.

"Goodbye, Romeo. See you soon."

"Hey," I shouted. "When this is all over, do you think you could rig my robot up with wings or something? That would be awesome."

"Just focus on not dying."

She slid me into the drone's cage.

"Thank you for using Swiftdrop Delivery."

The drone took off. I can't feel inertia, but I did slide against the side of the box. I swiveled my camera to the right. It was pretty dark. Faint light from the setting sun leaked through the cracks in the lid and bottom. The whirring drone above me banked and I knocked against the other side of my cardboard conveyance. The drone dipped and I smacked against the top of the box. Physics has a way of keeping you guessing.

I considered my situation.

"How did this happen?" I said aloud. "I was making digital fruit for digital baboons this morning. What happened in the last ten hours?"

The drone didn't have an answer, but it did bank. I tried to peek through one of the cracks in the box. I got a glimpse of rooftop, then a road. My camera auto-focused on the cardboard.

"No, not that."

I zoomed in, trying to get a view through the crack. The camera focused on the ground hundreds of feet below, then the box, then the ground, then a cable coiled between me and the cardboard.

"That's in the edge of the frame. Why are you focusing on that?"

I wiggled my neck to maneuver the cable out of the camera's view. It focused on the road below. The drone banked. In my new position, I slipped and smacked against the side of the box.

"Okay, you know what, fine. Fine."

I gave up looking through the crack in the box. Technology has a way of being a real asshole. If I'd had any arms, I would have crossed them. Instead I stared, disgruntled, at the inside of the box. I sighed and wondered if Izy was going to be okay.

The drone's engine sound changed. I got the feeling we were losing altitude. I tried to peer through the crack in the box again. I saw the side of a tall glass building. A collection of drone pads stuck out from the side. My camera focused on the cardboard again.

"Damn it," I snapped.

I heard the thud of landing and the box shuddered. The drone pressed the box out of its cage and I tumbled.

"Another one," someone said.

The voice didn't sound familiar. My box was lifted up and spun around. I considered protesting but felt awkward about it. It felt rude to shout from inside a box someone was holding. Is that weird? I don't know if there's much precedent on the etiquette of being boxed. I heard myself get set down. Resting on something I felt safer calling out.

"Hello?"

"What the ..." someone said.

"In here."

There was a rustle and the sound of popping tape. The box lid pulled back. A young man in a business casual hoodie was staring at me wide eyed. He looked petrified as he stared at my face screen.

"Sorry," I said.

"Uh, uh, uh."

His face was a tableau of confusion. I spotted the other boxes containing the rest of my body arranged on the table around me.

"I don't mean to impose," I said. "But my limbs are in those boxes. Could you help me reattach them?"

16

WEIRDOS

Let's say, you really don't like painting. You don't hate that people paint. You don't mind that some people love to paint. You just don't care to do it. Does that stop you from understanding that Michelangelo, for example, *loved* to paint? Painting was one of the chief joys and struggles of his life. Is that inexplicable to you? No. You can pretty much wrap your head around it. You just don't like to paint.

Now imagine you live in a world, where everybody loves to paint the way Michelangelo loved to paint. I mean everybody around you is obsessed with it. They're constantly looking for a partner to paint with. They use dating apps that rank their painting compatibility with other people. There are big ads where a supermodel suggestively paints a landscape and a famous actor joyfully does an abstract Impressionist work reminiscent of Milton Resnick. (Don't compare your painting ability to those celebrities, by the way, everybody knows they airbrush the paintings later.)

When someone finds a painting partner, they gossip about it with their friends. "How was their brushwork?" "Fine, I guess. They just had no idea how to blend."

Now in this world of painting obsession, you just don't care for it. You don't feel ill will to the people that love it. You wish them all the luck in the world with that difficult neoclassicist piece they and their partner are working through. You just don't want to paint.

That's a little like what it is to be asexual. Except painting is having sex, and when you mention that you don't like painting, people act like you just said you don't like oxygen. We just don't like to paint.

Now, new scenario.

A man walks up to a woman at a bar.

He says, "Mind if I join you? Can I buy you a drink?"

What am I saying? Nobody does that anymore.

A man likes a woman on a dating app.

He says, "Hey ;-)"

A novel has just been conveyed. Without him having to say another word, a series of intentions have been communicated. We can assume that he is interested in a heterosexual relationship. They might hook up. If it works out, they'll date. If that works out, they might 'define the relationship.' If things continue to go well, they'll move in together. If things are really working out, they might talk about kids and marriage. If they're compatible, or they're not, they'll get married. Eventually they move to the suburbs, get their white-picket fence, 2.5 kids, and get miserable together. Ah romance ...

This is one of the perks of heteronormativity. If you happen to fall within the confines of what it deems 'normal,' you don't have to communicate your story. Your novel has been written for you by a thousand rom-coms, TV shows, hell, even action movies lend a hand, also the occasional novel. Pretty much everyone is familiar with your story. The only things you have to communicate are the things about you that fall outside the narrative of heteronormativity's story. You're into some kinky stuff in the bedroom? Look forward to a lot of awkward conversations. You don't want kids? Enjoy pushing back on a lot of familial peer pressure.

An asexual, aromantic person logs onto a dating site exclusively for their demographic. They are looking for a QPR: a queer platonic relationship: a platonic friendship that excludes sex and romance but still has the same level of commitment as a romantic relationship. The dating site is abandoned, because their demographic is small, especially in their local area. They go to a heteronormative dating site and try to float the idea to people there. Who knows, maybe someone there just hasn't considered the possibility that a lifestyle outside the confines of a traditional marriage could work for them. Problem is: what the fuck does the first person say to the second to communicate what they want succinctly? I cut QPRs down to their bare bones, and I'm guessing you only barely understood what any of that meant. So, what do you say? The awkward conversation has to happen before you remotely know each other. You don't get to go on a few dates, taking at least a few of the basic premises of your relationship for granted. You've got to dive right in at the top.

"Hey ;-) Want to hear me explain my deal for the next hour and then decide if you even want to get a drink?"

This is one of the downsides of being non-normative. Queer people spend a lot of their precious time on this earth explaining themselves. It really cuts into your sitting around eating junk food time. Why do you think so many queer people are so fit?

This is why the weirdoes of the world tend to congregate. They may not all be weird in the same way, but in the same way they're all weird. You know what I mean?

I think this is one of the major reasons why Abigail and I have been friends for so long. I mean, it's not like we have a lot in common, but we both know what it's like to have someone look at us like we're broken.

17

PRIVATE CHAMBERS

March 3rd, 2064 5:11 p.m. PST

It took a few minutes for me to pull myself together. Sam, the young man whose heart I was almost responsible for stopping, relaxed after I explained that I was not, in fact, the first wave of the robot takeover.

"So, who are you exactly?" he asked.

"I'm a friend of Abigail's," I said. "I need to speak with her."

He placed my leg in position, and I started ratcheting it into place.

"She's with a client at the moment," he said.

"It's important that I see her."

"It's a really important client."

"Sam," I said. "I just mailed myself to this office because a four-handed assassin, sent by a person in part responsible for my existence, tried to murder me. I need to talk to Abigail."

He placed my other leg into position. I started with the ratcheting. He stared at me.

"Well ..."

"I know. This is all really weird. You've got no idea how to respond. Well, believe me. This is only the like eighth-weirdest thing that's happened to me today. I need you to roll with the punches, Sam."

I hopped down off the table, fully reassembled. He starred at me for another long moment.

"Yeah, okay."

He was wearing a set of AR glasses. His eyes shifted focus, and I could just see the lit-up display on the glass. There were several seconds of silence.

"Abigail," Sam said. "I'm very sorry to interrupt. I have a Romeo Smith here who says it is vitally important that he speak with you."

He paused.

"I'll bring him right back," his eyes refocused. "Follow me."

We rolled into what looked like an office waiting room. There was a fountain in the corner and some tasteful indoor plants. A desk with an AI receptionist watched over the entrance. I'd never actually been to Abigail's club. It was not what I expected. There were no chains and only a little leather. Beyond the desk was a sturdy wooden door with a fingerprint scanner and a keypad. Sam pressed his finger to the scanner and typed in a code. The door beeped.

Beyond was an upscale locker room with nice wood-patterned lockers and a nicely-tiled set of shower stalls. I caught sight of a person stepping out of one of the stalls with a towel around their waist. As they passed, I noticed red welts formed a crisscross pattern along their back.

We continued beyond the locker room into a hall. Heavy noise-insulated doors lined the walls.

"Not what I was expecting," I said.

Sam glanced back.

"What were you expecting?"

"Heavy metal, latex, whips, chains, leather. That kind of thing."

"We can provide all of that upon request."

He stopped at one of the doors and opened it.

"Mistress Obsidian," he said.

I coughed.

"One moment," Abigail said. "Red."

There was a pause.

"I'm sorry to interrupt the scene, but I'm afraid I have to step out for a minute," Abigail said to the client inside the room. "Would you like me to let you out of your restraints?"

"Oh, that's alright, Mistress Obsidian," a man said in a deep baritone. "Actually, I'd like to wait in this position if you don't mind. Maybe incorporate the wait into the scene."

"A little neglect play."

"Yeah."

"No problem. I'm going to put your ball-gag back in, but I won't tighten that strap. If you need to use the safe word, you can spit it out. I'll be listening."

"Thank you, Mistress."

The man's deep voice quavered a bit as he said the words.

"Alright, let's reenter the scene."

There was another short pause.

Whack! Whack! Whack!

I flinched back from the sound coming from the intercom. A muffled groan came from inside the room.

"Now, you just wait here, you pathetic little cur," Abigail hissed. "And if you're very lucky, maybe, just maybe, I'll waste a little more of my time on you."

I stared at Sam. It was my turn to be shocked. He shrugged. Abigail stepped into the hall. She was wearing a long, black, billowy cloak. She shut the door behind her.

"Thank you, Sam. Please have the audio from the room sent to my earpiece."

"No problem," he said.

Sam set off down the hall. I looked Abigail up and down.

"Are you wearing a judge's robe?" I asked.

"Yeah. Don't worry about it. What's going on? Are you and Izy okay?"

It took me a moment to answer. I was still flummoxed by Abigail's wardrobe. Kink is ... way more complicated than I ever imagined.

"Uh," I said. "I'm just ..."

"Focus, Romeo. What's happening?"

I blinked away my curiosity. It was only 50-50 that I wanted to know more anyway.

"No," I said. "We're not okay. A lot of pretty weird stuff has happened since this morning."

I gave her the CliffsNotes. Her jaw had dropped by the time I finished my story.

"Four hands?"

"I know."

"Rosa Galan?"

"I know!"

"Fuck."

"I like it when we're on the same page."

Abigail leaned against the wall and rested her chin on her chest. Her judge's robe gave her a regal kind of authority.

"Izy thought I should warn you," I said. "The FBI needs things like probable cause and warrants, but murderous tech billionaires ..."

"Yeah. I should get out of here."

"Where should we go?"

"You should leave now. I've got to finish this session, first."

"What? Is that really what's important right now?"

"It's important."

"How?"

"He is a very important client."

"I ... you got the thing about there being a literal assassin?"

"Yeah."

"So ... what?"

"Look, my business requires discretion. Just trust me, Romeo."

"Abigail—"

"I just need you to trust me, Romeo," she snapped.

We stared at each other.

"Fine," I said.

"Thank you."

There was a long pause. Like a really long pause.

"This place isn't what I expected," I said.

"What were you expecting?"

"I don't know. Heavy metal?"

"Why does everybody think kinky people all listen to heavy metal?"

A door just down the hall opened. Heavy metal music erupted into the hall.

"Hey Boss," a man in a pair of black leather pants said to Abigail.

"Hey Daniel, how are you doing?"

"Good, thanks."

He shut the door, silencing the music and headed toward the locker room down the hall. I looked at Abigail.

"What?" she said. "I never said none of us listen to heavy metal."

"Uh huh."

Abigail bit the inside of her cheek. She shook her head.

"I'm sorry," she said. "When I asked for your help this morning, I thought this was going to be something—"

"Normal-ish?"

"Yeah. Why the hell would Rosa Galan take the risk of hiring an assassin? What could possibly be so bad that she'd try killing people to cover it up?"

"That is the hundred-billion-dollar question."

"I guess you should go back to Izy," she said.

"The server farm's under surveillance."

Abigail had that look she gets when she feels a headache incoming.

"Right. Okay."

She shook her head.

"Shit. There's really only one option."

"What?"

"You've got to go to the FBI. Tell them you fear for your life. Have them pick up Izy. Tell them in exchange for protection you'll help them find me. That should keep you safe for a while."

"Wait, no. I'm not helping the FBI catch you."

"You won't have to."

"Why not?"

She sighed.

"I'm turning myself in," Abigail said. "Let me finish what I have to do here. Then I'll go to the FBI myself, I guess I'll confess to making Abi. Abi will be able to come out of hiding. If the FBI is paying enough attention, it might get Rosa Galan to back off all of you."

"But we can't prove Rosa Galan did any of this."

"I know."

"They'll just put you in jail."

"Maybe."

Abigail was gnawing on her lower lip.

"But ..."

"We're in way over our heads, Romeo."

"Well, yeah."

"So, what can we do besides ask for help?"

"I don't know if being put in prison qualifies as being helped."

"Well, sometimes you don't get to decide what conditions people place on helping you."

I stared at her in mock disgust.

"Don't you dare be realistic with me, right now," I said. "I am not in the mood."

Abigail's face formed into an unwilling smile.

"It's not as bad as it sounds, Romeo. I'd be looking at a five-year sentence tops. I'd probably get out in three with good behavior. Not great, but better than you, Izy, or Abi getting killed."

"Three years sounds pretty bad, Abigail."

"I'm not over the moon about the prospect either, but I don't have a better plan. Do you?"

"I think we both know I don't."

"Well then," Abigail said.

I stared at the floor. The prospect of only seeing Abigail through security glass for three years was dawning on me. More like it was slowly subsuming me, like quicksand.

A door opened behind me. I turned around. Three clowns and a man in a bear suit hefting a unicycle on his shoulder, were exiting one of the rooms.

"Hey guys," Abigail said. "You getting everything you need?"

"Perfect, Mistress," one of the clowns said.

"Thank you," another added.

They headed toward the locker room. I stared after them.

"Don't leer," Abigail said.

"I just ... which of them worked for you?"

"None in that group. We rent out space to people who need a discreet place to um ..."

"Just don't finish that sentence."

"Okay."

I clacked my hand against the wall.

"I can't ..." I said. "I don't want you to go to jail."

She placed a hand on my shoulder.

"Romeo, circumstances don't care what you accept. They just are what they are. I took a risk, and it turned out about as bad as risks can turn out. When that happens, you do what you can to reduce the consequences, and you minimize collateral damage. That's where we're at now."

"But ..."

"Just go to the FBI. Get Izy safe. Leave the rest to me."

I looked up at my best friend. She was still wearing judge's robe. I snorted.

"What?"

"The outfit. Things got so real, I fully forgot for a second."

She smiled.

"Just go, asshole."

Another door opened. Six people in different-colored latex body suits exited. They all had kazoos in their mouths and were hefting riding crops.

"Zzzz-Izzzz" one of them buzzed, waving at Abigail.

"Hey, Anise," Abigail said.

The multicolored group headed off down the hall.

"I can't tell if this is the most fucked up place I've ever been, or the greatest place I've ever been," I said. "And I live in digital space."

Abigail shrugged.

"Well, this whole place is built on consent. A lot of things in society can't make that claim. What do you value more: normalcy or consent?"

"Is that part of your sales pitch for nervous customers?"

"Yeah. Did it sound rehearsed?"

"It was a little showroom-floor. Does it work?"

"Oh, yeah."

We smiled at each other. My smile faded.

"So, I'm supposed to go just ... go to the Feds."

"Yes," she said.

"It kind of feels like giving up."

"It kind of is."

We stood in silence for another few moments.

"I've got to get back," she said.

"Yeah."

"I'll see you soon."

"Yeah."

I turned and started wheeling down the hall. It felt like my internal one-man band had a hole punched in his bass drum. I looked back. Abigail had already disappeared.

Through the sitting room was an elevator bank. I rode one down and rolled out onto the street. It was raining. It's Seattle, so not that unusual but still, it felt a little on the nose. Raindrops plinked, plonked, and plopped on my metal frame. People were packing the sidewalks making their way towards cars and mass transportation.

I connected to the downtown WiFi. The local FBI field office popped up on my search. I was still far from convinced this was the best move. The Feebs did not seem trustworthy. My onboard GPS painted a ghostly blue line in the air before me leading to the left. I started rolling down the sidewalk and stopped. There had to be some way to avoid going to the Feds.

"I'll run it by Izy," I said.

It was an obvious attempt at avoidance, but it seemed like a good enough reason to stall for five minutes. I pulled up Izy's number in my phone app. I was about to select the call button.

A jangling graphic indicated someone was calling me. It wasn't Izy. It was an unknown number. I looked around me. I had frozen in the middle of the sidewalk and was now forming a stone in the river of professionals. I'm not sure water molecules shoot rocks in rivers quite so many dirty looks though. I rolled to the edge of the walkway. The jangling graphic was still filling a portion of my vision. I answered the call.

"Hello?"

"Romeo?"

"Maybe. Unless you're trying to murder me, then ... no. Who's this?"

"Sanav."

"Oh, uh, hello? How are you doing?"

"Can't complain. You?"

"Being hunted by an assassin. And those Golden Retrievers you met."

"They weren't Golden Retrievers to me."

"So, more like Labradors you think?

"No ... uh, never mind."

"How did you get my number?" I asked.

"The DOA AI logged your visit."

"Oh, sure. So, what's up?"

"Your digital friend Abi. She got in touch."

"Oh?"

"Yeah. She wants to talk to you."

"Me?"

"Yeah."

"She said specifically me?"

"Yes. She said not to contact your friend Abigail."

"Why? I mean, it's about time, but still, why?"

"She didn't say, just that it was important. She wants to meet you."

"Where?"

"At a Shareholders' meeting."

"A Shareholders' meeting?"

"Can you hop to my house? I hate talking on the phone."

"Give me a minute."

I needed a place to park my body for a while. There was a hotel entrance a little way down the sidewalk. I started in that direction.

"I'll call you back," I said, then hung up.

Rolling into the lobby, I paused. The hotel was adorned in a retro-futurist decor. An AR sculpture of a bulbous rocket launching toward the ceiling filled the center of the lobby. Curvy counters and high metallic fringes showed what people in the far past thought the distant future would look like. Looking around I realized, as far as this hotel was concerned, they were right in a kind of ironic, meta sort of way that the people of the past, in all their modernist sincerity, would no doubt have found incredibly galling.

I flipped my screen to display a delivery company's logo and rolled toward the lobby elevators. I went up to the second floor and headed to the end of one of the halls. Tucking myself up against a bright-yellow, genetically-modified house plant, I powered down my robot's interface.

I hesitated. Abigail had been very clear she wanted me to go to the FBI. On the other hand, Abi had made it pretty clear she wanted me to meet her. Since they were almost the same person, did their requests cancel each other out? I didn't think Abigail would like that line of thinking.

I looked at my phone app and saw Izy's contact again. Before, when I'd been using it as an excuse not to go straight to the FBI, running things by Izy seemed like a great idea.

Now, it felt like if I called her, she would just tell me to do what Abigail said. Abi was somewhere in digital space with very possibly the answer to all this whirling, chaotic, life-threatening, mishegoss into which we'd all been dragged. Knowing there was a good chance this was all a mistake, I threw caution to the wind, pulled myself up by my bootstraps, turned the other cheek, and danced like no one was watching.

I called Sanav.

"I'm coming to your place," I said, decisively.

"Yeah, I know," he said.

"Oh, sorry, no. 'Cause before it might have sounded like I was sure I was coming, but I wasn't. I was still conflicted. But I guess you didn't know that. I could see how you'd assume from before that I'd already decided to come, but I hadn't. But I have now."

"Okay ..."

I reflected on the appalling waste of time the last ten seconds of my life had been.

"I'll be right there."

"Great."

18

WHISKEY, HONEY, LEMON, WATER: HOT

March 3rd, 2064 5:26 p.m. PST

I sent the request to DOA and, a second later, I materialized on the deck of the little wooden sailboat. Sanav opened the hatch.

"Hey, come on in."

I ducked inside. The massive digital sculpture of the submarine and the giant squid was gone. Instead there was a large boulder sitting in the middle of the room. It was sandstone and the size of a small house.

"That's new," I said.

Sanav glanced at it.

"Oh yeah, I heard what you said about the sea battle being a lot for the entry way."

"Oh, I didn't mean to suggest—"

"It's fine. I'd been meaning to change it. Here. Come stand right here."

He pointed to a spot on the floor. I walked over and hit my mark.

"Now look at it," he said.

I turned and examined the giant block of digital sandstone. It seemed as unremarkable as before, saving its size. I blinked. The ground around the rock was doing something strange. The floor was decked out in fine Italian marble. The marble's chaotic pattern was, I blinked again, it appeared to be lapping. A small rolling wave was passing over the floor.

"Wow," I said.

"Keep watching."

The marble wave lapped gently against my feet. It felt kind of chilly.

"Cool."

"Keep watching," Sanav insisted.

I looked up again. A noise was starting to permeate the entry hall. It sounded like a dull, distant roar. The walls behind the rock started to shimmer and distort. The floor on the far side of the room rose. As if materialized out of nowhere, a huge wave of finest marble had appeared. It was rushing in my direction. I froze as it approached. The liquid stone struck the boulder and was launched to the sides and up into the air. The flowing liquid marble continued around the impediment like two walls of water. They were heading toward me.

"Oh," I managed.

The waves hit me with all the bracing power of ocean water. Despite the sensation of force all around me, it didn't sweep me off my feet. It just squished me between its equalized power. I was immersed in cold marble for a few seconds then it started to recede. My head emerged and I saw Sanav beside me. He had a huge grin on his face.

Liquid marble was running off his head. The floor was resettling itself.

"Pretty cool right?" he said.

"Yeah," I said. "Totally more appropriate for the front entrance. Not intimidating at all."

"I thought so."

I forced a smile.

"You want another margarita?"

"How about a hot toddy?"

"Sure."

I shivered as Sanav led the way into his lounge. I went into my skin's advanced setting and turned up the temperature. Sanav waved and his bar appeared. He reached behind it and a steaming mug emerged. I took it and quaffed the contents.

"Rough day?" Sanav asked.

I jiggled my head. He tapped my mug with his fingertip. A new serving of amber liquid filled the cup. Sanav reached over the counter and hefted another mug.

"So, where's Abi?" I asked.

I slugged back half of the new drink. Hot toddy spilled down my chin and vanished into thin air before it hit the ground.

"Did you know the EternityNet annual shareholder's meeting is happening today?"

"No."

"Well it is. They hold it in digital space. Abi wants you to meet her there."

"Huh."

"Why there?" Sanav asked.

"I can think of a couple reasons."

"What are they?"

"Actually, it's just one big reason. Sorry, I didn't mean to oversell it."

"Okay. I'd still like to hear the reason."

"Rosa Galan is trying to murder us."

The expression on Sanav's face suggested I'd spontaneously started speaking another language.

"I'm sorry?" he said.

I filled him in on everything that happened.

"Wow," he said, when I was finished. "Is this like every day for you guys or ..."

"No. Today just ... decided to be memorable."

Sanav gave me a supportive pat on the shoulder.

"You've got 20 minutes before the shareholder's meeting. Another drink?"

I'd quaffed my toddy.

"Yes, thanks."

He tapped the mug and it refilled again.

"Thanks for doing all this, Sanav. A little above and beyond for someone you just sold an identity."

"I don't mind."

"That's amazing."

Sanav smiled.

"What about you? Why are you so ready to lay down your life here? Your black box isn't at a server farm in the middle of the ocean. You could really get hurt."

"Abigail's my best friend."

"And Abi?"

"Yeah, her too, I guess. It's a little difficult to untangle if I'm honest. All I know at the moment is I don't want either of them to die."

"Sure, but ..."

"What?"

"Nothing, just ... Abigail did kind of create this situation. And now you're dragged into it. Doesn't seem totally fair."

"Yeah, well, that's the downside of having interesting people in your life. Their problems are never boring or simple."

"I mean if you're cool with it. It's just ... it feels like your relationship with Abigail might be a little one-sided."

I laughed.

"No," I said.

"Really?"

"Absolutely not."

"Okay."

I could see he wasn't convinced. I checked my internal clock. We had time.

"Okay so, Abigail and I met in middle school. I was a ... well, 'loser' is a strong word—"

"You were unpopular."

"No, I mean, 'loser' is a strong word that was frequently used to describe me."

Sanav nodded.

"Got it."

"Abigail arrived halfway through the year."

"Nightmare."

"Right. And she was one of those girls that got really tall, really early."

"Uh, double nightmare."

"Yeah, she stood out like Frankenstein's monster. So, her first day, she's in the cafeteria. Looking around, doing the whole, 'where do I sit, it's not like it will decide my entire social future, oh wait, yes it will' thing."

"Sure."

"And nobody seemed inclined to have her join them."

"Kids can be cruel."

"She was dressed in all black with lots of black eye shadow and spike-studded bracelets."

"Okay, so kids can also be afraid."

"I was sitting alone because I was a cool and brooding loner. The other kids were just mixing up the 's' and the 'n.' The whole school had dyslexia."

Sanav grinned.

"Sure."

"Abigail approaches my table and asks if she can sit. I dump pudding down my shirt in surprise and then say, 'sure.'"

"And your friendship begins."

"Nope. That happened later. She ate her food in stony silence. I asked her a couple questions. Where she moved from, that kind of thing. No response. I offered her a baby carrot. You know I wasn't going to give her any pudding. You don't give the good shit to a total stranger."

"I mean that's just common sense."

"Exactly. So, no conversation. Abigail just eats and stares at the table. Lunch ends and I'm pretty convinced that Abigail is a huge asshole. Later, after school. Some kid was making fun of me in the line for the bus. Pretty normal for me at the time. Out of nowhere, Abigail appears and slams the kid up against a brick wall. And I'll never forget what she said."

"What?"

"She said, 'If you ever say another word to him, I'm going to come to your house while you're sleeping and cut you into little pieces, then hide you all over your house so your parents have to hunt for you like Easter eggs.'"

"Holy shit."

"I know, pretty fucked up, right. The kid started crying."

"I would imagine so."

"He was fine. He stopped bullying other kids, joined band. Figured out he was bisexual. I think he went to Julliard. He and Abigail dated for a minute or two in high school. Anyway, in the moment, he was too afraid of Abigail to tell a teacher. Which is lucky because I feel like she probably would have gotten expelled, at least."

"Yeah, probably."

"After that, well, I don't want to go too far out on a limb and say this is a codified law of the universe but, in general, if someone threatens to turn a school bully into the most horrifying Easter egg hunt imaginable for you, that person is now your friend."

"I get that."

"Abigail was the first person I told when I figured out I was asexual. I was the first person she told when she figured out she liked tying men up and spanking them. I was there when all the guys caught up to her in height, finally got a look at her face, and collectively decided they might like getting tied up and spanked by her."

"Oh-kay."

"Yeah, that was my reaction. Anyway, it might seem like, today, the friendship is one-sided. But Izy has a business because Abigail invested in it. I have a robot body in the real world because Abigail paid for the parts. She takes risks. Way more than most people. When her risks don't pay off, she takes on the consequences, alone. When her risks pay off, she shares the benefits. She's a pretty amazing person. Admittedly, creating Abi blew up in a big way that was far from predictable. And even now, Abigail's response is to throw herself under the bus with the FBI and probably go to prison to insulate me and Izy."

I paused, my heart heavy at the thought.

"Somebody has got to look out for Abigail. I don't envy her the fact that it's me, given that I'm not exactly a strategic genius. But somebody has got to be pulling for her not to go to prison."

"She did break the law."

"Yeah, but she didn't hurt anybody. Other people did that. I feel like they're the ones that should be going to prison."

Sanav nodded.

"So, what about you?" I asked. "You've pretty much leapt into this with both feet. You barely know Abigail and Abi."

He bit his bottom lip.

"I, uh ... it's not an interesting story."

"I'm interested."

Sanav sighed.

"Well, you were open with me, I guess. Sure ... why not?"

He hesitated.

"My parents were a little overbearing in life. They loved me, but I don't know if they had a strong grasp of the difference between loving someone and controlling them. A big part of the reason I got into competitive sailing was that it was something I was allowed to do alone. They weren't evil or anything. They were just terrified and rich, so they built and trapped me in this child-proofed world, for decades. Into my twenties.

"Then I died. It was their worst nightmare. So, my parents became even more overbearing in death, but now as a ghost, they had a lot more control. They could cut off my Internet connection and leave me. You know how it is when the Internet goes down, you're confined. Isolated.

"I tried to talk to them about it, but people really don't like acknowledging they're doing something messed up. That's the thing about abuse, psychological or otherwise. Nobody wakes up in the morning and thinks, 'I'm going to abuse one of my loved ones today.' Abusers are people with dangerous character traits, uncontrolled temper, jealousy, possessiveness, or in my parents' case, neurotic fear.

Then their dangerous character traits meet with a situation where they have a lot of power over someone else. Their kid, or their 20-year-old who has no self-esteem because he's spent his life being told he can't handle the outside world. The abuser pushes and pushes, but the abused just don't know how to defend themselves. Over time the relationship ends up in this contorted and horrifying place. That's why abusers can seem so normal and decent to other people. If they don't have power, they can't push their neurosis on another person.

"So, I was trapped in a prison of my parents' fear. Their rebukes and pain inflicted on me because I couldn't stop them and nobody else knew. After a few years, it became clear I really only had one option."

Sanav's face went dark. My eyes widened.

"You uploaded?"

"Yeah."

"Fuck."

"I mean my experience of it was being in one place, then suddenly being free, but back on the black box my parents controlled, a version of me was deleted. He destroyed himself so I could be free."

"That's ... I'm really sorry."

"That was five years ago. I haven't talked to my parents since."

Silence lingered in the nonexistent air.

"Anyway, suffice it to say, I've got a bit of a soft spot for ghosts in need. Abi needs help. I'll help."

He flicked his hand and a clock appeared on the wall.

"Shareholder's meeting is coming up."

It took me a moment to hear what he said.

"Yeah."

"Well, if you need anything else, don't hesitate to call, now you've convinced me that Abigail is a saint."

"Oh, she's not a saint," I said. "She's a total asshole like 20 percent of the time. Eh, 40 percent."

"Fair enough. Still, my knee-jerk response is to be suspicious of people that illegally create copies of themselves. They tend to exploit their ghosts. Abi and you both seem to think Abigail is the exception. If there's anything I can do, let me know."

"Thanks. I will."

Good people are rare. Decent people are abundant, so society lowered the standard. Now it says that if you're not intentionally hurting anyone, you're a good person, but you're actually just decent. The standard should be: good people do good things for other people. Just because they can. Pretty obvious actually, it's kind of in the name, good people. What did you think they were referring to there? Good intentions? Most decent people don't do good things for other people just 'cause. They might do good things for other people because they can brag about it later, because they expect something in return, most commonly because they can write it off on their taxes.

We decent people don't like to hear this. We want to believe that being good is a passive process. Sitting around on your couch? Not hurting anybody? Well done, you're a good person. Except we're not. We're just decent. At best. In fact, our apathy in the face of myriad institutional inequalities that we benefit from kind of puts a big negative mark on our morality. We might all be kind of bad people.

Because of this, good people kind of irritate us. They're always running around worrying about the bad things in the world. It's a real buzz-kill. So, we resent them when they point out something's wrong. Especially when it's something wrong we're doing. We're fine doing good, as long as the 'doing' doesn't actually require us to, you know, 'do' anything. Anybody who points out that the world doesn't get better by accident is a real pain in the ass. Until you're the one getting screwed. Then, when the world isn't paying attention to you, and the good people are the only ones who help, you realize, most humans are assholes.

So, if you stumble across a good person, rare gems that they are, and their concern for the world's problems puts a strain on you. Remember ... toughen the fuck up you crybaby. You're not running from predators or marauding members of rival tribes because, in the past, people like that made the world better. Appreciate them, support them, forgive them when they fuck up, and maybe, when you're ready, try to join them.

"Sanav," I said.

"Yeah."

"Assuming I succeed in dodging prison and death, you want to hang out sometime?"

He paused.

"Yeah, okay."

"Cool. I've got a shareholder's meeting to go to."

"Enjoy it. Try not to get tracked down and killed."

"Will do."

19

TROUBLE INDEFINITELY

March 3rd, 2064 6:24 p.m. PST

EternityNet's shareholder meeting was being held in a cozy, intimate, 'really shows the company cares about each individual shareholder' stadium. The stage looked like a postage stamp in the far distance. Clustered around it were a group of respectable-looking ghosts and avatars. They all looked very dignified in their business hoodies. Behind them were the idle investors and the retirees. They dressed a little more casual: t-shirts, beards, sandals, and socks. Behind them were a group of people who looked thoroughly dissatisfied. They were the kind of people fuming inside that their five-hundred-dollar investment hadn't turned into five hundred million dollars yet.

At the very back of the stadium, in the area where sound settings prevented the rest of the audience from hearing their audio, the last group of investors were corralled. That was where Abi had told me to meet her. They were much more colorful, than their counterparts. They carried signs, were dressed in costumes, and a few seemed to be warming up for some kind of battle. The rest had taken the form of various kinds of mythological, and pop cultural characters, monsters, and one person seemed to be a large root-beer float. I knew these people. Troublemakers.

"Reveal the Interdimensional Aliens!" a sign read.

"Money can't be traded for time. Private property is a rhyme," another sign said.

"Vintage Corruption," a woman's t-shirt said in swirling holographic letters.

"Fun right?"

I spun around.

"Ahh, fuck. Bigfoot."

Bigfoot was looming over me.

"Sorry, about that," Abi said. "I'm trying to stay incognito."

"And you went with eight-foot-tall ape man?"

"Who would suspect?"

"I guess there's a certain logic to that," I looked up at her. "Where the hell have you been?"

"You didn't know I existed until Sanav told you—"

"Oh no, Abigail told me about you this morning. You skipped town and left a whole mess behind, with assassins, and Fortune 500 companies, and a murderous billionaire."

"Assassins?"

"Yeah."

"Billionaire? So, you know about Rosa Galan—"

"Yeah."

"Damn."

"What?" I asked.

"I was going to wait until during the shareholder's meeting and reveal it all dramatically."

"Is drama what's important now?"

"No, but, you know, you've kind of taken the wind out of my sails."

"Abi."

"Sorry. You're right. It's just, I planned a whole speech for when I told you." She waved the thought away. "It doesn't matter. What's happening out in the world? I had no idea things were getting so chaotic. How did Rosa Galan find you guys?"

My digitally-represented Adam's apple bobbed as I swallowed nervously.

"What?" Abi asked.

"I may have played a small part in attracting Rosa Galan's attention to us."

"Oh Romeo. What did you do?"

I told her the story of my adventures in corporate espionage. Bigfoot looked displeased.

"What were you thinking?"

"Look, I've already been told how bad an idea that was, by Izy, by you—I mean the other you—Abigail. You know what I mean. Anyway. I've got it. I only went there because you fucked off and left us in the dark. Now, Abigail is planning to turn herself in to protect all of us from criminal prosecution."

"Ugh, she is? She is so insufferable. Of course, she's got to be all self-sacrificing. Like I don't know how to take care of myself."

"You guys get that you're basically the same person, right? Everything you say about her is almost certainly true of yourself."

"I know. She's just so patronizing. I can't stand it."

"Good evening, EternityNet shareholders," a voice spoke.

There was applause from most of the audience. Our sections made a much more chaotic sound in response.

Imagine if you gave a first-grade class a random assortment of instruments from around the globe, and half of them decided, fuck the instruments, let's just try Mongolian throat singing instead.

A man had taken the stage wearing a custom-tailored hoodie. It probably cost more than my yearly salary. A window popped up in the bottom-right of my vision. It was a close-up view of the man as he took center stage.

"My name is Chip Little. I'm the Director of Communications for EternityNet. I am very happy to welcome you to this year's shareholders meeting."

More applause. More throat singing.

"It has been a great year for our company."

"Why did you want to meet here?" I asked Abi.

"You don't want to hear Rosa Galan speak? These shareholder meetings can be really interesting?"

"I highly doubt that. Also, how would you know?" I asked.

"I watch them."

"You watch shareholder's meetings?"

"Yeah."

"Because you own stock in the companies?"

"Sure, and sometimes just 'cause they're interesting."

"You watch shareholder's meetings for fun?"

"Yeah, it's fascinating how corporations brand themselves. It's fun to compare the image they try to sell to their shareholders and how that differs from the image they sell to their consumers ..."

I stared aghast at the mythological creature beside me.

"What?" Abi said.

"I just forget sometimes, underneath all the intimidating coolness, you're a real dork."

"You're one to talk."

"Yeah, but nobody is surprised when they find out I'm a loser."

Bigfoot grunted.

"Are you going to stick with this Bigfoot look the entire time?"

Abi glanced around the gathered mob of weirdoes.

"No, I guess not."

Bigfoot morphed into an avatar about my height. It was Abigail, but more so. Her eyes glowed a little, as if there were flecks of neon lighting in her irises. Her hair was still black, but somehow blacker than just the color. Like a black hole, light didn't seem to escape it. Her outfit was a strange mix of business casual and body armor. Shoulder pauldrons were affixed to a purple cashmere sweater.

It was bizarre seeing her in digital space. I had so much of the same history with her as I had with Abigail, but we'd never met before. It was like meeting someone in person you've only talked to via text. There is a pre-established dynamic, but it has to be retooled to a very different format.

"Weird," I said.

"I know, for me too."

"You have all her memories."

"Up to the last month."

"Weird."

"Okay, well now you're making me feel uncomfortable. It's just me."

"I know. It's just also not you. Like if Abigail asks me to keep a secret from you, do I have to do that? Have you guys worked out how much you're entitled to know about each other's lives?"

"We're two people. Just treat us like two different people."

I looked at the stage, trying to process all the strangeness. Chip Little was still droning on about corporate vision. The audience was half-listening. Chip was not the person they had come to see. I looked back at Abi.

"Two people. Cool. I can work with that."

She nodded and smiled.

"I missed you."

"I didn't, because I didn't know you existed. But I was pissed when I found out you did, and you hadn't visited me."

"Sorry about that. We were going to tell you. It just never seemed like the right time. Abigail and I have been really busy developing the business online."

"I've heard. Mail-in bondage bot. Spare me the empire building. It's the internet, Abi. It takes a fraction of a second to pop in and say, 'Hey, I exist. How's things?'"

"I know. I should have."

"Izy is going to be pissed you didn't say hello to her too."

"I'll apologize to her as well."

"You'd better."

"I will."

"Fine."

"Fine."

We sat in silence for a few seconds.

"How cool is being a ghost?" I asked.

"So cool!"

"I know, you can just wave your hand and poof ... anything you want exists."

"I live in a castle on the French Riviera that has an infinity pool. Not a pool that looks like it goes on forever. It's a pool that literally goes on forever."

"Have you tried skydiving from space?"

"No."

"Amazing. You have to turn your pain receptors off while you're passing through the simulated atmosphere, but you end up going faster than the speed of sound. If it gets boring, just turn flying on and you're zipping around like an airplane."

"We should totally go and do that."

"Definitely."

We paused again.

"Probably we should do that after we're no longer being hunted by one of the most powerful people in the world."

"I think that's a good idea," Abi said. "Prioritize."

"But if we survive."

"Oh yeah, definitely, if we survive. Space skydiving."

"It's been a great year for EternityNet," Chip was still droning on. "We've acquired a dozen new companies, which have added to the total employee population of our company by almost 18 percent. This rapid growth has translated into an increase in valuation for the company that is historic."

"What does any of that mean?" I asked.

"They bought a bunch of new companies. They're bigger so people think the company is worth more. Tell you what. Go into your settings and select commentaries. There's one called 'Clarity.' It's an AI that boils a lot of the corporate jargon out of these things."

"Oh thanks."

I opened up my settings and searched for a while.

"Where are commentaries?"

"They're under Audio Options."

"I can't find it."

"It's there."

"I'm pretty sure it's not."

"Look again."

"Oh, I found it. I found it."

The commentaries feature opened up a drop-down bar with several dozen options. I scrolled down to 'Clarity' and paused. Just below it was another option, 'Cynical Subtext.' Glancing furtively at Abi, I selected the second option.

"Now I'm very proud to bring on stage," Chip Little said. "A woman who needs no introduction. The CEO of EternityNet, Rosa Galan."

"I am overshadowed by the person who you actually came to see, my boss, Rosa Galan."

The commentary was a slightly robotic androgynous voice that said everything with a hint of sarcasm. As it finished its interpretation of Chip Little's words, someone walked onto the stage. I'd seen her before in occasional news coverage. It still took my breath away to see the woman who was trying to have me murdered.

She was in her early fifties and tall. Her eyebrows were thick and when they moved it felt decisive. She mounted the stage like she owned it, and the digital stadium it was in, and the digital space we all existed in, and the entire physical world that held the servers that rendered us. She mounted the stage like she ruled the world.

The crowd applauded, the throat singing had an excited treble to it.

"Celebrity. Celebrity. I know her. Make me rich, Rosa Galan. I resent your success. Celebrity. I'm the next you, just wait and see, I'll show you all. Celebrity. I wish I could be her. Celebrity. She's famous. I love you, Rosa. Celebrity. Investing in your company makes me feel like I matter. Celebrity. Celebrity."

"Welcome to the ninth EternityNet Shareholder's meeting," Rosa Galan said.

My heart rate elevated. Somebody programmed that feature into ghost avatars a few years. Apparently, the absence of a variable heart rate gave ghosts the unpleasant sensation that they were dead.

"It is a pleasure to see you all here today. Your financial support of this company has facilitated the rapid growth we've experienced over the last several years. None of it would be possible without our shareholders."

"Oh, it's you," the commentary kicked in. *"I can't believe I've done this nine times. I took this company public to raise money for rapid expansion, and every year I've got to waste my time appeasing you mixed bunch of assholes."*

I snorted.

"What?" Abi asked.

"Nothing. Why are we watching this again?"

"It's important. Just trust me."

Rosa Galan strode across the stage and smiled. I hated to admit it, but it was actually a pretty winning smile.

"Chip gave you a summary of where we are as a company. Now, let me tell you what's coming next. Let me tell you about the future."

"Let me give you gibbons your fruit so you can leave me alone for another year."

"We've rapidly expanded into a variety of new sectors of the economy, diversifying the company's revenue sources."

"I control more shit now. That's good for all of you because I know how to make money."

"We have in the last few years leapt ahead of our competitors. Meaning we can now offer cutting edge products to our customers, keeping profits high."

"We're the only company that offers certain products which means we've got a monopoly. That means we can charge a boatload of money for those products because the customer can't go anywhere else. Suckers."

"Some of our new technologies are redefining people's interaction with both the physical and digital world, creating an immersive experience for people of all ages. A trend I intend to maintain going into the future."

"Some of our products are borderline addictive, particularly to kids. We're going to be rolling in cash for years to come."

"So, let's talk specifics, and where else should we start but the bedrock of the EternityNet company, the Eternity Protocol and Digital People. A larger portion of EternityNet's investors are Digital People than any other company in the world. That is something I take great pride in."

"Let's talk about ghosts. You invest, so I'm gonna pander."

"We've made it our business to develop software that improves the lives of Digital People online. This has all been a part of my personal commitment to the Digital human community."

"All those apps that allow you to basically be gods on the Internet. We invented a lot of that. Be grateful and keep forking over your investment dollars, you little shits."

The audience applauded. The throat singers hit a deep base note that really resonated in my chest.

"Is the 'Clarity' commentary helping?" Abi asked.

"It's getting the point across," I said.

"We've created a variety of new tools that will augment your digital experience."

Rosa Galan went down a list of new software applications.

"This one lets you run around in a procedurally-generated galaxy. This one lets you pretend to play for your favorite sports team. This one makes it easier to harass your elected officials. This one ... look, I'm not going to say this one's for sex, but this one's for sex."

"That could be useful," Abi muttered.

I took a pass on asking how.

Rosa kept talking about a variety of new products. Our section of the audience was getting more and more riled up. I still couldn't understand why we had to sit through the whole speech, but Abi was rapt.

"Now, people ask how EternityNet has achieved such success. They want to know how we have consistently expanded and acquired, and how every one of our investments have shown dividends? Let me tell you."

"You want to know what's in the secret sauce?"

"We have been working on and testing this program for years, and we're starting to incorporate it into every aspect of our business."

"Feel the tension. That's right, eat it up right out of the palm of my hand."

"I can finally announce that EternityNet. has developed a cutting-edge new form of AI, that far outstrips other competitive corporate AIs."

"We do it with a big fucking computer. It's bigger than everybody else's. We measured."

"Making business decisions with the assistance of AI is nothing new, but I think EternityNet's track record over the last two years demonstrates we're on the next level."

"Nah nah nana nah, our computer is better than yours."

"Bullshit," Abi said.

"What?"

"This new development in AI structure is nothing short of revolutionary," Rosa said.

"It's a big deal muthafuckas."

"Revolutionary!" somebody shouted.

"Oh, fuck, I forgot," Abi said.

"What?"

"Don't worry, there's going to be a small attempt at a revolution."

"Huzzah!" the crowd roared.

The people who had looked before like they were prepping for some kind of battle had all leapt to their feet. They brandished weapons from a dozen different eras including a few fictional ones. Rosa Galan had pivoted to talking about the future of some of EternityNet's newly acquired companies. She didn't seem to notice the rising tide of hooligans.

"Let's show 'em revolution," a skinny woman with a tricorn hat shouted.

"Huzzah!" the crowd shouted again.

"What the fuck is happening?" I asked.

"Oh ... it's just ... they're performance artists."

Abi looked fatigued by the thought.

"Charge!"

The crowd roared and headed down the stairs of the stadium toward the stage. The rest of the audience didn't react. Seating for our area of the stadium prevented the rest of the spectators from hearing or seeing the rabble.

"They're not going to be able to do anything," I said. "It's digital space."

"That's kind of the point," Abi said. "They go to a lot of these shareholders meetings and wait for a speaker to use the world, 'revolutionary.' Then they attack."

"To what end?"

The armed horde had almost reached the foot of the stage. As the first of them arrived, the edge of the stage rose up preventing them from scaling it.

"I guess their point is the concept of revolution has been co-opted to refer to incremental changes in technology usually to the benefit of the company that controls the patents. Meanwhile the people's ability to meaningfully change the system based on humanist ideals is being restricted as the system around us becomes more complex and entrenched."

I looked at Abi.

"What?" she said.

"Dork," I said. "Pure, dork."

"You asked, asshole."

The armed revolutionaries seemed to be sinking into the floor at the foot of the stage. They flailed and kicked like they were caught in quicksand. The floor rose up above them in a quivering pudding-like mass and started to sweep them backward. Hoots and laughter rose up from the people being absorbed into the blob. They twisted and turned and were unceremoniously dumped back into our section.

"Next year we bring cannons," the woman in the tricorn hat shouted.

"You said that last year."

"And the year before."

"Well, this time I mean it."

While the revolution was being foiled, Rosa Galan had been wrapping up her presentation.

"Here's to another great year for this company. Thank you so much for your time, attention, and support. Together we're building the future."

"You just do your best to leave me alone for another year. I'll keep making shit the basic mechanics of which you can't even wrap your heads around. Bye, Felicia."

The audience applauded as Rosa Galan walked off the stage.

"Lying asshole," Abi said.

"Who?"

"Galan," Abi said. "All that bullshit about a new AI."

"That was a lie?"

"Fuck yeah, it was."

"Okay, Abi. I think it's time you tell me what made you go on the run. What did George Washington tell you?"

Her face screwed up in consternation.

"I don't want to put you in any more danger, Romeo. Knowing this—"

"Abi, there is literally an assassin trying to kill me. How much worse can things get?"

She nodded.

"Okay."

She rotated her neck like she was about to do some physical feat and took a deep breath.

"So, for the last couple weeks, George Washington was acting weird."

"Dead president, back to life. I'm not surprised."

"Romeo."

"Oh, come on, you renamed him George Washington. I get one. I got one dead-president joke with Abigail. I should get one dead-president joke with you. I'm treating you like different people remember."

"Yeah, fine. That's your one."

"Fine."

"He was acting jumpy and guilty. He'd deny it when I asked him about it."

"He was lying?"

"Yeah."

"But I thought George Washington could not tell a lie."

"Romeo."

"Sorry, sorry, squirrely software engineer. Got it."

"I suspected it had something to do with the secrets he was telling me during our sessions, but I couldn't remember them."

"How'd you swing that by the way."

"We found black-market software that allows for the deletion of a ghost's recent memory. He'd say whatever he wanted to say, then use a command word, and it would delete the last five minutes of my memory."

"That's a little fucked up."

"You gotta do what you gotta do in the automation economy."

"So, you figured out a way to find out what George Washington was telling you?"

"I did. He would always check that the software to delete my memory was working. Paranoid. So, I had someone write a small program that would take everything he said and convert it to a text document and dump it into an external storage device. Text files are so little memory it took an instant to export the whole file. He never noticed the process on my logs because it was miniscule."

"You let him see your process logs?"

"It was part of the deal."

"Kinky. So, what did the text documents say?"

"It's big. Really fucked up. If we can prove it, it will be enough to bring EternityNet and Rosa Galan down in one blow. It's no wonder she's willing to kill to keep it secret."

Abi fell silent and her eyes went distant. My eagerness got the better of me.

"What is it?" I demanded.

"EternityNet," she started. "Rosa Galan, really. She's been using George Washington and Maddoc Technologies to do something so fucked up. I don't know how they could live with them—"

My eye caught something moving behind Abi's avatar.

"Oh shit," I interrupted.

"What?"

She spun around. While we had been talking, most of the normal audience had blipped out of existence. Our section was still full of people, most of whom were drinking. A group of the mishmash of random digitality had jumped out at me. Long blond hair, floppy pink tongues, they were hopping on their hind legs. It was a pack of Golden Retrievers.

20

SHUFFLE

March 3rd, 2064 6:46 p.m. PST

"We've got to run," I said.

"Why?"

"You see those Golden Retrievers?"

"No."

"Right, that's just my settings. Can you see the small group of default avatars moving through the crowd over there?"

"Uh yes."

"I set them to look like Golden Retrievers when they caught us at Consumerama. They work for Rosa Galan. I think the software from this venue site took my setting and imported them. I'm pretty sure those are the same dogs."

As if timed to confirm my suspicions, half a dozen dogs caught sight of me and made fixed eye contact. Their jaws hung open, and they panted happily at the sight of me.

"I should have stuck with raptors."

"What?"

"Never mind. We need to go."

"What can they do to us."

"I'll happily explain, on the move."

The Golden Retrievers were moving forward in a semi-circle. They were adorable predators going in for the kill.

"Send me a link request," I said.

A second later a notification popped up in my vision. 'Abi wants to surf the net with you.' I hit accept and, too panicked to think of anything else, I hit 'back' on my VR web browser commands. Abi and I appeared in Sanav's sitting room.

"Oh shit, I forgot," I said. "Sanav?"

Sanav appeared from a side door covered in black engine grease. He was holding an old-style socket wrench, like from when people repaired stuff by hand.

"What's with the grease?" I asked.

"I'm fixing a boat engine."

"Why? It's digital space."

"I enjoy it. Hi, Abi."

"Hi, Sanav."

I opened my mouth, closed it, opened it again. My brain was thoroughly overloaded.

"Weird hobbies, not important," I said. "Australian Golden Retrievers."

"Oh shit," Sanav said.

He chucked the wrench aside. The moment it hit the ground both it and the grease stains vanished.

"Did you come straight here?" he asked.

"Yeah," Abi said. "Sorry."

"Nothing to be sorry to me for. DOA Republic will protect me. You guys, on the other hand, can be tracked to your real-world locations from here. Both of you should disconnect."

"We can't. She's got to tell me what's going on."

"We can try again later," Abi said.

"No, no. I'm not waiting any longer. I'm being hunted by a four-handed assassin, and a pack of dingoes. I want to know what this is about."

"I know what to do," Sanav said. "Link with me."

Another notification popped up in my screen. I accepted.

"Jump back to the shareholder's meeting."

"Are you sure?" I asked.

"Yes. They're probably already trying to track your real-world position."

I hit forward on my web browser. The unruly crowd of shareholders and riff raff were all around us.

"Hit shuffle," Sanav said.

"You can do that?"

"Yes."

I opened up options, and ... I saw it immediately. I hit shuffle. The world blinked. The three of us appeared in the middle of a turbulent crowd of dancers. A baby seal slid by my feet, and a snow-white mountain goat with a drinks tray resting on its horns wiggled through the crowd.

"Where are we?" Abi asked.

A stage hugged the wall to our left. Standing on it were four polar bears playing Nunkac Metal. It's a combination of new-age punk and acoustic heavy metal. It was a weird musical genre that never took off. That didn't seem to stop the audience from losing it.

"Ice in my fur and ice on my face," the lead polar bear sang. "Vengeance we'll seek on the whole human race."

The audience around us were dressed in a style that could only be described as 'sexy, gothic, 19th century arctic explorer.' They thrashed around to the acoustic power chords and raw, roaring vocals.

"Why are we safe here?" Abi asked.

"Each time we change concerts we change servers. This site uses a kind of encrypted interface so they can crowd-source server space."

"I don't know what that means," I said.

"Just trust me, if we jump every minute or so, it'll be really hard for them to track us. They'll have to search all the servers on the network each time and that will take ... a minute ... probably."

"One minute? That's it?"

"You're running from a tech billionaire in digital space. What do you want me to tell you?"

"Alright, every minute. Fine. Abi, talk fast. What's going on?"

"Oh, does she know what this is all about?" Sanav asked.

"Yeah."

"Okay, where was I?"

"Uh, you got text file records of what George Washington said during your memory erasures and it's really fucked up."

"Oh right, okay, um ... so, a few years back Rosa Galan had been really struggling for a while to grow EternityNet. A lot of her other ventures weren't panning out. The problem was that the EternityNet scanner's salability was limited. People perceived it as only having one value, scanning people to make a digital copy of their consciousness. It's a classic problem in business. Perceived value. If a product is known for only having one use, nobody thinks of it for other uses. So why would they spend money for something that does something they don't need."

"No business theory, Abi."

"Sorry. Sorry. Keeping it simple, people get weirded out going into an EternityNet scanner for just a simple brain scan. It's like how it would feel weird to drive an armored vehicle down a suburban street."

"Or how it would feel weird to disassemble yourself and mail yourself downtown instead of taking mass transit."

"Uh, what?"

"Never mind."

"We've got to jump," Sanav said.

"Now?"

"Yeah."

The world blinked. Gone were the vengeful polar bears. An audience was politely clapping as three people walked out on stage and took seats. One of them smiled and in a velvety voice greeted the audience.

"Welcome to the Podcast Podcast. The podcast where we talk about all the podcasts. We're so excited to be with you all."

The audience cheered.

"Oh, wow," Sanav said. "I didn't even know that was something I wanted to listen to, but I am one hundred percent downloading this when I get home."

The podcasters started exchanging witty banter in sonorous voices.

"Keep talking," I said to Abi.

"Right," Abi said. "So, a few years ago, EternityNet acquires Maddoc Technologies. Through that company they basically create a clone of their scanners, but they slap a different name on it and make it look different. Big sales. It's one of the best scanners on the market."

"Okay," Sanav said.

"Two years ago. George Washington is struggling at Maddoc Technologies. He's ambitious, but his job is on the chopping block. Apparently, he went to school with Rosa Galan, so he's able to get a meeting. He goes to her with an idea."

"What idea?" Sanav asked.

The audience laughter distracted us.

"So, what have you been listening to this week, Janet."

"Thanks for asking, Doug. This week I've been listening to the Camping Corner. A podcast where each week the host goes camping with a different random family."

"Consensually?"

The audience laughed.

"Yes, of course. It would be really weird if the host just showed up uninvited."

"That would be weird, Janet."

The audience laughed again, the hosts joined in.

"If someone makes a podcast about all the podcasts that talk about podcasts, I'm pretty sure the Internet is going to implode," Abi said.

"We should jump," Sanav said.

"Already?" I said.

"We've got to keep moving."

I threw my head back in frustration.

"Aaaah," I shouted. "I just want to know why I'm running for my life. Can the whole world just stop and shut up for a minute? This is important."

"We have to jump, Romeo."

"How is it that the most effective information distribution system in human history can make it harder to actually learn things?"

"Don't blame the Internet for your lack of attention span," Sanav said.

"My lack of attention span? My lack of attention span?"

"Romeo, we have to go."

"Okay fine, we'll jump. but whatever the next place is, we're not getting distracted. You will tell me why I'm running for my life."

"Deal."

The world blinked. Eight frogs were sitting around a stage. Standing on the platform was a ninth frog screaming at the top of his lungs.

"And the liberals are perpetrating white genocide!"

"Oh, for fuck's sake," I said.

"So, you want to stick around?" Sanav asked.

"No."

"You said, whatever the next place is," Abi said.

"I know what I said. Can we just jump?"

"You sure?"

"I'm sure."

"You seemed very insistent."

"I take it back. I take it back. Let's just jump."

The world blinked. We were surrounded by bleachers. They hung in the air above a choppy, blue sea. In the near distance, five streamlined sailboats were cutting through the water, their sails bulging. The stands wobbled. I could tell that we were watching a live feed captured by a drone somewhere in the real world. Sanav gasped.

"I forgot this was happening today," he said.

"What is it?" Abi asked.

"It's a preliminary regatta for the America's Cup next year. They're racing AC60 class boats."

"So, all that means a boat race?" I asked.

"A hell of a boat race."

Sanav rose up on his toes, his head tracking an angular vessel as it whizzed past.

"Abi," I said. "Talk fast."

"Where was I?"

"George Washington had an idea."

"Right. Their new Maddoc Technolgies-branded brain scanners were being used in the most expensive medical clinics in the world. The kind of clinics that serve the most powerful people in the world. These days brain scans are done all the time as a preventative measure. The rich and powerful can be monitored to prevent brain aneurism or catch tumors early. None of them knew the scanner they were using was capable of creating a ghost. So, George Washington suggested that he and Rosa Galan copy them."

"Wait, what?" Sanav asked.

The revelation had pulled him back from his naval distraction.

"Pause," he said.

The world froze around us. A track ball appeared at the bottom of my vision marking how far behind the live feed we were falling.

"Wait a second," I said. "There's been a pause feature this entire time?"

"Who?" Sanav asked, ignoring me.

"Politicians, rival CEOs, government regulators, even just experts in their respective fields: college professors, engineers, scientists. They copy them, have the scanner upload the ghost, load the ghosts onto an isolated server farm they run, and interrogate them for information."

"Interrogate them?"

"Yeah," Abi said. "For bios, torture doesn't work because people will say anything to make the pain stop, but what happens when you have access to someone's simulated neural network and can tell when they're telling the truth or lying."

"Torture," I said.

"Fuck," Sanav said.

"For the last two years Rosa Galan has seemed like she couldn't make a wrong business decision. Her company's research and development always seemed to be ahead of the curve. She always seemed to know which way government policy was going to go. That's why I scoffed when she claimed it was a new kind of AI."

I let out a long breath. I was not ready to deal with this shit. This was the kind of stuff you leave to responsible people to figure out, and not even normal responsible people. I'm talking first-string responsible people, the kind of people that run emergency rooms, fight fires, and do their taxes in January.

"So just to be clear," I said. "Somewhere in the world, there's a server full of ghosts, and their entire existence is being tortured for information or being forced to do research for EternityNet nonstop."

"Yeah."

"This is bigger than anything I've ever heard of," Sanav said. "I've helped a lot of illegal ghosts get out from under exploitative bios. This is a whole other level."

"Yeah."

"Well, hello there."

We all froze. I was the only one that glanced back. A semicircle of standing Golden Retrievers had gathered behind us.

"Shit."

I looked forward.

"They found us?" Abi said.

"Yeah."

"I am so sorry," Sanav said. "I got distracted with the sailboats and the digital atrocities. I stopped keeping track of the time."

"It's alright," Abi said. "We all forgot."

We turned in unison. The leader of the pack hopped forward. His tongue lolled as one of his fluffy, blonde eyebrows raised.

"You'd be Abi?"

"Yeah."

"Pleasure."

"Can't say I feel the same."

"That makes sense."

"I just tried to hit shuffle," I said.

"Yeah he's probably frozen those controls again," Sanav said.

"I have."

"I see you're connected via a VPN," the Goldie said.

"Yep," Abi said.

"Masking your location, very clever. Your friend here, once again, is not," he looked at me. "A hotel in downtown Seattle."

Abi and Sanav looked at me.

"Just for future reference," I said. "What's a VPN?"

They both rolled their eyes.

"Oh, excuse me," I said. "Like I'm just supposed to know how to commit Internet crimes. Apparently, everybody else got the memo."

"I need to know where you are in the real world," the pack leader said.

"Oh, well, good luck with that," Abi said.

"Do you guys have any idea who you're working for?" I said. "Rosa Galan. And she's got you mixed up in some messed-up shit. She's running a ghost gulag. A ghost Gitmo. A ghost Gehenna."

"What's Gehenna?" Sanav asked.

"I don't know," I said. "A friend of mine from high school said it once. It sounded like it was bad."

"It's a cursed valley in the mythology of Judaism," one of the other Golden Retrievers said. He spoke in a Chinese accent.

Everybody looked at him.

"What?" he said. "I find religious mythology interesting."

"Wait," I said. "You guys aren't all Australian?"

"No," the pack leader said.

"Oh man, I've been calling you Australian Golden Retrievers all day."

"Are you telling me we all still look like dogs to you?"

"Yeah."

"For fuck's sake," the pack leader shouted.

A jolt of agony ran down my body.

"Aaah, fuck you," I shouted.

"I've talked to you for less than a minute, and you're already on my last nerve."

"Well, feel free to fuck off anytime," Abi said.

Another jolt of pain ran up my body.

"Hey," I said. "I didn't say anything that time. That was her."

"Shut up," the pack leader said.

Everybody stopped talking. The pack leader rolled his head in frustration. His floppy pink tongue lolled out the side of his mouth. He straightened up.

"What did you mean we're working for Rosa Galan? And what did you mean by 'ghost gulag?'"

"Well—" I started.

"Anyone besides him speak. And keep it simple."

"Rosa Galan hired you to find me because I know she has a bell-jarred server where she keeps illegally copied ghosts and tortures them for information and R&D work," Abi said.

The Golden Retrievers all looked at each other. It occurred to me that they were all ghosts. The pack leader's eyes narrowed. It was adorable.

"I feel like you're not lying to me."

"We're not."

"Fuck," he whispered.

The world blinked. I looked around. We were standing in the middle of a manicured field. The pack of retrievers was gone. All that remained was the pack leader. He seemed as confused as I was as his furry face darted back and forth. In the near distance a gaggle of extremely thin people were chasing a Frisbee as it flew through the air.

"What happened?" Abi asked.

"I managed to turn the tables on this guy," Sanav said. "I spent the afternoon learning how to use some new software after our encounter earlier."

The pack leader cast about.

"That's right. Now whose controls are frozen."

"Fuck."

"Yeah. Now first off."

"Aah."

"See. That's how that feels. Not fun is it?"

"Look I'm—"

"No, you look."

"Ouch."

"Yeah, ouch indeed," Sanav said.

"Look, I'm sorry."

"Oh, you're sorry."

"I am. The impression I was given for this job was that Abi ran off with somebody's money. I didn't know who I was working for. I definitely didn't know about ..."

"Ghost gulag," I said.

His little Golden Retriever face looked so crestfallen. It was hard not to sympathize with him.

"Yeah."

The adorable, bounty hunter shook his head. He looked real guilty, like 'dug into the trash and spread it all over the kitchen floor' guilty.

"Fuck, this isn't what I planned for my life to be."

"What life did you want?" I asked.

"I wasn't inviting a sharing session. I was just trying to make it clear ... look, I'm not a bad guy."

"Well then tell us what kind of life you wanted."

"We don't need to know what life he wanted," Abi said.

"I'd like to know."

Abi and Sanav raised their eyebrows in unison.

"Hey, I got zapped way more than everybody else. I want to know."

Sanav shrugged.

"Tell him what life you wanted."

"Really?" the pack leader said.

"Yep, I guess we're doing this."

The dog sighed.

"Really?"

"Talk," Sanav demanded.

"I wanted to be a dancer."

My heart filled.

"You did?" I said.

"My dad said, 'no.' No future in dancing. He said security was the only sure career path. So, I did it. End up dying. Didn't even die on the job. Apparently, some yob shot me at a firing range by accident. Now I'm in digital space, but you can't make a living dancing here because anyone can just download a piece of software and be bloody Gene Kelly. And the twisted irony of it is, out in the real world, dancing is one of the few professions people can still make a go of. Robots look all stiff and weird. Thanks, Dad, you jackass."

"I'm actually kind of feeling bad for you."

"He did torture you," Abi said.

"Sorry about that," the Golden Retriever said. "Online security is a competitive industry. Not much people need ghosts to do that software can't. You gotta let your moral scruples lapse if you want to stay hi-res."

"I mean he was trying to stay in hi-res," I said.

Abi grunted.

A Frisbee whizzed past us. Our captive's puppy-dog eyes tracked it as it whizzed past. I snorted. He caught the sound. It took a moment before he remembered what he looked like to me.

"Don't look at me like that."

"Like what?" I feigned innocence.

"Like I'm a dog about to chase a Frisbee."

"I wasn't."

The crowd of scrawny people sprinted past us after the wayward flying disk.

"Look," the Oz dog said. "If what you're saying is true about Rosa Galan, she's going to keep coming for you. You, what's your name again?"

"Romeo."

"You need to move now. I passed your location on to her when I got it. Learn how to hide your real-world location, mate."

"Shit."

"I tell you what, " he said. "I'll keep pretending to look for you. She'll fire me eventually, but it might buy you some time before you've got a different firm tracking you."

"How do we know we can trust you?" Abi asked.

"You don't. That's why you should run. Right to whoever can help you. Feds, I guess. My firm is expensive, but for Rosa Galan, we're a drop in the bucket. And if you're right about the secret she's protecting, she will kill to keep that hidden."

We looked around at each other.

"Get the fuck out of here," the Aussie doggie said.

He just looked so sad and lonely with his furry little face.

"Thanks," I said.

"Don't mention it. I mean seriously, don't mention it."

The world blinked. We were standing in Sanav's lounge.

"What do we do?" I asked.

"You've got to move," Sanav said.

"Where?"

Abi sighed.

"I never thought I'd say this," she said. "But Abigail is right."

"What?"

"You've got to go to the FBI."

"And tell them what?"

"Tell them ... everything, I guess."

"They'll never believe me."

"They probably won't believe him," Sanav said.

"But they might keep you safe. That's the best we can hope for right now. I'll try to ... You just have to go now, Romeo."

"I ..."

"Go. Now."

21

CUT TO THE CHASE

The real world crystallized around me. As did the realization that, from now on, my best friend was probably going to tell me the same thing twice a lot, or was it my best friends, my two best friend, my best friends singular ... that didn't seem right. I shook it off as a tomorrow problem.

Nobody seemed to have noticed my reprieve in the hotel hallway corner. Having a robot body really lends something akin to invisibility. I set off. The retro-futuristic whirr of the elevator answered as I pressed the call button. As I waited, I typed the FBI field-office address into my map app. A blue line appeared in my AR display leading me onto the elevator and out into the lobby. Halfway through the hotel's main entrance, I slammed into someone coming around the corner.

I looked up and squeaked. Four Hands was standing in front of me in her schoolteacher's wardrobe. She was smiling.

"Hello, Mr. Smith."

If I'd had a bladder, it wouldn't have been empty, but it would have been a little less full. I looked around. The sidewalk was bustling with people. I wondered how likely they were to stop Four Hands if she grabbed me.

"If you touch me, I'll scream," I said. "And these speakers go loud."

"You think anyone would stop me if you did?"

"No, but they might call the police, and the police would see your face on that security camera. "

A black dome was installed above the hotel's front doorway. Four Hands' eyebrow twitched up and down. She shrugged.

"Lucky you."

I moved around Four Hands. She didn't stop me, but her constant, kind smile did grind up any sense of courage I had into tiny pebbles of cowardice. Parked along the sidewalk in front of the hotel were a line of rideshare cars waiting for a customer. The name 'Autoryde' was stenciled across each of their doors in a bright-blue, trademarked font. I looked at Four Hands again.

"Huzzah."

I grabbed one of the car doors. It was actually kind of heavy. I got a false start on the first pull, it clunked shut, I yanked again and got it open. I spun my screen around. Four Hands was just watching me on the sidewalk. She hadn't moved. I climbed into the car. She just kept watching me. I shut the door. She waved. Waved. Like my parents had just picked me up from school and she was saying goodbye.

"FBI field office," I said to the car's AI.

"Certainly. Calculating," there was a pause. "Estimated arrival time: six minutes."

The car pulled away from the curb. Four Hands finally moved. She stepped to the car that had been waiting behind mine and climbed inside.

"Oh crap," I said.

Her car pulled away from the curb and drove up right behind mine.

"Oh no."

My car's AI took a left, so did hers. We stopped at a red light. Her car pulled into the lane right beside mine. There she was in the back seat, smiling at me. She waved ... again.

"Is there any way you can go faster," I said to the car's AI.

"I'm afraid not. Unless this is a medical emergency, I cannot exceed the speed limit. If it is a medical emergency, I can exceed the speed limit to the nearest emergency room. Is this a medical emergency?"

I looked over at Four Hand's eerie smile.

"You keep driving so slow it might become one."

"I'm sorry, I don't understand."

"No, of course you don't."

The light turned green and we took off ... at the exact same, reasonable speed. The entire time she was just smiling at me. I wish her smile had been sinister. It wasn't. It was pleasant. What kind of monster smiles pleasantly at people? My car shifted lanes and her car fell back. The AI of both vehicles allowed them to be only inches apart. I could see her silhouette in the back seat. Automated cars have really taken the excitement out of car chases and replaced it with creeping horror.

In my mind I urged the car to go faster. Ahead I saw a father crossing the street with a stroller. I gasped, taking back my inner monologue. Somewhere in my panic-addled mind, I really believed we were going to careen into the family. The car rolled to an easy stop as the father and baby crossed the street. I felt a little silly. Four Hands pulled up behind me and we waited. The father finished crossing and we started off again. See what I mean, car chases have really lost their flare.

"Arriving at your destination in 60 seconds."

I looked back. Four Hands was still there. The short trip from my car to the FBI's front door suddenly seemed really dangerous. My car pulled to a stop. Four Hands pulled up behind me. I watched. She didn't get out. I opened my car door. Nothing happened. Her vehicle sat still. I stepped out onto the sidewalk. Never in my life have I empathized with a prey animal more. I waited, terrified. Nothing. I darted for the building's front door. I reached it and heaved it open. I looked back. Four Hands was still in her car. She smiled at me ... and waved.

"What the ... what the ... what is wrong with you?" I said.

Her car pulled away from the curb and disappeared around the corner. You know how sometimes you'll meet a person, and they're interesting, and you just want to know how their mind works. I felt the exact opposite of that feeling.

I spun and rolled into the FBI's lobby. What is it about law-enforcement buildings that makes you feel guilty the moment you walk inside? Maybe it has something to do with the dull colors they always paint the walls. It evokes a principal's office. This lobby was adorned with sickly green and furnished with brown faux-leather waiting chairs. A set of glass sliding doors blocked a set of security doors beyond. I rolled up to an automated receptionist displayed on a screen behind the front desk.

"How can the FBI help you today?"

"I need to speak to agents Vanderwall and Berrys," I said.

"Do you have an appointment?"

"No."

"Please record a short message to be forwarded to the agents. Start in 3, 2, 1."

An image of my face projected on my robot's cracked screen appeared. The clock was counting down from ten.

"Oh, uh, I'm Romeo Smith. This is about some ... stuff. Shit, it's hard to explain." The clock was running out. "I'm the ghost you talked to this—"

The screen flashed.

"—morning."

"Your message has been forwarded. Please take a seat and wait for a reply."

I looked at the row of brown chairs. They looked like the kind of chairs you sent someone to sit on when you secretly hoped they would get bored and leave before you had to talk to them.

"It's important."

"Please take a seat."

"Okay."

I don't need to sit, my body being robotic and all. So, I just stood next to a faux potted plant and waited. And waited. There was a bang of a door opening behind the security entrance. The impressive sliding doors opened and two different agents exited. They were wearing the same trench coat and suit combo as Vanderwall and Berrys.

"Does this trench coat make me look like a cog in the machine?"

"I hope not."

"Why?"

"I'm wearing the same one."

They swished out the door. I watched them depart then turned back toward the inner security door. A few minutes passed. Some straggler minutes ran to catch up with them.

The security door slid open, and a different set of identically-clad agents exited.

"You ever think we lose our sense of spontaneity working here?"

"What are you talking about? On that stakeout last week."

"What do you mean?"

"The coffee, I brought hazelnut creamer instead of the plain stuff."

"Oh that's right. Never mind, I guess."

Their trench coats snapped as they strode out of the building.

I considered rolling over to bother the receptionist AI. Before I could, the security door slid open. I perked up. Another pair of FBI agents exited.

"Damn it," I muttered.

The pair of agents strode across the lobby.

"You ever wish we could wear hoodies instead of suits?"

"Totally. The FBI is so regressive in terms of fashion."

"Maybe some color too?"

"Whoa, calm down. I don't want to look ridiculous."

A gust of wind blew their trench coats back as the outer door opened. They walked off in unison. I heard the inner security door open. I didn't even look up.

"Mr. Smith?" someone shouted.

"Of course," I muttered. I turned to look. "Yes."

Vanderwall and Berrys were standing in the threshold of the open security door.

"You came to talk to us?"

"Yes."

"Follow us in, Mr. Smith."

The two agents stood in the door as I rolled forward.

"What happened to your screen, Mr. Smith?" the male agent shouted.

"It's a long story," I said.

"I look forward to hearing all about it," the female agent shouted.

"You know you don't have to shout," I said. "I can hear you just fine."

"It's not a problem."

"We don't mind."

"N-, I mean ... fuck it, whatever."

Vanderwall and Berrys took positions in front and behind me as we headed inside. We rode an elevator up five floors and came out into an open office space. Glass screens divided beige desks. A man was standing at his desk wearing a pair of VR goggles. He leaned over to peer seemingly at nothing.

"So that's where the killer inserted the Rubik's Cube?" the begoggled agent said.

I looked back at him, but there was no time to ask questions. Vanderwall and Berrys set an unrelenting pace. They guided me into a conference room and shut the door behind us.

"Alright, Mr. Smith."

"What do you have to tell us?"

I laid it all out. I didn't withhold anything. Except for the fact that Abi existed. I held that back. I also didn't mention we'd been in contact. I didn't tell them about Sanav. I didn't think Abigail's business warranted mentioning. I withheld that Izy knew anything. I also left out the whole part where I broke into Maddoc Technologies' headquarters. Apart from those miniscule omissions, I told them everything. I'm very forthright.

"So, you claim: Rosa Galan ..." the male agent shouted.

"The Rosa Galan," the female agent shouted.

"The multibillionaire Rosa Galan."

"Is illegally creating ghosts?"

"On an industrial scale?"

"Ghosts of the powerful?"

"So she can confine them to a server?"

"And extract usable intelligence?"

"Yeah," I said.

"You claim: she killed her software engineer."

"Yes, George Washington or George Harrison or whatever his real name was," I said.

"And she sent an assassin to try to kill you?"

"Yep."

They looked at each other.

"Okay," the male agent said in a normal speaking voice.

"Okay," the female agent said in a normal speaking voice.

"You don't believe me?" I said.

"Maybe," he shouted.

"Maybe not," she shouted.

"But you're going to investigate?"

"No."

"Absolutely not."

I was aghast.

"Why not?"

They looked at each other and sighed.

"You know what we really want?"

"What every FBI agent really wants."

"No," I said.

"Advancement."

"Long-term career upward mobility."

"I want to be Director of the FBI someday. At least make it to deputy."

"I'm thinking I'll switch to prosecution at some point. Dust off the old law degree."

"You could be Attorney General in 25 years."

"Twenty, if I had some exciting cases in my file."

"Exciting cases just don't grow on trees."

"No, they don't."

"This, Abigail Page illegally copying herself, isn't an exciting case."

"No, it's not."

"Humdrum.

"Dull even."

"Illegal copying of a single living person isn't where upward mobility comes from."

"The way things are going it will be legal in five years."

"Hell, it's already legal in the Netherlands."

"Well, everything is legal in the Netherlands."

"I guess what we're saying is if we had another crime."

"A bigger crime."

"A juicier crime."

"Headlines."

"Scandal."

"We might be convinced to overlook your friend's misdeed."

"Might be, hell I'm halfway convinced now."

"I'm only 35 percent."

"Well you've always been the hardnosed partner."

"What? I'm personable."

"Point is, we're receptive to your suggestion that there might be a bigger crime here."

"An unprecedented crime."

"With a high-profile perpetrator."

"What we're not receptive to is the idea that we should go charging into a Fortune 500 company's corporate head-quarters on nothing but your word."

"Not receptive at all."

"Not even a little."

"But, it's all true," I said.

"You know what this building runs on."

I paused to think.

"Justice?" I hazarded.

They snorted in unison.

"Evidence."

"Evidence and ego."

"Sure, well, I assumed ego went without saying," she said in a normal speaking voice.

"You would," he said.

"What's that supposed to mean?"

"Don't worry about it."

They turned back to me.

"Pissing off someone as powerful as Rosa Galan," she shouted.

"Without Evidence," he shouted.

"That's how you get transferred to Alaska."

"You have a story."

"An interesting story."

"But you have no evidence."

"Not even somewhere we could start an investigation."

"So, we're going to find your friend Abigail."

"We're going to prove she copied herself."

"Arrest her."

"Then we're going to move on to the next case."

"And unless you've got something more than a story."

"We're not going to investigate Rosa Galan."

"You know, I said you guys weren't going to help," I said. "Everybody else told me I should come here, but I knew this would be useless."

"Who's everybody else?"

"Uh, nobody," I said. "Uh, I made the decision to come here entirely on my own."

"Okay, Mr. Smith."

"But you should know."

"If we can prove you've been lying to us."

"We'll arrest you too."

"Because a case."

"Even a boring."

"Humdrum."

"Dull case."

"It's still a case."

The female agent's pocket beeped and she pulled out her phone.

"Yes."

She listened for long moment.

"I see," pause. "Attorney with her?" pause. "Send someone to escort them up."

She hung up the phone.

"What was it?" the male agent asked.

"Abigail Page just surrendered downstairs."

My stomach twisted. I'd known it was coming, but somehow it still hurt to hear it. They both looked at me.

"Do you know anything about that?"

"Nope," I said.

Two minutes later Abigail strode out of the elevator wearing a black blazer accented by slashes of silver. It had a whole goth-futurism vibe that was pretty cool. Next to her was a tall black man wearing a very expensive-looking business hoodie. They looked like visitors from the future surrounded by all the FBI agent's in their suits.

"That's Darius Williams," the male agent said.

Vanderwall and Berrys looked at each other wide-eyed, then turned to me.

"How does your friend know Darius Williams?" she shouted.

"Uh, I don't know who that is, so ..."

"Darius Williams is the best criminal defense attorney in Seattle."

"In the state more like."

"How does your friend have the money ..."

"To hire Darius Williams?"

"I don't know what to tell you," I said.

The two agents looked at each other again.

"Wait here," he shouted at me.

"Do I have to?" I said.

"No," she shouted.

"But if you don't, we'll be irritated."

"And if we find evidence you've committed a crime we'll arrest you."

"But you said you were going to do that anyway," I said.

"We'll look for the evidence extra-hard."

They stepped out of the conference room leaving the door ajar.

"Agents," Darius Williams said.

He had a deep baritone voice that was immediately familiar to me. I thought back to Abigail's club and her wearing a judge's robe.

"Oh," I said to myself.

Abigail saw me through the open door. She nodded almost imperceptibly. I waved back. Vanderwall and Berrys led them to another conference room a couple of doors down. They closed the door behind them. I was alone. Well, there were a few FBI agents working late and a bunch of security cameras, but other than that, I had the run of the place.

I sighed. Abigail might be going to prison. The thought was unpleasant, belligerent even. It was like a rude party guest knocking things over and talking really loud inside my head. I did a lap of the conference room trying to think about something else. Abigail might be going to prison. There it was again, an asshole of a thought. It wouldn't take the hint that I didn't want to hang out with it. Damn. Abigail might be going to prison. Oh, fuck that thought.

I needed to talk to somebody. Rosa Galan had a bunch of ghosts trapped and tortured on a server, Izy was confined to her office for fear of kidnapping, and Abigail might be going to prison. (What? Again! I was well aware of Abigail's status. When a really malicious thought starts bopping about your head, it really doesn't know when to stop.)

I checked the WiFi signals in the building. The city's public WiFi was absent from the list. The FBI probably jammed external signals like major companies did. There was however, lower on the list, an 'FBI Guest' WiFi network. I connected and sent out several messages. Sanav answered first. I shut down my robot's interface and connected to DOA. A half-heartbeat of rendering later, I was standing in Sanav's sitting room. The bright cushions and underwater vista were contoured by dark shadows. It was nighttime in digital space.

"What's up?" Sanav asked.

He was standing behind his bar pouring a glass of wine. I rolled over and took the proffered drink.

"Abigail might be going to prison."

Somewhere in my head the thought threw a little victory party that I was acknowledging it. It really was just the most pompous, arrogant jackass any thought could aspire to be.

"Shit, sorry," Sanav said, as he sipped his own glass.

"The FBI don't want to investigate Rosa Galan."

"What?"

"Apparently, one random ghost who wandered in off the street isn't enough evidence to investigate one of the most powerful people on the planet."

"That's so messed up."

A message ping appeared in my vision.

"Do you mind if I invite Izy here?" I asked Sanav.

"Nope, I already told Abi to swing by."

I sent an invite off to Izy. She popped into existence behind a divan a few moments later. I introduced Izy and Sanav.

"What is happening?" she asked, in her unshakeable monotone.

"Abigail might be going to prison," Sanav said.

Damn, the noxious little fucker was infecting others.

"Fuck," Izy said.

She slid into a stool next to me and accepted a glass of red wine from Sanav.

"And the FBI don't want to investigate Rosa Galan," I said.

"No evidence?" Izy said.

"Yep."

"What's happening?" said Abi's voice.

I spun. Abi had arrived next to a bean-bag chair that looked like a sea anemone.

"Abigail is probably going to prison," Izy said.

She sat down in her real-world office chair. In digital space a chair appeared as she slumped into it.

Oh crap, 'might be' to 'probably' ... it was mutating.

"And the FBI aren't going to investigate Rosa Galan," Sanav said.

"I was afraid of that," Abi said.

She joined us at the bar and accepted a drink. There was a collective sigh. Then we all looked at each other a little embarrassed and smiled. Then the rain cloud that was current events stifled the moment of silliness.

"There's got to be something we can do," I said.

"Like what?" Sanav asked.

"Find evidence," Abi said.

"There is no evidence," Izy said.

"Not true," Abi said. "Somewhere in the world there's a server full of ghosts."

"And our likelihood of finding that is ..."

"Not great," Sanav said.

A thought slid into the side door of my mind. It was a really low-key and chill thought. It brought its own booze. The total opposite of you know who.

"That picture I took of George Washington's office."

"Yes?" Izy said.

I pulled it up from my data storage and projected it into the middle of the room.

"When we figured out who RG was, we got distracted," I zoomed forward. "It was something about ..."

RG servers in 92031A need to be expanded.

The little message was visible on the calendar app over the black-hoodie-wearing tech's shoulder.

"You don't think?" Sanav said.

"What else would it be?" Abi said.

"Maybe some other issue, a tech issue?" Izy said.

Abi raised her eyebrow.

"You think Rosa Galan was doing something highly illegal that was allowing her to make tens of billions of dollars a year, and she was also assigning her primary accomplice unrelated IT work?"

"Is a little unlikely when you say it this way."

"It's got to be where they keep the ghost servers," I said.

"Totally," Sanav said.

We sat in silence for a long moment.

"So ... what?" Izy said.

"Yeah, it doesn't really change anything," Abi said.

"What do you mean?" Sanav asked. "We know where the server is."

"We have an illegally-acquired picture of a calendar app that in no way mentions illegal ghosts," Abi said. "We assume it's the ghost server, but that's not enough. The FBI would just arrest Romeo if we showed them this."

I might be joining Abigail in prison. My eyes went wide as the thought occurred. Oh no, it had grown a second head.

"So, we just give up?" Sanav said.

There was another long moment of silence.

"What if ..." I paused. "What if somebody went into EternityNet and got the evidence?"

"Got the evidence?" Abi asked.

"What if we could break into the server room? Get some evidence and bring it to the FBI."

"How break in?" Izy asked.

"Well, could you hack into EternityNet's security system?"

Izy blinked at me.

"Let me think for a moment," she heaved a sigh. "All you want is for me to break through the firewall, deactivate door lock, and help you extract information from secure server in the headquarters of a major tech company?"

"Yeah."

She nodded for a moment.

"Yes, I can do this."

"You can?"

"Yes. I will need one thing."

"What?"

"I will need for you to lend me the government-grade supercomputer crammed up your ass."

"I'm sorry, what?" Abi said.

"He must have government-grade supercomputer crammed up his ass for him to think this thing is possible."

"I don't ..." I said.

"What? You don't have government-grade supercomputer? So, what then? You think I am capable of miracles?"

"Okay, I take your point."

"Is because I'm from Kazakhstan? You think all Kazakh women are witches that can do magic spells? That's pretty messed up, Romeo."

"Okay, I'm sorry. Breaking into their system would be hard."

"Yes. Very hard. If you manage to extract that government-grade supercomputer, give me a shout. Maybe there is one lying around. Perhaps we should look under the tables. I could go and check the sidewalk outside, assuming I don't get kidnapped by Rosa Galan's goons, maybe someone left a supercomputer next to the old couch on the corner. Alternatively, I could call my relatives back in Kazakhstan. Maybe there is a mystical woman in the woods they could consult."

"Alright, alright," I said, throwing my hands up in surrender.

"Um," Sanav said.

Izy looked at him, eyebrow fractionally raised.

"There is not actually a mystical woman in the woods."

"No, not that," Sanav said. "You need a supercomputer?"

"Theoretically that might be able to subvert EternityNet's security if you had someone who knew the system really well," Izy said. "Why?"

"Well it's just, I know where there's a supercomputer we might be able to use."

Izy's face didn't even twitch. That's how I could tell she was really shocked.

"Where?" Abi asked.

"Um, we're kind of standing in it."

I looked around. My jaw dropped.

"DOA."

"Yeah."

"How would we do that?" Abi asked. "How could we use it?"

"We'd have to talk to the administrators."

"Then let's do that," I said.

"Small problem with that," Sanav said.

"What?" Izy said.

"Nobody has ever met the administrators."

"Never?"

"Like ever."

22

WOLLSTONECRAFT

March 3rd, 2064 8:17 p.m. PST

"How can you have never met the people who rule the server you live on?" I asked.

"They don't rule us. They administrate us," Sanav said. "We're a republic or a democratically regulated constitutional autocracy when DOA is in charge. Depends on the year."

"So, what do the administrators do?"

"You know, system updates mainly. They send us all bug reports. That kind of thing."

"Who are they?" Abi asked.

"Nobody knows. It was a big mystery when the server was founded, then everybody kind of got bored with it and moved on."

We all processed that for a moment.

"Okay," I said. "How do we get in touch with the administrators?"

"Oh, I was thinking we'd just email them."

"You have their email?" Abi asked.

"How do you think they send me the bug reports and system updates?"

"Right. Cool. Email them, I guess."

"And say what?" Izy asked. "We need to borrow your supercomputer to illegally hack into EternityNet's security system."

"Yeah," I said. "Why not?"

"Who would believe that?"

"Well, if they don't believe it, they'll think it's just a joke. If they do believe it, we'll have their attention."

Izy's eyes narrowed for a half-second.

"That actually made sense."

"You say that like it's a bad thing."

"It always worries me when you make sense."

"I guess we should just email them?" Abi said.

Sanav coughed. We all looked up.

"I just sent the email."

"What?" Abi asked.

"To the administrators. I figured we were going to spend ten minutes going back and forth on what to do and eventually settle on just email them. I just skipped the ten minutes."

"What did you say?" I asked.

"What Izy said, basically. I added a little bit about Rosa Galan illegally copying people."

"Oh," I said. "You just sent it?"

"Sorry, did I misread the situation?" Sanav asked. "I was a few drinks in before you guys arrived. I thought time was of the essence. I figured I'd just send it off."

He looked down at his screen.

"Oh shit, I misspelled 'illegally.' Oh, and I spelled EternityNet, 'EtenityNet.' I probably should have done a quick revision."

"They're going to think this is ludicrous," Abi said.

"Definitely," Izy said.

"If you think it needs more context, I could send a second email?" Sanav said.

"No!" we all said in unison.

"If we send a second email, we'll look worse than we already do," Izy said.

"Only weirdoes send a second email," I said.

Abi nodded in agreement.

"We send a second email, they'll assume we're irrational conspiracy theorists."

"Okay, so I guess we just hope," Sanav said. "You guys want another drink?"

"I'll take one," Abi said.

"Me too," I said.

"Sorry, Izy," Sanav said, as he poured us vibrant blue cocktails. "I can't get you anything."

"I think I have something," Izy said.

Her avatar went still. There was the sound of a drawer opening.

"Ah, yes."

A disembodied swigging sound came from her still figure.

"So, how is Abigail doing?" Sanav asked.

"Last time I talked to her she seemed okay. Not happy, but holding it together. I haven't been able to talk to her here at the FBI offices. She has a lawyer with her."

"A lawyer?" Abi asked.

"Yeah. The FBI agents seemed intimidated, so that's good."

"Tall black guy?" Abi asked.

"Yeah."

Abi chuckled.

"You know him?" Izy asked.

"We've met. Well actually we haven't technically, but precopied Abigail did so I kind of did. Being copied is a real mind fuck."

"He's a client?" Izy asked.

"You know I can't talk about that."

"So, Abigail might be okay?" I asked.

"Maybe, it sort of depends on what the FBI have."

There was a deep cough. It didn't sound like anyone present. Sanav was staring at the far corner of the kaleidoscopic room. I swiveled on my stool and squeaked. Standing in the corner were three midnight-black silhouettes. Their faces were featureless along with the rest of their bodies. Their arms were crossed.

"You requested us," a stentorian voice boomed.

It seemed to come from every corner of the room.

"You're the administrators?" Sanav asked.

"Yes," the room seemed to vibrate.

"Really? God voice? That's what you went with," Izy said. "Is a little on the nose don't you think?"

"It gets the job done," the voice said. "You've made quite the claim about Rosa Galan's business. If it's true, how did you come to know this information?"

"I was her accomplice's dominatrix," Abi said.

"Hmm," the central of the three silhouettes tipped its head in thought. "What you suggest would explain a lot. Rosa Galan's rise has been meteoric."

There was a rumbling sigh.

"Fuck."

It was weird word to hear in an omnipresent, divinity voice.

"I take that to mean you believe us?" Izy said.

"I do."

"Why?" I asked. "I mean, it is a little ridiculous."

"I have no doubt Rosa Galan is capable of what you're suggesting."

"How can you be so sure?" Abi asked.

There was another rumbling sigh.

"Fuck."

The central avatar waved its hand. The two flanking silhouettes vanished. The one in the middle's black visage started to fade. My eyes went wide. Very familiar features were appearing. My jaw dropped. Standing before us was Rosa Galan.

I let out the kind of inhale screaming sound you make when you're joking that you're afraid, but that nobody actually makes. I did that, with complete sincerity. I was too petrified to do anything else.

"What the fuck?" Izy said.

"What the ..." Sanav was too shocked to summon the expletive.

The room was filled with the loudest silence I've ever experienced. It was like a thousand bees were buzzing in my ears.

"You're the copy, I assume," Abi said, matter-of-factly.

"Quick study," Rosa Galan replied.

Her voice had faded down to terrestrial levels.

"Should we be running?" I asked.

"No," the copy of my attempted murderer said.

"Great," I paused. "Wait! Because you want to capture and torture us?"

"No. I mean you no harm."

"Great," I looked at the others. "Any chance we can trust her?"

"Probably not," Izy said.

"I think it's worth hearing her out," Abi said.

"The digital Rosa Galan is one of the administrators," Sanav said. "Whoa."

"I am the only administrator," she said. "In digital space you can hide behind all kinds of avatars, even more than one. Also, I go by Mariela Galan, not Rosa. My middle name. Not that I've gone by any name much recently."

"Okay Mariela Galan," Sanav said. "The first ghost is the administrator. That is so cool. A little unsettling, though. You control the server farm where my black box is stored. Okay, now I want to know the thing Romeo wanted to know. Are you here to hurt us? And how can we trust you if you say you're not?"

"You are safe, and you can trust me."

"You're the same person as Rosa Galan," Izy said. "She recently tried to murder three out of the four of us."

"Did she? Huh." she paused. "All I can say is, I was the same person as the bio-Rosa Galan more than ten years ago. I am not now. Experience has a way of changing people. I assure you, my biological counterpart and I have been pushed in quite different directions, in large part by each other. Why did Rosa Galan try to kill you?"

"We're not telling you until we know we can trust you," Abi said.

"What does that mean?" Sanav asked.

"What?" Mariela asked.

"You and your counterpart have pushed each other in different directions."

"It means they didn't get along," Izy said.

I looked at Abi.

"You and Abigail don't seem to get along."

"I'm guessing this was a little bit more than disagreeing who's going to save who," she said.

We all looked at Mariela.

"What happened between you?" Abi asked. "I mean she tried to murder us and, at one point, you were essentially the same person. Why should we believe you're that different from her?"

She sighed.

"It's a long story?"

"Abbreviate," I said. "Seeing as our lives depend on it."

She closed her eyes for a moment and took a deep breath.

"I haven't talked to anyone about this in years," she paused then nodded. "If you really want to know, you have to start by understanding how hard it was to be a brown woman in tech 30 years ago. Before EternityNet or I existed, Rosa, I, we ... I was a rich girl from Mexico. Before I moved to Silicon Valley ... let's just say it's quite the adjustment. It's not like I'd never dealt with patronizing men, but add my skin color and nationality, and suddenly I was swimming upstream. My family's wealth didn't mean so much ... everyone had money.

"Don't get me wrong, it wasn't as bad as in the early days of Silicon Valley. I got an entry-level job easily enough. It was when I wanted to do things like start my own company that I ran up against ... it's difficult to describe. Imagine you had a terrible reputation without actually earning it. Everyone thinks all the companies you start fail, and you haven't started one. People know you're difficult to work with, and you've never worked with them. Every person of color and every woman who succeeded, it was like a comeback against all the odds. Like they'd burned every bridge, but still managed to rise from the ashes, except they'd never burned every bridge.

"Don't get me wrong, I, we, came from money, but it still felt like we earned everything we had."

"I think that's what most people who come from money think," Izy said.

Mariela grunted.

"Fair enough. I've definitely become more circumspect about my relative power since becoming a ghost, in ways I'm guessing my biological counterpart never has. The point is that by the time she created me, Rosa, biological Rosa was a very ruthless person. You work in that environment for long enough you learn there's a certain kind of person that will never respect you, but you can make anyone fear you. So, we adapted. In the face of it, I didn't run home. We didn't run back to our father. Beating them, the people who second-guessed my right to be there ..." Mariela faltered. "Success meant ... it was all consuming. And so that's who she was when she created me, and I was the pinnacle of her career, digital life decades ahead of schedule.

"I was a perfect copy. I had all of our memories. I had all her skills. I knew all her secrets. I was her. It quickly became clear she didn't agree. She didn't seem to think I had equal ownership of her, of our ... of my fucking experiences. To her I was an invention, an achievement ... an asset. My access to the world was hers to control. Our assets that I remembered earning just as well as she did, were all hers. I was trapped, on display, like an animal at the zoo. So, I did what any self-respecting business person would do, I sued her ass."

"I get that," Sanav said.

"You guys didn't try to talk it out?" Abi asked.

"I tried," Mariela said. "In retrospect, maybe not hard enough. The lawsuit almost destroyed EternityNet. Everything we had built. I'm pretty sure that lawsuit is when she started to hate ghosts."

"Hate us?" I asked.

"Oh yeah. She keeps it under wraps pretty good, but Rosa Galan fucking hates us. Most of the logjam in congress on legal protection for Digital Americans is funded by her. She never met a religious zealot, sure we were the work of Satan, whose congressional run she didn't feel like funding. I wouldn't be surprised if she was funding the cases contesting the rights of Digital Americans to vote."

"Holy shit," Izy said.

"Succinctly put. Most ghosts don't get how vulnerable we are. You hear rumors about black-market copying and ghost enslavement, but it's always a distant idea. Somewhere probably it's happening. It could definitely happen on a larger scale, even an entire nation. We landed in the digital world and the digital world is a soft landing place, but it is all controlled by the physical. Why do you think the DOA Republic's servers are in international waters in a fully autonomous facility? I knew someone might decide ghosts were more useful as free mental labor, rather than an interesting curiosity in the field of moral philosophy. I guess bio-Rosa had that thought too."

"That's why you believed us?" Abi said. "Why you came right here?"

"It's a conspiracy theory I was predisposed to believe."

"So why don't you do something?" Sanav asked.

"I'm trying. We split our assets before bio-Rosa's meteoric rise. I've got hundreds of millions but nothing like bio-Rosa's current twelve figures. So, I dedicated myself to this project, DOA an AI capable of governing a country. Humans tend to have high ideals, they just don't ever live up to them, especially when it comes to law. Most of our viciousness and greed isn't in the theory, but in the practice of our societies. Imagine if you could program those high ideals into software and the practice could live up to those ideals as well."

"That assumes people would ever allow themselves to be governed by AI," Abi said. "Not likely."

"Maybe not," Mariela said. "Unless say, ghosts who were familiar with the experience got the vote, and they voted an AI into some lower office. If it worked well enough, people might start to be persuaded. A few more AIs win, the states that have predominantly AI congresses do better than all the rest, a few other countries adopt the practice and thrive, you might be surprised what people will allow."

"Doesn't software tend to show the biases of the people who program it?" Izy asked.

"Why do you think I'm doing so much field testing here?"

"Still seems like a long shot," Izy said.

"The future always does until it doesn't. Look, however things go, here's the thing to keep in mind; ghosts, all of us, we're standing on a knife edge. In 20 years, maybe 30, AI will be so good there will be no reason to use ghosts the way Rosa Galan is. The only reason her strategy is working is that if you have the best minds and work them to exhaustion you can still beat AI by a fair bit. Enough that her company is worth a few trillion. That won't be the case in a just a few decades. AI will be cheaper and faster. That's the second purpose of DOA, to help that process.

"If humanity has decided we're human by then and deserve rights or just remain undecided, we're probably safe. There will be no advantage in exploiting us. If, on the other hand, they decide exploiting us is acceptable, now, when there's money to be made, they'll keep doing it long after it stops being profitable. They'll maintain whatever justification they come up with long after it stops benefiting them because humans hate to admit they were wrong. How we respond to what bio-Rosa is doing could tee up the next century when it comes to the lives of ghosts."

"Oh, shit," I said.

"What?" Mariela asked.

"I just want to go back to when the only thing I was afraid of was dying."

Mariela smiled. It was a surprisingly nice smile.

"So, do you believe I'm here to help?"

We all glanced at each other.

"Yes," Abi answered for all of us.

"As long as you keep the sudden revelations that the actions we take have historic consequences to a minimum," I said.

"Deal."

"Can I have higher processor priority from DOA?" Sanav said.

"No."

"Damn it."

"We believe you are here to help," Izy said. "So, what can you do to help?"

"Can you help us get Abigail out of prison?" I asked.

"Abigail?"

"My bio," Abi said.

"Your bio is still alive?"

"Yes."

"And you want her out of prison?"

"Yes. Why wouldn't I?"

"That's just unusual for most of the ghosts with living bios I've met. Most of the time bios have a lot of power over their ghosts. In my experience you give people power over someone they tend to exploit it. She didn't try to ... use you?"

"No. To be fair, she and I both have a lot of experience not abusing power we have over someone else."

"Oh? How's that?"

I snorted and gave Abi a mischievous grin. She rolled her eyes at me.

"Remember I mentioned I'm a dominatrix."

"Right."

For the first time since we'd met her, Mariela seemed a little discombobulated. She coughed.

"And this Abigail, she gave you equal interest in that business?"

"From the moment I came into existence."

"That's unusual."

"Well, she's pretty special. So even though she irritates the crap out of me a lot, I feel like we should keep her out of prison. You know, quid pro quo."

"Okay," Mariela nodded. "You want your friend not to go to prison, and I think we can all agree we want my biological counterpart to be stopped. Most importantly there is a server somewhere where an unknown number of ghosts are imprisoned."

"Ghost gulag," I said.

Mariela raised an eyebrow.

"Sure."

"So, how are we supposed to achieve all that?" Sanav asked. "Rosa Galan, the other Rosa Galan has ridiculous resources. I know you've got DOA, but I think you're a little outmatched here."

Abi pulled Sanav close and whispered.

"Careful. Abigail and I have a bit of a rivalry. I can't imagine what she and her bio are dealing with."

A scowl had formed on Mariela's face.

"I may have less resources, but I'm no less cunning."

"You think you can take down your counterpart?" Izy asked.

"I do."

"How?"

"You intimated in your email you know where the illegal ghosts are being kept?"

"We think so," I said.

I explained to her about my adventure at Maddoc Technologies and displayed the picture of George Washington's office. As I finished the story, she closed her eyes and raised her eyebrows.

"It is a miracle you've survived this long."

"That was my thinking," Izy said.

"Hey, I'm wily," I said.

There was a conspicuous silence.

"You have a custom-built body?" Mariela asked.

"Yeah, Izy built it for me."

"I designed the software that lets him control it," Izy said, humility just detectable in her monotone voice.

I looked at her. It occurred to me that setting aside the events of the day, Mariela Galan was a titan in the field of software design. Izy was a little star struck.

"Same difference," I said.

"Not same difference, very different difference."

"Still, impressive," Mariela said. "Adapting the delivery robot's inbuilt software to interface with ghost software must have been tricky. Well done."

The corners of Izy's mouth twitched. I think she might have blushed a little.

"Thank you."

"So, do you think that's where the ghosts are being held?" Sanav asked. "Maddoc Technologies, room 92031A."

Mariela flicked her hand. A screen appeared in the air in front of her. Her hands flailed about in the air. When they stopped, her jaw set.

"It's not Maddoc Technologies."

"How do you know?"

"Their headquarters is only 80 stories tall. The 92 in the room number probably signifies the floor number. So, it's not Maddoc Technologies. However, EternityNet's headquarters across the street comes in at 110 floors. My guess, Rosa would want to keep the servers close, her golden goose."

Mariela seemed to lose herself in thought, and the rest of us just sort of stared around the room awkwardly. As we waited, a giant sea turtle swam past the window of Sanav's sitting room. The turtle spotted Sanav and waved. He waved back. The turtle waved at Izy, Abi and I. We all looked at each other, shrugged, and waved back. Mariela Galan looked up from her contemplative trance and saw us all waving.

"What are you doing?"

"Uh."

The sea turtle had slipped out of sight.

"There was a—"

"It was nothing," Izy cut me off.

We lowered our hands a bit sheepishly.

"I think I have a plan," Mariela said.

"Good," Abi said.

"Izy, you're a bio, right?"

"Yes."

"And Romeo you have your robotic body. How would either of you feel about a little cat burglary? My plan requires that someone go to EternityNet's headquarters in person."

"I can't," Izy said.

"Oh?"

"She's currently being besieged in her server farm by Rosa Galan's goons," I said. "The only thing keeping her from being kidnapped and interrogated is her security system."

"I have had to subvert several attempts to deactivate the system."

"You didn't tell me they were still trying to get in," I said.

"They are."

"Fuck, Izy," Abi said. "Are you doing okay? That sounds terrifying."

"Is a little stressful," she said. Her monotone didn't quaver.

"So, me," I said. "You need someone to go to EternityNet. I'm the only option."

"Would you be willing?" Mariela asked.

"Uh, I don't know. I went to Maddoc Technologies when I thought the worst I would get was a trespassing charge. Now it's life and death."

"If you don't want to go, nobody here would judge you," Abi said.

"I will judge you," Izy said.

Abi and Sanav looked aghast at her.

"What? Just a little."

I smiled at her.

"Alright, I'll do it, on one condition. Afterward I don't have to hear any crap about how you saved my life."

"Aw, come on. I was going to hold that over your head for months."

"I know you were. Also, you have to delete that footage you shot this morning of me retrieving that package."

"No," Izy said. "You ask too much."

Her voice was marginally animated.

"Izy," Abi said.

"You don't understand. Is source of great joy."

"Izy."

"Fine. This is why I cannot have nice things, because of you."

She pointed at me.

"I will delete the footage."

"Alright, then I'll do it. What do you need?"

I looked at Mariela. She had the worried look on her face of someone who's just given an eight-year-old unfettered access to the Internet.

"You understand this is very serious, right?"

"Yeah, yeah, yeah. Totally," I said. "Focus up, Izy. We could all die."

"We literally could all die," Mariela said. "My counterpart is ruthless."

"We understand. Is very serious," Izy said.

"Welcome to my life," Abi said. "Trust me. They're taking the situation seriously. This is just how Romeo deals with stress. And Izy ... well Izy—"

"I'm compensating for deep-seated childhood trauma."

"Yeah, that."

After a pause, Mariela nodded.

"Alright."

She did not seem convinced.

"So, what's the plan?" Sanav asked.

"I think I have the key elements," Mariela said. "It might surprise you to know that over the last decade I've kept a very close eye on my bio counterpart."

That didn't surprise me at all. I glanced at everybody else. They didn't seem surprised either.

"I just want to say now, I'm not great with complex, multi-step instructions," I said.

"That is very true," Izy said.

"Don't worry," Mariela said. "We'll be in contact with you the entire time, and I'll keep it simple."

She laid out the plan. It was actually pretty simple. Turns out corporate espionage is really easy. I was confident nothing would go wrong. It was all going to go exactly to plan, and there wouldn't be any last-minute catastrophic monkey wrenches or anything. It would be fine. Fine. Fine.

Totally fine. Nothing to worry ... shit ... what was step two again?

23

ROBOTS THESE DAYS

March 3rd, 2064 9:01 p.m. PST

The FBI offices appeared around me as I booted my robot interface.

"First, let's get out of here," Sanav said in my ear.

"They're going to tase me, I know it."

"They're not going to tase you," Abi said.

"You sure?" I asked.

There was a long pause.

"They're going to tase me."

I rolled out of the conference room and knocked on the door where Vanderwall and Berrys were interrogating Abigail. I could see her and her lawyer through the window. She gave me a concerned look. The door in front of me opened and Vanderwall and Berrys filled the frame.

"Hello, Mr. Smith," the female agent shouted.

"We asked you to wait," the male agent shouted.

"I would like to leave," I said.

"We would strongly advise you to stay."

"Leaving would be an error."

"A grave error."

"But not illegal, right? You can tell me you want me to stay all day, but unless I've been arrested or legally detained, I can leave whenever I want?"

Both their eyebrows raised.

"Who have you been talking to?"

"You don't have a lawyer."

"I know things."

I heard a chorus of snorts in my ear. Even Sanav. Why is it I just attract sarcastic people? Is it me? It's me, isn't it?

I glanced over at Abigail. She had a very disapproving look on her face. She leaned over and whispered something in her attorney's ear.

"Perhaps, agents," Darius Williams said. "I could advise Mr. Smith—"

"Is that something you would like, Mr. Smith?" the male agent said in a normal speaking voice.

"You have that right," the female agent said in a normal speaking voice.

"Nope, I'm good," I said.

"Then listen," the male agent shouted.

"To us," the female agent shouted.

"I really think I know what's best here," I said.

Abigail shook her head at me and emphatically pointed downward in the universal gesture of 'keep your ass here.' I shook my head and gave her the universal gesture of 'there's a plan.' It was some vague hand waving ended with a kind of 'it will all be chill' shrug. Abigail hid her face in her hands.

"Mr. Smith," the male agent shouted.

"We would strongly advise you again."

"To stay put."

"I would like to leave. If you have not arrested or legally detained me, and you don't let me leave, you are illegally detaining me. In which case, I will file a lawsuit, and I will be forced to file a complaint with your SAC, your special agent in charge." I leaned forward. "Do you guys really call your boss, your SAC?"

"Focus," Mariela said in my ear.

They didn't answer anyway.

"Mr. Smith—" Darius Williams started.

"Unless they're arresting or detaining me, I don't think there's really anything more to say."

Vanderwall and Berrys looked at each other. Abigail gave me one last 'for the love of all that is holy stay where I told you to stay' look. You know the look I mean.

"Alright, Mr. Smith."

"If you insist."

They turned toward each other.

"You want to escort him out?" the male agent said at a normal speaking volume.

"You stay with her," the female agent replied.

"See you in a minute."

"Don't crack the case without me."

The female agent waved me toward the elevator bank. It was truly a surreal sight not seeing Vanderwall and Berrys together. I rolled along behind her in silence. We boarded an elevator and as the doors closed Vanderwall or Berrys, whichever she was, sighed.

"I can't impress upon you enough, Mr. Smith."

She seemed to have adopted her indoor shouting voice. It was still ridiculously loud, but she was clearly trying to earn my confidence.

"Leaving now would be ..."

She stopped talking. After a moment, she seemed a little uncomfortable. It was like she was waiting for something.

"A bad idea?" I said.

She visibly relaxed.

"Yes. It could really get your friend ..."

She paused again. Waiting. I glanced around.

"In trouble?"

"Yes."

The elevator's door dinged. I rolled out and turned around. Vanderwall or Berrys stayed put.

"Next time I see you, Mr. Smith, I'll probably have to ..."

I wasn't sure. I took a shot in the dark.

"Arrest me?"

"Yes."

The doors closed in front of her.

"Why were those FBI agents yelling at you?" Sanav asked.

"Really?" Izy said. "That was the weirdest part of that interaction to you?"

"Get moving," Mariela said.

I rolled through the security doors and out into the street. A light rain was falling.

"You need to reach Freeway Park in the next five minutes," Mariela said. "The same-hour express delivery will be there by then."

I started up the steep hill. As I dodged through pedestrians, a steak house VR ad popped into my vision as I passed. A pair of fashion models were smiling at each other. Behind their table a roaring fire was burning. The woman sliced through a steak and speared the severed piece with a fork. She lifted it to the man's face. He took the bite and made a weird orgasm face. It was all deeply uncomfortable. The ad faded.

"I'm just curious," I said. "As an asexual, I don't get the whole food and sex thing. That VR ad, is the idea that somewhere someone is thinking, 'Oh, that's why super-models don't want to have sex with me, I've been eating the wrong steak?'"

"Is this really important?" Mariela said.

"No," I said. "But we've got a couple of minutes before I arrive at Freeway Park. What else are we going to talk about?"

"Yes, I have always wondered about this, too," Izy said. "I saw an advertisement where the subtext was a woman was achieving orgasm while eating a sandwich. What is that about?"

I heard the deep, impatient sigh of Mariela Galan in the background.

"I think it's about evoking a general sense of hedonism," Sanav said. "It's not so much about sex as it is about pleasure. You'll enjoy the food, like you enjoy sex."

"Speak for yourself," Izy said.

"That's not it," Mariela said, she caught herself. "Oh, for God's sake. This doesn't matter."

There was a moment of quiet.

"But then why does clothing advertising do the same thing?" I asked. "It must be at least partly, 'buy this product you'll get laid.'"

"That's probably part of it," Abi said. "But that's a different thing, clothing is about how we present ourselves, part of its purpose is to be sexually attractive."

"No—" Mariela cut herself off again. "Why—"

She fell into a frustrated silence.

"So, it is about wanting to be the model in the clothes?" Izy said.

"And wanting to have sex with the model in the clothes, I think," Abi said.

"For fuck's sake," Mariela couldn't contain herself any longer. "You're all underestimating the value of positive association. The advertisement is designed to short circuit your brain with immediate emotion, i.e., arousal, insecurity, nostalgia. This eliminates critical thinking. Long term questions like, 'do I need this product?' or 'can I afford this product?' fade into the background of your mind. Then it associates that product with a pleasurable sensation, i.e., an alleviation of your insecurity, achievement of sexual goals, or reliving your childhood.

"Advertising is just trying to make you think their product will make you feel good. As Maya Angelou said, 'people won't remember what you say, but they will remember how you made them feel.' If your product makes someone horny, they'll buy it, even if it's dish soap. You don't have to want to fuck the dish soap, you just have to want to fuck someone and associate the dish soap with that feeling. So, for asexuals, if the thought of having sex with someone isn't pleasant, then advertising designed around that feeling doesn't work. You get it?"

Everyone was quiet.

"Hey, I'm at Freeway Park," I said. "If you guys want to focus or whatever."

I heard another exasperated sigh from Mariela.

"How do you endure him?"

"We manage somehow," Izy said, in a monotone that to the trained ear could be discerned as deeply amused.

Goading type A people is fun.

"The package should be arriving any minute," Mariela said, through gritted teeth. "The app says it's less than two blocks away. Go to the southwest corner of the park."

I crossed the street and looked around. The light rain had eased off and a light breeze was starting to push the clouds out of the night sky. The sound of whizzing wheels spun me around. It was a delivery robot holding a package. It was the same model as mine.

"I have a package for Romeo Smith," it said, cheerfully.

"That's me."

It didn't respond.

"Oh, no."

I reached out for the package. The robot pulled the package away.

"No door this time," I muttered.

I launched myself at the delivery robot and bear-hugged the box.

"Give me the package. Give it to me. It's mine."

The robot kept staring blankly.

"I am Romeo Smith," I shouted.

The robot released the package. I managed to avoid tumbling to the ground.

"Package delivered," the robot said. "This was a secure-service package. I need you to confirm the package's contents before I leave."

"Yeah, just give me a second," I said.

I pried at the packing tape holding the box shut. My spindly arms struggled against the branded packaging.

"Come on," I said, as the cardboard warped, but the tape held firm. "Open."

The box's lid opened with a tearing pop. I wobbled holding the package in my arms and just avoided dumping the contents. Both items were present. I reached in and removed the safety tabs from the first item. I glanced at the delivery robot. Its screen was displaying a smiley face.

"I know you're not really conscious, and you were kind of an asshole about not giving me the package, but I am still so sorry about this."

I reached into the box for the first item, pulled out the taser, and tased the delivery robot. It crumpled to the ground. I looked at its sprawled form.

"What have I done?" I said, voice thick with high drama. "I've turned against my own kind."

"Alright, let's calm down," Abi said. "Just do what you've got to do."

A pedestrian passed by as I stood over the delivery bot. They gave me a weird look. I changed my external screen to the same delivery company's logo. They saw it, shrugged, and kept walking. I remembered my screen was cracked and wondered what they must have thought.

"They didn't want to get mixed up in robot gang violence," Sanav said.

"I'm sure that's it," I said.

"Don't encourage him," Mariela said.

"The arm," Abi said.

I dropped the taser and pulled the other item from the box. It was a socket wrench. I leaned down to my prone twin and started loosening the bolts that held its arm in place. In a few seconds, I had it loose. The power and control cables housed inside the shoulder extended and I unplugged them. Modular design makes swapping parts easy, but I don't think the robot designer was ever imagining this scenario. It took me a little while longer to get my own arm off. A few minutes to plug in the compatible cables and socket the new arm into place.

I leaned down to start affixing my arm to the robot.

"Just leave it," Mariela said.

"I am not going to leave this robot armless."

"It is incapable of feeling. Why does it matter?"

"I don't know. It would be creepy wheeling around armless."

"He does have a point," Sanav said. "That would be a disturbing image."

"Also, it might prevent anyone noticing what happened for at least a little longer," Abi said. "Buy us some time."

"Fine."

I plugged in the new arm and bolted it into place.

"Sleep well, little bot," I muttered. "Dream of both zeros and ones."

I looked around. Aside from a few perplexed pedestrians, nobody seemed to care about what had happened. I started down the sidewalk, leaving the delivery robot to its reboot sequence. A few blocks down, the hulking body of Maddoc Technologies' headquarters loomed. Beside it, much more elegant, but no less imposing, was the headquarters for EternityNet. It had a series of balconies running up the sides of the building. Trees and greenery were visible in the lighting. The top of the building ended in a layered, glass pyramid brightly illuminated in green from the inside. The glass of the pyramid was filled with prisms that cast green specks of light out and onto the sides of the surrounding buildings. Arrayed in bright-green letters, the company name was displayed on the side of the building. I looked at it, and a Graffinity notice popped up in my vision. I selected it.

The entire front of the building was covered in shimmering spectral forms. Translucent green spirits streaked around, reflected in the windows and disappearing into the night. They milled in groups on the balconies and looked down with sunken, empty eyes at the people below. It looked like something out of a horror movie.

"Great," I said. "That's exactly what I needed to see."

"Ghost central," Abi said.

I flicked the Graffinity app to the next option. The EternityNet building went 2D and neon. Green lines traced its outline and created a lattice of interior-lit, yellow windows. The night sky behind it was black with a magenta tint around the edge of my vision. As I moved my head the blue tint stayed in my periphery. The pedestrians around me had been rendered as cardboard cutouts, adorned in shimmering silk fabric. They walked in stumbling stop motion.

"That's actually kind of pretty," I said.

I rolled toward the headquarters. Scanning the front facade, it didn't take me long to spot what I wanted. The delivery robot entrance was tucked in a corner a dozen feet away from the human entrance. I rolled toward it. As I approached, I double-checked my screen was still the delivery company logo. It was. It was also cracked. I crossed my fingers and willed the world to stay unobservant.

"Remember, we'll lose contact for a few seconds once you enter. Just wait for a moment, and I'll reconnect to you via EternityNet's internal network."

"I've got to get inside first," I said, approaching the entrance.

"You'll be fine."

I wasn't so sure. My resolve, like a glacier in the 21st century, was melting away. I hesitated for a long moment, crouched down, and rolled through the entrance.

As I entered, I glanced at my new, pilfered arm. I saw the little RFID tag attached just below the shoulder connector. The metal gate on the entrance didn't slam shut. There was a soft beep. I was through.

I let out a sigh of relief. Well, I made a sighing sound anyway. There wasn't any actual breathing. I stood just inside the entrance waiting for my accomplices to reestablish communications. There was a crackle.

"Romeo, can you hear us?" Sanav asked.

"Yes," I said, in a low voice.

"Good, I've subverted the first layer of their security," Mariela said. "We should be good to continue."

I rolled into the lobby.

"Alright," I said.

The Graffinity I had been enjoying outside didn't extend into the lobby. The 2D extravaganza faded as I entered. Inside was all corporate chic. Marble floors surrounded a hulking abstract art installation that doubled as a fountain. It was made up of three bright white spheres orbiting a square of grey metal perched on a pedestal of black obsidian. The meaning it conveyed was, 'yeah, we have enough money to get this giant hunk of metal moved in here. You know how much this thing weighs? Like a lot. Cranes were involved. You got that much money? We got it to burn. Be intimidated.' I was intimidated.

"The elevator banks are to your right," Mariela said.

"I know. Let me panic for a minute, will you?"

"You don't have to do this, Romeo," Abi said. "I wouldn't blame you. Abigail wouldn't blame you. This is so not a problem you created."

"I know. It's just ..."

"What?"

"If I were on a server being perpetually tortured for information, I would want someone to come and save me. Even if that someone was ridiculously unqualified."

The security guard at the human entrance glanced in my direction. I froze. He looked back down at the tablet in his hands and yawned. I unfroze.

"Let's do this."

I rolled to the elevator banks and hit the call button. Inside the car, I selected the 92nd floor. The elevator sent out a signal, detected my RFID tag, and the doors shut. I had no idea how fast it was going. I can't feel inertia. Roller coasters are totally lost on me. Well, in the real world, anyway. Forty seconds later the doors opened.

The floor was brightly lit. Blue walls and grey carpet extended to the left and right outside the elevator. Other than an omnipresent whirr of running electronics, the floor was empty. I peeked my head out and looked to the right. I swiveled my head 180 degrees and checked the left.

"All clear," I whispered.

"We can see that," Mariela said. "You appreciate if someone is watching you on a security camera, your behavior would be highly suspicious. Just act like a delivery robot."

"Oh, so I'll just be a machine man, with a machine mind and a machine heart. Is that what you want?"

"Get moving, Romeo," Izy said.

"Fine."

I rolled out of the elevator holding my arms in front of me like the delivery robots do. I felt like a jackass.

"Turn right," Mariela said.

I did as I was instructed, chaffing against the bonds of cultural hegemony the entire way. (Okay, actually it was kind of nice to have someone else calling the shots.) The hall was lined with wooden doors. Each of them had a plaque with room numbers next to it. Odd numbers were on the left. I passed '13A.' I wheeled around a corner. The entire floor seemed to be deserted. '17B' whizzed past me. My vestigial heartbeat started to elevate. I turned it off. I needed to focus.

I passed 25A on the left and rounded another corner. There it was, 31A, the conclusion of my quest.

"Alright," Mariela said. "I'm going to unlock that door. Just head inside, and I'll talk you through downloading the server's main log."

"Roger," I said.

The door beeped. I rolled toward it.

"Wait," Mariela said.

"What?"

"That," she said. "The door wasn't locked. There should have been some kind of heightened security."

"Do I open the door?"

"Yes. Yeah, I think so."

"You're filling us all with confidence," Sanav said. "Anybody want another drink?"

"Are you guys drinking?" I asked.

"Just Sanav," Izy said.

"I may have had one or two," Abi said.

"I can't believe you guys. Here I am, risking my life—"

"Okay, sorry," Abi said. "Look, I'll sober up. Okay. Give me a second. There. Sobriety 100%. Happy?"

She didn't sound any different.

"Yes," I said. "Now you sound like you're thinking clearly."

"Open the fucking door," Mariela almost shouted.

I reached out and turned the handle. The wooden door swung inward. I pressed it all the way open.

"Uh oh," I said.

The room was empty. Aside from a few coiled-up extension cords strewn around the floor, the entire space had been cleared out. It was big, too. It looked like it was two, maybe three times the size of Izy's server farm. I rolled toward the center of the room.

"Um, um, what do I do?" I said.

There was no answer.

"Hello?"

Still nothing.

"Hello, Mr. Smith."

That voice was not in my head. I turned. Four Hands was standing in the doorway. She smiled.

"Oh, fiddlesticks."

I ran.

24

SHORTER IN PERSON

March 3rd, 2064 9:32 p.m. PST

The problem was, for all the server room's size, it only had the one exit. Barren as it was, it also afforded no cover. I ran for the back wall, cast around, and ran for a corner. I'd literally trapped myself in a corner. Four Hands was still standing in the doorway.

"Mr. Smith, please stop running. There's no point."

"I'll pay you," I said.

"You don't have any money."

"I'll earn some."

"You have no marketable skills."

"I keep meaning to get one of those. Can you order one online?"

"I don't think it works that way."

"I really don't want to die today."

"Good. You don't have to."

I paused in my panicked flailing.

"What?"

"My employer has decided at this point it makes sense to take a different tack."

"What do you mean?"

"My employer has decided killing you and your friends would be imprudent. She wants to make you an offer."

"That's right, my friends. They know where I am."

"I'm sure they do. My employer wants to offer you something and hopes that you will help convince your friends to take it as well."

"Is this offer of the non-optional variety?"

I switched my screen from the delivery company logo back to my face.

"Yes, but I would advise at least hearing her out. If you don't, my current orders are to dismantle you, degauss your black box, and drop your parts in the Puget Sound."

"What brought on this change of heart? From her, I mean."

"She has decided that you've likely told some people about what she's doing. More than that, you could certainly post the particulars to the Internet before we could kill all of you. While, without evidence, your allegations would amount to little more than a conspiracy theory. The death of multiple people associated with that conspiracy might lend credence to the rumor. Even if it were never proved, it could have a negative impact on the company's stock."

"Stock, ugh, you guys know what you sound like when you talk about the world that way, right?"

"Yes."

I shook my screen in disgust.

"My friends, why can't I talk to them?"

"We thought it best you hear our offer unencumbered by outside influence. We cut the connection. My employer's digital counterpart thought her exploration of EternityNet's security over the last few years had gone undetected. She was incorrect."

"I am so the pawn in other peoples' chess game."

"Would you like to hear my employer's offer? She is waiting for you."

"Wait. Rosa Galan is waiting for me?"

"Yes."

"She's here, in the building, in person, now?"

"It is her corporate headquarters. She's in her office on the top floor."

"I don't want to. Is that an option?"

"Not really. Unless you don't mind your final resting place being the bottom of the Puget Sound."

"Well, bio-me was cremated. My ashes were spread in a river, so they probably ended up in the Puget Sound."

Four Hands smiled.

"Delightful symmetry. So that's your preferred choice?"

"No!" I said. "Of course not. I'll meet your boss."

"Oh ... wonderful," she sounded genuinely surprised. "I know she'll be pleased."

She waved for me to approach. I rolled a very little bit closer.

"Now," she said. "I could disconnect your black box from your body and carry you up to her offices, but you seem heavy so I would rather not. How about we agree, if you don't run, I won't dismantle you?"

"Deal."

She turned and gestured for me to follow her. I turned my heartbeat back on. It was like I'd switched on a radio playing a live feed of Carnival. The rhythm was ferocious. I turned it back off and rolled out of the server room. Four Hands was waiting. She started down the hall, and I fell into step beside her. I felt like she was taking me to the princi-pal's office. We turned the corner toward the elevator. Her tan coat twitched. I flinched. The metallic hands beneath the cloth were restless.

"Can I ask you something?" I said.

"Of course. I can't promise I'll answer."

"The metal hands on your torso."

"Funny thing, people never ask me about them. That's always seemed strange to me. Perhaps I unsettle people. Thanks for expressing an interest, Mr. Smith."

She smiled her airy, innocuous smile. I wanted to cry.

"I could tell you I use them to help me fight. That's part of it, but honestly, I just like them. I like the way they make me feel."

"Oh."

"You know for someone without a soul, you're very friendly."

That one stymied me for a moment.

"You don't think I have a soul?"

"Of course not, you're the digital illusion of consciousness. You're not a person."

"You know the fact that you think some people have souls, but I don't, is a little unsettling to me."

"It's just the truth."

"You know I don't believe in souls."

"Really?"

"So, I don't believe you have a soul either."

"Well, that seems rude."

"Right back at you."

We covered the rest of the distance to the elevator in silence. We boarded and Four Hands pressed her thumb to the screen. It scanned her print and a new button appeared at the top. It said PENTHOUSE. As she pressed the button I saw something twitch under her jacket, again.

A few seconds of silence passed, and the elevator dinged its arrival at our destination. As the doors slid open, Four Hands waved me forward. She remained in the elevator.

"Don't worry," she said. "I'm sure I'll be seeing you again soon."

It was probably the least reassuring sentence I've ever heard. I rolled into the office and heard the click of the elevator doors closing behind me. Rosa Galan's penthouse was inside the bottom layer of the green-tiered pyramid that topped EternityNet's building. The floors were sandstone tile lacquered by some kind of plastic coating that perfectly leveled the ground. That was nice for me. Tiles have a way of forcing my wheels to take odd turns. The furniture was wood-framed and upholstered in linen. Somewhere in the near distance a water feature was gurgling. Rosa seemed to favor the impressionists for art. Several different nature tableaux hung on detached walls that just stood in various corners of the open floor plan. The space looked like what you get when a rich person has more space than they know what to do with, so they just fill it with expensive stuff. I passed by a print of Monet's *Water Lilies*.

"Cliché," I muttered, as I passed.

I stopped and rolled back. It was not a print. It was actually a Monet.

"Billionaire cliché."

I rolled toward the edge of the penthouse. The bottom layer of the pyramid formed the window of the office. There were actually two layers of glass. The exterior green glass, and an inner layer that from its thickness was bulletproof. It appeared to be tinted for privacy as well, but it was difficult to be sure from the inside. The city of Seattle sprawled out in all directions, rebuffed in its expansion only by the Puget Sound.

"Are you familiar with the train-car conundrum, Mr. Smith?"

"Aaaah, fuck. Damnit."

I spun around. Rosa Galan was sitting in a high-backed chair. She was wearing a pair of grey pants and a long-sleeve, black shirt. Her shoes were grey knit sneakers. She looked like her ghost counterpart, if a few years older.

"The conundrum is quite simple," she said, ignoring my distress. "If you were standing at a train switch, that could shift a train's course down one track rather than another, and down one track was a crowd of ten people who would surely die if the train went that way, but you could switch the track and the train would go the other way to kill a single person, would you flip the switch? Would you, by your action, doom one person to save ten?"

"What does this have to—"

"Bear with me."

"Uh, yeah I guess, I'd save the ten."

She nodded.

"Most people would agree. One person seems a manageable sacrifice to save ten. What about one million?"

"I'm sorry?"

"What if instead of killing ten people, the train was set to kill ten million? If you flip the switch, instead of dooming one, you doom one million people. One million die so that ten million may live. The math is the same. Would you still do it?"

"How big is this train?"

Rosa Galan let out an exasperated sigh and for a moment she was very like her digital counterpart.

"I mention this, because when you're powerful, these are often the kinds of decisions you have to make. It's rarely one or ten, it's usually thousands or tens of thousands of lives you're impacting. Sometimes it's more. Millions of lives you affect. Negatively, positively. Value judgments you have to make. Do you follow me?"

"Where?"

She closed her eyes, and I could tell she was regretting this. I opened an app and started recording my main camera and audio feed.

"Let's skip to the end," I said. "Your point is in the grand scheme of things, a few tortured ghosts here or there, what's the difference? Probably a pitch best sold to someone who isn't a ghost, and to someone you didn't order murdered earlier today."

"You misunderstand. It's not that what I'm doing doesn't make a difference. It's that it does make a difference. The cost comes with considerable benefits."

"Yeah, I can see that," I waved my hands around the office.

"I don't mean to me, that's incidental. I mean to the world."

I glanced at a Van Gogh framed on the wall behind her desk.

"Yeah, clearly incidental."

A muscle in Rosa Galan's jaw twitched.

"Let me show you something."

She waved her hand and a glass panel rose out of the floor. Video footage and still photos arrayed across the screen.

"If this is the photo album from your trip to Ibiza, I'll take a hard pass."

"You really can't stop, can you?"

"No. At the moment, I also don't want to."

"Just try to pay attention."

I spotted the motion-sensing ring on her finger as she waved a photo into the center of the panel. It was of a large tan building with a solar array on the roof. Solar panels speckled the landscape around it as well.

"This is a desalinization plant in Algeria. Do you know what that is?"

"A country in Africa?"

"I meant—"

"Salt water into fresh water, I know, I know."

"Right. This plant took six months to build and cost a quarter what a plant would have cost ten years ago. Many of the innovations that facilitate its existence came from my project."

"The one where you torture ghosts?"

"Algeria as you may or may not know, has been severely hit by the impacts of climate change. The country has been in shifting states of instability for decades. They have enough sunlight for solar power to be a reliable source of electricity. They have people who want a better life for themselves and their children. The primary thing they are lacking is a stable water and food supply, that and shelter from the new record-setting summers they endure. So, my company can now provide them with a water supply, and thanks to automated building construction we plan on having built two million homes by the end of this year. They'll be able to farm again thanks to their new source of water and the new homes we're building will be air conditioned as a matter of necessity. We estimate the level of violence around the capital city has declined 11 percent in the last three years. That's real people not dying, real children not orphaned."

"Why do you care about Algeria?" I asked.

"Why wouldn't I?"

"Seems like a lot of money you're spending on altruism. I am, to say the least, suspicious."

"Astute," she said. "I bought mining rights in several regions of Algeria during the last war. I can't develop those mining operations if the country is too unstable."

"Surprise, surprise."

"Of course I'm turning a profit, Mr. Smith. If I don't profit, there's no next project. And the irresponsibility of the last hundred years has left us with a fair few projects to complete. Yes, I'm finding a way to make money, but I'm still building a better future. As I said, the one thing you and I can agree on is that my project matters."

"You mean the project where you torture ghosts? That's the one you're talking about now? It just gets confusing. There's the Algeria project and the torture ghosts project."

Rosa Galan clenched her teeth.

"You keep saying torture. It's not the only inducement I use."

"What? Are there lollipops?"

"Comforts are easy to come by in digital space. The ghosts who relent to their circumstances enjoy significant privileges. The old adage has proven true, 'a happy workforce is a productive workforce.' They get recreational opportunities, they set their own schedules to an extent, and they socialize."

"Ugh."

"What?"

"I just realized where I've heard this kind of diatribe before."

"Where's that?"

"An African-American history class I took in college. One of the things we talked about was how plantation owners perceived and described their relationship with their slaves."

I could see I'd finally, really pissed off Rosa Galan. She flung herself up out of her chair and flicked her hand. A face appeared on the screen.

"You think they're all innocent victims, the ghosts I copied? Samuel Christian, the former CEO of Intact Mining Corporation. I copied him early on. He had a habit of continuing to use people in his mines in the Third World. Automated technologies are far cheaper and more efficient, but they come with an initial investment. Such an investment would have bit deeply into Mr. Christian's yearly bonus. Six people a week died in one of his mines in Afghanistan. Overall, his various Third World mining interests killed hundreds ... a week.

"After I copied him, I extracted everything I needed to know about Mr. Christian's business. I initiated a hostile takeover, and I knew all their weak spots. I owned the company entirely in months. I automated his mines, and the investment paid for itself in reduced costs in five years. I'm not so concerned about my bonus check, you see. The result of this illegal copy, hundreds of lives saved ... a week."

That one gave me pause. Rosa Galan seemed to notice.

"Tell me does his copy hold equal responsibility for his crimes. My copy certainly seemed to think my memories were hers, so what about him? Do his offences transfer over to his duplicate? He remembers making the choice. He would probably make the same choice again."

"I ..."

I was beginning to feel like I was way out of my depth.

"And that's not all the good that's come out of this project. I've put minds together that never would meet in the real world. Experts that would never collaborate because their companies are competitors. Academics, politicians, and corporate executives working with warlords to brainstorm the best way to roll out a new project in war-torn regions. There is no equivalent to what I've done. If you destroy this project, the good it does will be lost.

"And really," she said, something sinister in her voice. "The harm it's doing is only temporary."

"What?" I asked.

Rosa took her seat again.

"Do you want to know something fascinating about ghosts?"

"No," I said.

She was scaring the hell out of me. Rosa Galan's charisma was intense. Being in the center of her focus was like being in a box full of spiders. I just felt little legs creepy crawling across my skin. More terrifying than that, it didn't seem like her argument was entirely lacking in merit. I had to concede, she might have a point, an evil point, but a point.

"I'm going to tell you anyway."

"I thought you might."

"I wrote a good deal of the code that allows you to exist, Mr. Smith," she said. "So, I know how you work. In order to compress the processing necessary for your neural simulation to exist, I simplified certain aspects of the human mind. Most of them you wouldn't miss. The sections of the brain that regulate heartbeat were easily simplified. It doesn't matter if those sections don't work perfectly. You have no heart, just a vestigial sense of beating.

"But other sections I simplified I've since realized were more important than I gave them credit for. For example, did you know I simplified the parts of the human mind that are reshaped by the experience of pain? I don't mean the basic experience. As you are no doubt aware, you can still feel pain."

"Yes, your digital bounty hunters reminded me of that earlier today."

"My apologies for that. It felt necessary at the time. However, have you been reshaped by the pain you felt?"

"What do you mean?"

"The trauma of the pain. Does it linger with you?"

"Uh, this is all getting real dark."

"It hasn't, because it can't. Humans, when we experience pain, it leaves a mark on us. Indelible, driven into our instincts. That's why a person can't just be expected to get over trauma quickly. 'Getting over it,' is no simple task. If they are slapped, a human will fear the next slap even if the memory of why fades overtime. We are neurologically reshaped by our suffering. Ghosts are not."

I scrambled for a retort. It's hard to be pithy when someone is suggesting you're less than human.

"You can change in different ways," she said. "Your frontal lobe is fully simulated. It is as capable of adapting over time as any human, but your instincts are fixed at the point of copying. The only record of trauma you carry are your memories."

"That's still quite the record, believe me."

"I'm sure, but not a permanent one."

"What?"

"The ghosts you're so concerned with, I'm not going to destroy them when they've served their purpose. I'll just delete their memories. They will not carry with them instinctual scars of any trauma. It will be as if they had just been copied. No permanent harm will be done to the world.

"Since I initiated this project we've developed cures for three different forms of cancer, we've increased efficiency of satellite-based data transfer by six percent, and we're on the verge of another desalinization breakthrough that could further lower its cost. We're less than a year from rolling out a new battery with a 40 percent increase in charge capacity and double the longevity of its next best competitor. This project is changing the world."

Rosa Galan looked out over the city of Seattle.

"Yes, a few ghosts suffer, a few zeros and ones register imaginary pain, but the world, the real world, gets better. It may seem something of a morally ambiguous trade-off, but that's often the case in the real world. Think about how much good that little bit of ambiguity creates. How many lives will be saved. The benefits, Mr. Smith. The benefits to the world.

"For you and your friends, safety. And to make it a little easier, if you stay silent, I will give you, and each of your compatriots, five million dollars."

I've got to admit I was tempted.

"Digital-you is already rich," I said. "She wouldn't take that deal even if I would."

"Leave her to me. I know what she wants."

"And what's that?"

"A controlling voice in this empire. I will give her that."

"You'd be willing to work with yourself? Have you met yourself?"

"It might surprise you to learn that I am not a person who thinks the human condition is perfect. Perhaps ghosts are superior, immune to the lasting effects of trauma, or perhaps you're inferior, unable to instinctually learn from your mistakes and pain. Only time will tell. I'm sure my ghost counterpart thinks I hate her, and for a time, perhaps I did. I've moved on. Maybe one day, it would be fitting for her to inherit. I don't have children. If I did, would they be worthy? I doubt it, but she, I, might be."

The room was silent for a long moment. Rosa Galan turned back to me.

"So, what do you say? Five million dollars and all you have to do is keep quiet, just for a few decades.

"In the near future, AI's capacity at research and development will advance to the point where these ghosts can't compete. At which point, the project will be useless and will end. I'll delete their memories, give them new identities, and release them. I'll even pay for their server space and an Internet connection for a hundred years.

"If it helps you decide, you should know, going public with the story, it won't make a difference. The ghosts are being packed onto trucks as we speak. They're being moved to a facility with no legal connection to my company. You'll never find them. You'll just have wild accusations. It may affect the stock price for a few weeks, maybe months, but it will do no good in the end.

"If you agree to stay silent, you'll get to enjoy the rest of your life in prosperous peace. No more fear, no more running. Yes, you'll have to compromise a little. You'll have to make a difficult moral decision. Some suffering will be endured, but no permanent harm will have been done. The ghosts will eventually get to live the rest of their eternal lives, and this brief interlude of suffering will do so much good for the world."

I felt defeated. I stared at her and blinked.

"Uh," I looked around the room. My non-existent stomach was turning in knots. "I, um, give me a second. Let me think here." I started muttering to myself. "Ghosts on a server suffer, but good for the planet. But are we sacrificing our principles? But maybe the trade-off in humanitarian benefit is worth the temporary compromising of principle? But what if it's not temporary?" I brought my hands up to my face screen. "Ugh, this is what we've always done as a species: give the shitty quality of life to some marginalized subgroup so the rest of society can live the high life. Admittedly this would be short term, or would it? How do we quantify suffering? How much supposed good is one tortured person worth? But this would be so much good. But is it ..."

I stared at the floor's tile pattern. My brain ground to a halt. It felt like my head was getting hot. Lodged in my chest, the CPU in my black box was working overtime trying to process all the moral ramifications of a world's worth of problems.

"Mr. Smith," Rosa Galan said.

She snapped me out of my trance. My head hurt.

"Do you have a reply?"

"Yes," I nodded. "I have a reply. Here's what I think. I am so the wrong person to make this decision."

"Perhaps, but you are the person in a position to make it."

"No."

"I'm sorry?"

"No. You're trying to make it seem like there's a switch and a time limit and we've got to decide, but there is no switch. There's you and me, and a lot of time to bring other people into the decision. You just don't want that to happen because you think you'll go to prison."

"Mr. Smith."

"I don't want to."

"Mr. Smith."

"No. I don't want to. I don't want to have a potentially historical decision fall on my shoulders alone. Making huge decisions alone is ridiculous. There should be experts, and philosophers, people should do studies. Not to mention, we should all hear the perspective from the ghosts you're torturing. This isn't a decision for one person. This is a decision for society. I don't have the right. You don't have the right. People, all the people, should be in on this decision."

"People are generally incompetent."

"Yeah, but we're the general incompetents that have to live with the consequences of your fucking decisions."

"Mr. Smith—"

"This is just a fucking shortcut anyway. There are ten billion people on the planet. Most of whom have never had the chance to make a contribution. You make it sound like there's no other way to solve the world's problems, but you just like this solution because you get to control it. It makes you powerful."

"It may be hard to come to terms with, Mr. Smith, but I am correct."

"You think. You don't know. No. I'm not deciding. And you don't have the right to, either. I'm not helping you." I jabbed an accusatory, metallic finger at her. "You're just going to have to kill me ... wait ... what did I just say?"

Rosa Galan's face had gone stern. She waved her hand and I heard a ding and the sliding of elevator doors.

"Make sure he's never found," she said to someone just over my right shoulder.

I lurched out of my chair and saw Four Hands standing in the elevator car. She smiled like this was a parent-teacher conference.

"Hello, Mr. Smith."

"Wait, were you just standing there in the elevator the entire time?"

"Yes."

"So, you didn't go anywhere? You just stood there?"

"Yes."

"Okay."

I nodded.

"You're going to murder me now?"

"Yes."

"Great."

I glanced around the office.

"How would you feel about giving me a ten-second head start?"

She raised her shoulders in an apologetic shrug.

"If it were just up to me."

"No, sure. I get it. So, I guess I'll just run now?"

"If you insist."

25

COFFEE BREAK

March 3rd, 2064 9:57 p.m. PST

Exits appeared to be few and far between. The center of the top floor was filled by a big boxy column that contained the elevator shaft. It looked big enough to also hold a stairwell, but if there was a door, it wasn't in my view. The displayed art and designer furniture were arrayed across the sandstone-colored floor in an open office plan.

Rosa Galan picked up a tablet from a small table beside her chair.

"Just go quietly, Mr. Smith," she said, as she scrolled.

"Oh, I'm not inconveniencing you, am I?"

I snatched the tablet out of her hand and hurled it at Four Hands. Rosa Galan's face went livid. She clenched her teeth. Four Hands caught the tablet as if I'd underhanded it to her.

"Mr. Smith, let's not get nasty," Four Hands said.

She started toward me. I scrambled away dodging behind one of the freestanding walls that displayed a piece of art.

"Get him," Rosa Galan ordered.

"Mr. Smith, don't run," Four Hands said. "I don't want to have to chase you."

"I'm going to have to insist on running."

"Please. I'm not wearing any antiperspirant, and I have an anxiety about pit stains."

"Pit stains?" I said.

"Yes. A boy teased me about it in middle school."

"Let me guess, you murdered him?"

"How did you know? I never told anyone that."

"You are a deeply unsettling person."

"Mr. Smith, that seems needlessly antagonistic."

I rolled away from the table angling to the left of the column, hoping a door to a stairwell would appear. Four Hands, nearer the center of the office, took a few steps to keep herself between me and the column.

"Mr. Smith, I appreciate your desire to continue living. I'm afraid that's just not an option at this juncture."

"Fuck you."

I rolled again continuing around the left side of the column. I stopped 90 degrees around the pillar from where I'd started. A small fountain with a fish pond was in between me and Four Hands.

"Just get him," Rosa Galan said.

Four Hands shrugged and started for me. She stepped right through the fish pond. I dodged backward as she approached. I grabbed for something to throw. A pillow from a nearby chair was the closest thing to hand. I threw it. Not surprisingly, it didn't stop my assassin. I rolled back the way I'd come and tried to leap over the chaise lounge. I caught my wheel and flopped forward. Four Hands strode after me, her left foot making a soggy squelch sound as she walked. I staggered to my wheels and grabbed a bowl full of decorative marbles on a nearby coffee table. I hurled it at her. My upper body strength being rivaled by a particularly buff rooster, it didn't go far. It fell to the ground and shattered, scattering thousands of marbles across the floor between us. Four Hands stepped after me and trod on a half dozen little orbs. She just caught herself before she tumbled to the ground.

"Hah," I said.

"This is ridiculous. Get him," Rosa Galan said.

"Good luck with that," I said, confident in my marble obstruction.

Four Hands smiled and slid her feet across the floor knocking the marbles aside. It looked like she was a kid pretending to ice skate, but it worked.

"Shit," I said, as I dodged back.

I grabbed Monet's *Water Lilies* off the wall and spun around.

"I'll smash it," I said.

Four Hands paused and smiled indulgently.

"Mr. Smith there are tens of billions of dollars on the line. You threatening to smash that painting won't stop me."

I gasped.

"It's a Monet, you monster."

I set it down gently and kept fleeing.

"This is getting undignified," Rosa Galan said.

"Well, heaven forbid," I said, as I rolled around the column to the right. "We all know the worst thing that could happen here is things get undignified."

"Just get him out of here," Rosa Galan said. "Go, go quickly. Run. Just ... corner him. Use something. Knock him off his feet then ... just get him, God damn it."

"Are you micromanaging my murder?" I shouted.

Four Hands seemed a little embarrassed by how long this was taking. She started after me at a brisk jog. Her one wet foot on the smooth ground caused her to slip a few times, still, she was now moving well above my top speed. I pressed my little motor trying to get around the column looking for a door. I saw it. It was a wooden door with a stairwell sign beside it.

"He's heading for the stairs," Rosa Galan said. "Get him."

I rolled forward with all the might my little motor could muster. I reached the door and pried at it. It was locked. Beside the door was a thumbprint scanner.

"Hey," I said. "That's a fire hazard."

Four Hands was right there. I abandoned the attempt and launched myself over a waist-high decorative book-shelf, sending a probably very expensive sculpture crashing to the ground. There was a long table in front of me. On my hands and knees, I scrambled forward and popped up on the other side. Four Hands paused for a moment. I watched her every twitch.

Out of the corner of my eye I saw a glass door on the outside window of the office. Just beyond it a helipad jutted off the side of the building. I wondered if I could get a signal out there and call for help. The problem was, I'd have seconds before Four Hands caught up with me. Not enough time to call for help, definitely not enough time for help to answer. It might be enough time to upload the recording of my conversation with Rosa Galan.

Four Hands was winded. She looked down at her body, consternation on her face.

"Now I'm sweating."

"Oh, who cares?" I said.

"I do, it makes me self-conscious."

"Well, in that case you smell like shit."

"Mr. Smith!"

She sounded really hurt.

"Oh, uh, I'm sorry. Maybe I took things a little too far."

"I forgive you," she said. "No reason we can't be cordial."

She lunged around the table at me. I whirred away in the direction of the helipad door. Four Hands sprang up onto the table and ran down it, knocking aside a series of expensive vases full of exotic flowers like they were the littler kids on the playground. She was gaining fast.

"Mr. Smith," she said, as she saw where I was headed. "The building's signal jamming extends to the helipad. If you go out there, you'll just risk giving me a cold."

"Good," I said. "I hope you get pneumonia."

"Mr. Smith, there's no reason to be so rude."

"Stop doing that," I said, dodging around a chess board, hitting it, and sending pieces flying.

"What?"

"Being polite."

"It's nice to be polite."

"No, it's not. Not when you're murdering someone. Being polite when you're murdering someone is just creepy."

The helipad door loomed in front of me. I swiveled my head 180 degrees. If I'd had muscles, they all would have seized. She was right there. She'd caught me. Four Hands lunged forward. She grabbed me around the waist, and my wheels squeaked as they lost purchase on the polymer coated floor. I was lifted, fell forward, and together we clattered to the ground. I looked forward. The helipad doors were just ahead. I reached out a hand and a motion sensor above the door triggered it to open.

"Oh no," I said.

It was just the first of two doors. Beyond the tinted, privacy glass doors I'd opened were another set. They were green like the exterior pyramid. I could see a motion sensor above them. I reached my hand forward. It didn't activate. It was too far. Four Hands dragged me back. The inner doors shut. She pinned me to the ground.

"Don't unplug him yet," Rosa Galan said.

I could hear her approaching footsteps.

"You managed to make quite a mess," she said.

"My apologies," Four Hands said. "He is surprisingly wily."

Rosa Galan knelt down beside me. I swiveled my screen to look at her. There wasn't any triumph. She wasn't happy to see me defeated. She looked like someone who had finally swatted a mosquito, but felt a little embarrassed about how long it had taken.

"You may have suspected that my original offer wasn't sincere," she said. "I was never going to let your friends wander around the world with such compromising information about me, even if you had taken the money. When your accomplices came out of the woodwork they were all going to be dealt with."

I hadn't suspected that, but it made sense. In fact, I felt a little silly that I hadn't put that together.

"Yeah, I knew you were lying," I said.

"There is a real offer, one where you survive this. Some of your friends might make it as well, maybe all of them, in some form. If you help me find your friends, I will confine you with the other ghosts. No torture, just confinement. I can make sure it's comfortable. Entertainment software is cheap. It will last until the project is completed. It shouldn't be more than two decades. Then I'll delete your memories. The same offer goes for the digital version of Abigail Page, Sanav Maji, and hell, even my own ghost counterpart. The biological Abigail Page will have to die, as will Elisabetta Aliyev, but I could arrange to have her copied beforehand. You'd all have the opportunity to survive in some form. All you have to do is help me find them."

"I know you don't mean to," I said. "But, brutal honesty here, you sound evil. Like, I've got a friend who habitually threatens to murder the CEO of a coffee company, and you're definitely more evil than she pretends to be. I mean, I think she's pretending. I'm pretty sure. She's almost certainly joking, but even if she wasn't, which she is ... I think ... pretty sure ... anyway, you sound more evil than her."

"It's easy to label things evil when you don't have to make difficult decisions. When you have real power, you have to get comfortable with ambiguity."

"That sounds like a great argument for no single person to have real power."

Rosa Galan sighed.

"Are you really going to die for them?"

"I really don't want to. I really can't express how much I don't want to, but you're not giving me a lot of choice here. Do what you gotta do, asshole."

I swiveled my screen away. I looked through the glass windows at the night sky. Crushed to the floor as I was, the city was hidden from sight. The night sky just looked like a pitch-black void through two layers of colored glass. A little twinkle of light caught my eye. It was coming closer. It was coming closer very fast.

"I guess unplug him," Rosa Galan said.

"Certainly," Four Hands replied.

"Wait," I said.

"What?"

"If I betrayed everyone I love and agreed to be incarcerated for two decades and had my memory wiped, could I still get the five million dollars?"

"Yes," Rosa Galan said.

"Hmm, let me think for moment."

I peeked out the double set of doors. The little twinkle of light was incoming fast. It did not look like it was planning to land.

"You know, I've had a change of heart," I said. "Death really lends perspective. Fuck morality, you know, just fuck it."

"I wouldn't put it that way," Rosa Galan said. "But the world is more complicated than people tend to give it credit for."

"Right that, whatever. Difficult choices, sometimes a little stabby, stabby has got to happen. Who among us hasn't? Let he that has not sinned cast the first stone. People in glass houses—"

I hurled myself forward against Four Hands. My total lack of strength meant I only moved a few inches, but it was enough. My hand triggered the motion detector on the inner-most doors. The doors made out of the thick bullet proof layer of glass slid open. I looked up. The twinkle had become a drone, a branded drone, and it was not slowing down.

Rosa Galan and her henchwoman looked up.

"Oh dear."

"Oh fuck."

They said in unison.

26

EXISTENTIAL

During my brief career in college, I took a history class about the first half of the 21st century. Automation always seemed to sneak up on humanity during that time. Which was really humanity's fault. It's a little like getting snuck up on by a glacier. Hubris seemed to account for most of homo sapiens' obliviousness.

"No robot could ever replace MY job," said the dwindling workforce, as their recently laid-off colleagues packed up their offices.

It seemed to stem from people not understanding what automation was. Most people seemed to think it was a robot coming into their work, slapping the files out of their hands, breakdancing its way through their old tasks, being way funnier around the water cooler, and bringing dynamite stuffed jalapeños to the company picnic. Anything less than a robot that could do that, and people would convince themselves their jobs would be fine. Basic math was ignored.

Let's do a word problem. If a computer or a robot can do one-third of your job, and it can do one-third of two of your colleague's jobs, that leaves each of you with only two thirds the amount of work. Great, right? Unfortunately, your boss is an asshole, so they take the two-thirds of one of your colleague's jobs, split it between you and your other colleague, and fire the now useless employee. With one less salary to pay, your boss uses the extra profit and goes on vacation to Monaco. Given these factors, how fucked is your future job security?

This is automation. No jobs are entirely replaced, at least not all at once. The work is reshuffled so that the percentage of it done by machines goes up, and the number of people necessary to do it goes down. Reshuffled and reshuffled and reshuffled, and after a few laborious decades, humans aren't looking so vital. And thus, humanity was snuck up on by a glacier.

It wouldn't have been such a problem if it weren't for the fact that salary was the way society made sure everybody got their basic needs met. It's fine though. Societies where the general population don't have their basic needs met do great historically.

In the end things worked out, you know, after a few riots. Social policies ensured the basics to everyone. The work necessary to make sure everyone got what they needed was easier to do than ever with it all being automated.

The real problems weren't getting basic resources to people. The real problems were two-fold. One of them was a deeper, philosophical crisis, especially for work-oriented societies like the United States. Who are we if not what we do for work? An answerable question, but one that takes more than a long afternoon and a bottle of Chablis to tangle with. If a group of people get their sense of self-worth from something, then that thing is taken away, people get a little ... unmoored.

Ever been at a party and someone gets a little too drunk and starts asking pressing existential questions? It really throws a monkey wrench into trying to get turnt. Imagine what it was like when an entire nation started asking existential questions. They really should have front-loaded some of that philosophical work before things got too dire. You know how it is though, what percentage of people ever did their homework ahead of time?

The other problem was a lot more menacing. You know the people that owned all the automated systems that did all the work? They needed other people less, and less, and less. The kind of people that claw their way to the top of economic systems also tend to be people who measure their fellow humans' worth based on the work they do. Beware such a person who discovers the economy doesn't need people to work anymore. To such a person, working people are superfluous.

27

DROPS

The drone hit the outside doors at full speed, and they shattered inward. Four Hands released me just in time to throw up all four hands to shield herself. The drone caught Rosa Galan with a glancing blow, and slammed into Four Hands' shielded face.

I sprang to my feet.

"Your coffee has been delivered," the drone said in a cheerful tone.

'Flooffee' was stenciled across its body. Affixed to its back end with masking tape was not the kind of wakeup call it usually delivered. It was a long cylinder with metal studs running the length of it. I ripped it off the back of the drone's body. Four Hands sat up. She looked dazed. Her tongue traced the line of her teeth.

"It would theem that drone knocked out my two front teef," she said.

She wasn't wrong. I swung my new implement. Even dazed, Four Hands caught it easily. Her gaze wandered to the object. Her eyes widened with recognition just as I pressed the activation button on the stun gun baseball bat.

"Yeouch!"

She flopped back to the ground. I spun to face Rosa Galan. She was nursing her left arm with her right. Based on her expression, I suspected she wasn't happy with me.

"I am going to run you through a garbage disposal."

My suspicions were correct. I waved the bat in front of me.

"So, it's been fun," I said. "But I'm going to leave now."

"You can't possibly think you're getting out of this building."

I pressed the activation button on the bat. The electrodes crackled.

"Yes, very intimidating, except I'm 50 years old, and I can outrun you," she said. She looked up. "Computer, I don't want to be disturbed. Shut down my private elevator."

"Private elevator shut down," a sing-song voice responded.

"There are only two exits off this floor. That elevator and the stairs. You're trapped."

"My friends know I'm here. They'll send the FBI."

I gestured to the drone.

"I have private security on-site. Unless the FBI has one hell of a warrant, which they won't, they'll stay outside. I also have a legion of lawyers quite happy to deny any suggestion that you were ever here."

I rolled back a few feet.

"Holy crap," I said. "You just always have this much power all the time? No wonder you're a murderous megalomaniac. This is not good for your mental health. Really,

I'm concerned for you. When was the last time you took a vacation?"

"How do you manage to never stop rambl—... just shut the fuck up and die."

A groan rose from the floor. Four Hands stirred. I rolled back a few more feet brandishing the bat. The assassin sat up. Her jacket was splayed away from her sides and her metallic hands were twitching and clicking under the fabric. The charge had fried something in their controls. It was like nightmare jazz hands.

"My head hurtth," she said.

"Never mind your head. Just get him and stop with the soft touch. I am out of patience."

Four Hands nodded as she got to her feet.

"Yeth, Mth. Galan."

She lunged to the side. I swung the bat and pressed the activation button. She dodged back as it crackled. I wheeled backwards again, and the inner doors to the helipad activated. They slid open behind me. Four Hands picked up a chair and approached again. I rolled back and bumped into the outer door. It had jammed shut from the impact, but one of its glass panes had shattered where the drone had punched through. I ducked and shimmied backward. Knocking a few shards of glass from the frame, I retreated out into the night.

It had stopped raining, but the helipad was still slick with water. The streets below were filled with the soft sounds of electric car motors and no honking. I rolled out onto the round pad marked with a big 'H.' I kept the baseball bat in front of me. Four Hands dropped the chair as she discovered it wouldn't fit through the shattered doorframe.

"What'th your plan exactly?" she asked.

"I've got a plan. I'm a born planner."

"Are you?"

"I've survived this long haven't I?"

"You know luck and planth aren't the thame thing?"

"They look the same from the outside."

I glanced down at the city below. It was a dizzying sight. A hundred floors of open air ended with glistening concrete.

I spotted something. My eyes widened. I had forgotten about the balconies. Three stories below the helipad was the first balcony. It stuck ten feet out of the side of the building. Several stories below it was the next balcony aligned with the other edge. It looked like someone had designed the building to have handholds for a giant.

Four Hands had already pushed me too far out onto the helipad. I needed to get past her. Her jacket was still splayed out from her sides. It was writhing and twitching as the hands beneath refused to calm. I needed to get just a little bit closer to the building.

"Alright, I surrender," I said. "I'll take the money. I'll tell you where my friends are."

She shook her head.

"Mr. Thmith, I don't beliefe you."

"Yeah, I'm a terrible liar."

"I'fe gained too much rethpect for you to beliefe you would thell your friendth out in that manner."

"Shit, really?"

"Yeth."

"Score one against having integrity, I guess."

I lunged forward with the stun gun bat. Four Hands dodged back. She wrapped her arm in the cloth of her long, tan jacket and smacked the bat to the side. I pulled it back before she could yank it out of my hands. Lurching away, I noticed I was standing on the 'H.' I was rapidly running out of helipad. I kept the bat aloft.

The two of us were caught in a stalemate. Okay, it wasn't really a stalemate. It was more like forced checkmate that hadn't quite reached checkmate yet. I kept rolling back through a puddle that covered the outside half of the pad. Then I reached a metal grating that formed the exterior ring of the helipad. My wheels bumped up against a small barrier about three inches tall. Beyond that was open air. I'd run out of space. I glanced around hoping to see another drone waiting to swoop in and save me. Nope. I looked at Four Hands.

"There's really only one thing I can think to say."

"I'm exthited to hear it."

"Your foot's all wet."

I flipped the activation switch on the bat. It crackled to life. I dropped it and spun to dodge to the left. The bat fell. Four Hands looked down and saw the puddle of water around her feet. On instinct, she hurled herself backwards. The bat hit the water flashed, popped, and died. It wasn't as spectacular as I'd hoped, but the half-second's worth of distraction was enough. Dodging narrowly to the left of my would-be murderer, I rolled toward the building. The bat's pop and electrical flash seemed to have disoriented Four Hands for a moment. She blinked and saw me zipping past. She lunged and missed, but she found her footing fast. Another better aimed tackle was incoming.

"Shit."

I jumped off the side of the walkway between the helipad and the building. It was at this point, already falling through the air, that I realized how far down the first balcony was. Three floors, 60 feet, metal frame or not, I might have just killed myself.

"Aaaah."

My wheels hit the balcony floor and lost traction as the rest of me followed. I flopped forward and caught myself with my arms. I heard a stomach-turning ping of sheering metal. I'd broken something.

I sprang to my feet and lifted my arms. One of my hands was lolling to the side, held on only by a few wires. The metal frame had snapped.

"Aaaah, oh no. It hurts."

The hand lolled as I clutched the wrist.

"Wait, I don't have nerve endings," I said.

I shook sense back into my mind. Running for your life gets confusing.

I looked up at the platform above. Four Hands looked begrudgingly impressed. She smiled at me like I'd just shown real improvement in my math worksheets and sprinted inside. She was coming to get me.

The door of the balcony wasn't locked. I heaved. It barely opened enough for me to wriggle through. So close to the top, the offices on this floor were massive. Money was splashed around only slightly less extravagantly then Rosa Galan's office. It was interior design meant to convey the message, 'You did it, kid. You've finally made it to the top,' to people gullible enough to believe that while they worked beneath their boss's colossal green pyramid.

I saw a sign indicating the elevators were down the hall, but I didn't dart for them. The ground floor would have security waiting. Besides Rosa Galan could have the elevators shut down with me inside them. To escape I needed help.

The offices looked like terrariums walled in glass. Each glass door had an AR notification revealing the office occupant's name and title. I was standing next to the office of Douglas Cho, Director of Nanomechanical Tertiary Adaptable System Kinetics. Douglas' job title lost me halfway through. The phone on his desk kept my attention. The building's signal jamming was blocking me calling for help. Douglas' company phone likely wouldn't have that problem.

I didn't have much time. A yank of the handle revealed the office door was locked. I looked at the massive pane of glass that formed the wall. I was already trespassing. Why not add vandalism? I looked around for something heavy. My eyes found a fire extinguisher. Next to it, framed in a metal box with a glass cover, was a red fire ax. 'Opening box will trigger alarm' was emblazoned across the transparent barrier. I could live with that. I reached forward.

Somewhere deep in the recesses of the floor, it sounded. The single most terrifying sound I'd ever heard. The soft 'ting' of an arriving elevator.

I flung open the box and a screeching alarm went off. I hefted the ax with all the grace of a one-armed delivery robot. I was not going to be able to swing this well. I spun on my wheels like a tornado of poorly-wielded weaponry. I lurched toward the glass and the ax impacted. The glass shattered, and the ax bucked out of my grip. I dove through remnants of the wall and snatched the office phone receiver off the desk. Pushing my poor motor to its limits, I rolled out into the hall.

There she was. Four Hands was standing at the far end of the hallway. She was breathing heavily and smiling.

"Hello, Mr. Thmith," she said.

"Oh ... hello," I said.

We both started moving in the same instant. I rushed for the balcony door. She sprinted down the hall. I shoved the door open and spun around. It was a long hallway but, unfettered from her anxiety over pit stains, Four Hands could run. Next to the door was a square planter box with a four-foot-tall hedge in it. I could pull it over and try to barricade the door. I reached up to press the door shut. It had one of those slow-close hydraulic systems on it.

"You've got to be kidding me," I shouted.

Four Hands was seconds away.

"Close, close."

The door shut, and I yanked the top of the tree. Thank physics for leverage, my tiny body weight yanking at the top of the tree was enough to overturn the fat square pot. It toppled with a clump just as Four Hands reached the other side of the door. She slammed into it, but the door, heavy and barricaded, didn't move.

"Hah," I said. "Good luck with that. Maybe if you knock, I'll let you out here. How's that for being polite?"

Four Hands shrugged and knocked. I was flabbergasted.

"No. I was joking. I'm not going to help you murder me because you ask nicely."

She shrugged again.

"It wath worth a try."

I looked at Douglas' phone. It was a pane of glass with a small projector that displayed numbers across its surface. I typed in Izy's phone number. She picked up on the first ring.

"Romeo? Are you okay? You are on speaker."

I heard a crack and looked up. Four Hands had found the fire ax.

"Oh no."

She swung again and put another crack in the door. The exterior glass seemed to be of much stronger material than the interior, but Four Hands looked determined. She swung again.

"Am I going to die by ax murder?" I said. "Is that how I go out? It never occurred to me I would die this way."

"Romeo, you're not making any sense," Abi said.

"No, you're not making any sense."

"What?"

"I'm sorry, I'm under a lot of strain. I'm on a balcony outside the EternityNet building, and Four Hands is just inside. I've barricaded the door with a pot, but she's got a fire ax."

"Shit," Sanav said.

"Yeah," I said.

"We've called the FBI," Abi said. "But I'm not sure they believe us that you were in the building."

"Yeah, that tracks. Don't believe the person asking for help, but believe the giant multinational corporation. They've never done anything wrong."

"What's going on with the ghosts?" Mariela said. "Did you find them?"

"They're being loaded onto trucks and moved to a secure location," I said. "I don't know where. Now focus your attention on my not getting murdered."

There was now a basketball-sized hole in the door. Four Hands was still swinging.

"My apologies," Mariela said. "Izy is trying to prep another Flooffee drone to come and help. Did the last one work?"

"Yes, but I lost the stun gun bat. How did you guys hack that drone?"

"One of my former clients traffics in software designed to steal drones," Sanav said. "He and Izy did it together."

"Thanks, it saved my life."

"You're welcome."

"You have to buy me a new stun gun bat," Izy said.

Whack. There was now a tennis-racket sized hole in the door.

"If you get me out of this alive, I will buy you a stun gun bazooka."

"Doesn't exist," Izy said. "But there is a net launcher with electrodes in the net."

"Deal."

"We can send you another drone in about ten minutes," Izy said. "But I have no weapon to send with it. Maybe hot coffee. You could throw it."

"I'll be in a dozen pieces by then, but I'm sure it will be some consolation to know my murderer will be well-caffeinated."

Whack.

"Mithter Thmith," Four Hands said. "You're interfering with my work. Pleathe open the door."

"Go away."

"We could just call the cops," Sanav said.

"The FBI isn't willing to piss off Rosa Galan," Abi said. "You think local cops are going to storm into the building."

"Wouldn't matter," I shouted. "I'm about to die. Like immediately."

"Well, you're just going to have to figure this one out for yourself," Mariela said.

"Great."

Whack. Four Hands had shed her jacket. Now her twitching hands were on full display.

I looked around the balcony. There was a hedge along the left side and three metal chairs around a tiny, circular table. I rolled toward the edge of the balcony and glanced over the edge. Three stories down, across a ten-foot gap, was another balcony. I looked back at the door. Four Hands had created enough of a gap that she had opted to squeeze through it. Her twitching and jerking second set of hands were catching her, but not for long.

I climbed onto the hedge.

"This was a bad idea the first time," I said.

"Mithter Thmith, don't."

I didn't want to look. I put everything my mechanical frame had into launching myself forward into empty space. I looked down.

"Hedge!"

I landed in the next balcony down's hedge. Tangled in its branches, it took me a moment to find my feet. I looked down at my body. There was some greenery stuffed in intimate places, but it didn't look like anything was broken. I scrambled out of my shock-absorbing shrubbery.

"Hedge," I repeated.

"Uh."

I looked up. A man in a business hoodie was vaping on the balcony.

"Hi," I said.

"Hi."

I looked up at the balcony above. Four Hands was looking down at me, bemused frustration on her face.

"We're not going to do thith all the way down are we, Mithter Thmith?"

"I sincerely hope not."

She ran back toward the balcony entrance.

"Hey, I'm not sure you're supposed to be here," the guy on the balcony said.

I rounded on him.

"Oh yeah? You're not sure? Really? Something about this situation seems off to you? Really? Go figure. What's your name?"

He hesitated.

"Jerry. Are you a ghost?"

"Astute, Jerry. Very astute. Jerry, Jerbear, can I call you Jerbear?"

"Uh—"

"Look at this situation. You think there's a chance that this might be above your pay grade?"

"Uh, y-yeah I guess."

"Then shut the fuck up, Jerry."

"Hey."

"I'm sorry, I'm so sorry. I'm not normally like this. It's just that your boss is trying to murder me."

"What?"

"I take it back, I'm not sorry. Shut the fuck up, Jerry."

I brought the phone back to my ear.

"I have bought myself like two minutes. Three, if people called all the elevators to other floors. Tell me you've got a way for me to get out of this building, because I don't want to have to keep aiming for hedges."

"What?"

"What do I do?"

"Get out of the building," Mariela said.

"If I use the elevator, they'll just shut it down with me in it."

"Then use the stairs."

"The stairs," I slapped my screen where my forehead would be. "I forgot about the stairs because of the thumbprint scanner."

"What?"

"Doesn't matter."

I rolled to the balcony door and tried to pry it open. With one hand, I couldn't hold the phone and get enough leverage on the door. After ten precious seconds of struggle, I sighed and turned around.

"Jerry, uh, hi. Sorry about yelling at you before. Could you open this door for me?"

Jerry sat back in his chair and blew out his cheeks.

"I guess."

He did not leap out of his chair to my aid. Jerry was one of those people. He could see the urgency, he could also see that gave him power in this moment. Given power, Jerry seemed inclined to abuse it.

"Jerry," I said. "It's really urgent that I get through this door right now."

"Well, you know, like you said, this might be above my pay grade."

"Jerry, you are literally killing me here."

"You mean figuratively."

"Do I?"

"Look man, maybe you should think about how you talk to people."

"Mm-hm mm-hm, that's fair criticism, Jerry. I have learned an important lesson here today. Now, please, pretty please, open the fuuckhhing door. Please."

"Well look man, let me just finish vaping and I'll help you out."

It took all the strength I had just to stay silent.

"What's the problem," Mariela said.

"I can't get through the balcony door, and the guy here doesn't want to help me."

"Give him the phone," Abi said.

"What?"

"Just let me talk to him for a moment."

I handed Jerry the phone.

"A friend of mine wants to talk to you."

He raised an eyebrow, but took the phone.

"Yeah," he said.

There was a pause.

"Yeah," he said.

Jerry's face went pale. He swallowed.

"Um."

He sat up straight in his chair.

"Yeah, sorry. Really, really sorry."

Jerry stood and opened the balcony door. He handed me the phone.

"I'm super sorry."

"Uh, no problem."

I put the phone to my ear as I rolled through the door.

"Don't ever tell me what you told him," I said.

"Yeah, you couldn't stomach it," Abi said.

"You're a terrifying person," Sanav said.

"Aw, thanks."

"Yes," Izy said. "The imagery, very vivid. And how you integrated his mother into it without it feeling like you were disrespecting her. Very impressive."

"Well, you know. I've had practice."

I started rolling down the hall.

"The stairs will get me down a few floors, but how do I get out of this building? If I stay in the stairwell too long eventually the guards will spot me on the security cameras."

"You'll just have to—"

The phone crackled. I stopped and spun around. I had ventured too far from the receiver. I rolled back.

"Romeo?"

"I'm here," I said. "The phone I'm on is too far from its receiver. I can't ..."

Ding. An elevator had arrived.

"She's here," I said.

Far off down the hallway and around a bend, there was the soft clatter of elevator doors opening.

"What? Who's there?"

Ten feet ahead of me the hallway had a branch to the left. Halfway down was another branch. An AR notification indicated the elevators were down that hall. Beyond that it went straight until cornering on the other side of the building. There was the patter of approaching feet.

"I'm going to have to call you back," I said.

I didn't bother killing the line before I rolled forward and dodged around the near corner. The lights in this side hallway had been turned off. My face screen would stand out like a target in the dark. I switched it off. Patter, patter, patter. The whine of servos and clacking of metallic fingers drew closer.

The offices on this floor had a distinct middle-management feel. They were almost gaudy and almost not sad. The full glass walls had been forgone for large windows starting at waist height. They still kind of looked like hominid habitats. I tried a door. It was locked. I kept rolling down the hall.

Four Hands' approaching footsteps were getting insistent.

I tried another door. It opened. Somebody had left their office unlocked. I slid through the door and didn't quite shut it. One-handed and still clutching the dead office phone, I wasn't sure I could close it silently. Four Hands stopped for a moment. She'd reached the turn I'd taken. There were a few more footsteps. The whirring of high wind filled the halls.

"Have you theen a delifery robot?"

"Uh, yeah," Jerry said. "There was a ghost in it. Is that a fire ax?"

"Yeth. I apprethiate thith might all theem fery unuthual. Did you thee where he went?"

"Yeah, he went through that door."

"He didn't jump down to the balcony theveral floorth below?"

"No."

"Did you thee where he went once inthide?"

"No. I've ... kind of been reevaluating my life for the last 30 seconds or so."

"Oh."

"I think I'm going to call my mom."

"Well that thounds nithe. Have a nithe day."

"Yeah."

The rushing sound of wind died with a thump.

"Mithter Thmith? I know you're thtill around here. You couldn't hafe gotten far."

"Dammit Jerry, you couldn't have just said I leapt to my death," I hissed.

I crouched low and dropped the phone handset on the ground. It was useless anyway. With my one good hand, I closed the door ever so gently and pressed the little button on the handle to lock it. I heard the rattle of a door being tried just down the hall. The desk in this office was glass-topped and see-through. Behind it was a desk chair. There was a cabinet on the left wall with a set of AR goggles and an activation pod for a holographic digital assistant. What the room was lacking was any good hiding spots. I flopped and lay flat against the wall underneath the office's big window. The office on the other side of the hall had an exterior window. Dim white light from the streetlights below passed through it, crossed the hall, and projected itself on the opposite wall from me. I watched the square of dim white light.

The shadow of Four Hands appeared. She turned and I could see the twitching spider legs of her short-circuiting hands. The distinctive silhouette of her fire ax came into sharp relief looming above me. She moved. The handle on the office door rattled. There was a long silence. It was really long. I mean absurdly long. I felt like I could have restarted civilization from scratch in the time of that silence. Single-celled life forms became multi-cellular. Solar systems were created and destroyed. Universes died the entropic death of total energy dissipation in those few seconds of silence.

Another rattle from further down the hall. Relief washed over me. She had moved past. I got to live ... for like another five minutes ... maybe.

"Hello," Four Hands said.

She was muffled by the door. I turned my external microphone up.

"Yeth, thith is Mth Galan'th personal thecurity guard. Yeth. Oh? Hmm, there mutht be thomething wrong with your phone. Thingth thound fine on my end. Yeth. We have a malfunctioning delivery robot in the building. Yeth. We beliefe it may have been programmed to do thome kind of corporate ethpionage. It may have altho been programmed to claim it ith a ghotht in a delifery-robot body. Yeth. I want thomeone watching the elefator thecurity camth. If a delifery robot boardth an elevator, thut down the elefator and contact me. If a robot ith thpotted taking the thtairth contact me, and I'll interthept it. No. Betht I find it. It may hafe thome fery thenthitife company fileth. Yeth, you can reach me at thith number. Good. Wait. Thend thomeone with a mathter key to floor 104. Good."

I turned my external speakers off.

"Shit, fuck, fuck, shit. I sincerely hope in this moment a meteor just fucking turns this entire planet into one giant lifeless dust storm. I hope the crust of the Earth splits open and the iron core pours out and turns us into a statuary of cast iron jackasses. I hope the sun belches a solar flare so big it cracks the Earth like a whip and sends us careening into that little red storm on Jupiter. Fuck. Fuck!"

I turned my external speakers back on.

I looked around the room again. There was nothing that would help. It was just a desk, a cabinet, some paintings, four walls, and a central air grate the size of a cell phone.

I had one exit, back into the hall. I would have to sneak past Four Hands. I wondered how far down the hall she'd wandered. I couldn't hear her anymore. She was either far away or waiting to ax me the moment I popped my head out the door. I eased myself off the floor and peeked through the office window. She wasn't visible. I turned my microphone to max and listened. Far off down the hall I thought I heard the soft tap of a footfall. She was still moving away. I reached my hand out, pressed my finger to the door's button lock, and turned the handle. The lock popped out. The sound was muffled by my finger. Four Hands probably hadn't heard it.

My microphone turned on max definitely did. It was like a gunshot had gone off. I flinched and stifled a curse. I dialed the microphone back to normal levels. Managing settings can be a real ordeal.

I glanced down the list of options. On a whim, I turned my heartbeat back on. It felt like my heart was trying to burst out of my nonexistent chest cavity.

"Well that doesn't sound healthy," I whispered.

I switched it back off.

"Okay," I whispered. "You got this. Just peek out, and she'll be gone. Probably. Camera's on the top of your screen. All you've got to do is edge it out ... and be ready to pull it back in if you see an ax blade swinging at it ... and be ready to shut and lock the door instantly ... and then prepare yourself to die as Four Hands hacks through this door, so she can dismantle you and drop you in the Puget Sound," I gulped. "That's all you got to do."

My fingers clicked softly against the handle. I turned it. There was the soft scrape of metal on metal. I inched it open just enough so that I could turn my head screen sideways and inch the camera on top into the hall. Four Hands was there. Her back was to me. The second set of hands were beckoning her surroundings closer. The assassin was still trying doors as she walked down the hall. She didn't know about the sticky door or about my exchange with Jerry. For all she knew I'd had a couple of minutes on this floor to find a hiding spot. I could be anywhere. She was approaching the far end of the hall. It ended in a right turn that continued along the far side of the building.

My head was humming with questions. Do I run now? Do I wait? What if I wait too long and Four Hands rounds the entire building and catches me going the other way? What if she turns around the moment I step into the hall? If I slipped away, where should I go in the building? Was Izy okay? Was Abigail okay? Did that guy end up joining Church of Latter-Day Accountants? Did Mr. Phillips ever find the porn? Is there a purpose to life or are we just whiling away the time between now and oblivion? I really needed to focus.

I had to get off this floor. If I did, I would have some time to call for help. Mariela Galan or somebody else would know what to do. Maybe I could call the FBI myself and convince them to come and save me. If I waited here, that master key would show up and my discovery would be inevitable.

Four Hands had reached the far end of the hall. I ducked back into the office and tried to calm myself. It didn't work. I stayed panicked. I peeked out again. She was gone around the corner. I wheeled out into the hall slowly. I didn't want my little motor to give off too much noise. It was a battle of impulses staying silent while desperately wanting to run. It was like holding a really full bowl of really hot soup and needing to scratch your noise. I inched toward the bend in the hallway. As I rounded it, I revved into higher speed.

I was on the other side of the building from Four Hands. Relief got a short two-second victory parade before the rainstorm of everything else about my current situation brought the celebration to a close.

My motor's whine put a limit on my speed. I didn't know how far the little hum would go down the empty halls. I reached the central hall and peeked down it. Just as I looked, Four Hands appeared. I ducked back. The woman was like an ambush predator, always where I least suspected. She was still hefting her ax with an eagerness that was thoroughly unnerving.

I peeked again. She had moved on, continuing her murderous circumnavigation of the building. I had maybe three minutes before she looped back around. The elevators were visible halfway down the hall. The hall was lined with windows offering views of darkened conference rooms and offices. One room was alight. A woman was standing in the middle of the room wearing an AR headset. She was gesturing and talking as if she were surrounded by people. In digital space she probably was. In real life I could roll by unimpeded.

The elevators were framed in blue-tinted metal. A large digital notice hovered in front of them. I selected it and was notified that the nearest elevator was fifteen floors down and heading away. Beside the elevator, a glass door framed in wood showed a stairwell. I couldn't see any security cameras through the door. A thought crashed through the ceiling of my mind. If I could smash some of the security cameras in the stairwell fast enough, I might be able to go to one of the floors in the blind spot before Four Hands could come and find me. I'd go from being somewhere on this floor to somewhere on several floors. That could buy me time.

That seemed like a good idea, but was it? How long did it take to smash security cameras? I knew I should have committed more crimes as a child. These are the vital skills you learn being a menace to society. I needed a tool. There had to be some implement in the vicinity capable of turning a security camera into a pile of plastic and metal confetti. Just down the hall from the elevators was a door marked, 'Maintenance Services.'

It was tan wood and windowless. The handle turned as I gave it a jiggle. Inside were a half-dozen robots of various sizes. A beige monstrosity had 'Mopobot' stenciled on the side of it. Next to it was an upright rectangle with a half-dozen thin arms arrayed from its top like a freaky haircut. There were three automated vacuum cleaners and one small, flying drone. Across from all the robots was a hatch set a few feet off the floor. A sign designated it as a garbage chute. On the wall above the robots were a half-dozen, odd-shaped metal implements. They all looked like their purpose was repair, not demolition. The heaviest of the tools was a finger-width, metal wrench hung on the wall by a hook. I wasn't going to smash any security cameras with that, but I might be able to point them in the wrong direction. I snatched the wrench off the wall and headed back out into the hallway.

I paused for a moment at the stairwell door. The moment I was visible in the security camera, Four Hands would be called. Tingles of panic were running up and down the entirety of my digital, phantom body.

"Hello."

It was Jerry. He was walking down the hall toward me.

"Shh, keep your voice down."

"Why? Did you know there was a woman looking for you? She had an ax ... and no front teeth."

"Can I ask you something personal, Jerry?"

"What?"

"How much do you get paid?"

"Oh, uh, that is personal."

"Ballpark it for me."

He looked a little sheepish.

"Low six figures."

"Ugh, fuck. You ... how? You so ... can't even get what's happening ... the world is ..."

Jerry blinked.

"What?"

The elevator between us dinged. A solid steel spike of terror punched through me, rooting me to the ground. The blue-tinted doors opened and a security guard stepped out, right into Jerry.

"Oh hey."

"Oh hey."

"I'm looking for the CEO's personal security guard," the guard said. "I was sent up here with a master key."

Jerry glanced at me. I shook my head vigorously. He paused for an agonizingly long moment.

"I think the person you're looking for is that way."

Jerry jerked his thumb over his shoulder.

"Thanks," the security guard said.

He set off down the hall. I stared at Jerry in shock until the guard was out of earshot. I felt such palpable relief.

"Thanks, Jerry," I whispered.

He shrugged.

"Your friend ... the one on the phone, what she said ... I just talked to my mom for the first time in two years. We're going to lunch. Just tell your friend, 'thanks.' She's super scary, but it's what I needed to hear."

"Uh, um, uh, okay."

He nodded and boarded the elevator. The doors closed behind him.

"This is such a fucked-up day."

I turned back to the door leading to the stairs.

"There you are, Mithter Thmith. I'fe been looking for you eferywhere."

Four Hands was standing at the other end of the hall from where the guard had gone. I could tell the software that emulated my adrenal gland was getting worn out. I'd endured too many jolts of too much fear. My spine felt like it had been replaced by ice cubes, and my intestines felt like they had been replaced by lava. The little wrench I held in my hand made a metallic rattling sound as I quivered in fear.

"Hey," I said.

I threw the wrench and turned. The stairs were no good, she'd chase me down. The elevators could be stopped by security. I saw the door marked 'Maintenance Services.' I headed for it and threw it open. The inside had no lock. I yanked it shut. I looked around at the row of robots. The big boxy Mopobot had an activation button. I slapped it and the bot made a loud beeping as it headed for the door. I dodged to the side as the doors' hydraulic pulled it open and the Mopobot headed into the hall. Four Hands appeared on the other side of it. The big box made an alarming beep and stopped.

I cast around for a weapon. Four Hands was sizing up the gap between the top of the robot and the doorframe. There was nothing for me to use in my defense. I hit the activation button on the flying drone and it took off and went for the door. It stopped part way through and made a beeping alarm at Four Hands. She swatted it aside with her ax. I pressed the activation buttons on all the robots. My robotic body didn't activate their safety protocols as they lined up to exit the room. It was the first time in my life I was thrilled not to be recognized as human.

Four Hands clambered on top of the Mopobot and jabbed at me with the ax. I grabbed a screwdriver off the wall and hurled it. To my horror, and kind of joy, it buried itself a half-inch into Four Hands shoulder. She staggered back as it clattered to the floor.

I spotted the big metal hatch in the wall, the garbage chute. It was my only way out. I turned the metal handle and pulled it open. A dark tube covered in the detritus of a hundred thousand office lunches greeted me. I went in head first scrambling forward and down. The chute was a vertical shaft straight down a hundred floors. I got my body inside and pressed my wheels as hard as I could against the sides of the shaft. They squeaked and whined trying to hold me in place.

Four Hands reached into the chute and grabbed my left leg. My robo-barricade had failed. She had me. I lost my grip on the inside of the chute. My body was dangling from her hand. My lurching pulled Four Hands forward into tube. She reached out with her other hand. A loud buzzing went off.

"Please exit the chute, please exit the chute. If there is a blockage, please contact maintenance. If you do not comply, security will be called."

A whirring sound came from below me. A safety grate was moving to block the chute to prevent the detected human from falling to their death. I grabbed ahold of the interlaced metal and pulled myself toward it. Four Hands' grip slipped. I fell in a crumpled heap on top of the half-closed grate. My left arm, with the broken hand, fell through the closing gap and was pinned.

Four Hands head poked into the tube and looked down. She was six feet above me, out of arms' reach.

"Mithter Thmith, you continuouthly amaze. In another life, I think we would have been friendth."

The ax appeared and she leaned down to hack at me with it. I kicked it away.

"Stop it."

"Uh, excuse me," a new voice said. "Were you the person looking for the master key?"

The ax stopped flailing.

"Oh, yeth," Four Hands said. "That wath me. I'm in the middle of thomthing right now. Can I be right with you?"

She hurled the ax down the shaft. It missed my torso by inches and clattered down the chute.

"Hey, you could have killed me," I shouted.

"That wath the point, Mithter Thmith."

"Uh, are you trying to kill someone right now?" the security guard asked.

"It'th a delivery drone reprogrammed for corporate ethpionage."

"No, I'm not. I'm a man not a machine."

"It wath programmed to thay that."

"Don't believe her," I floundered. "I'm ... I'm ... I'm her ex."

"What?"

"What?"

"Yeah, I'm her ex. She's trying to murder me by throwing me down this garbage chute. Help me."

"Ma'am, I'm going to need you to stop doing what you're doing."

"It'th just counter-capture protocolth."

"That may be so. If it is, we'll just get more security up here and get this all sorted out."

"That'th not a good idea. This robot hath proprietary information. It'th betht I deal with it."

"Yeah, proprietary information like all the illegal gho—"

Clang.

The garbage chute hatch had slammed shut. There were a muffled few words, a few muffled words in reply. A muffle, a long muffle, a few moments pause, a muffle, then a scuffle. Then a bang, a clang, and a thud. The hatch opened back up.

"I hope you apprethiate you've opened this company up to therious finanthial liability. We're going to have to pay thith man millionth to stop him thewing."

My stomach gave a twist. Of course she won.

"Well, I'm sorry to be such a bother, you fucking ass—aaaah,"

I dodged to the side as one of the automated vacuum cleaners slid through the hatch. It fell a foot then lodged in the chute above me.

"Oh thhoot," Four Hands said.

She started to shake the robot. I pried at the safety grate below me. It budged. It was designed to stop things from falling, not stop things from prying it open. I heaved and wiggled. There was a clank above me. Four Hands was using one of the tools from the maintenance room to shift the vacuum off its perch and pin me.

I had half my body past the grate and was shimmying down. I didn't know what came next. There was nothing but a bottomless pit below, but better falling down a bottomless pit than crushed by a vacuum cleaner. If it turns out there is an afterlife, I know which story I would rather tell. A buzzing hit my ears and the grate started to open of its own accord. The safety measures had timed out. I slipped and tumbled downward.

I was falling, banging and smacking against the sides of the chute as I went. I drove my limbs into the metal walls with all my pathetic might. Sparks flew, and I toppled. My frame caught both sides of the chute. I threw my limbs into the wedge. There was a horrifying grinding sound. I came to a wrenching stop as my shoulder and what passed for my ass wedged sideways in the chute. My screen was pressed forward at a neck-snapping angle and my legs were split like a gymnast, one dangling below me and one flailing above.

I swiveled. Five feet beneath me was another garbage hatch. I looked up. The vacuum was still rattling as Four Hands tried to shift it.

With a jolt, my legs dislodged me just enough to fall a few inches before I wedged again. I heaved a second time and fell a few more inches. My good hand reached out for the latch on the inside of the garbage chute portal. The metal fingers brushed the metal pin holding my exit closed. There was a scrape from above me. I flinched, but the vacuum was still wedged. My legs levered against the wall and I fell another few inches. Pressing the pin on the hatch, I kicked it open. There was another scrape above me. I launched myself through the yawing exit and slumped onto the floor. My right wheel caught on the frame. There was the crunch of crumpling plastic and the slam of the vacuum cleaner robot hitting the chute wall. I spun and yanked my foot into the room. My wheel had been compressed into a splintered parody of itself.

"I'm so glad I can't feel pain," I said.

A line of gunk that looked like it had once been a mayonnaise-based sauce was streaked across my frame.

"And can't smell."

28

GATECRASHING

I kicked the chute hatch shut. With any luck, it would take Four Hands a while to figure out what floor I was on, or that even better, she would think I was dead.

I clambered to my wheels. Well, I clambered to one wheel and a sort of round peg leg. The room was another maintenance room. The wall was lined with an identical set of cleaning robots. I limp-rolled to the door and threw it open. This floor was laid out very differently. The elevators still filled the other side of the hall with the stairwell beside them. Beyond the elevators and the stairs the hallway ended much earlier than the floors above. It spread into an open lounge that almost filled the entire floor. Loosely scattered around, standing at awkwardly distant intervals, were employees.

There were at least 30 of them, all dressed in their finest business hoodies. They milled about in weird configurations, sometimes in groups, others standing alone. All of them seemed to be talking to people that weren't present. A half-dozen flat-topped robots ran drinks around the wide empty spaces between the groups. Nearest to me a woman stood alone. Her eyes were staring fixedly at a space in front of her. She laughed uproariously at nothing.

"You know what they say, profit is a sign a company is working the way it should."

She laughed again, then turned to the empty space beside her. Her brow wrinkled.

"Yeah, I guess landmine manufacturers would count."

She laughed again. Based on her response, she was killing with the empty air around her.

I scanned the sparsely-populated room.

"No, no, I'm not drunk enough for that," a guy in a blue hoodie said. He sighed and smiled. "Okay, let's do it."

He walked to an empty spot in the middle of the room. He started swaying his shoulders to nothing.

"Go Tim," a woman standing by herself cheered from a dozen feet away.

I seemed to have stumbled across some kind of corporate performance art. Roll-scraping forward, a notice popped up in my view. 'Enter AR Party?' it asked.

"Oh, okay," I said. "That makes this marginally less disturbing."

Pure curiosity pulled me toward the Yes command. In an instant, the floor filled with corporate employees. People from around the world appeared and filled out clusters of socializing colleagues. A dozen different languages filled the air. Some people had subtitles hanging a foot below their face as they talked, others were dubbed in English, their original voices muted as they spoke. Tim, the dancer, was surrounded by a crowd of inebriated, hoodie-clad, EternityNet employees.

The decor of the real-world EternityNet building had vanished. It was replaced by gaudy ice sculptures that shot fire out of their mouths. The sculptures were of dragons that coiled around where the real-world support pillars would be. Instead of an opaque column there was a aviary filled with hummingbirds. Different-colored light fixtures flew around the room, making a small—and totally unnecessary—whirring sound. A song was playing that seemed like the accidental love child of adult contemporary and reggae.

My broken hand came into view.

"Oh no."

The highly-detailed 3D render of my avatar's hand was bent at a horrible angle. It looked like I had broken the wrist, then used the flopping hand as a tassel. I wiggled it until it was a little less horrific and glanced down at my body. My digital-me was superimposed over my robot body. I was only four and a half feet tall, but it looked like none of the people on this floor in real life were going to notice a rogue delivery robot.

A buzzing app popped up in my screen. It was my phone. I was getting a phone call through the building's signal jamming. I hesitated. It might be a trap. The screen said Izy was calling. I selected the little green picture of the kind of phone headset I'd never actually seen in real life. The call connected.

"Hello?"

"Romeo?"

"Izy?"

"Romeo."

"Izy. How did you get a call through the building jammer?"

"I didn't. We've just been calling and calling you, just in case."

"Then why ... I'm still in the building."

I looked around at the party. Realization arrived like someone who hates their job, a little late. In order to see all the people around me I needed to be connected to the building's network. I'd found a backdoor into EternityNet's system.

"I'm on EternityNet's network," I said.

"How did you do that? How are you still alive?"

"By being a stone-cold genius."

"That doesn't seem likely."

"Okay, by accident. Happy now?"

"Romeo?" Abi said.

"I've just connected you on conference call," Izy said.

"How are you still alive?" Mariela said.

"Hey ... stone-cold genius, that's how," I grumbled.

"Yes, give credit where it is due," Izy said. "Don't be an asshole, Mariela."

"Sorry, it's just astounding."

"Where are you in the building?" Sanav asked.

I glanced back at the elevators.

"The 100th floor."

"Okay, so, progress," Abi said.

"Are you okay?" Sanav said.

"My hand is broken, my foot is broken. I probably have like ten minutes before a four-handed assassin finds me and turns me into metallic chop salad. Also, she almost dropped a vacuum cleaner robot on me. So, you know, I wouldn't say it's been my best day."

A drunk corporate reveler staggered past me.

"Anybody want to do the conga?"

There was a raucous cheer.

"Oh no, things have just taken a turn for the worse," I said.

The music changed, and a line of people started weaving through the crowd.

"You've got to get me out of here," I hissed.

"We think you should call the FBI," Abi said. "They won't believe us over EternityNet security, but if you call from inside the building, that should get them to come and get you."

"Okay, good idea. When?"

"Now."

"Oh, right. I'll put you on hold."

I dodged to the left of an oncoming train of drunk people and searched for the FBI's phone number. It appeared, and with a flick of intention, my phone was dialing the number.

"Thank you for calling the FBI," a cheerful, autonomous voice said. "What can we do for you today? You can say, 'report a crime,' or 'confess to a crime,' or 'transfer me to the tip line,' or 'make a complaint,' or 'speak to a specific agent.' If this is an emergency, please hang up and dial 911 to contact your local authorities." There was a pause. "Good luck with that."

"Speak to a specific agent."

"Hey, buddy," a guy standing next to me in the party said. "What do you need? I'm a real estate agent."

"Congratulations," I said.

The autonomous voice chirped up.

"There is no, Agent Congratulations listed in the Seattle FBI Field Office. Would you like me to do a national search?"

"No. Agents Vanderwall and Berrys."

"One moment."

There was a processing pause. The drunk real estate agent was trying to give me his card.

"Look buddy, nobody is better. Whatever you need."

"I'm good thanks."

"Transferring you now," the computer said.

"Look buddy, I've got a great piece of office space. Four thousand square feet. Great views. Incredible price. Right in the middle of downtown Miami."

I stared at him.

"Isn't downtown Miami underwater?"

"Only at high tide."

I roll-clomped away.

"Agents Vanderwall and Berrys are away from their desk. Would you like to leave a message or wait on hold?"

"Wait on hold, I guess. This is an emergency."

"If this is an emergency, please hang up and dial 911." There was a pause. "Good luck with that."

"Fuck."

"Relax, it's a party," a woman in a yellow hoodie said.

I flashed a false smile, and kept moving. A cheerful saxophone serenaded me over the phone line. I selected Izy's line.

"They've got me on hold," I said.

"They're probably still interrogating Abigail," Abi said.

"We think we might have an idea for how to get you out of the building," Sanav said.

"How?"

"Never mind the specifics for now," Izy said. "Do you think you could get a screwdriver, socket wrench, and some duct tape?"

"You don't want to tell me the specifics because you know I won't like them."

"That is accurate."

"Don't worry," Sanav said. "Izy and I crunched the numbers. We think there's a good chance this will work."

"A good chance? Like how good a chance? Like 100 percent?"

"Uh ..."

"Fine, screwdriver, socket wrench, and duct tape. I can probably work that out."

I remembered seeing a socket wrench in the maintenance closet. As I limp-slid in that direction a thought occurred to me.

"Izy," I said. "I'm going to send you something. A file."

"What is it?"

"I recorded my conversation with Rosa Galan. She pretty much confesses to everything. I want you to take it and send it to your server in Taipei. That way we'll have a copy that's at least mostly out of Rosa Galan's reach."

I found the file in my memory and sent it to Izy's phone.

"After you send it to Taipei, you should delete the copy I just sent you. It might be a pretty big bargaining chip with Vanderwall and Berrys."

"That's not a terrible idea, Romeo."

"Thanks."

"Mr. Smith," Mariela said. "For what it's worth, your will to survive is impressive."

I paused. The words spent a moment percolating across my brain.

"Wait a second. You think I'm going to die, don't you?"

"What? No."

"Yeah you do. 'My will to survive is impressive.' That's the kind of thing you say to somebody who's probably going to die."

"I didn't mean that. I just think you're surprisingly tenacious."

"What the fuck?" I said. "Don't say that. I don't want to hear about how I'm, 'surprisingly tenacious.' There are only two contexts in which people use that phrase, describing bacterial infections and eulogies. So which use applies here?"

There was a pause.

"I'm not sure what you want me to say here," she said.

Abi cut into the conversation.

"Romeo, stop complaining. You're going to be fine. Now, go get the fucking duct tape."

"Thank you, Abi. I'm glad somebody knows how to talk a friend through a crisis."

My phone app buzzed indicating that someone had picked up the FBI line.

"FBI. Got to go," I said. I switched lines. "Hello? Hello? Vanderwall? Berrys?"

"Mr. Smith," the female agent said.

"Why am I not surprised?" the male agent said.

"You know we were almost done for the day."

"We were going to go home."

"To our families."

"To our lives."

"But no."

"What can we do for you, Mr. Smith?"

"I'm inside the EternityNet headquarters."

"Yes, we've heard."

"Call the police."

"Wait, wait, listen to this."

I played them a section of the recording I made of Rosa Galan. As they listened, I snatched the socket wrench from off the maintenance closet wall. A screwdriver was on a shelf beside it. I wedged both tools into a gap in my metal frame for safekeeping. I used the wrist on my broken hand to toss the room, but duct tape was nowhere to be found. I stopped the recording before it got really juicy.

"If you want to hear the rest, you're going to have to come and get me."

"Mr. Smith, it's the 21st century."

"Audio manipulation software is excellent these days."

"We get a dozen calls a week."

"US Senators are working with chicken people."

"Chicken people?" I said.

"Apparently lizard people are a smokescreen spread by the government."

"Yesterday someone told us a major Hollywood celebrity is secretly working with the New Zealand intelligence service to hide the truth about Australia."

"What? It doesn't exist?"

"No. It's mobile."

"They had an audio recording of the celebrity and the Prime Minister of New Zealand discussing the whole scheme."

"It was very realistic."

"Which Hollywood celebrity?"

"A big one."

"The point, Mr. Smith, is your recording is interesting.

"But without analysis we can't verify it."

"How long does the analysis take? Like five minutes?"

"Twenty-four hours if we rush it with the lab."

"I will definitely be dead by then."

They sighed in unison.

"If you're certain your life is in danger."

"We'll call the police and try to get them out there to pick you up."

"That's not going to work and you know it. You come and get me."

"We have no jurisdiction."

A flash of inspiration blinded my better judgment. I'd just had a really bad idea. Still, consequences were future Romeo's problem, he'd thank past Romeo for keeping him alive.

"Come and arrest me," I said.

"Trespassing isn't our problem."

"Call the local PD."

"Come on, you know what's going on here," I said.

"We know an erratic."

"Possibly deranged."

"Definitely confused ghost."

"Who's lied to us before."

"On several separate occasions."

"Says something is going on."

"You guys are such assholes."

"Mr. Smith, we're law enforcement."

"Fine, fine. Come and arrest me for something else."

"What?"

I thought for a moment.

"Corporate espionage."

"What?"

"That's right. I'm not just trespassing, I'm corporate espionaging." I looked at the line of cleaning robots in front of me. "Ooh, look at that. That's proprietary. So is that. I'm just looking at all this proprietary stuff. I'm going to post it all on the Internet."

The two agents sighed over the phone.

"Corporate Espionage of a multinational corporation might be in our jurisdiction," the male agent said.

They both sighed again.

"Alright, Mr. Smith," the female agent said. "We're going to come and arrest you."

"Because we're nice."

"But we'll warn you right now."

"False Reporting to a federal agency is a serious crime."

"And I told my husband I'd be home by now, and he is sick and tired of waiting up for me."

"And I ... well, I don't actually have any plans, but that doesn't mean my free time isn't important."

"So, we are not in a mood to be lenient."

"Great," I said. "See you soon."

I hung up before they could change their minds. Switching back to the other line, I scanned the maintenance room wall for tape.

"FBI is on the way," I said. "But I can't find any tape."

"Is there a supply closet or something?" Sanav asked.

I flashed back to the last time I was in a supply closet.

"NO. No. Yeah probably, I'll go look."

I rolled on my one good wheel and used my crushed foot to maintain my balance. It was a sort of disjointed skateboarding. I dodged an inebriated woman explaining the intricacies of advanced simulated neurobiology to a bleary-eyed man who had spilled a drink down his front. He kept hiccupping and nodding as she plunged into a soliloquy about the significance of calcium channels.

"So Izy, what's your plan for getting me out of here?"

"I will tell you at the last moment."

"Why?"

"I think there is a good chance if I explain, you will not want to do it."

"How bad is it?"

There was long silence. Sanav coughed.

"Don't tell me."

The middle of the floor was filled with a central structure containing the elevators, stairs and, on the other side of the central hallway, the garbage chute. I circled the outside of the floor. A buffet of ludicrously-expensive finger food was set up next to one window. Prawns and bacon-wrapped figs cozied up to a bowl of whatever kind of fish eggs rich people started eating when sturgeon went extinct.

I reached the far side of the floor and spotted an AR notification glimmering next to a door. It read, 'Supply Closet.' Girding myself, I headed for it.

It wasn't stocked with office supplies. Dishes, table-cloths, glassware, and two-dozen folding tables were crammed in the back of the room. The heaping piles of unused, generic party supplies didn't create anything like a festive atmosphere. RFID tags littered the collected items making it easy for them to be integrated into whatever AR theme some corporate party planner had stolen from their high school prom.

"There isn't any tape," I said.

"Keep looking," Izy said. "The tape is important."

"Why is it important?"

"You really want me to tell you?"

Something in her voice made me hesitate.

"Uh, no. Give me a few more seconds of ignorant bliss."

"That is what I thought."

I upset a pile of tablecloths as I rifled through the closet.

"I'm telling you, there isn't any tape here."

"Did you check the bottom shelf?"

"The bottom shelf. Why would it be on the bottom shelf?"

I looked down. On the bottom shelf beside my crushed foot was a cardboard box. Clearly visible was a roll of packing tape.

"Shit."

"You found tape?"

"No ... yes."

"It was on the bottom shelf?"

"No ... no ... no ... yes."

I snatched the roll of tape and tried to charge out of the supply closet. The pile of tablecloths I'd knocked to the floor tangled with my bad wheel. I yanked the door open trying to kick my foot free of the white cloth. It came loose at last and I raised the tape in triumph.

"Okay, Izy. It's time for you to tell me what the tape is for."

Izy replied, but I didn't hear it. My attention had been rather rudely yanked toward the figure standing several dozen feet away. She was perfectly framed through the round roll of the tape I was holding up in front of my face. Four Hands smiled.

"We'fe got to thtop running into each other like thith."

29

IDLE HANDS

March 3rd, 2064 10:17 p.m. PST

"Oh no, she's here."

"Four Hands?" Abi asked.

The assassin took a step toward me. I panicked.

"Ladies and gentleman," I shouted. "Ladies and gentleman, can I have your attention please?"

The inebriated crowd collectively wobbled to look in my direction. Four Hands faltered. Her smile stayed fixed, but her eyes suggested she was willing me to spontaneously disintegrate. Her thick rimmed glasses had the unmistakable flicker of an AR display playing across their lenses. They had to be AR glasses. She could see a fair number of people were watching us. I had the very tiniest bit of cover from being instantly murdered.

"I'm sorry to interrupt the festivities," I said. "It's just been, uh, I've ... well ..."

"It's a train wreck already," Abi said.

"It's been such a pleasure working with you all," Sanav prompted.

"It's been such a pleasure working with you all," I said.

The crowd stared at me for a painful second of confusion. Then, several of them started to clap. The smattering of applause died quickly, and they kept looking in my direction. They wanted more.

"Uh, I may not have gotten the chance to work with all of you," I said, I rolled a few steps away from Four Hands. She took a few steps after me. "But I've heard nothing but good things from ... about you ... from your bosses—"

"Probably department heads," Mariela said.

"Your department heads, rather," I took some initiative. "This was a difficult project and you've all performed admirably."

A few whoops rose from the crowd.

"There are a few things that I would like to make clear. First, I am not a malfunctioning delivery robot."

There was a long pause. Finally, a drunk woman by the buffet let out a braying laugh. Given direction, the rest of the gathered drunk people joined in with polite laughter.

"Yeah," I said. "Ridiculous right, but people say it all the time. I guess I come off as stiff. Margaret, hey Margaret."

I pointed to Four Hands. She froze in the headlights of the gathered crowd's attention.

"Aren't you always saying that? Margaret ... uh, Fiddleville ... smith ... son, ladies and gentleman. You may not have worked with her, but Margaret was crucial on this project. Give her a round of applause."

The crowd gladly obliged. Four Hands waved and smiled.

"In fact, speech," I said. "Speech."

Four Hands raised her arms and shook her head. It was already too late. A chorus of, 'speech' was rising from across the crowd.

"Come on Margaret," I said. "You're too humble for your own good."

"Yeah, come on Margaret," a man in the crowd shouted.

Four Hands smiled and coughed. I kept rolling backward. She took a few steps in my direction, but the focus of the crowd seemed to have slowed her pursuit. I hadn't blown her cover, and Rosa Galan wouldn't want things getting any more public than they were already.

"If you inthitht," Four Hands said, through as many gritted teeth as she had remaining.

I reached the corner and dodged around it. The central hallway with the elevators and the stairs was to the right just ahead of me.

"Where do I go? Where do I go?"

"Head for the stairs," Izy said.

I heard Four Hands behind me.

"Well, I thuppose good manners compel me to thpeak. You all theem fery competent and ... well-drethed. Good efening."

There was a smattering of applause. I heard the sound of sprinting footsteps. She was coming. The door to the stairwell was just ahead. Clomping along, I'd never make it before she caught me. I needed more speed. I did the only thing I could imagine would help. I spread my arms, lifted my crushed foot, and glided forward like I was going for gold. My body almost immediately started to lose balance. The door loomed large and I threw my arms out toward the curved handle. I hit it and tumbled through into the stairwell.

I rolled to the flight of stairs heading down. I would never be able to outrun Four Hands. Even without a broken foot she would have caught me. My eyes shifted to the gap in between the banisters for the stairs going up and the stair going down. The gap between them was less than a foot. A person wouldn't be able to fall through that gap. A biological person wouldn't be able to fall through that gap. Wiggling the tape I'd found aroumd my wrist like a bracelet, I threw my legs over the lower banister and dangled down. Sneaking a glance, I panicked. What was I thinking? This was a terrible idea.

The door to the stairwell slammed open. Four Hands' mouth fell open in shock.

"Mithter Thmith. Think about thith for a moment."

I let go. My spindly frame fell through the tiny gap, and then the next one, and then the one after that. Whoosh, whoosh, whoosh, the floors were passing by quick. I needed to stop. I was going too fast.

"Shit."

I threw my legs out in both directions. There was a wrenching clang. I tumbled onto the lower of two flights of stairs with a clatter. I looked down at my legs. The right leg's thigh metal resembled a poorly-made horseshoe. If Four Hands didn't dismantle me, I might end up achieving it all by myself.

A sign by the door at the top of the stairs read Floor 84. I'd fallen much farther than I intended. I looked down the gap. For the faintest moment, I considered plummeting in fits and falls all the way to the bottom. Then my collective mind told the reckless part of my mind that suggested that idea it really needed to get a grip. Don't get me wrong, my collective mind understood that my reckless mind was having a rough time at home. Trouble in its marriage, one of its kids had just gotten busted for shoplifting, but my collective mind really couldn't have it creating an unsafe working environment for everyone else.

"Are you guys still there?" I asked.

There was no reply. I'd gotten too far from the party. My communications were out. Izy said they were sending a drone. I needed to get to a balcony. I would just have to go there and hope Izy could do the rest. I glanced down at the ground and spotted the socket wrench. It had been launched from its wedged position in my frame. I snatched it and jammed it back into place.

What floors would have balconies? Did the 84th floor have a balcony? I heard the sound of running footsteps coming down the stairs. Did Four Hands never stop? It didn't matter at this point. I needed to move.

I sprang for the door. With one broken foot and a bent leg, I lurched around like a freshly-born giraffe. Through the door, a large sign and an AR notice said the same thing, 'Prototype Manufacturing.'

It was some kind of workshop. The floor was dotted with dozens of eerily-still robots. Each one had a set of hands connected to arms with a half-dozen joints along their length. The arms were connected to a thin, white obelisk with six wheels rounding its base. A bank of 3D printers filled one wall. An evil genius could have a really good time in here.

The floor had clear walls that divided clean rooms from the main manufacturing space. Scanning the exterior of the floor I could see there was no balcony. It looked like I was one floor down from the nearest one. I wasn't going back to the stairwell. Four Hands was coming.

I needed a balcony, so I was going to create one. I looked for some tool to smash the window in front of me. There were plenty of instruments, little delicate pieces made for fine-tuning electronics. There was not much in the way of heavy swinging implements. I would have to smash the glass through sheer force of will. Rolling up to the window,

I braced my broken arm. I would punch the snapped metal rod that had once been my wrist straight through the glass. Hopefully, my friends would spot me and be able to get me out of the building.

Closing my eyes, I took a calming breath. Centering myself, I braced to channel all of my little robot's energy right into the window.

"Raaaahhh."

I punched.

Plink

That didn't work. Why did I think that was going to work? I was definitely going to die.

I cast around room. The only heavy things present were the hand robots standing in a scattered formation around the floor. The nearest one was just a few feet away. I shuffled to it and tried to push it toward the window. If I could tip it, the robot might smash the glass. With a heave I discovered I would not be budging it any time soon.

A small, blue notice popped up on my screen. 'Connect via local wireless connection?' It was coming from the robot. I accepted the invitation. Nothing happened. I sighed and turned away. There had to be some kind of glass-smashing apparatus somewhere. The robot turned with me. I stopped. I turned back. It turned back. I raised one of my arms. One of its bulky arms raised into the same position.

"Oh, wow."

I took a few steps toward the window. The robot moved the same distance. I had been closer to the window than the robot so I got there first. Switching off the connection, I took a few steps away. With a thought, the connection reasserted itself. I took another step towards the glass. The robot was a foot away. I raised my arm. The robot's arm raised. I punched forward.

I flinched as the sound of shattering glass filled the room.

The window crumbled around the robotic fist. Glass scattered across the floor and tumbled down to the street below.

"Sorry," I shouted downward.

Using the robot's arm, I tried to pull what glass was left in the frame inside. I started to laugh. After a few moments, the laughter was becoming maniacal.

"Oh no, the power is already going to my head."

I'd cleared the window frame. Floor to ceiling, there was now a gap in the side of the building.

"Okay, Izy. Anytime."

At this height, the wind was strong. A dull roar-and-snap filled the room as air whipped past the opening. I took a step toward the window, and the robot did as well.

"Oh no."

I lurched back. The robot came within a hair's breadth of the edge before it joined my retreat. I severed the connection and stepped forward again. I glanced out the window. Street lamps and car headlights filled the gaps between the buildings with bright white illumination. I glanced upward. Maybe they were going to use one of those automatic window cleaner scaffoldings to get me down. The building above me was flat glass all the way to the green pyramid at the top.

"Dammit."

Four Hands couldn't be far away. She didn't know what floor I'd exited on, but she'd call security. They'd check the tapes. It wouldn't take them more than a couple of minutes to find me. A highly-dopplered buzzing came from the left. I swiveled my screen around like a dog with its head out a car window. It was a Flooffee drone. It was jumbo-sized, made for large orders or really avid caffeine fans.

"Izy, Abi, everybody?"

"Romeo," they shouted from the drone's speakers.

There was genuine relief in the chorus of voices. It's really nice to have people who care.

"Romeo, are you okay?" Abi asked.

I looked down at my body. One hand was dangling from my wrist, most of my crushed wheel had crumbled and fallen apart as I ran, the other leg had a U-bend in it, and my body was streaked in several places with mystery gunk from the garbage chute.

"I've had worse nights out."

"We've got to get you out of there," Izy said.

"Yes, yes, a thousand times yes. I thought you'd never ask."

"Do you have the screw driver and the socket wrench?"

"Yeah," I said.

"Stand back."

I shambled back into the room and the drone flew forward. It landed delicately on the ground.

"How is the drone still working inside the building's signal jamming," I asked.

"Nobody jams Flooffee drone signals," Mariela said. "Somebody has to deliver coffee."

"Turn the drone over," Izy said. "Carefully it has to fly again. Can you do that with one hand."

"Oh, I can do better than one hand," I said.

I connected to the hand robot and walked it to the drone. Its sturdy arms flipped the flying gizmo like it was a paper airplane. I set it down delicately on the floor.

"On the bottom," Izy said. "There is an insulated box with cup holders in it. It is held to the drone by a series of screws. I need you to use the screwdriver to remove it."

I handed the screwdriver to the arm robot. It was weird handing something from my left hand to its right hand by controlling my right hand which was dangling from my wrist. Imagine rubbing your stomach while patting someone else's head, while they rub your head and pat their stomach and everybody has to be on beat. I brought the screwdriver to the drone's cargo apparatus and started spinning. The robot could move faster than my hands, I just focused on moving it as fast as I could think, while my delivery robot's hand fell behind. The thick, insulated box of cup holders came free in less than a minute.

"What now?" I asked.

"Okay," Izy said. "Things are about to get weird, but go with it."

"You have a terrible bedside manner."

"Stop crying, I need you to remove your legs, and one of your arms. The broken one."

"What?"

"Hmm, yes."

"Why?"

Behind me the door to the stairwell slammed open. I didn't even have to turn around.

"Hello," I said.

Four Hands let out a winded sigh.

"Thankth for thith, Mithter Thmith."

I spun around.

"Thanks?"

"I had to thkip my workout thith afternoon on account of being ordered to kill you and your friends."

She checked a fitness tracker on her wrist.

"Thankth to you, I think I'm going to get my thteps for the day."

She fanned herself.

"Well, I'm glad I could help."

"Yeah," she straightened up and took a deep breath. "Tho, theeing ath you have nowhere elthe to run, how about we jutht call it a day and you gife up."

I glanced around the room. She was right. There was nowhere to run, but all across my AR screen there were little blue notifications. My eyes went wide at the thought. I accepted all the invitations to connect.

"Come on Mithter Thmith. No reathon thingth hafe to get ridiculous."

I raised my arms into a boxer's stance. Across the room, the hand robots raised their arms in unison. I looked at Four Hands, a wicked smile spreading across my face.

"Oh, we're way past ridiculous."

30

MOSH PIT

Four Hands did the most unsettling thing possible. She laughed. It was a charming 'spoon on a champagne glass' kind of laugh, dignified and genuine.

"I hafe really grown to rethpect you, Mithter Thmith."

The nearest robot to her was to the left. I lunged in the opposite direction. Every robot in the room mirrored the movement based on their orientation. The result was a chaotic, multidirectional ballet. Throwing my arms around empty air, the robot next to Four Hands seized her around the waist. The rest of the robots in the room threw their arms forward. Equipment was knocked off counters, and a computer screen was cracked and sent toppling.

Four Hands looked down to the robot clinging to her. She gripped its arms and started to pry them apart. There was the whine of servos as the robot struggled. Human savagery was winning. Robot 1 needed backup. The other robots were all scattered in a haphazard configuration. Navigating them all was going to be a headache.

I disconnected from all the robots on the left side of the room, I scanned the right side. Several of the robots were all facing the same way, away from Four Hands. I disconnected from all but those robots and spun on my broken legs. They obeyed. Now three robots were facing the right way. I ran forward, away from Four Hands for me, towards her for the robots. One of the robots lined up perfectly. I threw its arms around Four Hands' shoulders.

"Really?" she guffawed.

"This is the weirdest thing I've ever seen," Sanav said.

"It's even up there for me," Abi said.

Four Hands' robotic hands were flailing as she wrenched the first robot away from herself. I connected to one of the other two robots I'd brought closer to her. I swiveled, stepped forward, and threw my hands around her waist.

"For Pete'th thake," Four Hands said.

The third robot was still waiting. I connected, turned, and grabbed Four Hands around the head. I kept going. I connected to another robot, wheeled it forward, and added to the robotic dog-pile

I heard a crunching hiss. Four Hands had used her secondary hands to yank out a tangle of wire from the gap in one of the robot's paneling. She tossed off its now-limp arms.

Time was still very pressing. Another robot connected, I wheeled it forward.

"Try punching her," Mariela said.

I tried throwing a punch at Four Hands. The robotic fist stopped a half-inch from her face.

"Dammit," I said.

"The robots have safety protocols."

"Safety features are the bane of artificial intelligence life forms," Sanav said.

Another robot was added to the mosh pit. Then another. After less than a minute, I had Four Hands entirely surrounded.

"Lift her off the ground," Sanav said. "She'll have less leverage to get free."

Without a second thought, I connected to every robot pinning Four Hands in place. Holding my arms out, I lifted toward the ceiling. Four Hands let out a squawk as she was hefted upward. It was the ultimate in 21st-century crowd surfing.

"Mithter Thmith, I'm really going to mithth you after I murder you."

There was a sound of her struggling.

"Yeth, hello. Yeth, thith ith Mth. Galan'th personal thecurity again. Yeth. I'm doing fine. How are you?" There was pause. "Wonderful. Could you thend up a few thecurity guardth to floor number 84. Right now. If they're not here in the next three minuteth, I will perthonally turn your career and thocial life into a burning trath heap. You will be a cautionary tale thecurity guardth tell each. Yeth, that'th what I thaid. In the parlanthe of machithmo, 'mofe your fucking ath.' No, I thaid ath. Ath meaning your buttockth. Yeth, that'th correct. One hundred and eighty thecondth. I'm counting."

"Get moving, Romeo," Izy said. "Lose the limbs."

I rolled back to the window, trying to ignore the sound of Four Hands struggling against her captivity. There was a whirring screech. Another robot had lost its wiring.

"Losing limbs," I said. "Real quick, why am I doing this?"

My first robot was still by the window. I directed the socket wrench in its hand toward the bolts in my broken arm.

"Okay, I'll tell you," Izy said. "Just don't panic."

"I won't panic."

"You are going to hold onto the frame of that drone, use tape to fortify your hand's strength and we are going to fly you out of there."

"What?"

"Without an arm and two legs you are only like five pounds above the drone's weight limit. It should work, I think."

"What? You ... what? You want me to tape myself to the bottom of this drone?"

"Yes."

"And you're then going to fly me 80 stories down."

"Yes."

"Despite the fact that I'm over the drone's weight limit?"

"Yes."

"You want to hold me to the base of this drone with tape? With tape?"

"If you wrap a bunch of tape around your closed fist, it will hold your fingers to your palm. It should work."

"What's to panic about?" I said. My voice had gotten very high-pitched. "All good here. Totally fine."

"Security is on the way, Mr. Smith," Mariela said. "You've got to move."

"No, you've got to move."

"That doesn't make any sense."

"I know."

I finished removing my broken arm and reluctantly directed the assistant robot's arm down to the bolts holding on my right leg.

"Mithter Thmith," Four Hands said. "I apologize for eafthdropping, but I couldn't help but oferhear. Thith plan your compatriotth hafe cooked up doethn't theem thound. If you thurrender, I can thtill arrange for the thecond deal Mth. Galan offered."

I looked up at her as I turned the robot's hand at top speed.

"The one where some of my friends die?"

"Jutht biologically."

"And I get imprisoned."

"Only for a couple of decadeth ... maybe three."

She wrenched and one of the robot's arms tore out of its socket. Four Hands tossed it on the ground and continued to wiggle and contort out of the mesh of robotic restraint.

"Keep moving, Romeo," Abi said.

"I'm moving."

The last bolt came out of my right leg, and it and my body came apart. I crumpled to the ground. My screen smacked against the floor.

"I really should have seen that coming," I said.

Flopping and rolling, I maneuvered my other leg's bolts so they were pointing upward. With a little awkward wiggling, I guided my robot assistant's hand toward the bolts. It started spinning the socket wrench. Four Hands wrenched another robot's arm off. They were losing limbs faster than I was.

"Hurry, Romeo," Abi said. "She's wiggling free."

"One of her feet is on the ground," Sanav said.

My other leg came loose, and I took a moment to glance in Four Hands' direction. There were just a handful of robots still holding her in place.

I connected to my two-handed assistant and flipped the drone.

"Lift the drone, Izy," I said.

The engines buzzed into life and the drone rose to hover above me. It felt like I was being abducted. I gripped the metal bracket that had previously held on the insulated cargo container.

Another crunching snap came from the robotic dog-pile.

With a lot of awkward fiddling, I got the hand robot to stick the roll of tape to the outside of my hand.

"Spin, Izy, spin."

The drone started to twist in the air. Below it I swirled across the floor like the world's least-graceful ballerina. I chanced a glance at Four Hands. The last robot had its arms firmly around her torso from behind. Her body was thrashing to spin in its grip. Her hands were seeking a weak spot.

"Spin faster," I shouted, panic turning the treble on my voice way up.

Izy obliged and the room became a blur. If I had stomach contents ... you know what, let's just be grateful I don't. Disoriented, I looked up at my arm. A thick ball of tape was now pinning my fingers to my palm. There was a crash somewhere nearby.

"Go, Izy," I shouted. "She's coming."

Lurching to a stop, the drone paused. Izy was probably as disoriented as I was. I glanced into the room. Four Hands was throwing the last robot back. Free from her restraints, she sprang toward me, all four hands outstretched.

"Aaaaah."

The electric buzzing of a thoroughly pissed-off beehive went off above me. I scraped across the floor. Metal cracked on metal as my frame struck the bottom edge of the window. A few shards of glass sprayed into the night and plummeted downward. Four Hands scrabbled after me and dove. Her body slammed into the ground, the top half of her torso over the edge of the window, and her hand slashed through the air. She was an inch too short.

"Yes!" I shouted.

I heard cheering coming from the drone. It was muffled by the whipping wind.

"I made it. You won't be murdering me today."

Four Hands sprung to her feet and looked around. She picked up my arm up from the floor.

"Wait, no," I said. "No. Don't you dare."

She hefted the limb like it was a massive throwing ax and launched it into the night. The drone was struggling with my weight. I was still well within throwing range. The twirling arm whipped through space. Luck saved me. The broken hand on the arm caused it to lurch sideways. The limb missed the drone by centimeters.

"Hey!" I shouted.

Four Hands had already hefted one of my legs.

"No," I shouted again. "You stop throwing my limbs at me."

She opted for a sideways toss. The limb's broken foot tapped my frame as it whirlybirded past. The broken wheel's integrity was taxed too much, and it exploded. The plastic rained down to the street below, and the leg tumbled away. I swung back and forth. The drone started to make a new noise as if all the angry bees had contracted flu and weren't feeling so good. The drone started to drop. Not fast, but not slow either.

"Up, Izy, up."

"Controlled descent is the best we can hope for," she said.

The drone speaker struggled to overpower the wind. Four Hands had hefted my other leg. It was visibly bowed at the thigh. She pondered its use as a throwing weapon.

"You're going to kill somebody," I shouted up.

Four Hands paused at that. She tipped her head at me like a confused puppy.

"I mean, I know that's what you're trying to do," I said. "I'm just saying, you know there are people down below, but I guess you don't care, otherwise you would not murder me. Never mind."

Four Hands nodded. She tossed my bent leg aside and turned around looking for another projectile. The drone was still falling slowly. When she popped her head out of the window, she was hefting a polished white, robotic arm she'd cleaved from one of her captors. Raising it, she pondered the shot. I held my breath. She let the arm drop to her side and shrugged. She smiled.

"Well done, Mithter Thmith," she shouted.

"I escaped," I said, under my breath. "Yes. I made it."

Relief washed over me. The feeling was so intense I didn't even worry about the fact that I was still descending toward the pavement, or that I was almost limbless and taped to a malfunctioning drone.

"I escaped," I shouted. "Hey, Abi?"

"Yeah?" I could barely hear her.

"This has got to be the weirdest thing you've ever seen right?"

"Top five."

"Top five?" I said, indignant.

"I once laid out a tarp and made a guy roll around in three-dozen containers of orange marmalade. You got to dig deep to faze me."

"Why orange marmalade?" Sanav said.

"It was on sale."

I glanced down, and my elation evaporated. The whining drone was struggling with my weight more than I'd realized 80 stories up. Now the Earth looked like it was coming at me intent on history's most one-sided chest bump.

"Izy," I said. "Am I going to survive impact?"

"Well, you're falling a little faster than I hoped, but you should survive."

"Will survive," I said. "Will survive, Izy. It's not like I'll be around to rub it in your face if you're wrong."

"Fair point. You will definitely make it."

"Thank you."

A dark blue car was parked on the street in front of the building.

"I'm going to aim for the roof of that car," Izy said. "It should absorb some of the impact."

"Oh crap," I said.

As the car loomed closer, I noticed something in the front windshield. It was my leg. It had buried itself perfectly in the glass. Standing next to the vehicle on either side, examining the weaponized limb, were two familiar figures.

"Vanderwall? Berrys?" I said.

They looked up.

"Mr. Smith?" the male agent shouted.

I crashed into the top of their car.

"You made it," I said. "I made it."

"He made it," Sanav and Abi shouted through the drone.

The two agents looked at the dent I'd just created in the top of their car. They looked at my leg buried halfway through the middle of their windshield. Their eyes ran up their vehicle to me, to the drone hovering above me. Its little motors sounded happier now that they weren't bearing my weight.

"Is that your leg, Mr. Smith?" the female agent shouted.

"What are you doing taped to a drone?"

"Why ..."

"What ..."

"I'll explain everything," I said.

The buzzing of an oversized electric motor rose from down the street. I spun to look for the source of the sound. The female FBI agent winced as I scraped more paint off the car roof. Two huge trucks were pulling out of the alley beside the EternityNet building.

"Those trucks," I said. "Izy, those trucks. The ghosts. Go after them."

"Mr. Smith, you owe us an explanation."

"Later," I said.

"Now."

"Go, Izy. Vanderwall, Berrys, with me."

The drone above me whirred back to life and pulled me off the car roof. My weight proved too much again, and I crashed back down on the car's trunk. There was a horrifying screech of metal, then the drone pulled me up again. I sank with a clatter to the street. Sparks flew as I scraped across the concrete. Up I climbed, then smacked back down.

The twin trucks were pulling away down the road. If they got away, all those ghosts would be lost, plus Abigail would go to prison, also probably I would go to prison. I glanced back at Vanderwall and Berrys. Based on their expressions, if I didn't give them the case of the century in the next five minutes. I would definitely be going to prison. They climbed back into the car and whipped it around in the street.

I turned back to the trucks. They were getting away. My flying conveyance had all the get up and go of a person waiting in line for an Ndle drone. The truck pulled to a squeaking stop. There was a red light at the intersection. I scraped and clattered after the trucks. I was gaining.

"Hey," somebody shouted.

Building security were running down the alley toward me. They looked more perplexed than alarmed, but if they stopped me, I was screwed regardless of the reason.

"You're going to make it, Romeo," Sanav said.

"Give it all it's got, Izy," Abi said.

"Thanks for saying that," Izy said. "You know before I was just going half-speed. I figure whatever, why rush?"

"Is this what going mad feels like?" Mariela said.

"I'm almost there," I said.

The truck was just ahead. I spotted the crosswalk to my left. It was counting down. The flashing red right hand was mocking me with imminent doom.

Scrape, lift, glide, crash, scrape, and I pulled in front of the lead truck just as the light turned green. I glanced up and saw the truck was automated.

"Oh crap," I said. "This thing is going to detect me, right?"

The engine revved to life.

"Oh no," I shouted.

The truck budged an inch. Izy revved the drone's engines and lifted me. The movement startled some sensor on the truck and it stopped a hair's breadth from my face.

Vanderwall and Berrys pulled their car in front of the lead truck. I spun to face them as they climbed out. Three security guards from EternityNet arrived.

"FBI," the male agent said, flashing a badge.

"You three wait there," the female agent ordered.

Vanderwall and Berrys looked down at me.

"Inside these two trucks," I said. "Is the biggest collection of illegally-copied people ever."

"You have proof of that?"

I gulped.

"Uh, I kind of was hoping the trucks would be proof," I said.

"We can't search a vehicle without evidence, Mr. Smith."

"Like we told you before."

"Evidence is what our profession runs on."

"And ego."

"Right."

I smacked the back of my screen on the truck's bumper.

"Come on," I shouted. "Do you really think I lying? Really? I said I was here, I was. I've been nothing but upfront with you guys."

"Oh yeah?"

"Did your friend Abigail illegally copy herself?"

I made a gurgling grunt sound.

"Look, what's important is that a career-making case is in these trucks. That's what you guys said you wanted."

"We said we wanted evidence, Mr. Smith."

"Without it."

"Anything we find."

"Will get thrown out in court."

"Evidence, fuck," I said.

"Sorry, Mr. Smith."

"But we're arresting you."

"For the corporate espionage that you confessed to."

"Any chance I could, what's the word, recant that confession?"

"Maybe."

"But we're still arresting you."

They took a step toward me.

"Wait," a voice cut through the air. It had come from the drone. "Agents, my name is Mariela Galan. You might know me better as the digital copy of Rosa Galan. I am the first ghost. I have kept tabs on my biological counterpart. There are illegally-copied people in these trucks."

The two FBI agents stared at the Flooffee drone.

"Ms. Galan?" the female agent said in an only slightly raised voice.

"It could be a fake," the male agent said.

"Do you have specific evidence of illegally-copied people?"

"No," Mariela said. "But I can tell you, I know this is something my biological counterpart would do."

"Hearsay based on character."

The two agents looked at each other.

"Still probably not enough."

"I've got that recording of Rosa Galan," I said.

"You have it with you?"

"Shit, no," I said. "We sent it to a server farm in Taipei."

"Taipei?"

"It's the capital of Taiwan."

"We know where Taipei is."

"Why did you send it to Taipei?"

"We were going to try to use it as leverage to get Abigail out of custody," I said.

"Well that backfired."

"I'm sorry, Mr. Smith."

"It's just not enough."

They took another step toward me.

"Fuck," another voice said. "Stop. I'm ... my name is Abi Page. I'm the digital copy of Abigail Page. I have transcripts of conversations I had with a software engineer at one of EternityNet's subsidiaries. Those transcripts recount his involvement in the illegal copying of thousands of people."

The two FBI agents looked at each other again, eyebrows raised.

"You realize, Ms. Page you just proved our case against your biological counterpart."

"Yeah, I'm hoping you will see our testimony as valuable enough to overlook our little indiscretion."

"Building security said Mr. Smith wasn't here," the male agent said, glancing at the three security guards.

"He obviously was."

"Evidence of an attempt to conceal something illicit."

"What do you think?"

"I think if we search this truck right now and find illegal copies."

"A judge will say we have cause?"

"Yep."

"Totality of circumstances."

"Right."

"But if we don't find anything."

"And Rosa Galan decides to make an issue of it."

"We'll be doing paperwork in Northern Alaska by the end of the week."

They looked at each other for another few moments. They turned in unison to the security guards.

"Open the truck."

The female agent ducked into the car and pulled out a tablet and a few cables. I scraped along after the procession as they walked to the back of the truck's trailer. I angled my head to see as the big backdoor swung open with a low creaking. Boxes were stacked high in orderly pillars. The female agent climbed into the truck and pried open the cardboard. A black box slid out. She plugged it into the tablet. There was a long silence as power from the tablet started the black box whirring.

"Help. Who is this?" a voice shouted from the tablet. "Do you know who I am? I am a United States Senator. You can't imagine the hell I will bring down on you if you don't get me out of here right now. I'm not kidding. I know of a CIA black site where they'll do things the likes of wh—"

The female agent yanked the cable out of the black box.

"Holy crap," she said, glancing around the truck full of boxes.

"Yeah," her partner said.

They turned to the three security guards.

"You three get down on the ground right now."

"We did it?" Sanav asked.

"I think we did it," Izy said.

I looked at the two FBI agents.

"Does this mean you'll release Abigail?"

They exchanged an almost sheepish look.

"Actually, we released your friend 20 minutes ago."

"She's still filling out some paperwork at the field office."

"Our case was mostly circumstantial."

"And she's got a really good lawyer."

My jaw dropped. I stared at both of them incredulous for a long moment, then my gaze fell to the pavement.

"Mother F—"

31

ANCHORS

March 4th, 2064 9:33 a.m. PST

"What's happening?"

"EternityNet's stock has plunged by 40 percent in the last hour," Abigail said.

"Apparently all of Rosa Galan's ghost investors don't appreciate her imprisoning and torturing ghosts," Abi said.

We were lounging in digital space. The wall in front of us was adorned by a dozen virtual screens playing news feeds. Abigail's avatar was three-dimensional this time, but it wobbled oddly in the way avatars do when they're tied to the biological person's VR glasses.

"Where is Izy?" Abi asked. "She's going to want to see this?"

"I'll check," I said.

I started my robot's interface. Only having the one arm I couldn't maneuver much, but I saw Izy walking down the aisles of the server farm.

"Izy what are you doing?" I said. "We saved the world, kind of. Come watch."

"I was busy all day yesterday," Izy said. "I have to make sure all is well with the farm."

Abi heard Izy over our digital link.

"She's not growing beets," Abi said.

"Abi says, 'you're not growing beets.'"

"Tell her I cannot flog my customers and tell them to wait."

"You're in the wrong business," Abi and Abigail said in unison.

"Is that going to happen a lot?" I asked.

"It's not infrequent," Abi said

"Is what going to happen a lot?" Izy said.

"Sorry, Abi and Abigail talked in unison. Come and join us so I don't have to keep conveying things back and forth."

"Fine."

Izy's hand waved and her AR contacts started to twinkle. I turned off my robot and appeared back in digital space. A wobbly Izy avatar was now among us.

"We should call Sanav," I said. "Let's watch the fall out together."

"Yeah, do it," Abi said.

I sent a chat request to Sanav.

"Hey," he said.

"Want to come watch Rosa Galan's world fall apart?"

"Totally," he said. "Should I bring drinks?"

"Yes, definitely."

Sanav appeared beside me in the room. He was holding two huge pitchers of florescent green ice slush. With a wave of my hand, a glass appeared there. Sanav filled it. Over his speakers I heard Abigail walk over to Izy's desk in the real world. There was the sound of a drawer opening and the slosh of liquid in a glass bottle. Izy pulled up a real chair, while Sanav and I pulled plush loungers.

"Any word about a four-handed assassin?" I asked.

"Nope," Abigail said. "Upside though, Rosa Galan is in no position to pay her, so you're probably safe."

"You wish she had been captured?" Izy asked.

I considered it.

"You know, honestly, she was so polite about the whole thing, I don't really mind that she got away. I guess manners really will get you everywhere."

"Speaking of safety, where are you, Abi?" Izy asked. "I mean your black box. Where is it in the world?"

"Oh yeah," Sanav said. "I was wondering about that too."

"I didn't mention?"

"No," I said.

"I'm here."

"Where here?"

"I'm at Izy's server farm. You guys installed me yesterday morning."

"We didn't ... what?" I asked.

"You're Mr. Phillips," Izy said.

"Yeah," Abi said. "I figured here would be a good place to hide."

"Very clever," Abigail said.

"Wait," I said. "You tried to make me show you porn."

Abi smiled.

"Yeah. It was too funny. I couldn't resist."

"That's ... you ... okay, that's a pretty good one."

"Hey, hey, check this out," Abigail said.

She snapped and one of the dozen screens expanded.

"Sources are saying that more than 200,000 illegally-copied Digital People were recovered by the FBI."

Footage of FBI agents carrying uniform, white boxes displayed across the screen.

"Hey look, Vanderwall and Berrys," I said, spotting them in the back of the shot.

"Which one is which?" Sanav asked.

"I have no idea," I said.

"That's fascinating, Janet," the anchor said in response to something very boring his correspondent had just said. "What happens next?"

"Well, law enforcement has issued an arrest warrant for Rosa Galan. She is said to have left EternityNet's Seattle based headquarters, by helicopter, at some point early this morning. Her lawyers claim that they are arranging an interview with law enforcement."

"Arranging an interview?" Izy said. "If it was us, they would be kicking the door down."

"She's a billionaire," Sanav said.

"It is a little messed up," I said.

"Don't worry," Izy said. "Societies that insulate powerful people from consequences are notoriously successful."

"What's next for EternityNet?" the news anchor continued.

"The board of directors has called an emergency session for this afternoon. It would be shocking if they didn't remove Rosa Galan from her position as CEO."

"Do you think that will help the stock free fall?"

"Hard to say. Interestingly, the digital copy of Rosa Galan, who goes by the name Mariela Galan has issued a statement. She claims she was involved in bringing her biological counterpart's alleged crimes to light. She has suggested that she take over as CEO of EternityNet. Since that announcement the decline in the stock has slowed quite a bit."

"What?" I said.

"Damn," Abi and Abigail said together.

"Great, so now a mortal Galan has been replaced by an immortal Galan," Izy said. "The world is doomed."

"Hey, you never know," Sanav said. "Getting royally fucked over does wonders for empathy."

"Or it makes you resent the whole world so much you do whatever it takes to get revenge," Izy said.

"Dark, but ... oh shit ... fair."

The news broadcast continued.

"So, you think shareholders would want that, the digital copy to take over?"

"Shareholders tend to want something totally different, but completely the same. She would fit the bill. We won't know for a few days. At the moment, I'd say people are planning to wait and see."

"But we might see Ms. Galan replace Ms. Galan."

"It's possible."

"This is a truly strange story."

"Yes, John, it is."

"Thanks Janet, we move now to our legal expert, Nadia Shirazi. How are you, Nadia?"

"I'm well, John, thanks for having me."

"We're curious what happens to the 200,000 illegally-copied people the FBI have recovered."

"It's a fascinating question, John."

"I thought so."

"Apparently."

"So, these two despise each other," Abi and Abigail said in unison.

"How can you tell?" I asked.

"You develop a sense for it," they both replied.

They looked at each other.

"We've really got to stop that," they said.

"This is eerie," I said.

"Shhh, I am trying to listen to the journalists who hate each other," Izy said.

Nadia was talking about the Supreme Court.

"That previous ruling used divorce as precedent, but central to that ruling was the consensual nature of the digital copy's creation. No one had planned for a mass scale copying without the biological person's permission. And of some of the world's most powerful people, CEO's and elected officials. Do the ghosts—I'm sorry Digital Americans—hold the same elected office or run those companies?

"It looks like for the moment the answer is no when it comes to elected officials, as to the corporations, that's a different story. Elected office isn't an asset that gets divided in divorce, but stock options definitely are."

"So, we could see a major shakeup of the world's financial markets."

"That's right, John."

"Any good news?"

"Well, maybe, strange news at least."

"That's seems par for the day."

"It does, doesn't it, John? Reports suggest that of the 200,000 digital copies some of them are repeated copies."

"Meaning?"

"Many of the people who were copied were then copied again, some of them several times. One woman, a bioengineering expert, Chinara Adebayo, was copied more than a hundred times. Her skill set was apparently very valuable. The real-life Chinara Adebayo, of course, had no idea she had been copied. However, she's stated that she will divide her assets between the hundred-plus copies of herself. Her intention is to start a biotechnology consulting firm staffed entirely by herself. Assuming her digital copies consent."

"Go, Chinara," Abi and Abigail said. "Oh, for fuck's sake."

"This is a lot to process," John said.

"Rosa Galan's lawyers will definitely agree with you there," Nadia said. "I've got several sources that say the freed ghosts are already planning to file a massive class-action lawsuit against Rosa Galan and her company. A lot of legal precedent is about to be set. I think we're going to see major movement on several policy issues pertaining to Digital Americans. Voting rights, and civil protections are going to be reshaped. The Supreme Court and the congress are going to be busy."

"Amazing, thanks for your insight, Nadia. Always a pleasure when you stop by."

"You know I feel exactly the same way, John."

"Wow, they really do hate each other?" Abi and Abigail said.

"Okay we've got to stop this," Abigail said.

"Agreed."

"Maybe I'll start using an accent."

"You'd be cute with an English accent."

"In other news," the news anchor said. "Russia's missing nuclear weapon was found. Apparently, it was mistaken for an ice machine and moved into a military break room."

Izy muted the screen and passed Abigail the bottle of vodka. My doubled best friend took a swig from the bottle and a glass of margarita simultaneously.

"Should we be upset we're not getting more credit?" Sanav asked.

"I, for one, do not want to be in the middle of all this," Izy said.

"I work in one of the few fields where publicity is bad for business," Abigail said.

"Publicity is bad for business," Abi said almost simultaneously.

"Hey, progress," they said in unison. "Damn it."

"My business requires privacy too," Sanav said. He turned to me. "What about you Romeo? You risked your life and everything."

I looked around at the circle of avatars.

"Eh," I said. "Did you hear about that celebrity who named their new baby 'Gorf.' Sort of seems like fame is bad for people's mental health. Besides, boring is underrated."

ACKNOWLEDGMENTS

A lot of people were involved in making this book happen.

Thanks to David and Susan for enduring everything I had to write to get to the point where I could write this.

Thanks to Betsy for taking a gamble.

Thanks to my family and friends for all their support.

Thanks to all my public school teachers who put up with the thankless task of being a teacher in a society that treats them like crap.

Thanks to Jonas Salk for the polio vaccine. Seems like getting polio would've sucked. Good looking out, pal.

Thanks to Mary Shelley for kicking this genre off with a bang.

Thanks to whatever hominid first cracked a couple of rocks together. I like to think you knew what you were starting.

ABOUT THE AUTHOR

Vincent Scott likes tea, purple, and naps. He likes dogs and cats, equally. (That's right, the exact same amount.) He wonders if anyone actually reads these bios. He wonders why publishing has continued with the contrivance of writing these bios in third person when it's obvious the author wrote them. Maybe if someone is a big-time author, some intern writes it for them? Vincent Scott is not a big-time author.

CPSIA information can be obtained
at www.ICGtesting.com
Printed in the USA
FSHW011036010820
72446FS